D0700472

Also By Cathryn Grant

NOVELS

The Demise of the Soccer Moms

Buried by Debt

The Suburban Abyss

The Hallelujah Horror Show

Getting Ahead

Faceless

An Affair With God

THE HAUNTED SHIP TRILOGY

Alone On the Beach

Slipping Away From the Beach

NOVELLAS

Madison Keith Ghost Story Series

Chances Are

SHORT STORIES

Reduction in Force

Maternal Instinct

Flash Fiction For the Cocktail Hour

Cathryn Grant

SLIPPING AWAY FROM THE BEACH

Haunted Ship Trilogy Book Two

Cathryn Grant

D2C

D2C Perspectives

This book is a work of fiction. References to real people, events, establishments, organizations, or locales are intended only to provide a sense of authenticity, and are used fictitiously. All other characters, and incidents and dialogue, are drawn from the author's imagination and are not to be construed as real.

Email Cathryn at Cathryn@SuburbanNoir.com or visit her online at SuburbanNoir.com

ISBN: 978-1-943142-20-0

Mary

Mary knew there was a ghost haunting the concrete ship. The S.S. Palo Alto had been built too late to be of use in World War I. It was used briefly for dancing and dining in the early 1930s before a violent storm damaged it and The Great Depression eroded its appeal. It was permanently moored at the end of the pier on Seacliff Beach, decaying under the onslaught of sun, salt water, and thrashing waves.

Very few people believed Mary, but very few believed anything a woman had to say when she was experimenting with drugs like a carefree teenager. They laughed off her beliefs as drug-induced hallucinations. Mary's references to a ghost were simply a middle-aged woman's hope for assurance there was some kind of consciousness beyond the grave.

But she'd known there was a ghost long before she inhaled a whiff of marijuana, long before she'd put a drop of LSD on her tongue. She'd known since she was a little girl, watching as the "cement boat" was towed up to the beach. She'd seen it, she'd felt it, and she'd heard it speak.

Haunted

I've been here for a long time — alone on the California coast, near the center of Monterey Bay, on the shore of Seacliff Beach. I'm the ghostly breath of fog that blows across the water, hugging the horizon, quickly shrouding the blue sky, blanketing the sand. I'm closer than the pebbles and sand and broken logs of drowned trees. Only a handful of the millions of beachcombers and surfers, swimmers and sunbathers, have felt my presence. Only those with eyes. Not the eyes in their heads, but internal eyes.

I'm here, watching. I'm here, listening. I'm here, speaking, if anyone wants to pay attention.

It's commonly believed that ghosts haunt a particular place because they're looking for closure, they want to find rest, they need release from something unresolved so they can pass on to the afterlife. But that's not how it is at all.

1967

Coming home for the summer was a misnomer. Nothing felt like home. Five years ago when Thomas had left home for his freshman year at UC Berkeley, he'd driven away from the large house perched on the cliff where he'd grown up. When he returned at Thanksgiving, his father was living in that house with a younger version of his mother. It was no longer home and he couldn't bring himself to walk through the front door, smelling food that had been prepared by his father's mistress. Instead, Thomas went to a small house a few yards from Rio Del Mar beach where his mother now lived, seemingly calm and unaffected by the loss of her husband and her home and the complete dismantling of her world.

Five years, and the house still felt unfamiliar to Thomas.

This time, he was arriving with a year of graduate school under his belt. Part of him wished he'd found an apartment for the summer with a few other guys. But Berkeley was exploding with hippies and psychedelic experiences even more than Santa Cruz. Aside from that, he couldn't face trying to locate appropriate roommates. Home, as foreign as it was, remained the only choice for now.

He turned onto the narrow street and pulled up in front of his mother's house. It didn't fit her, but he couldn't say why. He hoped she'd grow into it. He hoped she'd meet another man, someone more suitable than his father. He didn't like the untethered vibe she gave off. He laughed. He hoped his vocabulary wasn't going to be degraded by words like *vibe*. But he had to admit, it was an appropriate description in this case.

The front door was painted a lurid red. Two windows faced the street. Her glass animal collection lined the sill of the smaller window near the door. The colored glass pieces were sprinkled with dust. His stomach knotted. When he'd talked to her a week or so ago, she'd sounded vague, as if she wasn't really listening. The sense that something in her life had changed nagged at him all through his final exams. He hadn't seen her since Christmas. The dust on the backs of her glass cows and horses filled him with fear.

He got out of the car and stood beside it, staring at the red door. The plaintive strains of an electric guitar drifted over the roof of the narrow two-story house, coming from the deck that faced the beach on the opposite side. The music played at an octave that made his ears ache.

He lifted his suitcases out of the trunk, walked to the door, unlocked it, and stepped inside. The aroma of cookies baking and a hint of disinfectant softened by the scent of artificial lemon suggested everything was normal. At first. The sound of voices, too many voices, came from the deck. He set his suitcases on the tiled floor and stepped inside, closing the door and locking it behind him.

Leaving his suitcases in the entryway, he walked into the

kitchen. The music was louder, piercing. Cookies were stacked on cooling trays and a collection of beer bottles stood near the sink, but otherwise the room was spotless. He looked through the opening over the bar, into the living room which was not so spotless. Couch pillows were scattered around the floor. Beer bottles stood on the coffee table and a thick glass ashtray overflowed with cigarette butts and ash. Several sleeping bags were in a heap near one of the armchairs. The table in the dining area was stacked with plates and a cluster of red-stained wine glasses.

People were sitting and standing on the deck that ran the length of the living room and dining area. Most of them looked to be close to his age. Some of the males — he couldn't quite bring himself to call them men, even the one or two who looked like they fell somewhere between his age and his mother's — were dressed like him, with neatly trimmed hair, pressed shorts, and shirts. Others wore their hair long and were dressed in ragged blue jeans. They were bare chested. One looked like a girl, a string of blue and green beads covering his collarbone. All of the girls had long hair, and they all wore bikinis. As Thomas moved around the bar into the living room, past the messy table, he saw that one girl wore cutoff jeans short enough to look like the bottom half of a bikini. She wasn't wearing a top. He turned, not wanting to stare at her breasts, pale white next to her lightly tanned shoulders and ribs.

He crossed the living room and stopped at the doorway. The screen was open, welcoming flies into the house where they were happy to investigate the dirty plates and glasses. Any minute they'd make their way to the cookies in the kitchen. He closed the screen and spoke through it. "Mom? Mother?"

Somewhat reluctantly, his mother separated herself from a group of young girls. She wore a skimpy turquoise bikini. She looked as good as the girls around her, who appeared to be at least twenty years younger. He felt a confusing mixture of pride, shame, and anger. He didn't want to consider what each of those things meant.

Mary crossed the porch, her bare feet firm on the redwood planks. "Thomas! Come meet my friends."

"What's going on?"

Neither one of them made a move to slide the screen door along the track.

"A party."

"I can see that. All night?"

Mary laughed. "Why do you ask?"

"The sleeping bags."

She opened the door. "Come outside and meet everyone."

"Who are all these people?"

"My friends."

"They look like they're my age. "

She laughed, too hard and too loud. "Not all of them."

"Are you tipsy?"

She laughed harder. "Tipsy? Such a silly, old-fashioned word."

"Are you?"

"I've had some champagne, yes." She giggled. "And maybe

something else, something more natural."

Her eyes were hidden behind enormous sunglasses, the frames the same color as her swimsuit.

"Is that what I smell? Marijuana?"

She shrugged, lowering her shoulders in a languid sweep that looked more like the start of a dance move than a response to his question.

"Is your party almost over?" He took a few steps away from the door.

She moved her shoulders in that same disjointed fashion again. "I don't decide when it's over. And what does that really mean? *Over?*"

Thomas turned and glanced around the living room, certain someone had crept up behind him and was listening to their conversation. He felt like a character in Alice In Wonderland, a male Alice to this petite Cheshire cat. He took a slow breath. "When are they leaving?"

"When they feel like it."

The music wasn't as loud as earlier, the shrill guitar faded, replaced by something with a deeper beat and a guy with a smooth voice. He knew this song, but the title wouldn't come to him. He heard it everywhere, it was constantly playing on the radio. He took her wrist and pulled her toward the doorway. "Can I talk to you in the other room?"

"What for?"

"I want to talk to you."

"I know. But what about?"

"You're acting strange."

"We're all strange. Life is strange. I don't have anything to hide. My friends can hear whatever you have to say."

"I don't think they should."

She smiled as lazily as she'd moved her shoulders. "Oh come on, Thomas. Get a beer and take off those hot shoes and socks and join us."

"I need to unpack."

She waved her hand like she wanted to brush his words out of the space between them. "There's plenty of time for that. The sky is blue, the air is warm. You spend too much time inside classrooms. You need some sunshine."

He stepped back farther and pulled the screen closed, but not in time to prevent another fly from zipping inside the house. "I'll put some of my things away first."

"I'm afraid all the rooms are being used."

"Being used by who?"

"Whom. Used by whom." She giggled.

"Isn't the back bedroom mine?"

"When you're here."

"I'm here now."

"If you don't mind sharing with Caroline."

"Who's Caroline?"

Mary turned. She pointed across the deck at a girl sitting on the railing. She had long brown hair and sunglasses that were larger than Mary's, giving her the appearance of a cartoon bug.

"Okay, but who is she?" As he spoke, he realized she was the one in cutoffs. She was wearing a top now, a red kerchief that wrapped around her breasts.

A man came up to Mary, older than the others, maybe thirty-five. He draped his arm around her shoulders. He looked at Thomas and smiled.

A violent shudder ran through Thomas's stomach.

The man's fingers gripped his mother's bare shoulder. The fingers tightened as he massaged her flesh. His index finger moved slightly, inching toward the strap of her bathing suit. When it was securely settled beneath the turquoise strap, it stopped moving.

"This is Gordon," Mary said. She tipped her face up toward the man and kissed his jaw. "This is my youngest son, Thomas."

"What's up?" Gordon said.

"Hullo." Thomas wondered whether he should have given a proper greeting, but there was nothing about this man that deserved respect. "Mom. Can I please speak to you for a minute?"

"We have all summer to talk," Mary said.

"I know, but I just got here. Did you forget I was coming today?"

"Of course not. I'd never forget you."

He moved away from the door. "I'll go unpack."

"Sure, honey. It seems like it's important to you. To get settled."

Thomas saw her drift away from the door, sliding her arm around Gordon's waist, leaning into him. Gordon wasn't a large man, under six feet, but Mary looked tiny and fragile beside him. It always shocked him — how small his mother was. It was difficult to reconcile her shape with the knowledge she'd carried and given birth to four sons.

He went to the coffee table, grabbed the necks of several beer bottles, and picked up the ashtray. He went into the kitchen and dumped the contents of the ashtray into the garbage. He piled the beer bottles, including those cluttering the counter, on top of the bottles already in the trash. He ate one of the chocolate chip cookies and returned to the living room. It took three more trips to get the beer bottles, wine glasses, and plates into the kitchen. He'd wash them later. He grabbed another cookie and went to the front hall for his suitcases.

The house had two master suites, one on the first floor that his mother used. The second floor suite looked out at the water. The third bedroom was at the front of the house, above his mother's room. He stepped into the ocean-side bedroom. The white shutters above the window seat were closed, keeping the room dark and cool. The pleasant temperature didn't erase the odor of overused sheets and soiled clothing piled on the armchair in the corner. The dresser was covered with soda bottles, seashells, pebbles, and several pairs of sunglasses. The blanket and sheets were pulled out from the mattress, piled in a huge mound near the foot of the bed. Two suitcases stood open near the closet, spilling their contents onto the floor.

How was he supposed to share a room with one double bed? Did his mother intend for him to pack up this girl's things first?

Was she leaving today? He walked down the hall to the other bedroom. It was also filled with discarded clothing. The carpet wasn't visible, every inch covered with sleeping bags. What was going on here? Judging by the stale smells, it appeared that all of her party guests had spent several nights. He needed to talk to his mother without their curious, listening ears, but it seemed she felt no obligation to explain what was going on.

He went out of the bedroom to the stairs and sat on the top step. He put his head in his hands. A dull ache spread out across his forehead, creeping down behind his eyes. He'd wanted to unpack, and now, his sole desire was to lie down and sleep, but there was no place he could stay undisturbed. Worse, there was no place that appeared to have clean bedding. He couldn't wait in the living room with all of them talking and laughing and the music throbbing from the stereo. Should he go find a motel room for the night? Call a high school friend, if any of them were in the area? Music drifted up the stairs, the beat hammering his skull. He felt as if he'd been flung head first into parenthood — responsible for telling his mother to behave herself, to send her friends packing, to clean up the mess, putting her under house arrest for using illegal drugs. He laughed.

The party showed no signs of winding down. The screen door slid open and he heard two people taking as they walked through the living room toward the kitchen. A moment later he heard them again, bottles clinking against each other, and the screen door sliding closed. No doubt more flies had entered the house while they were getting their beverages, the door yawning wide and unattended.

There was nothing to do but join the party. He went back to the bedroom that was supposed to belong to him, shoved his suitcases into the closet, and yanked the sheet and blanket up to cover the bed. There was something exposed and slightly embarrassing about its uncovered state, as if whatever had happened there was on public display. He went into the bathroom, took a clean towel out of the cupboard, and splashed cold water on his face. It made the headache easier to bear.

Downstairs, he opened the refrigerator and took out a beer. He found the opener, pried off the cap, and took a long swallow. His headache slid away. He would have preferred a more civilized drink, but it was mid-afternoon, far too early for that.

As he walked through the living room, he resisted the urge to replace the cushions and roll up the sleeping bags. None of this mess was his and he wasn't responsible for helping his mother clean up when she refused to provide any explanation about where she'd met all these people and how long they were planning to stay in her house.

The moment he stepped onto the deck, Caroline sidled up to him.

"Hi. Mary said you're her son!" Her laugh was more of a shriek, echoing the gulls gliding over the water, looking for a spot to settle on the concrete ship.

"Yes." He extended his hand. "Thomas."

She patted his hand. "Ooh. How formal. I think I'll call you Tom, since I'm sure we'll be seeing a lot of each other."

"I don't know how much we'll be seeing each other, but I prefer Thomas."

"Okay. If you say so. I'm Caroline Miller. Your mom…" she laughed. "I can't think of her as your mother. It seems like she and I are the same age. We're best friends."

"How old are you?" Thomas said.

"Twenty-six."

"Are you married?"

She laughed. "Noooo."

"Why not?" he said.

"Are you married?"

"I'm still in school."

"How do you know I'm not in school?" She tugged on the kerchief that was acting as a top.

"*Are* you?"

"No. Marriage is outdated. I mean, I'd like to get married if it was an equal partnership, something spiritual, with a man who's meant to be my soul mate, someone who has the same vision I do. Some day. But it's not the only option for a girl now."

"Do you have a job, then?"

"I'm still figuring things out."

"How do you support yourself?"

"We share." She swept her arm out to the side, gesturing toward the other partiers, the deck, the house, possibly the ocean itself.

"Who are all these people?"

"Friends. The curious. Seekers."

He took a long swallow of beer.

Caroline lifted her hair off her shoulders and arranged it so half of it fell down her back, and a few sections were draped down the front of her, partially covering the ridiculous piece of fabric she considered a top.

"How did you meet my mother?"

Caroline shivered. "Don't call her that, it's freaky."

"What am I supposed to call her?"

"Mary."

"How did you meet her?"

"At a party."

"Where?"

"Aren't you nosey," Caroline said. "At a party. I don't remember which one. She's very cool. She understands me. We can talk about anything. *Anything*. It's amazing."

"Cool," Thomas said. He put the top of the bottle between his lips but didn't drink. This girl talked about his mother as if she were a kid, two degrees away from being a teenager. Even her sons were well beyond that designation.

"I know. Far out." Caroline took his wrist and squeezed it. Beer sloshed in the bottle. "Wanna joint?"

"No. Thanks."

"You seem uptight. I think it would be nice. We should get to know each other. Since we're both connected to Mary."

"I'm not uptight. Just tired. I have a headache."

"A smoke'll help."

"I don't think so."

"I get wicked headaches. It always helps me."

"I don't smoke dope," he said.

"Oh. Why not?" she let go of his wrist and snaked her arm around his waist. "You are really uptight, man. I can give you a massage."

"I don't think so."

"Okay. That's cool. What do you want? Something else?"

He didn't want to know what she meant. He didn't want to be here. He wanted all these people to leave, right this minute. He didn't even want to finish his beer. He put the bottle in his mouth and tipped his head back, letting the cool liquid flow down his throat as fast as possible. "Why are all your things in the bedroom?"

"I'm staying here. Me and my friends. Mary's friends."

"All these people?"

"No. Not all of them. But a lot of us. That's why Mary is so cool. She knows we all need to share what we have, and she's so generous."

"She made the cookies, too?"

Caroline grinned. "Yes! Groovy cookies. Perfect for munchies."

"I'm sure," Thomas said.

"You sound annoyed."

"That's my bedroom. She knew I was coming home for the summer, and that's the room where I always stay."

"No problem," Caroline said.

"What does that mean?"

"Plenty of room for both of us."

"There's one bed. And I like my privacy."

She laughed. "Privacy is so old-fashioned. We're a community."

"Is that right."

"You'll love it. Lots of mind-blowing conversation, good food. It's like we were all meant to find each other."

"I have a headache," Thomas said.

"That's what you said. A toke will definitely help. I promise."

"Not for me," he said. "Can you clear your stuff out of the suite on the second floor? I need to take a nap. And please change the sheets."

"What?"

"I need to rest."

"It's cool. I'm hanging out here for the rest of the day. I won't be going to bed 'til two or three." She let go of his wrist. "Sleep tight." She stood on her tiptoes and kissed his cheek, so close to his mouth, her lips brushed the corner of his. She bit his earlobe gently. "I don't have cooties. Enjoy my bed."

Thomas waited for her to cross the deck before he went inside. He left his nearly empty beer bottle on the coffee table and climbed the stairs. He found an extra bedspread in the hall closet, flapped it open, and smoothed it out over the rumpled blankets. He closed the door, locked it, pulled off his shoes, and laid down on his back. It took a long time to fall asleep.

Two

Mary liked having a lot of people in the house, but for the past day or two, there were too many. And all of them wanted to be around Gordon. She hadn't had a moment alone with him, except the three minutes when she was introducing him to Thomas. Those few moments were unpleasant — she'd felt Thomas staring at them, the heat of his judgment boring into her forehead. He didn't understand. As much as Thomas knew about what his father had done, he was still a child in a lot of ways. He knew very little about sex and love, and women and men. He probably couldn't imagine his mother desiring a man. Needing a man. But she couldn't live for her children any more. They were adults with their own lives. It was her turn. In the blink of an eye, she'd be too old for any man to want her.

Right now, she could pass for thirty. It was remarkable — forty-seven years old, and no one guessed it, although her twenty-two-year-old son jarred the image. She'd taken excellent care of her body. A lifetime of walking on the beach, hiking in the nearby foothills, eating mostly vegetables and an occasional piece of fish. She looked better than all of these girls who subsisted on hot dogs and potato chips and beer. Too much beer.

She glanced down at her stomach. Her flesh wasn't as firm as the other girls' of course, but she was lightly tanned, and that forgave a lot of soft skin. Her hair was long and silky, bleached to a pale color by the sun. She took baths laced with baby oil and spread lotion over every inch of her skin in the morning. She didn't smoke cigarettes, which kept her voice clear and light. At first, a smoker's voice sounded rough and sexy. But she had plenty of friends who were smokers, and the sexy quality was quickly replaced by hard edges and a loose, sickly cough. It was a mystery why cigarette smoke, or maybe something else wrapped tightly inside those sexy tubes, drew wrinkles to the surface of a woman's skin.

Gordon hadn't slept in her room last night. He'd stayed up until sunrise, hanging out in the living room, talking. He'd crept in beside her just as she was waking. She wasn't sure who all had stayed up with him. She'd fallen into bed at two-thirty, so tired her eyes felt like blocks of wood nestled in her skull. That was where her age showed. By midnight she was longing for rest.

Her home was crowded with friends. With everything changing, friendship had a different meaning than it had when she was a child or even a young mother. Then, friendships were carefully orchestrated among people who moved in the same social circle, neighbors, families with similar incomes and in most cases, identical ethnic backgrounds. Groups of friends were better defined as cliques. She'd lost her place in the clique when Henry walked out of her life. There was no place for single women, especially divorced women, worst of all, abandoned women. The men looked at her as something extraneous or someone deserving of inappropriate comments, glances, and occasionally, touches accompanied by outright propositions. Women saw her as a threat or an object of pity. They acted as if she had the plague. The odor of death would permeate their marriages and leave them alone and destitute — shunned — wandering the fringes of their former group of friends like rabid dogs locked outside a fence where they couldn't cause harm.

It hurt more than any of them would ever know. As if the searing pain of your husband, with whom you shared four children, tossing you out of his bed and the house where you'd made a home for him wasn't enough, her friends turned on her like a pack of wolves. She could see in their slightly lowered eyelids, their darting glances to one another that danced around her own eyes, never meeting her gaze, that they blamed her. There was something defective in her. Perhaps her clothing covered a hideous deformity. She must have failed to satisfy her husband's needs. Possibly she was boring, or a shrew that he couldn't bear to be in the same room with. Their husbands would never…their husbands were faithful… what drove a man to seek a woman outside of his marriage? To tear apart the family, to reject the mother of his children? Men wanted stability and a comfortable fortress to retreat to at the end of the day. They wanted support and affection, welcoming arms, good food, and a listening ear. Mary must have failed to provide one, or all of those things. Their silent judgement was like a shard of glass in her throat every time she approached one of her so-called friends to meet for coffee or lunch or shopping.

And the loneliness. Sitting on her deck, looking out at the

ocean. Watching television alone. Reading a book. She used to enjoy knitting, the click of needles and the weaving of soft yarn, transformed with tight little stitches into something warm and useful and beautiful. Her older boys each had two children, but she wasn't inspired to knit sweaters for the little darlings. Before, she would knit while Henry talked about his day. Now, she could knit and listen to the stereo, but after a while, her thoughts floated above the music and turned in on themselves, aching for the sound of a human voice. The music swelled around her, reshaping her brain into something unrecognizable, rattling inside her skull. Without human contact, she began to feel she didn't exist.

One night, she'd gone outside and stood on the deck. She stared at the dark ocean crashing against the shore, at the ghastly white ship that had taken her mother. An abandoned ship that was haunted by unknowable beings. Now, she was one of them. Something that didn't exist in any meaningful way. Living beings exchanged thoughts and smiles and caresses. Only those hovering between two worlds were voiceless, hiding unknowable feelings, unable to feel the sensation of another body.

The beach was deserted and the lights of the houses on either side of her were barely visible behind thick drapes or solid pine shutters, closing out the night, and closing out any hope of her glimpsing a human being. And maybe it was better that way. She wasn't sure what it would feel like to see a man and woman in their living room, talking to each other, drinking cocktails, holding each other on the couch.

The waves continued unabated. The ocean didn't care whether anyone heard their crashing, their steady rhythm, unchanged since the world came into existence, continuing until the human race managed to destroy the globe and all breathing life with mountains of toxic garbage or a nuclear explosion.

Thoughts drifted through her mind, unrecognizable as her own — a suggestion that her purpose in life was over, that she should venture out onto the boat and extinguish her breath in the same way her mother had.

You bore children. You raised them. They don't need you now. Your husband doesn't need you anymore. It's time to say goodbye.

She'd gone back into the house, picked up the phone, and dialed three friends in succession. Each one answered, greeted Mary politely, then informed her it wasn't a good time for a phone conversation. Finally, she'd called Thomas at his dorm. They'd talked for several minutes, but the sound of voices in the background and his obvious distraction slowly emptied her mind of anything worth saying. Thomas seemed to be at an equal loss for words. When she hung up, she'd felt she had her sanity back under control, but the loneliness was an ache that threatened to crush her. She mixed herself a martini and when it was half finished, she was sleepy enough to crawl into bed.

These accepting, loving kids had erased the pain. They really were kids, but what did that matter? They liked her. They were grateful she offered a place where they could crash and a place to party, a refrigerator full of food and beer, the ability to cook delicious meals. They listened to what she had to say. They didn't treat her like a mother or a middle aged woman, or someone too old to have fun. She'd gradually modified her vocabulary until her speech sounded similar to theirs. She wore the same drapey blouses and sandals they did. She loved smoking marijuana. It was more pleasurable than a few too many glasses of champagne. The good feeling lasted longer and didn't lead to stumbling, rude behavior, followed by nausea. She floated pleasantly, content to simply *be*. Wanting nothing.

Although right now, she wanted something very much. She wanted Gordon. Despite the fact that the world was changing — fewer boundaries defining relationships, couples coming together and moving apart without fights and jealousy, she still wanted a man that belonged exclusively to her. She was fairly certain Gordon wanted the same thing. He wasn't a kid either. Despite the ideas of free love and getting rid of restrictions such as marriage licenses and the obligations imposed by vows made in churches, people still needed companions. They needed someone to call their own, someone with whom you could share deeper thoughts and feelings. You couldn't make love with every single person you knew. After a while, it would be confusing and exhausting.

She'd met Gordon on the concrete ship in early June. She'd been standing near the side looking into the water. He and a few others were sitting at the farthest accessible point. He had longish dark brown hair barely captured in his stub of a ponytail. His sideburns were long, but the rest of his face clean-shaven. He was slim with well-defined muscles. Although it was daylight and the risk of being caught was high, he and his friends were passing around a marijuana cigarette. She'd watched from the corner of her eye as Gordon took the tiny stick, put it to his lips and sucked in smoke, holding his breath for a moment. He'd slowly released a cloud of smoke as he passed the tiny cigarette to the boy at his left. She hadn't turned away quickly enough and he glanced in her direction, catching her watching him. He gave her a lazy smile that melted over her chest. His eyes looked hungry, staring at her as if she were the most beautiful woman he'd ever seen. He'd gestured for her to join them. Without thinking, she walked across the ship and sat beside him, not caring that two of his companions looked as if they were barely out of high school, not caring that all of them but Gordon were young enough to be her children.

Taking a puff from the shared cigarette was frightening, but she didn't want to give the impression of being old and disapproving, afraid of experimenting. She'd never smoked a real cigarette, so she had no idea what was coming when the smoke wound its way into her lungs. She'd coughed until her throat felt as if a cat had scratched her esophagus. Her eyes brimmed with tears and her nose ran, but they hadn't laughed. They'd waited patiently for her to take a second hit, watching with partially closed, dilated eyes, as if they wanted to drink in her experience and make it part of their own.

When the cigarette came to her the second time, Gordon had put his hand on her thigh. A river of warmth opened up inside of her and she wanted to lean into him. She managed to remain upright as her throat clogged with liquid. No one had touched her like this in more years than she wanted to think about. Tears rushed into her eyes, not from the smoke this time. Gratitude and shame and desire washed through her in equal quantities. He held the joint for her. The side of his thumb brushed against her lips and she could barely manage to draw the smoke into her body.

The abandoned ship seemed to vibrate beneath them, as if it wanted to welcome them to the depths below, form a shell over them, and close out the rest of the world. She began to feel as if the people surrounding her — she'd forgotten all of their names except Gordon's — were the closest friends she'd ever had. And maybe they were. They smiled at her, they didn't ask her marital status and they didn't seem to care when she said something foolish. No matter what she did, closed her eyes, held the smoke in for too long and coughed like she was trying to expel blood, or sat without speaking, they smiled at her.

That night, she and Gordon went for a long walk and made love on the beach. She was still high, or something like it. Maybe making love with Gordon felt different because it was different. He'd noticed the essence of her. He'd whispered her name repeatedly. He'd taken his time, drinking in her body, her mind, her soul. For a moment, her mind slipped sideways. She wondered if Henry was different with his new wife, or if he'd continued having sex with the same mechanical efficiency as always. She closed her eyes and let the memory float away.

Gordon was confusing, though. He didn't act as if they were a couple. He didn't touch other girls beyond a hand on a shoulder, or a kiss on a cheek, but he talked to them constantly. Whenever she saw him, he was deep in conversation with a girl. Sometimes Mary would walk down to the beach and observe him from a distance, seated on dry sand, talking and gesturing, surrounded by three or four girls who looked at him with devoted gazes that suggested he was their teacher, their guru. At the same time, the girls' lips looked as if they wanted more from him than ideas and opinions and stories. They wanted *him*, not just his insights from his years spent teaching high school. Not just stories of his drop-out moment of enlightenment, after which he'd traveled around Europe and Asia, acquiring more stories than Mary thought she'd be able to acquire in a lifetime.

She hadn't managed to find the courage to ask for a definition of their relationship. At night, he came into her bed. During the day, he belonged to everyone.

Today, she planned to ask him directly. Maybe.

She went into the kitchen and made a pot of coffee. Most of her new friends weren't coffee drinkers, but she needed at least one cup to get the day going. Some of them roused their bodies with pills. The pills scared her. She wished the few who saw pills as a road to a satisfying life would find another place to stay. Still, it was important to accept everyone, not judge their choices.

Gordon liked coffee. She hoped he'd smell it and join in her in the kitchen while it brewed. They could go out onto the deck and drink a cup while the others slept. She washed the plates and set them in the dish drainer to dry. She wiped down the counter and carried the overflowing trash bin out to the garbage can in the rear corner of her one-car garage. She went back inside and opened the refrigerator door. There were plenty of eggs. She'd scramble a large pan of them.

When the coffee was ready, she was still alone in the kitchen. She filled her cup. She took out a second cup and saucer and set them on the counter. She could carry the coffee to the bedroom and wake Gordon. He wasn't annoyed when she woke him before he was ready, but neither would he be eager to get out of bed and join her. Best to drink a cup and wait to see if the aroma tickled the inside of his nostrils and drew him toward consciousness.

She stepped around the bodies curled and sprawled inside sleeping bags across the living room floor. The coffee shivered in her cup. As she tried to steady her hand, the bottom of the cup rattled softly against the saucer. No one even turned over, no eyelids fluttered. She stepped outside and settled on the chaise lounge. She wished Gordon was beside her, watching the fog change shape, settling into a long gray and brown tube of vapor cushioning the horizon.

The coffee was cooling fast. She drank half of it in a few sips. She'd never gotten around to speaking to Thomas the night before. She wasn't sure where he'd ended up sleeping. She couldn't imagine he would have agreed to be in a room with others. He was funny about wanting things just so. He'd wanted his own room from the day he learned to talk, and had been reluctant to share a dorm room when he first went away to college. He'd overcome that, but she was pretty sure he would never allow Caroline to stretch out her sleeping bag beside the bed where he slept, much less stay in the same bed with him. He must have chased her and the other girl into the already over-crowded third bedroom.

As if her thoughts had summoned him, she turned and saw Thomas standing on the other side of the glass door. He slid it open and stepped outside.

Before the door was closed, he spoke. "What the heck is going on here?"

Mary took a sip of coffee. "That's not a very nice way to start the day."

"I tried to talk to you yesterday and you avoided me."

"Why don't you get some coffee. And refill mine." She smiled and held up her cup. He took it and went back inside. Her chance for time alone with Gordon was gone. Maybe this afternoon. If the fog stayed out where it was, they'd all go for a swim and perhaps she could entice Gordon to leave the others and bob in the waves with her, talking between breakers.

Thomas was standing at the door holding two cups of coffee.

She got up and opened the door. "Is anyone else awake?"

He shrugged and settled on the chaise lounge next to her. "Who are they?"

"My friends."

"Your friends? They're my age."

"Not all of them."

"Why are a bunch of people young enough to be your kids

staying here? How long has this been going on? When are they leaving? Are you aware that they're smoking pot?"

"Slow down."

"I have a lot of questions."

"The friends I had when I was married to your father abandoned me."

"And this is the answer? Throw a house party for a bunch of kids? Strangers?"

"Some of them have become quite good friends. Caroline. Beth. Gordon."

"About Gordon..."

"Quite a few of them have only been here a few days. I expect most of them will leave on Sunday."

"Most of them?"

"Gordon and Caroline and Beth will be here all summer, I think. Paul, too."

"Why?"

"You don't have the right to interrogate me."

"I think I do. You're my mother."

She laughed. "This is my house. I can invite anyone I want to stay here. It was very lonely, you know."

"I'm sorry about that."

"It's not your fault."

"That's not what I meant," he said.

She sipped her coffee.

"I just don't get it."

"It's simple. I was cast out of society."

"Don't dramatize it."

"I'm not. So I made some new friends. They're very accepting. I don't have to prove anything to them, and they don't judge me for being divorced. They don't even care. They don't pity me because my husband cast me aside."

"No one pities you. They know Dad's a jackass."

"You're wrong."

He took several sips of coffee. "About the marijuana. I don't know if you realize…"

From the corner of her eye, she saw someone moving on the other side of the glass door. She turned — Gordon. She pushed herself out of the chaise lounge.

"Do you know they're…" Thomas said.

She patted his head. "Later." She pulled open the door. "There's fresh coffee in the kitchen."

"Cool," Gordon said.

She left the door open. She didn't want to discuss pot, or anything else, with Thomas. Why did he have to get up so early? He'd stolen the few minutes she might have had alone with Gordon. She wanted to talk to Gordon, not her square, fretting son.

Three

Watching his mother scramble eggs, butter toast, and serve orange juice to the hoard of sleepy, ungrateful house guests made Thomas's stomach tighten as if he'd swallowed a large rock. It sat there, bearing down on him, interfering with his breathing. When they'd finished eating, most of them drifted out to the deck and began wandering down onto the beach. They didn't bother to carry their breakfast plates to the kitchen, much less offer to wash up.

He stood with a linen towel, wiping each plate as Mary dunked it in the rinse water and handed it to him. Caroline sat on the kitchen counter, bare legs crossed at the ankles. She was talking and braiding her hair. Each time he went to put a glass or a plate in the cabinet he had to excuse himself. She spoke breathlessly about a *mind blowing* music festival she'd attended in Monterey. *The music was out of sight. The people were so groovy*. The music *blew* her mind *wide open*, expanded it *beyond* the *limits* she'd known were possible.

He wanted to tell her to be more specific, but then, he didn't really want to know exactly how and why her mind was blown. He wanted her to stop talking.

The night before, he'd folded her clothes into a sloppy pile and placed them outside the bedroom door. He dragged her sleeping bag into the hallway. He stripped the bed and piled the sheets on top of her sleeping bag. He opened the shutters and windows to let in the ocean air. When the room was back to its original state, he locked the door. When he'd come out of the bedroom this morning, the clothes, sheets, and sleeping bag were gone. She hadn't said a word, keeping her monologue focused solely on the mind-blowing concert. Perhaps she had more affection for Mary than he'd assumed.

The dishes were washed, dried, and put away. The counters glistened, the same as his mother's counters had shone all his life without a spot of water or a stray piece of onion skin. Caroline continued talking and Mary encouraged her, asking questions, acting as if Caroline's unbroken string of hip phrases contained the most fascinating information she'd ever heard.

"We should get some sun and sand," Caroline said. She hopped off the counter and tugged the cutoff jeans away from her crotch. They appeared to be the same pants she'd worn the day before. He wondered if any of the clothes tossed around the bedroom had been washed since her mind-blowing concert weekend. She drifted out of the kitchen, behaving as if he weren't there — simply a dish drying machine, useless until the next meal. Was his mother doing all the cooking and cleaning for these cretins? It seemed so, although it might not be fair to judge since he'd been home less than twenty-four hours. Last night, a few of the guests had gone out and picked up pizza for dinner. All of that was put away when he'd come downstairs this morning, but he imagined his mother had cleaned up while she waited for the coffee to brew.

The living room stank of pot, sweat, dirty hair, and beer. There was nowhere to go but back to his room. He should call one of his brothers. It was doubtful they had any idea what was going on. As far as he knew, none of his three brothers had visited her since Christmas. Of course she was lonely. It wasn't surprising that some of her lifelong friends had excluded her from their social lives, but all of them? He didn't want to be responsible for taking care of her. He was the one who was supposed to be going to parties and experimenting and not caring about obligations. Part of him wanted to pack up and return to Berkeley. Suddenly, living with a handful of engineering students in an overpopulated old house didn't seem as troubling.

He climbed the stairs, exiled to his room. He opened the shutters and settled in the armchair in the corner. He pulled a copy of *You Only Live Twice* out of his suitcase and began reading, glad for the escape out of this house full of dopers and freeloaders, into the world of *James Bond*.

By eleven, the sun was shining directly on the chair. The side of his face was hot and his jaw itched. He closed the book and stared out at the concrete ship. Fishermen lined one side. There were people strolling around the worn boat, leaning over, peering into the water. Some of them might be his mother's friends. What did they do all day? Lie around on the beach, waiting for dark until they could get stoned? There were plenty of people like that at Berkeley. Didn't it eventually get old? What did they plan to do once they ran out of money? Were all the food and beer expenses coming out of his mother's bank account? His father had seen that she was well-situated, but still. Surely they needed cash to buy pot, and pills, and whatnot.

It was probably hypocritical to condemn them since he was still dependent on his parents' money. But he was getting an education, preparing to support himself, to contribute to society. He had goals and plans for the future. This crowd was only interested in music and sex and pot.

He stood up, went to the window, and opened it wider. The sky was clear without a trace of fog. Monterey was visible on one side of the bay and Capitola on the other. The expanse of water was the blue of paintings and colored photographs. He tried to remember what he usually did during his long summer days at home. There were lots of books, some television shows and movies. Occasionally he went swimming or surfing with a few remaining high school friends with whom he had less in common every year. He'd never had a summer job, another reason he shouldn't be delivering harsh judgment to the kids and newly emerged adults sleeping all over his mother's floors.

As he stepped away from the window, there was a knock on the bedroom door. He glanced at the knob — locked.

"Who is it?"

No one spoke. He grabbed his swim trunks out of the second dresser drawer and waited. "Can I help you?"

There was nothing but silence. He went to the door and opened it. The hallway was empty, and the door facing his was closed. He didn't hear any voices coming up the stairs from the living room. Hadn't they all gone out to the beach? He turned back, closed and locked the door, and changed into swim trunks.

Downstairs, the living room was in worse condition than the previous day — bedding covered the floor and most of the furniture. Clothing was tossed on the table. One of his mother's beautiful cream and blue china coffee cups with a cigarette butt swimming in the muddy liquid sat on the carpet near the floor lamp, unprotected from a careless footstep. He picked up the cup and saucer and went to the kitchen. He stabbed the butt with a steak knife and dropped it into the trash. He emptied the coffee into the sink.

From the back deck, he looked out across the beach. It was filled with people lying on towels, tossing balls, and splashing in the waves. If he'd been asked by the police, he couldn't have pointed out the people that slept a few feet away from him all night. He went outside and settled on the chaise lounge. He was too tired to battle the waves and the chilly water of Monterey Bay. He wished he'd brought his book with him, but he was tired of reading. He stretched out and closed his eyes.

When he woke, there was a shadow across his torso. He opened one eye.

"Hi." The kid who stood in front of him was tall — probably six-three. He had longish blonde hair and a nearly hairless chest. He was thin but not skeletal. Around his neck was a leather necklace with a thick pewter charm on it. Thomas couldn't make out what the charm represented — maybe an animal of some kind. A dolphin?

"Sorry if I woke you," the kid said.

"It's okay."

"Do you want a coke?"

Thomas adjusted the back of the chair so he was sitting up straighter. "Sure."

The kid disappeared into the house and returned with two bottles of cola. He handed one to Thomas. "I'm Paul."

"Thomas King. Nice to meet you. Thanks for the drink." He took a long swallow of soda.

He waited for Paul to give his last name, but Paul simply smiled and nodded his head several times. "Can I sit down?"

"Are you one of Mary's friends?"

Paul nodded again. He sat sideways on the other chaise lounge.

"How'd you meet her?" Thomas squeezed his hand around the bottle, hoping to keep it solidly in place. It was slick with moisture.

"She's cool."

"I know that, but where did you meet her?"

"She knows my friends, I guess."

"Who are your friends?"

"Jerry. Dawn. Caroline. George. Beth."

Thomas closed his eyes. There had to be a way to get his mother to understand this was not a good idea. In fact, it was a very bad idea. She was putting herself in danger. An army of strangers was moving in and around her house, using illegal drugs, possibly selling them. And if they weren't blatant thieves, feeding them must be costing a fortune. Not to mention the wear and tear on her carpets and furniture.

"Did you want to get back to your nap?" Paul said.

Thomas shook his head, but he kept his eyes closed for a moment longer.

"Should I put on some tunes?"

Thomas shook his head again. He opened his eyes and looked at Paul. The boy was young. Eighteen, maybe nineteen. "Are you in school?"

"Naw."

"How long have you been here?"

"It's hard to remember."

"Try."

Paul laughed. "You sound worried."

Thomas shook his head. He gulped down the rest of the soda.

"Want a beer?" Paul said.

"Are you twenty-one?"

Paul laughed. He stood and drank the rest of his soda. His Adam's apple bobbed and moved like a hamster scrambling around an exercise wheel. He took the bottle from Thomas's hand and opened the screen door. He went into the house, leaving the door open. Thomas wondered whether he was going to survive the summer. Either his mother had to wake up and take back control of her house, or he needed to figure out another option. If one more person left the door open, he'd smash a fat horsefly on the side of the offender's face.

Paul returned with a six pack of beer.

"One is fine for me," Thomas said.

"This way I don't have to keep going back and forth."

"They're going to get warm. Can you please close the screen all the way."

Paul jumped up and adjusted the door. He settled on the chaise lounge and shoved the rest of the six back beneath it. "There. It'll stay cool in the shade." He pulled an opener out of his pocket and pried off the caps. He held the bottle out and waited for Thomas to take it. "Cheers to summer."

As if to argue with him, a gust of cold wind whipped across the deck. It seemed to come from the direction of the concrete ship. Thomas looked at the people fishing and walking around on it. None of them seemed to be reacting to a rush of cold air. He shivered. "Cheers."

Paul downed half the beer. He set the bottle near his left foot and leaned forward. "I never saw you before last night."

"I just got here." There was no need to explain who he was. Not yet. It would be more interesting to see what developed, to see whether he gave the impression he was just another freeloading partier.

"Cool. Where from?"

"Berkeley."

"Wow. *Berserkly*. What's it like there?"

"Like any school, I guess."

"You take classes?"

"I'm a graduate student."

"Far out."

Thomas rolled his eyes.

"I'm from Boise. In Idaho."

"I know where Boise is."

"People are more cool on the coast. More open, ya' know?"

"I've lived in California all my life, so I guess I don't know. Not really. But I've heard."

"I thought you were cool the minute I saw you," Paul said. "Something clicked."

"Clicked?"

"I felt we might have had similar experiences…that we look at the world the same way."

"How on earth would you know that?"

"Just a vibe."

"I'm an engineer. I don't believe in vibes."

"They're everywhere. The whole planet is vibrating — a new generation is taking over. It doesn't matter if you believe."

"If you say so."

"Besides, I bet you can feel it if you try. Can't you feel it when a storm is coming? Or when a guy you meet in a bar is a threat?"

"I get weather updates from NBC."

Paul grinned. He had straight teeth and thin lips which made him look sophisticated despite his bare chest and leather necklace. What kind of guy wore a necklace?

"What about a thug in a bar? You can feel that they're looking for a fight."

"I don't spend much time in bars."

"At a party?"

Thomas didn't want to admit there was definitely a vibe to someone who wanted to hurt you — they provoked an animal wariness. It was the same tightening of his muscles and acceleration of his breathing that occurred when he looked at his mother's house guests. Maybe it was the word he objected to — *Vibe!* If they were discussing instinct or something more scientific instead of a pseudo-psychedelic term, he'd agree. He felt a *vibe* right now, but he couldn't identify what it was. Could the kid be right? There was some common experience or outlook they shared and his body told him it was so, even though his mind was unable to provide information? He barely felt it. Did Paul feel it with more intensity because that was what drugs did to you? Put you more in tune with you instincts?

Paul nudged his foot against the side of Thomas's lounge chair. "Admit it, I'm right."

"I prefer to explain things with rational language."

"Sure. Okay. But I'm right."

Thomas finished the rest of his beer. "Yes. But I didn't get any *click* from you. I didn't even see you until you sat down here a few minutes ago." It wasn't the truth, but he felt he needed to protect himself from Paul's assumptions.

"I'm wounded," Paul said.

"Can I have another beer?"

"I thought one was enough?"

"It's hot."

"It is." Paul reached under the lounge chair and pulled a beer out of the cardboard container. He thrust his hips up from the chair and worked the bottle opener out of his pocket. He eased off the cap and handed the beer to Thomas, vapor still escaping from the cool interior.

Thomas took a few sips. He turned his head to look at the water. He felt uncomfortable under Paul's gaze, and he wasn't sure what to say in response to the comment about being wounded. It sounded frighteningly vulnerable. Why couldn't the guy keep it light? Wounded turned it into something painful and serious. What difference did it make? He was probably going on about *clicking* and common experiences because he wanted something. Cash. For pot. They all wanted something. He wondered again whether a shared house near the UC campus wasn't a better option. When he turned down that possibility, he'd had no idea what he was coming home to.

"I can tell we're both sensitive," Paul said. "We feel life more profoundly than others."

"Is that right? How on earth would you know that? You know nothing about me."

"I said, it's a vibe. Instinct, if you prefer."

"Well I have no instinct about you," Thomas said. It was a compounding of the lie, but he wasn't going to yield the upper hand. If the vibes were so great, the kid would figure out it was a lie. He smiled, then quickly twisted his lips into a less revealing expression.

"Really? None at all?" Paul grinned. He pushed his hair off his face. The top of his forehead glistened with sweat and the roots of his hair were damp. The moisture darkened the roots, giving them the appearance of tree roots in sharp contrast to the blonde strands surrounding the rest of his face, and the delicate blonde hairs in his sideburns.

Thomas shifted in his chair. Sweat was pooling on the small of his back, his skin starting to glue itself to the cushion. He shifted again, angling his body away from Paul's. He sipped his beer and looked at the endless blue expanse. Sunlight sparkled on the water where it rippled beyond the swells undulating toward shore. It wasn't unpleasant listening to Paul's smooth voice. Despite the strange ideas and the insistence that they had some kind of mysterious connection, Thomas realized he didn't want to be anywhere else. He was enjoying the beer and the heat and the shimmering, gliding conversation with an uncertain destination.

"Why do you think I wanted to sit here and share a few beers with you?" Paul said.

"Being polite to the host? I dunno."

"The host?"

"Never mind."

"I thought this was Mary's house? Are you like some super secret owner, a magnate concealing your identity, dropping out to start your own commune?"

"Not at all."

"Not a secret owner?"

"Correct."

"Then why did you call yourself the host?"

Thomas sipped his beer. His tongue had taken its lead from an unconscious part of his brain, now that a bottle and a half of beer was swimming around his skull. "No reason."

"There must be a reason."

Resisting any further would make him look like a dope once the truth came out. He wasn't sure why he cared what this hippie kid thought of him, and he didn't really, but he did care that he wasn't perceived as a sneaky jerk. "Mary's my mother."

"Wow. No shit. Hard to believe."

"I'm home from school for the summer. I was kind of surprised to find all these people here. So you'll understand why I didn't notice you in particular."

"Just one of the crowd."

"That's right."

"She doesn't seem that old," Paul said.

"No, she doesn't." He almost added that he had three older brothers, but it was important to her that she call these people her friends, and he had no reason to spoil that for her. He wanted them gone, but that had to be her choosing.

"No wonder you're so territorial."

"I'm not territorial."

"You are. I saw you the minute you walked in yesterday. You took over the room and I could feel your energy all over the deck. Everything changed."

Thomas was foolishly proud of the fact that he had such a compelling presence. He hoped it wasn't simply a sense of ownership and entitlement, but that there was something about him that dominated. Growing up with three strong-willed older brothers made him the least noticed. At least by his father. Maybe because his father had turned his interest outside of their family once Thomas began making his way through the teenage years. For whatever reason, Thomas had always been more connected to his mother. He was never quite sure of how he measured up to his brothers in his father's eyes. Once his father had shown his true nature, Thomas no longer cared what the man thought, but the sense of being unnoticed remained.

It was disappointing that Paul was tying the impact of his presence to the fact that he lived here. "So, not really a connection after all," he said.

"No, there was a connection. I know we're brothers under the skin. Just saying you took over the place when you walked in and now I know why. But there's more to it."

"Do you always have these deep, esoteric conversations with people you've just met?"

"No. I like you. I feel a connection."

"Why do you keep saying that?"

"It's the truth."

"You're making me nervous." Thomas laughed and finished his beer. He set the bottle on the deck. Even though he felt Paul was peering inside him, digging around in his brain for something Thomas didn't even recognize was there, he still had no desire to leave. He didn't want to go up to his room and return to the unambiguous world of *James Bond*, or even go for a swim. Of course, after two beers, swimming was no longer a good idea. He wanted to ask for a third beer but it would give

Paul the upper hand — admitting he wanted to get drunk in the middle of the day after all.

"Wanna smoke a joint?" Paul said.

"I don't do that."

"Why not?"

"It takes away all your drive."

"That's a myth."

"Is it?"

"Well you're not gonna want to go crack open a text book right after a few tokes, but it's not like it's permanent. It'll help you chill. More than beer. You need to chill."

"How do you know what I need?"

"No pressure. Maybe you'll change your mind later."

"I don't think so," Thomas said.

Paul pulled the six pack from under the chair, removed a bottle, opened it, and handed it to Thomas.

They drank their beers and Thomas looked out at the ocean, as if it might wash over the confusing, unsettling conversation.

Four

The people staying in her house had come into her life through Gordon. When she was honest, she acknowledged there were more people than she would have liked. She didn't mind Caroline and Beth. Or Paul — he was a sweet boy. But the others…she couldn't remember some of their names. Currently there were thirteen — five in the upstairs back bedroom where Thomas had unceremoniously shoved Caroline and Beth in with three other girls, and eight sleeping on the living room floor. She couldn't say whether it was the same eight people every night. The fact that she was stoned in the evenings and slightly tipsy most of the afternoon was not helping to maintain control of her home and the guest list.

It started simply enough — she was drunk on sex. The magical things his hands and mouth did to her body made her feel like an entirely different woman. She'd grown up with the impression that the sole purpose of sex was procreation. With Henry, she came to understand it was a burning need for a man, one of the highlights of his existence. She vaguely understood that some women felt the same way, but she didn't get it. Feeling Henry's skin on hers was pleasant enough, but it was a lot of effort and mildly uncomfortable, and ultimately, something to feign interest in.

Under Gordon's care, her body exploded. Now she understood the drive, the desire. She couldn't get enough of him. It felt like an addiction. She thought about him and replayed their love making constantly. A glimpse of his face across the room caused her stomach to collapse. Sometimes, she felt she could hardly breathe, she wanted him so badly.

That first night her arms and legs began shaking from the cold as they lay in each other's arms. She invited him into the house. A floating, disconnected piece of her brain inquired whether it was a good idea to invite a man she'd just met, while smoking pot no less, into her home. She shushed it, snapping to herself that the question sounded like something Verna would say — the woman who had married her widowed father, tried to replace Mary's mother, and ultimately drove Mary into what turned out to be a heart-shattering marriage. A man who may never have loved her. Henry had loved that she was attractive and a good mother and a gracious hostess and an excellent cook. She supposed she did have Verna to thank for that last bit.

Gordon had laughed — a weak, uncertain sound. "Not sure I'm up for climbing that hill when I'm stoned."

She gestured toward the row of houses lining Rio Del Mar beach. "It's right there."

"Really?"

"Yes."

He grabbed her waist from behind and gently bit her shoulder. "You're stoned too. You don't live in a beach-front house."

"Yes, I do."

"Don't believe it."

"Come on." She wriggled out of his arms. She picked up her straw bag and sandals. She stuffed the rumpled, sand-encrusted towel into the bag and took his hand. "I'll show you."

They walked across the beach. She led him along the pathway up the slight incline to Beach Drive. As they passed the darkened homes of her neighbors, she dug around in her bag with her free hand. She pulled out her keys. When they reached her red front door, she stopped, inserted the key, and opened the door.

Gordon followed her inside. She turned on the lights. He let out a long whistle. She turned away from him, wishing he'd delivered that admiring sound to her rather than her house.

Spanish tile covered the entryway and kitchen floors. The kitchen had rustic cabinets with iron handles, a primrose blue table with two chairs, and an eating bar that opened into the living room. The back deck, a strip of sand, and the ocean beyond were visible from the righthand end of the bar. The living room was spacious with a dining area that backed up to the kitchen. She'd decorated with modern wood-frame couches and chairs and a six-foot console that housed the TV and stereo system. The dining table accommodated twelve. On the opposite side was a short hallway leading to her bedroom and adjoining bathroom and beside that was the staircase to the second floor.

Gordon wandered around, whistling at each place he stopped — the sliding glass doors to the deck, the state-of-the-art television, the stereo system, and her spacious bedroom, done in blue and green. He paused at the foot of the stairs. "May I?"

"Of course." She smiled. Such a gentleman. She'd been silly to worry about inviting him inside.

He climbed the stairs while she waited on the first floor. He returned a few minutes later. "I didn't see any of your husband's things."

His quest for information lacked subtlety, but she didn't challenge him. "I'm divorced."

"He did right by you."

"It's what I deserve."

He lifted his eyebrows. "Better than sleeping in a tent. Or on the beach."

She laughed. "I certainly think so."

He dropped his backpack in the corner of her bedroom. They stripped off their clothes and fell into bed. Gordon put his hand on her belly. After a few minutes, he moved it and rested the side of his head in the spot he'd warmed with his palm. He turned and pressed his face into her skin, inhaling as if he wanted to draw the aroma of her out through her navel.

She giggled.

After a while, he suggested they smoke a joint.

She didn't want the odor in her bedroom, but the idea of doing something so unconventional kept her from speaking — In her bed! With a man she'd just met!

Tomorrow she'd open all the windows. It was easy to get a good cross-breeze going from the back doors into her bedroom where a large window faced the street.

He'd stayed with her for three days and then said he had

things to take care of. After knowing him such a short time, she didn't have the right to ask what *things*. She didn't want to question him like a demanding wife, or worse, his mother. It wasn't that she viewed him as belonging to her sons' generation, but the space of years between Gordon and her eldest was narrower than she wanted to think about.

When he'd returned at dinnertime the following day, Caroline, Beth, and Paul were with him. Mary had recoiled when she saw them, feeling the pinch of age — overcome with a vision of herself as a foolish middle-aged woman. These were kids. Maybe not teenagers, although Paul appeared to be under twenty-one. She was older by nearly two decades. Of course, Gordon was older than the girls by a decade.

He'd introduced them and asked if they could hang out for a few days.

"Sure," Mary said. "Of course. There's far too much space for just me."

The girls treated her like an instant friend. They didn't say a word about her age, or gush over a house they couldn't possibly afford. Paul was dreamy and detached and demanded nothing.

Mary offered to make Cioppino and the girls said they'd walk to the store for sourdough bread. They drank champagne and ate on the back deck even though it was foggy and the early June air was as cold as a winter evening. Caroline and Beth wore cut-off blue jeans that revealed goose bumps from their hip bones to their ankles, and tops that tied behind their necks. They clearly weren't wearing bras, and she wondered whether they were wearing underwear at all. She felt overdressed and old-fashioned in her sundress and cardigan sweater. Her feet were bare, her toenails painted pink, but it didn't help. She looked like their mother.

The maternal feeling went away after they smoked a joint and Gordon showed the girls the upstairs bedroom overlooking the beach. They could share the double bed and Paul would sleep in the other room. When Gordon slipped beneath the sheets of Mary's bed and his warm skin touched hers, the thing stuck in her throat dissolved. She closed her eyes and let him carry her off to a place where she wasn't required to think.

A few days after that, Paul returned from a hitchhiking trip that had taken him up Highway One past Bonny Doon. Two boys and a girl he'd met at a beach party were with him. Rather than asking Mary if they could stay at her house, Paul had dragged Gordon onto the deck where they spent nearly two hours talking, heads bent together. Fog billowed around them. With their longish hair and funky shirts, they had the look of pirates conspiring to capture an enemy's chest of gold. She laughed. It was a crazy thought — THC lingering too long in her blood. She shook her head vigorously. Her hair, longer than it had been since before she was married, flowed across her bare shoulders and arms.

Finally, Gordon came into the house. Paul remained on the deck, gazing at the ocean like he was standing at the bow of a ship. The pirate image returned to her mind. Gordon pulled her into her bedroom. *Their* bedroom, was how she liked to think of it. He kissed her hard. "I can't last two hours without needing you." His voice was hoarse, either from talking too much with Paul, or the damp salty air, or maybe his need for her. He held her so tightly she had trouble taking a full breath. "Those kids with Paul," he said. "They really need a place to crash. The girl…she was kicked out of the house. Isn't that awful?"

As she nodded, the fabric of his shirt sleeve tugged at her ear.

"There's plenty of room," he said.

"Yes."

"I'll give you some cash."

"Don't worry about it," she said. "Everything's fine. No child should be thrown out of her home."

"I agree. It's happening to a lot of kids now. Old folks don't understand how things are changing. They don't understand how liberating it is to rearrange your mind, how music takes control of your body. They don't get all the cool things that are happening."

Mary shook her head and swallowed hard. Tears pressed against her eyeballs, liquid threatening to fill the back of her throat and spill out of her nose and eyes. "Sometimes," she whispered. "Sometimes…"

He pulled back slightly and kissed her ear, his breath warm inside her head. "Sometimes, what?"

"Sometimes…"

He nibbled at the lobe.

"Sometimes I feel older than everyone. I am, of course. But I…"

He laughed. "Older? What does age matter? It's what's inside here."

He tapped his fingers on the back of her skull. They echoed inside her head as if he were rapping on a coconut. He moved away from her and took her wrist. He pulled her to the bed and slipped a joint out of his pocket. He lit it and handed it to her before taking a hit himself. She drew in the aromatic smoke and handed it back.

"We're all one," he said. "We're connected by the experiences we have together, not by what happened before. Not by whether we had kids or jobs or other relationships. None of that matters."

She wasn't sure about that. Her children certainly mattered, more than anything. Her whole adult life had been shaped around her children. But she understood what he was trying to say. She took another hit. She was overly attached to one idea, to her sons. The other things he mentioned were equally important. Besides, her boys were gone. This was her life now. She had a short time left to enjoy new things before her hair went gray and her body began to slip away from her frame.

It had been a long day. Too much sun, too much food, and now, too many puffs of dope. Mary was exhausted, and Thomas was poisoning her mood. He'd sat on the deck most of the day, dozing and drinking beer. She'd glanced up from the beach once and seen him staring at the water. Paul sat beside him, talking with animated, eager gestures. Thomas looked disinterested. Later, when she'd checked again, Thomas was alone. He'd been rude and unfriendly to everyone. A few years ago, she would have pulled him aside and told him to change his behavior, reminded him of his obligation to make their guests feel welcome. There was no reason she couldn't do that still, but it made her feel that motherhood separated her from the carefree life the others enjoyed. She wanted him to be polite without her having to reprimand him.

The others didn't seem to notice that Thomas looked at them with an expression of superiority. They couldn't feel him watching, silently criticizing. His steely eyes registered every sip of alcohol and every stiff, tight joint pulled out of a pocket. Every empty beer bottle or coffee cup left in the living room sent a visible ripple across his skin, the dark hair on his arms rising up as if he were a grizzly bear marking his territory. It was *her* house. If things were cluttered, if she had to wash extra dishes, that was her problem, not his.

What was wrong with him? He was twenty-two years old. He should be thrilled to meet new people, to try a little mind expanding of his own. The world was exploding into an amazing array of color and sound and new ideas. Thomas didn't remember how it used to be, when you didn't dare express an opinion contrary to authority figures, or paint your front door candy apple red for that matter. The music now made your whole body thump in response. It drove you to dance, turned your mind toward the invisible qualities of life — peace and freedom and caring and love. Those were the things that mattered. Not matching china and linen napkins and freshly vacuumed carpet. Barriers were breaking down and Thomas acted as if he'd been assigned to single-handedly rebuild them, erecting walls so that people peered through crevices with suspicion instead of compassion and acceptance. And what about sex? He was a young man. Why on earth wasn't he drawn to the realization that sex could be so much fun, unbound from rules and jealousy and obligation?

She wanted to smack him.

She didn't want to be thinking about Thomas. She had one focus this evening — she needed to remain alert and available to Gordon. She wanted time alone so the two of them could talk. When she got him away from the others they made love and quickly fell asleep. Much as she loved her new friends, thrilled that her life was overflowing with people, when a few weeks ago it had been sterile and broken, she needed to talk one on one. She couldn't always be part of the hive mind, dreaming and debating until everyone drifted to sleep just before dawn. She had a man who made her feel she was nineteen, but they needed more conversation. She needed to solidify their relationship and get to know him better, tell him more about herself.

Jealousy had no place in this new world, but its claws gripped her heart. Champagne subdued it somewhat. Pot helped even more. But the good feelings came in waves, and in between, she ached. Sharp pains shot through her stomach when Gordon walked down the beach with one of the other girls, his arm around her shoulders, leaning close as he listened to whatever she had to say. It hurt to see them fade, then disappear from sight, impossible to see whether they were walking or had stopped, if they were sitting on the sand, if his arm had progressed down the side of her body.

At sunset, all of them had headed out to the concrete ship. As they'd walked the length of the boat, Gordon hadn't even glanced in her direction. He'd pulled all the guys around him in a tight circle, their heads bent toward each other. They performed a silly chant about hunting and fishing and dancing to the rhythm of the earth. Their feet shuffled in time with the improvised verses that Gordon wove around them. She'd smiled and tried not to care, tried to think about her bond with other females, but these girls were nothing like her. They were so young! They didn't feel the obligation to cook and maintain some semblance of cleanliness in the house. They didn't worry about pairing off with a single boy. They were like boys themselves, eager to make love with whoever was beside them, whoever had stirred their emotions at a particular moment in time.

For dinner, she'd made a huge pot of spaghetti, but the rich food — pizza and spaghetti, hamburgers and hotdogs, had begun to pillow around her hips. She wanted to eat and enjoy, but the effects had begun to show when she wore her bikini. Still, her friends wouldn't be here forever. She needed to relax and go with the flow. Experience everything.

Now, they were sitting on the back deck. A stiff wind came off the water. They were drinking soda which made the air seem colder. Mary had dragged out spare blankets and the girls sat with the blankets wrapped around their shoulders. A joint was passed around. Then a second one. Paul was lighting a third. Gordon had filled several large bowls with potato chips. The only sounds were the occasional cough from smoke held inside for too long, the metal tap of a bottle opening, and the crunch of potato chips. The quiet sounds were backed by waves crashing on the sand.

The concrete boat gleamed white. Mary felt it watching them, observing their thoughts. The sensation didn't come from the pot wafting through her brain, she knew it was waiting, listening. It always had. Its heavy presence was inescapable, at least for her. She was never sure how much others noticed. She closed her eyes. A moment later she forced them open. She couldn't fall asleep. She felt the others might be drifting toward sleep, and soon, she'd have Gordon to herself. If she could stay awake. She reached for a bottle of coke and held it out to Paul in a silent plea for him to pry off the cap.

Within a few minutes, she'd drained the bottle. She stood up and stepped around to the railing, shaking her legs gently to loosen the tendons that had tightened with the cold and too much time sitting in a single position. She walked to where Gordon sat with his back against the railing. His head was tipped back, his eyes wide, looking at the stars. She rested her hand on his shoulder. Possibly her touch was too light because he didn't move his head. She squeezed gently. Without taking his gaze off the sky, he placed his hand on top of hers. She lowered herself to sit beside him and leaned her head on his shoulder. "Feel like sneaking away to my room?"

"Too wired," he said. "Isn't the sky incredible?"

"It is. I'm a little tired, so the stars look smeared." She laughed softly.

"Go get some sleep."

"I thought we could talk," she said.

He put his arm around her. "Sure. What's up?"

"Not here."

"Why not?"

She moved away from him. "It's nothing. Not important. I wanted to be alone together, but maybe another time."

"Alone. Together. That's funny, isn't it." He took her hand. "Together." He released her hand. "Alone. And yet, we're always alone in this world."

She put her hand to her mouth, pressing the insides of her lips against her teeth to avoid yawning. It was an interesting thought, and she would have liked to talk to him about it. Alone. "I think I'll go for a walk."

"Cool. Maybe I'll be tired by the time you get back. Or horny." He laughed. "Horny first, then tired."

She stood up, half waiting for him to suggest it might not be a good idea for her to be alone on the beach, stoned, and walking in the dark. She stepped around him. "See you."

"Rock on."

She walked down the steps and headed toward the water. The sand was cool and soft. She walked slowly, avoiding broken bits of driftwood and stiff seaweed that was barely visible under the half moon. The tide was high, so she stayed up on the dry sand, walking toward the concrete ship and the glistening wet wood of the legs supporting the pier. She hadn't been on the beach by herself since she'd met Gordon. It felt familiar and comforting. It had been quite some time since she'd encountered the ghost that inhabited the ship. She hadn't mentioned it to Gordon or the others. She imagined they might be fascinated by the possibility of an apparition drifting above the ship, moving about on the bow, wafting through the empty spaces below deck. They were open to every possibility, the whole pulsing, breathing universe. Why not that? And yet, when it came to mind, she pushed the thought away and said nothing. They might think she was mad.

The deserted pier towered above her. She moved onto the wet sand. Water splashed against the legs of the pier. From a distance, they looked frail, leaning slightly in the wet sand, too thin to support the weight above, yet up close they were huge and solid. They'd withstood pounding waves for nearly forty years now.

When she was directly beneath the pier, she paused. She heard it. Footsteps passing overhead, walking slowly, stopping for a moment. She shivered. She tried to hurry out to the other side, but her feet sank deep in the wet sand and she lurched forward, falling on her hands and knees. The sound of the waves grew distant, so soft they were more like the breath of someone sleeping. Water echoed as it sloshed against the boat. The feet — walking, stopping, walking again. The feet moved faster, thumping. They stopped.

He doesn't love you.

She squeezed her eyes tightly. She wasn't going to allow it to take hold of her thoughts.

He never will.

The ghost was wrong. The meaning of love had changed. She didn't need to own Gordon, didn't need him all to herself all the time. She could share him. She was doing that already. Love was so much bigger than a single couple. The world was a mess because people were selfish, hoarding, clinging. Love meant letting go of that. All of it.

She stood up and brushed wet sand off her knees. It stuck to her hands. No matter how vigorously she rubbed them together, the granules simply moved around, scratching at her palms, working their way beneath her fingernails.

Never.

All she wanted was companionship. Someone who wanted to touch her. New friends. They'd eradicated her loneliness and that was the only thing that mattered. She was happy. She didn't need a reminder creeping through her head, making her crave something she couldn't have. She just wanted to enjoy it all. And she was. There was no need for a *private* talk with Gordon. What would she even say?

Five

When Mary woke the next morning, Gordon was not beside her. She couldn't recall who had been on the deck when she'd returned from her walk on the beach — her thoughts had been consumed with silent arguments against the insidious whispers coming from the concrete ship. She didn't recall whether anyone at all had been sitting outside, if they'd been scattered around the living room, if the TV was on, or music playing, if they were sleeping or talking or zoning out. She didn't recall seeing Gordon.

She turned to look at the clock. Eight-thirty. She hadn't slept this late since she was child. She turned onto her right side and pulled the blankets over her head. Her mouth felt stuffed with cotton and her head was so heavy she wasn't sure she could lift it off the pillow. Her eyes were dry and it hurt when she opened them. She'd had more pot, or more champagne, maybe both, than she'd realized. She'd never failed to remember the details of an evening. The sound of footsteps walking on the pier overhead circled through her mind, alongside the disconnected, vivid dreams she'd woken from. Dreams populated by birds. If she thought hard enough, it might have been that each of the people staying in her house had taken the form of a bird in her dream. They'd flown madly overhead and she hadn't been able to look in their eyes, or touch even the tip of a feather.

After a few minutes of trying not to think about Gordon, she pushed away the blankets and shoved herself up to a half sitting position. She was wearing nothing but a slip. She didn't recall wearing a slip the day before, hadn't put one on all summer. She got up and filled the bathtub with steaming water. After a soak and a good scrubbing of her teeth, the weight of her head felt more bearable, but the rest of her didn't. She was afraid to leave her bedroom and walk into her own living area. She took a deep breath. The air smelled clean, empty. There was no suggestion of coffee or toast. Neither was there a hint of marijuana smoke. Were they all sleeping still? It wouldn't be surprising. But where was Gordon? When he wanted to rest, he came into her room. Did that mean he'd stayed awake all night, managed to remain alert past dawn and well into the morning?

The emptiness of her room echoed around her. The entire house could be empty for all she knew. They might be on the beach, walking on the pier, oblivious to the feet that thudded up and down its length in the darkness. They might have all moved out, found a better party place. Her heart tightened like a lead ball, pressing against her ribs, shoving its way up to her throat. Surely Thomas was still here. He wouldn't be sleeping, but neither had he made coffee. She assumed he was still here. Had he been on the deck last night? She pressed her fingers into the corners of her eyes, trying to bring back an image. She couldn't recall seeing him after sunset.

She walked to the door and put her hand on the knob. She

had a house full of companions, but the only one that could be truly considered a friend was Caroline — the only one who'd ever carried on a meaningful conversation with Mary, asked about her life, shared stories of her own. Gordon too, of course, but his easy manner made him seem remote except when they were making love, or touching each other's bodies in some concrete way.

The day that Beth, Caroline, and Paul moved in, Caroline had been the one to help Mary clear the table and stood ready with a towel, carefully drying each plate and utensil as Mary handed them to her. Without being asked, she'd swept the kitchen floor when they were finished. It seemed as if she cared about Mary's house, that she admired its beauty and quality and wanted to be sure it stayed that way. After cleaning up, they'd gone out onto the deck. Caroline brought a bottle of champagne and two glasses. The air was unusually warm, the sun still sending its heat up over the horizon. Beth had gone upstairs to sleep, and Paul and Gordon turned on the TV. They were watching a show that involved a spaceship populated with men and women wearing unisex outfits, visiting various fictitious planets.

Caroline closed the sliding glass door, silencing the TV. She peeled the foil off the champagne, untwisted the wire, and yanked out the cork. Champagne foamed over her arm, soaking the leather strap she wore for a bracelet. She shrieked with laughter and held the bottle away from her.

"If you take the cork out slowly, it doesn't explode quite so much," Mary said.

"What fun is that?"

"I suppose not much."

"Damn right." Caroline splashed champagne into each glass and handed one to Mary. "To girls!"

Mary tapped her glass against Caroline's and took a sip. They'd had champagne before dinner and red wine with their meal. She wasn't sure she should drink much more, but her new friends had already proven they were unconcerned with limits and she didn't want to miss any of the fun. They settled in the chaise lounges, looking out toward the water, even though it was impossible to see more than an occasional sparkle of foam under the moonless sky.

Caroline talked about the eight months she'd spent hitchhiking around the country and the neanderthal who'd stolen her guitar, ripping away her chance to earn money singing in coffee shops. She went on about what a bummer school was. She'd left college before she was finished. It was a drag thinking about how she was going to get money. "It's cool that you drink champagne. Very high class," she said.

It flickered through Mary's mind that Caroline was trying to start a conversation about money. It hurt to think that might be Caroline's only interest in her. She decided to ignore the threatening implication. "I like the bubbles."

"That's cute. Pot's a better high, though. Don't you think?"

"It's different."

"Ever tried acid?"

Mary laughed. She sipped her champagne.

After a few minutes, Caroline picked up the bottle and refilled their glasses. She didn't seem to notice Mary hadn't answered the question. Maybe it was all part of the live and let live approach to the world. If you didn't want to answer a question, it wasn't required or necessarily expected. Caroline settled back in her chair and took a long swallow of champagne. "You don't seem like a mother."

"Maybe because you've never seen me around my children."

As if she hadn't heard, or disregarded the explanation, Caroline went on, "My mother hates me."

"I'm sure that's not the case. No woman hates her child."

"You probably think that because you're a good mother. Lots of women hate their kids. Women have an animal drive to make sure their offspring fit into the herd, and if they don't, the mother rejects them."

Mary laughed. "Where did you hear that?"

"It's true."

"I don't know."

"My mother was a debutante."

"Oh, my."

"And I'm a slut. Or so she says. She was freaked that I'd bring disease into her house, so I needed to find another place to live. Apparently I'm dirty and diseased from letting filthy boys who don't comb their hair do nasty things to me."

"I'm sure she doesn't think that."

"She absolutely does think that. She told me."

"The world is changing very quickly, that might be hard for her."

"You seem to be coping. In fact, you're loving it."

"I think I've had different experiences than your mother."

"No, you're an intelligent human being."

"Thank you."

"Any woman who doesn't wear white gloves to garden parties and enjoys her body doesn't exist in my mother's world. It's like she doesn't even see me. Her daughter should look like her. She should be wearing pink and yellow dresses like my mother is in the photographs in fake gold frames that are plastered up and down the hallway. If you aren't in that frame, she doesn't see you."

"This makes me want to cry," Mary said.

"I used to cry. But what's the point?"

"It is good to move on, not let bitterness eat away at you."

"Damn right," Caroline said. She raised her glass. "To dirty hippies."

Mary clicked the edge of her glass to Caroline's, but she couldn't bring herself to share the toast. She liked the love and peace, but she didn't like unwashed bodies or hair that potentially hid lice eggs. She shivered.

"Are you cold?"

"No."

"If that guy hadn't ripped off my guitar. I'd be in San Francisco. A folk singer. Flowers in my hair. I'd be famous. Then she might have to think twice. But she'd still probably hate me.

For singing songs that weren't Frank Sinatra or honky stuff like that."

Mary laughed.

"You really don't seem like a mother at all. You like groovy music, you like to get high. It's cool to talk to you. I can say whatever I think. I feel like you're my best friend."

"Thank you," Mary said.

"It's true." Caroline held out her glass, waiting for Mary's to connect. They clicked their glasses against each other. Champagne splashed on Mary's fingers. "To friends forever," Caroline said. "Blood sisters. Did you ever do that with anyone?"

"No."

"We should do it."

"Maybe. Some other time."

"Now you sound like a mother." Caroline laughed.

"We can't have that."

"Definitely not, since the word *mother* doesn't have a positive connotation for me!"

"I'm truly sorry for you," Mary said.

"So, do you want to trip on acid with me?" Caroline swallowed the rest of her champagne and put the glass on the deck.

"That could be fun."

Caroline jumped up and went inside. Mary shivered again, although the air remained silky warm. What if she'd made a mistake? She'd heard LSD could kill you. People took it and thought they could fly and jumped off the roof. They attacked their own bodies, thinking bugs were swarming over their skin. But Caroline was experienced. She'd be here to help. Gordon and Paul, too. Would Caroline invite them along on the *trip*? She giggled. It was exciting and terrifying. But look what she'd managed to live through. There was nothing that could beat her down for long — her mother's suicide, her husband's betrayal, her step-mother's coldness and control. She could definitely relate to Caroline in that respect. It must hurt so much more when it was your real mother, but it still hurt when the person who was supposed to care for you truly despised you, no matter how much she tried to cover it over with pleasant words and gifts.

A moment later, the door opened and Caroline stepped onto the deck. She'd brought two sweatshirts with her. She handed one to Mary. She slid two small pieces of paper out of her pocket.

Mary tugged the sweatshirt over her head and held out her hand for the tiny square of paper pinched between Caroline's fingertips. "What do I do?"

"Put it on your tongue."

"I've heard scary stories." She thought of the spirit on the ship, sometimes appearing as her mother, sometimes as another, unknown entity. She should have told Caroline about that. At least Caroline's mother didn't come back from the grave to torment her daughter. Not that Mary's mother had been cruel, or failed to love her. Unless choosing death over raising your daughter was a failure to love. Maybe once they were tripping, she'd mention the ship and the things that didn't belong there.

She smiled. Nothing was as scary as encountering a ghost, feeling it slip inside your mind. Acid would be far less terrifying.

"Scary trips happen to scary people," Caroline said. "They start out with bad energy, and the acid draws out the demons that were already there."

"Are you sure?"

"Trust me. I had one not so great experience. Right after I talked to my mother. She infected the trip. But now, with you and me being friends, talking about life, liking each other, it'll be spectacular."

Mary felt a surge of warmth through her chest. How childish that hearing she was liked filled her with such a blissful sensation she could hardly breathe.

"You'll be fine. I'm here. And the guys are right inside."

"Did you tell them?"

"Naw. This is a girl trip." She smiled. "They'll figure it out later, but for now, just us. Friends. Exploring the universe together."

"That sounds nice," Mary said.

Caroline opened her mouth wide and stuck out her tongue. She touched the remaining scrap of paper to her tongue and closed her mouth.

Mary did the same.

Caroline scooted her lounge chair close to Mary's and sat down. She reached across the space between them and took Mary's hand. "I feel like Romeo and Juliet," Caroline said. "We're going to another place together."

"Don't say that."

"Okay. Sorry. We won't die. That came out wrong."

They were silent for several minutes.

"I don't feel anything," Mary said.

"Be patient." Caroline squeezed her hand and let go.

They sat quietly. The sky looked darker than ever. The stars glittered so sharply her eyes hurt. She closed them for a moment. She giggled. What was so funny? Oh, that stars could hurt her eyes. They were pretty, they wouldn't hurt her. She giggled and smiled at the friendly stars.

"I guess you feel it now," Caroline said.

"Do I?"

"You're laughing."

"I was laughing at the stars."

"Is that something you normally do?"

Mary laughed again. The stars pulsed at her as if they were laughing at her laughter. Soon, she and Caroline were giggling, shrieking like orangutans carrying on inside their cages at the zoo. The stars. The TV blinking silently behind the glass door. Although they weren't facing the door, she could see the TV, mouths moving, the screen flashing from one scene to another. How could she see it? The TV was behind her. Seeing it without seeing it, sensing the life shooting out of it. The stars were crackling now, snapping their fingers and laughing as hard as the two women. Mary and Caroline stood up at the same time, as if the stars had reached out their hands and pulled them to their feet. They walked across the deck and down to the beach. The sand tickled her feet and she laughed. Caroline laughed. They ran toward the water. They stopped halfway and took hold of each other's hands. They skipped forward, stumbling and awkward in the loose sand.

After a while, they took off their sweatshirts and sat down in the sand. For some inexplicable reason, they folded their sweatshirts and placed them nearby rather than using them to sit on. Part of her brain told her it was damp, it was too cold. But everything felt so good. She wanted to put her arm around Caroline's narrow shoulders, feel the soft cool flesh of her upper arm. Caroline's hair brushed across her face, smoke and sand filtered up into her head until she could taste them, singing through her brain like the soft strumming of a guitar.

The stars dissolved and began dropping into the ocean with quiet splashes. She wasn't tired. She didn't need to talk. Their minds were connecting without requiring speech. Caroline was humming softly and her fingers moved across her thigh as if she were plucking the strings of her missing guitar. She began talking, describing each of her mother's cocktail dresses in painfully precise detail. Mary didn't want to hear about the dresses or Caroline's mother. She wanted to laugh hysterically as they had earlier, like teenaged girls playing on the beach, living for the feel of sun and sand and water and knowing boys were looking at you with greedy eyes.

It was all too much, too many thoughts. She took a long, deep breath, trying to erase the images pinging around inside her head, moving faster and faster. The sound of the waves took over, crashing against her skull and then her ribs as if she'd swallowed the ocean.

Moments, or hours later, she was shivering. They stood up. "Let's go back."

Caroline moved away from her. She pulled her top over her head. She tugged off her jeans and dropped her clothes at Mary's feet. She turned and began running. She splashed into the shallow water spreading across the sand.

Mary called after her. "Wait. It's not safe."

Caroline ran faster. She plunged deeper, her progress slowed by the weight of water and the force of the waves.

Mary shivered. This was what they warned about. She never should have agreed to take this terrible drug. So small, almost invisible — a dot of liquid on a scrap of paper — yet so powerful it took your entire psyche and reshaped it into something else. Caroline thought she was a dolphin! She was going to swim out too far. The current could be like thick ropes, dragging you where you didn't want to go. Pulling you down. "Stop! Come back." Her voice screamed inside her head but she wasn't sure any sound came out of her mouth.

Caroline dove beneath a breaking wave.

Mary strained to see. Was that her? She couldn't be sure. It was too dark. She should go after her, but what good would that do? She'd have less chance of finding her, thrashing around in waves over her head, water spilling into her mouth, salt stinging her throat, her mind distorted. She shouted as loudly as she could, but the sound of the ocean swallowed her voice. She was crying. Her tears tasted sweet and thick. "Caroline. Come back!"

Caroline's body shimmered as she dove through the waves, the slow, graceful moves of a dolphin, heading toward the bow of the ship. Or was that a dolphin? Was Caroline gone, drifting along the sandy bottom, far below the surface as the water pressed down on her?

Mary trembled. She couldn't make up her mind whether to follow Caroline into the water, wait and try to call out to her, or run back to the house and cry for Gordon and Paul to help. She sobbed, her eyes blurred with tears, making even the outline of the waves impossible to distinguish. All she saw was black water and the black, starless sky. And the boat, white and solid, refusing to let go of the pier.

"Caroline! Blood sister!" She clawed at her arm, trying to tear ridges in her skin, hoping to dig into a vein, dots of blood bubbling up that she could share with Caroline as soon as she emerged from the water. They should have mixed their blood. It's what Caroline wanted and now it was too late. Forever too late. She ran to the edge of the water. Waves splashed up around her knees trying to pull her in. She felt the ship watching her, waiting to see what she would do. Watching. It was always watching.

For an eternity, she stood in the shallow water, waves lapping at her feet and ankles, occasionally slapping her thighs, splashing drops across her arms and face. Then, only a moment had passed and Caroline was walking out of the waves. Her skin glistened. Her hair was plastered to her skull. Mary rushed toward her and fell against her.

Caroline stumbled back and put her arms around Mary. "What's wrong?"

"I thought you drowned."

Caroline laughed. "You are like a mother, aren't you? I just had a little swim. It was lovely."

Despite the less than pleasant ending to their trip into another dimension, Mary felt closer to Caroline after that. Only for a moment, fear had taken over her heart, and there was a sliver of anger at Caroline's reckless swim and her subtle mocking of Mary's concerns. But overall, they'd had a glorious, mind-exploding adventure. They knew each other deep inside, every piece. Their friendship was beyond conventional social interaction. They'd shared their thoughts and hearts. Their very minds had merged. They'd laughed and played. She'd never had a friend like this.

Six

Thomas had spent the night in his room with the door locked. They were all down on the deck. He'd seen their hair glittering with moisture from the fog. Even with the windows closed, he heard them laughing and talking nonsense as the smell of marijuana drifted up toward the second floor. His mother had gone mad and he had no idea what to do about it. There was no one to alert, aside from his brothers, and what could they do? It was up to him, but she wouldn't even speak to him, much less consider anything he had to say.

He'd finished three *Bond* novels since he'd arrived. At this rate, he'd work his way through the remaining two he hadn't read and begin with the current crop of New York Times bestsellers. Or maybe revert to the classics. His education, with only the required humanities classes, was mildly deficient in that area. Right now, *Bond* was more appealing. Fast moving, always thinking *Bond* dulled the clamoring in his own head.

For some reason, he recalled a scene from his childhood — his mother placing a bowl of steamed clams in front of him. Even the sight of clams made his stomach roil — tight fleshy knobs resembling organs that had been harvested from deep inside the body. The tender necks sometimes an inch or two long...as if he could eat something like that. His brothers stuffed the vile things into their mouths while Thomas whimpered and gagged and listened to his father bark out orders to stop whining and eat what was put in front of him. Thinking about clams made him feel ill.

The house was silent right now. It was seven in the morning. He wasn't sure what time they'd drifted off to their various sleeping spots, but they were dead to the world at this point, unlikely to wake until lunchtime. He wanted coffee, but didn't relish tiptoeing down the stairs and averting his eyes from people sprawled on the floor, some of them less clothed than they should be, the tops of their sleeping bags thrown aside because all that body heat turned the spacious living room into a sauna. He rolled over and went back to sleep.

When he woke again, it was nine and the house smelled of coffee. His mother was up. That was good. He didn't like thinking of her with that guy lying next to her, putting his mouth on hers, his hands roaming over her body. He supposed she had a right, after what his father had done to her. But still…

He showered quickly, dressed in shorts and a blue sport shirt, and shoved his feet into a pair of canvas shoes. He found his mother in the kitchen.

"Coffee?" she said.

"Thanks. It smells good."

She smiled.

"Rough night?" he said.

"No, not at all. Why do you say that?"

"I woke up at three and everyone was still outside."

She held her finger to her lips. "Shhh. Lower your voice."

He rolled his eyes. It wasn't as if they needed to get their rest because they had jobs to get to later that day.

"I went to bed before that," she said. "I took a walk on the beach and it tired me out."

"Alone?"

"It was nice." She poured coffee into two cups and handed one to him.

"Should we go outside?" he said.

She glanced through the opening above the bar. "Don't step on anyone."

He smiled. She was still her same self. He sipped his coffee, scalded his tongue, and followed her out of the kitchen.

The sky was white with fog, turning the water slate gray, but there was no breeze. It was like settling down under a soft, cottony quilt. He took a few sips of coffee. "I don't want to be rude, but are all of them planning to stay here all summer?"

"I don't think so."

"But you don't know?"

"What does it matter?"

Hearing her say it turned something upside down in his brain. What did it matter, after all? He had no plans of his own. Why was he so concerned about it? The invasion of his space. The expense. The potential damage to the house. The damage to his mother's dignity. Perhaps she believed her dignity had been torn to shreds already. What more was there to lose after being replaced by a new, younger wife?

"I guess it doesn't. It's just wearing."

"Something happened last night," she said softly.

"Oh?"

He hoped that creep hadn't done something to hurt her. He'd kill him. His lungs tightened and for a moment he couldn't breathe. Where had that thought come from? He'd never even been in a fist fight. Did he really think he'd *kill* the guy? Why was he so filled with rage? Always, he'd thought of himself as a somewhat gentle, thoughtful person. The mind and education and intelligence were the important forces in life. Accomplishments came through deliberate actions, and problems were resolved through conversation and compromise. Was there something in the man himself that turned Thomas's thoughts toward murder? He wanted to laugh at the idea, but his mother would think he was mad if he began laughing at nothing. Such rage, even now as he analyzed what was happening inside his body. It burned in his eyes. The things he wanted to say to Gordon wrangled inside him, making him ache to pound his fists on the chaise lounge. Maybe the rage was at his mother. These people were using her and she was completely blind to that fact. She was behaving like a fool, thinking she was part of their group, that she had the same desires and thoughts as a bunch of incense-inhaling goons. He wanted to smack her. His violent impulses shocked him. He wished it were time for the fall quarter to start up. He could escape to books and lectures and thinking about things that had nothing to do with relationships and Human *Be-Ins* and psychedelic fantasy.

"The ghost…"

He turned toward her. "What?"

"I've never told you, but I've wanted to for a long time."

"Told me what."

"Have you ever seen…felt…"

"Felt what?" he said. The rage continued to build. He wasn't sure he could sit on the deck much longer, sipping coffee from delicate cups. He needed to unleash the ire tightening his muscles, hammering in his chest. And now she was dancing around some difficult subject. It wasn't like her. She usually was quite blunt. "Felt *what*?"

"The ship. It's haunted you know."

He laughed.

"Please don't."

"You can't be serious. It's not haunted."

"You've never experienced anything strange? Seen a form over it, a cloud?"

"Yes. I see clouds all the time. Fog. Rain clouds."

"Don't mock me."

"Smoking pot is not good for you. It damages your brain."

"It has nothing to do with pot, I saw it when I was a child."

He drank the rest of his coffee. "What do we have for breakfast? I'll cook, so you can have a break. And get some rest."

"I'm not losing my mind. And pot does not damage your brain. I felt it again last night. Heard it walking on the pier. I've always thought of you as the most intelligent of my children, open to different ideas," she said.

"Don't flatter me into listening to some hallucinogenic dream. Have you used other things besides marijuana? Please tell me you haven't."

"It's none of your business. I'm your mother, remember."

"Now you want to be a mother? After all this?" he gestured toward the living room. For all the stillness, the house could be empty. They slept like the dead, as if they didn't have a care in the world. Of course they didn't. They'd wake and Mary would feed them. She'd replace the toilet paper in the bathroom and pick up their empty beer bottles. She provided a beautiful home that allowed them to party on the beach and swim in the ocean all day and half the night without ever having to get in a car or look for a parking space or fill the tank with gas. They were children. She was the old woman in the shoe. He laughed.

"Don't laugh at me!"

"I wasn't laughing at you." It was a lie, but as angry as he was, he didn't want to hurt her feelings. It was becoming more and more evident that she was living with a crippling loneliness that he and his brothers had failed to recognize.

"I heard footsteps. Walking overhead on the pier. I've heard them before, but I started wondering if you'd ever heard them. Or..."

"Have you mentioned this to anyone else?"

"Not recently."

"Well don't."

"It's not a fantasy. Please consider... I really need to talk about it, and..."

"Talk to Gordon," he said.

"What are you saying?"

"I'm saying I don't want to get involved with drugs. In fact..." he stood up, "I think you're making yourself liable for encouraging criminal activity. I'm saying...Gordon seems to be your chosen gigolo."

"Please sit down."

"I'd rather not."

"I thought now that you were an adult we could have an adult relationship, adult conversations."

He sat down, defeated. "I don't understand this." He nodded at the glass door.

"I've explained."

"Gordon is at least ten years younger than you."

"So? How old is your hero, *James Bond*? And how old are the women he beds?"

"Beds? I can't believe you said that. Anyway, that's beside the point. *James Bond* isn't real."

"But you accept it. Why can't a mature woman and a younger man have a relationship?"

"I thought we were talking about a ghost?"

"I'm tired of you treating me with such an astonishing lack of respect. I can have a relationship with a man who's a little younger than I am. And I've experienced things on that ship that you can't imagine. I don't appreciate you acting like I'm a middle-aged, drug-addled idiot."

He wanted to shout — *stop acting like one!* But he didn't want to fracture their relationship. Besides, if he left her alone with these people, she might really be hurt. And not just emotionally, although that too might cause irreparable damage. She needed him, even if she didn't recognize it. "I don't think you're an idiot."

She handed her coffee cup to him. "I'd like a refill, please."

He went inside. When he returned with her coffee cup, she was standing at the railing. She wore a dark dress-like thing that looked as if it was made of a fishing net. Underneath was a white two-piece bathing suit. Her hair was in a single braid down the center of her back. For a moment, she didn't look any different from the girls sleeping all over the house. He understood why Gordon was drawn to her. She was slim and just as attractive as the others, but she had a quiet sureness about her the younger girls lacked. Maybe the reason he was so angry was he resented that she was sure of what she was doing and what she wanted, and he was not. Not at all.

"Here's your coffee."

She didn't turn.

He walked to the railing and handed it to her. She took the cup but left him holding the saucer. It was awkward and unbalanced in his hand.

"I first saw the ghost after my mother drowned. I thought it was her. It was her. But then, other times, I'm not sure. She…it… shows up when I least expect it."

He moved the saucer to his other hand. The fog was settling lower now. He glanced toward the ship. He could see it gave off a haunted impression, but it was fantasy. It was the story of the thing that created the haunting atmosphere — deserted, eaten away by the sea. It was built under a cloud of disdain for an imagination that conceived of the possibility that concrete could float. It was towed in and enjoyed for a brief time, but left for dead once the amusement company that purchased it realized the depression and the weather were invincible opponents. Abandoned. Maybe that's why his mother was drawn to it and believed a spirit lived inside.

"I know you think I've killed brain cells with drugs. I see it in your eyes. But you're wrong. You've never noticed anything unnerving about the ship?"

"All uninhabited structures are unsettling."

"This is different."

He turned and put her saucer on the iron table near the chaise lounge.

"I don't know why I brought it up," she said. "I guess I thought you'd understand. Or that you'd had your own experience."

"My experience is swimming down into the hold, that's all."

"Maybe you had to be here from the beginning."

After several minutes, he said, "Why?"

"Never mind. You should try smoking pot, Thomas. It's no different from alcohol."

"It's illegal."

"But why? Look at the damage alcohol has caused over the centuries."

"Exactly."

"But we still like it. You love beer. And whisky."

"I don't love it."

"You enjoy it."

"It's relaxing, but I hardly ever get intoxicated."

"Why is that so terrible?"

It was a good question, but he didn't feel he could answer until he had time to think about it. He'd never considered it.

The door slid open behind them. "Hey!" Caroline said. "You started the party without me?"

"Just drinking coffee," Thomas said. "It's not a party."

"Not yet! Where can I get me some of that?"

"It's in the kitchen." Was she just trying to be clever? Or was she still half asleep? Surely she wasn't suggesting he serve her a cup.

It appeared to be her expectation, because she waited several minutes before sliding the door along the track and slipping back inside the house.

Mary looked at him. "Are you leaving?"

"What do you mean?"

"You don't like my friends, you disapprove of our parties. I assumed you were planning to go back to Berkeley, or something."

"No. I'll get used to it."

"I think you will," she said.

The morning progressed as he'd expected. Mary cooked

breakfast. Mary washed the dishes. He didn't offer to help. If she wanted to wait on everyone, that was her choice. He hadn't come home to be a short order cook and chief bottle washer.

The fog had burned off and the sky was cloudless now. He went up to his room, changed into swim trunks, and took a towel and his book out to the beach. He spent the morning reading until he grew tired of sitting, swimming back and forth along the shore, then returning to his book, followed by another swim.

When he got hungry, he returned to the house. He was surprised to see it was a few minutes after two. The house was deserted. He hadn't noticed any of them on the beach, but couldn't be bothered to go back out to the deck and do a concentrated search. He walked into the hallway leading to his mother's room. The door was ajar. The bedspread was pulled smooth and tight, tucked under the pillows at the top. The dresser and nightstand had their usual sparse appearance. There wasn't a stray shoe or sweater in sight. The window was partially open and the curtain fluttered in the breeze. The street outside was quiet. It wasn't a good idea for her to leave her room with an apparent invitation for anyone to enter. He glanced around again but didn't see her purse. He went to the closet and folded the louvered door to the side. Her purse was tucked neatly between four pairs of shoes. He nudged it with his toe, shoving it toward the back. He slid the hangers around to arrange longer garments near the center where the purse would be partially blocked from view. He closed the door roughly. What did it matter? If someone needed cash, they'd look until they found it.

In the kitchen, soda bottles stood to the left of the sink, some half filled with dark liquid. There were a few plates with crumbs of toast and smears of jam. He stacked the dirty plates in the sink, made a ham sandwich, and went outside to the deck. He pulled a chair up to the small table and put down his sandwich. He'd forgotten a drink.

When he returned to the deck with a glass of soda. Paul was seated in his chair holding half the sandwich near his mouth, poised to take a bite.

"That's mine," Thomas said.

Paul took a large bite. "Sorry. Starving. No breakfast."

"There's plenty of ham and bread in the kitchen. I only used half a tomato, so you can have the other half."

Paul took a second bite.

"Stop eating my sandwich."

Paul put the sandwich on the plate and stood up. "Sorry. I was famished, thought I might pass out. I'll make it up to you."

"Too famished to walk twenty feet to the kitchen?"

"Yeah, pretty much."

Thomas slumped in his chair. He picked up the half-eaten section and handed it to Paul. "You might as well finish this half."

"Don't wanna get my cooties?"

"I prefer not to share food."

Paul smirked, took the sandwich, and pulled a chair up to the table. "I don't suppose you're offering to share the drink?"

"Absolutely not."

"So is that why you don't like smoking dope? Too many

mouths sharing saliva?"

"I never thought about that aspect. I don't engage in illegal activities. And I prefer not to damage my mind."

Paul appeared to have a permanent smirk on his face. He made a futile attempt to smile around it. "You might expand your mind. You could use expanding in a lot of areas."

"How would you know?"

"Just an observation."

They ate in silence. Thomas finished first, chewing and swallowing so quickly his stomach ached. He leaned back in his chair. "Where is everyone?"

"They went for a walk."

"The whole gang?"

"Yup."

"Why didn't you go?"

"I was waiting for you."

"What for?"

"I already told you."

"Your imagined connection?"

Paul nodded. The smirk was gone and he looked genuinely interested in what Thomas was thinking. "You're sure I can't have a sip of that drink? I'll use the other side of the glass."

Thomas handed the glass to Paul. He watched Paul take a few sips, feeling as if the kid was trying to creep inside of him, consuming his food and drink, then pushing his thoughts and opinions into Thomas's ears.

Paul stood up and dragged his chair around the table so the

two chairs were side by side.

Thomas didn't want another conversation about connection and clicking or whatever it was Paul had said the other day. Yesterday. It was only yesterday.

"I'd think a red-blooded male like you would be hanging out with us more, taking your pick of one of these incredibly pleasing girls."

"That's crude," Thomas said.

"But true."

Thomas sipped his drink carefully, letting the liquid sit inside his mouth for a moment, trying to discern any foreign taste that might have slid out of Paul's mouth and into the glass. His stomach was unsettled. Maybe he should hand the glass over to Paul and let him finish. But he was thirsty. He took another cautious sip.

"You already have a girlfriend?" Paul said.

"No."

"Why not?"

Thomas swallowed. He knew why, but he'd never been asked that question. Or at least not so directly, and not by someone he knew would refuse to accept a misleading response. It wasn't something he talked about. Ever. There was no one to talk to. Well, maybe one or two, but the opportunities had been rare.

It might be tolerated for all these girls to hop from one sleeping bag to another, for the boys to welcome them inside, enjoy them for one night, or ten, and then move on. Free love. Everything was cool. But everything was not cool. He was quite certain it would not be tolerated for two of the boys to slide naked into the same sleeping bag. Maybe in some places, but those places were on dark side streets, in large cities where no one recognized anyone.

"I take it the topic is off limits?" Paul said.

"Yes." Thomas put his glass to his lips and tipped it up. A thin line of diluted soda ran down the length of the glass and touched his tongue. He licked at it. The taste was dull, mostly melted ice with a hint of cola.

"Can I get you another soda?" Paul said.

"Yes, thanks."

Paul returned a moment later with two glasses of soda and ice, and a bag of chips tucked between his elbow and ribs. He set the glasses on the table, tore open the bag, and placed it on top of the empty sandwich plate. He took three potato chips and shoved them into his mouth, followed by a sip of soda. When he put the glass down, there was a smear of oil and salt from his fingers. For a moment, the only sound was the crunch of chips between their teeth and the occasional tap of a glass on the table.

In a low, almost hypnotic voice, Paul said, "You want to talk."

Thomas said nothing. The sun was directly in front of them, burning into his eyes. He closed them for a moment and studied the red glow caused by the rays working to penetrate his eyelids.

He felt Paul moving beside him. Paul's hand was on the arm of Thomas's chair. Thomas took a breath and held it inside. When it tightened his lungs, he let it go.

Paul put his hand on Thomas's forearm. He squeezed gently

and left his hand there for a moment. His hand slid lower. He ran his finger over the bone in Thomas's wrist.

Thomas pulled his arm close to his body but Paul didn't let go. He didn't want Paul to let go, but at the same time, he did. This couldn't happen. His mother. The other people staying here. His whole life. The sensation of Paul's fingers ran up his arm and spread across his chest. He felt his body preparing to let out a satisfied exhalation. He couldn't. Not now. Not…ever.

"We have a connection," Paul said. "You should…" He moved his hand to Thomas's thigh and slid two fingers beneath the hem of his swim trunks.

Thomas gasped. He opened his eyes and slid his finger beneath Paul's. He pulled the boy's hand off his leg and lifted it onto Paul's own leg.

"Okay." Paul stood up.

Thomas wondered whether Paul would apologize, ask Thomas not to say anything to the others.

Instead, Paul walked across the deck and down the stairs. He started across the sand, not looking back. The set of his shoulders was relaxed. His black t-shirt fluttered against his lean body. He walked with long strides and seeming confidence — not offended, unconcerned, perfectly comfortable in his own skin, and equally unconcerned with what was happening inside of Thomas.

Seven

Some of Mary's guests had left, but they'd been replaced by others. She was less and less sure of who was living in her house and who had dropped by for an evening. She was conflicted about how long she wanted them to remain. Of course she wanted Gordon. And Caroline. She liked Beth and Paul, and a few others. Some mornings she came out of her room and they seemed to have multiplied overnight. Still, it was exciting. The constant new faces, the lack of structure. It was unlike anything she'd experienced. They were so full of life. If Thomas preferred to spend the summer locked away in an upstairs bedroom, it was his choice. The world was vibrant with color and possibility. Her guests gulped in every moment as if their throats were parched.

Thomas was hiding out in his room, eating his meals up there, refusing to help her cook or spend even a few minutes talking to her friends. From time to time she saw him on the beach, reading or swimming. Sometimes he took a sandwich and bottle of cola out there, but other than that, he acted as if he were allergic to sunshine, allergic to meeting new people, and allergic to having fun. Or maybe he was avoiding her because he didn't want to hear about the ghost. She never should have mentioned it. Maybe he was up there writing letters to psychiatrists, trying to figure out what he should do with his mother, how he might go about getting her committed to an asylum. She laughed. When she was a child, that sort of thing took place, but not now. People controlled their own fates now.

She climbed the stairs, glanced at his closed bedroom door, and turned to the right. She went to the room where Beth and a rotating crew of other girls slept. Caroline was sleeping in the living room now, preferring a mixed crowd, or maybe simply more space and breathing room. Mary knocked on the door.

"Mmhm?"

She opened the door. Beth and two other girls were seated on the floor, their backs pressed against the side of the bed. "Anyone want to go to the market with me…help decide what we should fix for dinner the next few nights?"

"Maybe later," Beth said. "I just ate. I can't think about food."

"Have you seen Caroline?"

All three girls shook their heads. Beth's hair swung across her face. A strand of hair caught on her lip. She pulled it away and inspected it as if there was something to be learned from why that particular hair had clung to her skin.

Mary backed out of the room, closed the door, and went downstairs. She didn't want to be responsible for planning all the meals and she didn't like shopping by herself. It accentuated the fact she was the one with money, she was the one in charge. But if she pushed harder for help, it made her seem the adult to a bunch of children. It wouldn't be this way if there wasn't such a large crowd. They fed off each other — their lack of willingness to be anything more than sponges. All of them assumed someone else would step in. What happened to the idea of a community, sharing tasks, everyone contributing a small piece?

She went into her room and closed the door. She took off her sundress and pulled on blue jeans and a gauzy top. Maybe she could get some of the girls to go shopping for clothes. Her wardrobe was in desperate need of an upgrade. When the closet door was open, all she saw were dresses and skirts and sweaters that had been the latest fashion four or five years ago. She had a few things — sandals and woven shoes, a few peasant blouses, and of course, blue jeans. Two bikinis. But her dresses were all wrong, as were her narrow, fitted skirts.

Her purse was shoved toward the back of the closet. She pulled it out and placed it on the armchair. She yawned. She flopped down on the bed and put her hand over her face. Why was she thinking about clothes? It wasn't likely that Gordon would clarify their relationship if she dressed differently. He was already drawn to her, and he preferred her in a bathing suit, or naked, so what did her other clothes matter? It was all inside her head. Still, she would feel more a part of the group if she dressed like the others. It was bad enough being the homeowner. She rolled onto her side. Even now, Gordon was on the beach, playing with a huge beachball, all of them batting it around, not a thought for dinner.

Maybe she shouldn't worry about going shopping. Wait until they got hungry. She turned onto her back again and closed her eyes. A nap would be nice. Something would happen and then she wouldn't have to think about dinner, wouldn't have to make a decision. It would be done for her. She didn't have to be in charge, she was too impatient. She needed to let the day slide around her like the others did.

When she woke, the room was dark. She couldn't possibly have slept all day. Besides, it was summer, it didn't get dark until after eight. She rubbed her eyes and turned her head. Her neck was stiff, and it ached as she strained to look at the window. Someone had come in and closed the drapes while she was sleeping. The realization sent a shiver down her arms and legs, turning her toes and fingertips to tiny blocks of ice. She didn't like anyone looking at her while she slept. She hoped it was Gordon and not a virtual stranger. She sat up and blinked several times in an effort to clear her eyes of the bits of crust wedged in the corners.

She slid off the bed and pulled the cord to open the drapes. They dragged along the pole, thick and heavy, as if they didn't want to part and allow light into the room. She stood by the window and looked out. A pale yellow and white cat ambled along the sloped sidewalk that led down toward the public access to Rio Del Mar Beach. The cat stopped under the window and looked up at her. It wasn't likely the cat could see her, since the sheer curtains were still drawn, but it seemed to know she was there. It studied the window, waiting for her to chase it away, or possibly give it something to eat. The cat yawned. Watching it made Mary do the same and she laughed mid-yawn. The cat hurried out of sight.

She ran her fingers through her hair, pulling out loose strands.

She went into the bathroom and dropped the discarded hair into the trashcan. Looking at the fluff of dead hair made her think of the cat. She was shedding like an animal, her whole body ridding itself of useless cells and hair on a never-ending quest to remake itself. She thought of her guests and the things coming off of them — hair and skin, bits of fingernails and eyelashes. No wonder the house smelled overused and had a tired look to it. The furniture and floors couldn't bear the weight of all that dead stuff piling up in crevices and corners.

There was a heavy silence over everything, an absence of human life that she'd been used to before they moved in, and now felt ominous because it had become rare. She should enjoy the time alone in her home without feeling claustrophobic. The problem was, someone might appear at any minute, so she couldn't really feel settled into herself. And then there was Thomas, brooding upstairs like a relation to the hunchback of Notre Dame. She went into the living room. Someone had rolled the sleeping bags into tight coils, their straps snug around their middles. The dining table was swept clean of debris and the ashtray in the center of the coffee table sparkled in the sunlight pouring through the glass doors.

She went into the kitchen, filled a glass with water, and walked out to the back deck. The sky was clear, bright blue, the water almost turquoise. Immediately her gaze ran to the ship. Caroline and the rest of the group were out there, some sitting and talking, others walking about. She squinted, trying to pick out Gordon. He didn't seem to be there. She felt more alone than she had before her friends had moved in. She should go out and join them, but it seemed like too much effort. Dinner still loomed at the back of her mind despite her vow to not take action. Drifting. No obligation. Let it be.

"Hi. Did you have a good nap?"

She turned.

Gordon stood in the doorway. He walked to her side. He stroked her hair away from her neck and kissed the spot below her earlobe. She shivered. He kissed it again.

"I feel disoriented," she said.

"Naps do that."

"You never sleep." She laughed.

"Not a lot. Too much energy, too many things to experience."

"I suppose. Thank you for cleaning up."

"It wasn't me."

"Oh. Did you close my drapes?"

He shook his head.

"That's odd. Where were you?"

"I went out for a while."

"Where to?"

"Just had some things to take care of."

She wanted to know what things, where he'd gone, how long he'd been out. She wanted to know who had come into her room while she was sleeping. But it seemed she wasn't going to be allowed to know any of that. She wouldn't ask more. A bit of playing hard to get was in order. She'd take a lesson from the cat and remain aloof. She wasn't going to hound him into coming closer. She'd wait for him. There was no rush, was there?

"That boat is really cool," he said.

"Is it?"

"Don't you think so? A ship made of concrete. You wonder who would dream up such a thing."

"It was made during World War I, when steel was in short supply."

"Of course. Half the ingenuity of the human race comes out of building weapons of war. But it's still an interesting curiosity."

"It is."

"Have you ever dived off the side?"

"No. I'd never do that," she said.

"Why not?"

"Too dangerous."

"I saw some kids swimming down into the hold," he said.

"But they didn't dive off. The surf could smash you against the side before you knew what was happening."

"I'd like to try diving."

"It's dangerous."

"But fun. A thrill."

"Not a thrill that I want," she said. "But you go ahead, if you think you can manage it."

"I'll have to see."

She turned her head and smiled. He'd realized she was right after all, he was just too proud to admit it. Or too dominated by male ego. He didn't usually give off that kind of impression, but she supposed all men had it. The pride that couldn't even admit it was pride, the swagger and boldness that made them irresistible to women. She put her arm around his waist. He leaned against her.

"Want to go in your room and have another nap?" he said.

"Sure." She squeezed his waist. A simple question, and with it, all her feelings of being put upon dissolved and washed out of her body, as if she'd dived beneath a large wave that stripped her skin clean of sand and sweat.

They turned at the same time and went into the house. Thomas was standing in the center of the living room. "Looks better, don't you think? It doesn't take much."

She wanted to kick him. Why couldn't he do something nice and let it go, why did he have to brag and make a subtle dig at Gordon? She was sure that's what it was. And now, how could she and Gordon slip away to make love? Thomas was standing there, just as he had when he was five years old, demanding her attention. She knew she wouldn't be rid of him easily. "Thank you for picking up." She let her arm fall away from Gordon's waist.

Gordon took her hand.

"Where are you off to?" Thomas said.

"To get it on," Gordon said.

Blood rushed to her face and neck. Thomas's face was instantly and equally red. She let go of Gordon's hand. No one spoke. The blood flowed away from the surface of Thomas's skin as quickly as it had risen. He licked his lips and glanced at the TV.

Gordon took her hand again and tugged gently. Surely he didn't think…

"I should figure out something for dinner," she said.

"Why is that your job?" Thomas said.

"It's not my job. I'm just trying to be nice."

"When is someone else going to be nice?"

"Hey, calm down," Gordon said.

His grip on her hand was so strong she thought he was going to cut off the circulation to her fingers. She wiggled them, but he tightened his grip.

"You seem like the head guy for this gang," Thomas said. "Why don't you get them to pick up after themselves? Help out with food and such?"

"I'm not the head of anything," Gordon said.

"You can't all live here and mooch off of my…off Mary."

She wanted him to stop talking. How could she make him stop? Make both of them stop?

Gordon let go of her hand. "You know, you have a point. I'll make dinner tonight. Not that I can cook like you." He winked. "Barbecued hamburgers sound all right?" He looked at Thomas, smiling as if nothing uncomfortable had been said, as if they were all on pleasant terms with one another.

"You're buying the food?" Thomas said.

She wanted to reprimand him, but that would embarrass her more than it would him.

"I'd be happy to," Gordon said. "Why don't we go together?"

"Because you don't have a car?"

"I have a car. I wasn't suggesting you drive. I was suggesting the men could hunt, so to speak, and cook the meat. Equal roles for everyone."

Thomas gave one quick nod.

She didn't like where this was headed. Without her there to referee, what might happen between them on the drive to the market, inside the store? She could imagine every ingredient becoming a battle, imagine Gordon saying more embarrassing things and Thomas not reacting well. She shouldn't blame him, but she did. It was time for him to grow up.

Gordon went to the corner of the living room where he'd left his backpack. He rummaged around inside for quite some time before his hand emerged holding a leather pouch that looked more like a coin purse than a wallet. He stuffed it in his pocket and zipped the pack closed.

Thomas looked as if he deeply regretted his offer. "I'll drive."

"I'm perfectly happy to drive."

"How long since you had a toke?"

Gordon laughed. He pushed his hair off his face and rubbed his hand across the stubble along his jaw. "I'm not stoned."

"I'll drive." Thomas turned and jogged up the stairs.

Gordon turned to Mary. He took her face in his hands and whispered, "Tonight. I need you." He kissed her.

"I need you too," she whispered.

He kissed her harder, running his tongue along her teeth. She pressed herself against him, but all she could think about was Thomas. At any moment he'd reappear and be presented with another opportunity to interfere with her pleasure. She sighed and pulled away. Gordon kissed her nose.

She went out to the deck, finished her glass of water, and walked down the stairs to the beach. She planned to walk all the way to New Brighton Beach and back. Hopefully it would unwind the tangled, knotted, unpleasant threads clogging her brain.

Eight

While they sat on the sand eating burgers, she'd counted the people. Fifteen. In general, she preferred smaller groups of people. She wanted to connect and form closer relationships with her friends, not watch a bunch of strangers drifting around, all the energy consumed by small talk. She also wanted to try another acid trip with Caroline, and she wanted to spend hours in bed with Gordon, telling their life stories, but there were always other people in the way, always something going on. Not anything important or planned, but something — people talking or sleeping or watching television.

Now it was dark and cold and most of them didn't feel like sitting outside. The one rule she'd implemented was no more smoking pot in the house. Right now, most of them were in the living room watching *Bewitched*. They hooted and shouted over the laugh track, far more than the slapstick jokes warranted.

She'd settled down on the deck with Beth and Paul. At the last minute, Gordon had turned and gone inside, saying it was too cold after all. It seemed rude to change her mind and leave Beth and Paul, as if she were rejecting their company. She supposed she shouldn't be concerned with rudeness, but polite behavior was too deeply ingrained. She was a hostess and she couldn't escape the sense of responsibility.

Now, she sat cross-legged on cold wood planks, smoking pot with two very nice, but very young people, while Gordon stretched out on a comfortable couch in a warm room. Caroline was lying on her side at the opposite end of the couch, her lower legs resting across his thighs. She wore the cutoff jeans that were so short the pockets hung below the ragged hem. Her feet were bare and her toenails were unpainted. No wonder she'd been too cold to sit outside — she wore nothing but a bathing suit top and had refused to consider putting on more clothes. "I like wearing beach clothes at the beach," she'd said with a coy smile.

Had it been coy? Mary wasn't sure whether she'd mis-read the expression on Caroline's face. Caroline wasn't a coy person. She was the opposite — blunt and unpretentious. A little aggressive.

Caroline's hair was spread over the arm of the couch like a curtain, brushing the floor. Gordon's hands were clasped behind his head, his elbows extended out to the sides. He wasn't touching Caroline, not even in a casual, platonic way, but Mary longed to go into the house and push Caroline's legs off his lap, insert herself between the two of them, and lean her head on his shoulder, even though she found *Bewitched* terribly silly and an utter waste of time.

Paul handed her the joint. She sucked smoke into her lungs.

"Is Thomas staying all summer?" he said.

"As far as I know."

"He's sweet," Beth said.

Paul smiled.

Mary wasn't sure if she was supposed to thank Beth for the

compliment. Better not to exaggerate its importance. She wasn't sure how Beth had come to that conclusion. Maybe she hadn't spent enough time around Thomas to see the sneering, brittle looks he passed around more readily than the joint moved around their small circle.

Paul and Beth began chattering about Thomas and college. They marveled at the idea of sitting in chairs welded to tiny desks. There must be symbolism in the rigid attachment of chair and desk. They couldn't imagine listening to teachers who had no idea what was going on outside the classroom. It was incomprehensible that an event far enough in the past to exist in a textbook might be relevant. College was a form of slavery, a way to take kids that were already molded by years of government-sponsored education and insert hooks into their brains for life. College was there to funnel them into jobs where they would plod along and answer to the corporate masters until it was time to retire, old and broken and lifeless.

Their voices floated around her head, sounding farther and farther away, echoing from a great distance. Inside the house, Gordon laughed. He glanced at Caroline. Was his laugher about the TV show or something she'd said? Mary's eyes were glued to his face, watching his hands as if the intensity of her gaze could keep them propped behind his head. She hadn't noticed Caroline gesturing or moving her head to suggest she was talking. All she'd noticed was the white flesh exposed on the side of her hip where her shorts had ridden up, and that her legs remained on Gordon's lap.

Why didn't he push them away? A better question was, what did Caroline want from him? Was it innocent affection between two friends? There was nothing to indicate it wasn't, but if nothing was going on, why was her stomach twisted into a rigid coil?

Paul handed the joint to Mary. She took a quick hit and passed it to Beth. She recrossed her legs, putting her right shin on top of her left foot. Her ankle bones ached from pressing against the wood. She had a towel spread across her lap to keep her legs and feet warm. She tugged it to one side, stuffing part of it beneath her ankles, hoping to cushion them. Now, her ankles felt some relief, but the towel wasn't covering her left leg and it was instantly cold. She raised herself off the deck and tucked her legs to one side, swaddling her feet and lower legs in the towel.

"Are you cold?" Paul said.

"A little."

"Should I get you another towel or a blanket?"

"No, I'll be fine. I'm wishing they'd chosen something else to watch, because then I might want to go inside."

"Yeah, dumb show," Beth said.

"Not when you're on shrooms." Paul laughed softly.

So. That was why they were all laughing hysterically. She'd guessed, but hadn't understood the specifics. Gordon hadn't said a word. This time, Caroline had chosen to do it without her. She hadn't even asked whether Mary was interested. Maybe it wasn't a thing where you asked, although Caroline had issued a very specific invitation when they took acid. Why was she excluded this time? She hadn't heard any discussion of it, yet somehow Gordon and Caroline both knew.

"You didn't want to do it?" Paul said.

Mary shrugged.

Beth shook her head. "Not tonight. Pot makes me feel mellow, why would I want to screw up my brain in the hopes it might turn out good? It can just as easily go bad."

"As long as you have a trusted source," Paul said.

"Maybe. But not this time," Beth said.

Mary wished they would stop talking. She needed to think. She needed to figure out how she'd missed out on the planning, why she hadn't been invited. It was her house! Didn't they owe her some respect and courtesy?

That's not who they are.

She jerked her head toward the ship. She closed her eyes, squeezing the voice out of her head. These were her friends, she wouldn't allow the ghost to turn her thoughts against them. But she was in a relationship with Gordon. Why didn't he want to try mushrooms with her? Maybe he'd already done it a hundred times before, he and Caroline, and he didn't want to be burdened with a first-timer. Didn't they care about her? Wasn't she a fun companion to have along for the ride? Tears brushed the backs of her eyes. She wasn't going to cry in front of Beth and Paul. In front of any of them. But the rejection boiled inside like something thick, pressing against her heart and lungs, making her want to lie down and curl up into a ball.

Paul handed the joint to her. It was almost gone. She put it to her lips but didn't inhale. What would they do when it was gone? Beth might go upstairs and fall asleep, or write in the little notebook she was constantly opening to sketch a bird or jot down phrases for poems.

Paul dropped the stub into a cup. He straightened his back and widened his eyes. He leaned forward slightly, staring into Mary's eyes. "Hi Mary."

She smiled.

"Who are you, Mary?"

"Just me," she said.

"What do you want?"

Her eyes filled with tears. She knew Paul saw them. She held her breath, hoping to prevent them from spilling down her cheeks. After a moment, maybe longer, maybe much longer than she realized, she whispered, "What does anyone want?"

"Excellent question," Paul said.

"Yes, a most excellent question," Beth said.

"Something else," Paul said.

Mary tightened the towel around her feet and wrapped her arms around herself. She was freezing. Gordon had one hand resting on Caroline's leg. He wasn't looking at her, it didn't seem sexual, but Mary wanted to rake her nails across his face. Or Caroline's. She didn't know which one she hated more. Her question was the truth — what *did* anyone want?

The next morning, Mary woke to Gordon's naked body beside her. This time, she remembered the entire night quite clearly.

She'd left Beth and Paul on the deck, walked through the living room without glancing to either side, ignoring the bleat of the TV and the hoots of her friends. She closed her bedroom door and turned off the light. She drew the heavy drapes, took off her clothes, placed them in the dirty clothes basket, and slipped beneath the covers. She closed her eyes and was grateful for the pot making her drowsy. A glass and a half of champagne with dinner was helping it along.

A moment later, the door opened.

"Are you asleep?" Gordon said.

"No."

He undressed quickly and climbed in next to her. She didn't speak. She let him make love to her, doing whatever he pleased, while she kept her thoughts buried so deep she forgot what they were. Until now.

He was still asleep. She turned toward him and put her hand on the top of his head. With all the psychedelic drugs and all the advances in medicine — brain surgery, for example — you couldn't ever know what was inside another person's head. But that didn't stop her from longing to find out. The heat from his scalp worked its way through the bones of her hand and spread up her arm. She wanted to feel the blood moving through his head, the thoughts that were forming and reshaping in his dreams. The longer she kept her hand there, the more she despaired that she couldn't ever know what was passing through his mind, not now, and not when Caroline had been sprawled across his lap. With mushrooms sliding through his nerves, maybe even he didn't know. She yanked her hand away as if the blood pumping through his brain had burned her skin. She wrapped herself around him and pressed her face against his back. She ran her hand across his chest and then let it rest over his heart. It thumped in time with her own.

"You're wide awake." His voice was clogged with sleep.

"I feel like I slept twelve hours."

"Good." He sat up and put his arm around her shoulders. "The guys from Napa are leaving today. I thought we could send some supplies with them."

"What supplies?" She wanted to ask what guys, but it didn't matter.

"Well obviously some entertainment." He squeezed her shoulder and moved his hand until it found her breast. He curved his fingers around it. "Maybe some sandwiches? And a six pack."

"That sounds good." She slid out from under his arm. Fewer people. Although she didn't know exactly which guys were from Napa, but she thought there were five of them. If no others plugged the holes…she sat up. "What time are they leaving?"

He shrugged.

"I'll go make sandwiches."

"Nothing else you need to make first?" He slid down and put his mouth on her hip bone. She settled back into the pillows and gave herself over to him.

She wasn't able to make sandwiches after all. When she and

Gordon came out to the living room, the stereo was on, only the screen door was closed, and there were three people seated on the couch. Their eyes were closed and they moved their heads in response to the music. The volume was low, instrumental only. It was dominated by an electric guitar at the high end of the scale, reaching as far as it could until it felt like a tone coming from another dimension. Gordon walked over and sat beside them. The remaining sleeping bags, duffel bags, and backpacks made it obvious that the guys from Napa were already gone. She would have liked to send them off with something substantial to eat. She felt she'd created bad karma by wishing the crowd reduced in size, and now they'd be forced to bum for food or panhandle.

In the kitchen, Thomas stood in front of the coffee pot, waiting for it to finish perking. "I'm going for a drive up the coast today."

"That sounds nice."

"Do you want to come with me?"

"I don't think so. Maybe another day."

He looked hurt. Not angry or critical of how she was spending her time, simply hurt that she preferred Gordon and her friends over him.

"I'm lucky to have you as a son," she said. She blushed. She wasn't normally gushy with her boys.

He touched her arm. "I'm lucky too. Just looking out for you."

"I know."

She turned on the faucet and rinsed out three half-full beer bottles. She dropped them into the trash. "Did you close the drapes in my room yesterday?"

"No. Why?"

"Because you're taking care of me." She smiled.

"Maybe you closed them," he said. "Or Gordon."

"He didn't. And I remember the things I do."

"For now."

She sighed. "I don't like people watching me when I'm asleep."

"Can I pick up anything on my way back this afternoon?"

If Thomas hadn't closed the drapes, who had come into her room? She shivered, not liking the not knowing. "Yes, thank you. I'm low on champagne."

"You still love your champagne," he said.

She smiled. "The bubbles make me feel good."

"I know. As does the alcohol content."

She laughed. "Yes, there's that too." It seemed as if things between them were as they had been in the past. He didn't seem so angry.

"I'll get you some money," she said.

He poured coffee into the two cups he'd set on the counter. He picked them up and placed them on the bar. He pulled out one of the chairs and sat down.

"I'll be right back." She wiped her hands on the dish towel.

First, she opened the drapes. The street was empty. She picked up her purse off the closet floor and placed it on the bed. She unclasped the latch and removed her wallet. She lifted the flap and pulled out several bills, fanning them slightly between her fingers. Twenty-three dollars. She put the wallet on the bed and opened the purse wider. After digging around for several seconds, she found nothing. There'd been one-hundred-and-seventy-three dollars in there. Had she put it somewhere else? She opened the top drawer of her dresser. Pieces of lingerie were arranged like small pastel clouds. She poked her finger under the nightgowns but all she felt was the paper drawer liner. She closed it.

She picked up her purse, closed the bedroom door, and sat in the armchair. She yanked the purse open as wide as it would go and began taking things out — a compact and lipstick, keys, a fabric container for tissues. The pile on the dresser grew. She dragged her fingers across the bottom of the purse. Occasionally she dropped loose bills into her purse, when she was in a hurry. It was a bad habit, and this was what happened when she didn't follow the same routine every time she withdrew cash from the bank or received change from a clerk.

The last time she'd been to the store was three days ago. Groceries. She'd written a check. So when was the time before that? Slowly she put the compact and other things back into her purse. How could she have been so careless? It couldn't be the other thing. The thing teasing at the back of her head like a cobweb hanging from a corner of the ceiling, clumped up because someone had attacked it with a mop but hadn't removed all the pieces. It floated across her mind, scaring her with its steady tickling.

Thomas would never let her hear the end of it. If it were true. It couldn't be true.

She stood up and went to the bed. She picked up her wallet and yanked out her driver's license and several receipts, she spread it wide as if it were a child's mouth, stubbornly closed around a toothbrush when she was trying to clean his teeth. It was empty. The twenty-three dollars was all it contained, and she'd known that before she emptied her purse and yanked out receipts from the wallet. She stuffed the wallet back into her purse.

What to tell Thomas? He'd be suspicious if she suddenly changed her mind about needing champagne. Write him a check? If she acted cool, he wouldn't suspect. She could simply explain that she wanted to conserve her cash. It would be easy to fool him. It wasn't that he was a dupe — he wanted to trust her. People didn't want to think they were being lied to.

Maybe that's what Gordon thought about her. Or Caroline. Or both of them.

Nine

His mother must think he was still eight years old. Thomas hadn't been fooled for one minute by her offer to give him a blank check instead of cash. As far back as he could remember, she always had a healthy number of bills in her wallet. Despite his effort to shove her purse out of sight, someone had rifled through it. His bet was on the guys who were so eager to hit the road at seven that morning. Since when did any of those characters get up before the sun was climbing toward the top of the sky?

Driving felt good. He wouldn't think about theft or freeloaders. It felt good to escape the makeshift commune. That was what they called them, although from what he'd read, communal living was slightly more rustic than a two-story, glass-fronted home with wall-to-wall carpet and a redwood deck featuring a panoramic view of Monterey Bay.

As he exited Santa Cruz, continuing north on Highway One, he increased his speed. He had no idea what his destination was. Possibly he wouldn't stop until he was in San Francisco, although that would be a mixed bag. It was overrun now with flower children and musicians and people seeking free everything. At the same time, there were hidden bars where he would be welcomed. In those bars, for a few brief hours, several times a year, he could be himself.

He'd known he was *different* from the time he was…eight years old…now that he thought about it. All the talk among his brothers about girls and their boobies left him baffled. What was the big deal? Over the course of a year or so, he'd realized the big deal was that the whispered jokes and fantasies his brothers shared about girls became interesting when he considered his fifth grade teacher — Mr. Jordan. And the two boys taking surfing lessons with him. And dreamy James Dean, brutally ripped out of the world before Thomas's eleventh birthday.

Since leaving Santa Cruz, he'd passed five or six hitchhikers, most of them in pairs, but a few singles. Twice before he'd picked up a hitchhiker and ended up having sex in the back seat of his Fairlane. Hitchhikers offered perfect anonymity, but a lot of risk. They didn't ask his full name, where he came from, or where he was headed, at least not beyond wherever he agreed to take them. He was able to relax, free of the fear of being caught, being tossed out of the university, shunned by his family, arrested for indecency. He had no idea whether any of those things would really happen, but they were definite possibilities. At the same time, he'd heard the horror stories of drivers butchered in their cars and left like rotting cattle on the side of the road. Everything was a risk.

Most hitchhikers looked harmless with their long hair, often with headbands tied across their foreheads, almost as often, with guitars strapped to their backs. But you didn't know. It wasn't as if there were pictures in the paper or on TV to let you know what the murderers looked like. Most of them weren't caught, fading into the horizon to kill again. They might have the gentle mask of the guy he'd just passed. He stepped on the accelerator. Finding a place in San Francisco was safer.

The sun was glowing like the yellow ball shown on postcards. The sea sparkled beneath. Farmland along this part of the coast stretched to the cliffs before the landscape changed abruptly from pastoral to ragged, dark brown cliffs. Beyond the cliffs, white foam sprayed against enormous charcoal gray boulders.

Paul's firm, but undemanding pass had shaken him more than he'd realized at the time. It didn't seem fair that Paul appeared to feel completely comfortable with his attraction to men, not at all worried about being seen, being labeled, being shunned. He seemed equally relaxed with rejection. Although, maybe he knew it wasn't really rejection. It was shame and fear and absolutely the wrong place — his mother's house! What was the guy thinking? Or was Paul so unbound by convention it hadn't crossed his mind?

Since that afternoon, all he'd thought about was Paul. The clean-shaven face and golden blonde hair formed itself among the printed words when he tried to read. No matter what room Thomas entered, it seemed Paul was there, looking at him with a craving that made Thomas's entire body tremble, forcing him to rush out of the room. Paul's fingers were strong and supple. His nails were smooth ovals that looked as if he filed them. His eyes were like entire solar systems, filled with so many questions, so many thoughts it would take a lifetime to discover them all. He was only a few years younger than Thomas. And yes, he was drifting, no idea what to do with his life, but Thomas could help with that. He was more mature, settled on a path. The only problem was the drugs. And his mother. And the constant presence of too many people, watching. And the fact that their desire was deemed perverse, something to be hidden or, ideally, eradicated.

When he closed his eyes, he felt Paul's fingers on his wrist, then on his leg. He'd replayed the scene a hundred times, tried to imagine a different outcome. The outcome he envisioned was wonderful in fantasy — the house suddenly and inexplicably empty. But then there was after. Would Paul tell the others? Would he tell Mary? Would he talk to the others and they'd tell Mary? And how would she respond? It was entirely possible that her response would be welcoming. He'd never witnessed her hating anyone. She'd even seemed to forgive his father for ripping her life to shreds. She hadn't been fond of her stepmother, but there was no vengeance, no desire to let rejection or rage control her life. Besides, she had no problem inviting a young guy into her bed, no problem experimenting with drugs, no problem with complete strangers having sex on her living room floor.

She didn't like his rudeness to her so-called friends, but she adored him. She clung to him. She wouldn't feel her life was complete without him. With his other brothers living elsewhere, Thomas was the one she had a close relationship with. Part of that was because his brothers were married, settled into their adult lives, but he liked to think, and was reasonably certain, he was flat out her favorite. He always had been. Sill, he couldn't tell her. She'd be horrified.

The car sped along the two-lane road. Hitchhikers were more sparse now. The few he did see had probably crawled out of a backwoods camping area, ready to move on to the next adventure. They'd run out of money and needed to find a populated area for panhandling. Even in a commune, cash was necessary. Despite the mindset that food and medical care should be free, that music and a place to sleep should be free, drugs cost money. Big business controlled the pathway to nirvana. The terminology alone proved they were part of a business-minded structure — supplier. They might as well be in the auto parts business.

About a half mile ahead he saw another one. It was difficult to tell if it was male or female. The more of them he passed, the more he wanted to offer a ride, but it was a guessing game. He couldn't just leap to the question — *Hey! any interest in getting it on with a guy?* Some of them said okay simply for the money, but he preferred guys with a genuine interest. It was hard to tell. Even in a bar, it wasn't always clear if desire was stirred by money.

He resented that this was how it was. He didn't resent his desire for men. He didn't resent that he'd come out of the womb with a different genetic makeup than the majority of the population, but he resented that it had to be a secret, shoved underground and turned into something wicked. You couldn't help who you loved. Why was loving a woman and pursuing her like a bull in heat acceptable, but loving a man could get you arrested or locked in a mental hospital? At the very least, forced to talk to a shrink twice a week as they floundered with mind games, trying to reprogram your instincts or some such nonsense.

The hitchhiker was in focus now. It was still difficult to determine whether it was a male. The hair was shoulder-length, which was more likely male because most girls had hair down to their waists. At least the hippie girls did. Girls in his computer classes had short hair, formed into solid bubbles. He understood why the hippie girls wanted to be rid of that style. It looked uncomfortable — like walking around with a skull-sized seashell attached to your head.

He eased his foot off the accelerator. Only slightly. He didn't want to appear to be stopping…if it was a girl…if a crazed expression revealed itself.

A male without a shirt. A strangely smooth chest — unusual for a guy with such thick, dark hair. No beard. Thomas liked that. Beards made men look like wild animals, and not in a good way. Now he was going about forty. He needed to make a decision quickly. The guy held up his right hand, his fingers extended in a peace sign. His long fingers looked like Paul's.

Gravel crunched beneath the tires, spun out, and pinged against the fenders as Thomas made an abrupt turn off the highway onto the shoulder. He brought the car to a stop, stretched across the seat, and opened the passenger door. The boy sauntered over and ducked down to peer into the car.

"Where are you going?" Thomas said.

"North."

"Can you be more specific?"

"It's the journey, man."

"Good thing to remember. I can take you to Pacifica."

"Far out. I'm Luke."

Thomas hesitated. "I'm…Paul."

"Good to know ya, Paul." Luke opened the back door and tossed his backpack and a sleeping bag onto the seat. He slammed the door and climbed in next to Thomas.

"You're not a smoker, are you?" Thomas said.

"Not tobacco."

"Okay. Good. I don't like my car smelling like smoke."

"You look like a pretty uptight guy for offering a ride."

"Don't judge a book by its cover," Thomas said.

Luke grinned and closed the door.

Thomas pulled out onto the highway. The sky and the ocean looked different now — the sky more washed out, hardly blue at all, and the ocean almost navy, spots that were black with huge dislodged gardens of kelp, as if the bay were covered with bruises.

"What's in Pacifica?" Luke said.

"Nothing really. Just going for a drive and I thought I'd turn back before I hit the city."

From the corner of his eye he saw Luke nod.

"I know it's a journey and all that, but where are you thinking about going?" Thomas said.

"Seattle, maybe. Or Canada."

"You're in trouble? Fleeing the country?"

"Naw, nothing like that. I just think Canada's cool."

"Have you ever been there?"

"Nope. That's why I'm thinking of heading there."

Thomas tried to work out whether this was drug-fed logic or there was something in what Luke was saying that made sense. He supposed a place could be considered cool if you'd never been. Maybe more so than if you had, now that he thought about it. He tried to think how he might steer the conversation.

"Where do you live?" Luke said.

"Not around here. I'm staying near Santa Cruz for the summer." He stopped himself before he blurted out any details that might make Luke re-consider his plan to head north, thinking Mary's house sounded cooler than Canada.

"So where do you live? It's not a government secret, is it?"

Thomas laughed. "No." He tightened his fingers around the wheel. "I'm from…" He cleared his throat. "From Ohio."

"Ah, okay. No wonder you didn't want to say. What a drag."

"You said it."

"How do you like California?" Luke said.

"Not so uptight."

"I hear you."

"It's like a different planet," Thomas said. He eased off the accelerator, afraid they would reach Pacifica before he maneuvered the conversation where he wanted. It was tiring, trying to steer a car and a conversation, especially when he had to filter what he could and couldn't reveal, manufacturing white lies that he hoped hung together.

"I'm digging it here," Luke said. "I'm from Nevada myself."

"Viva Las Vegas." Thomas felt foolish for saying it, but it was the first thing that came to mind, as if it had been stuck there all his life, waiting for someone to mention Las Vegas.

"That's not all of Nevada. In fact I've never been there."

"Why not?"

"No interest. I live north, near the Idaho border. My old man runs a service station in the middle of nowhere — a single-pump operation sitting on Highway 93, waiting for people to buzz through. There's seventy people in our town, so trust me, I know what a drag some places can be. I couldn't wait to get out. Everyone knows every little detail of your life. And they all act like they're your parents. I meet lots of people who think it's great — all that wide open space. A kid can run around the desert and kill snakes and go crazy thinking up stuff. That part's good. When you're ten. But man, you can only ride a horse so many hours a day."

"You have horses?" Thomas felt like a little kid himself. He could hear the excitement and the envy in his voice. He'd never been on a horse, but it seemed like something that could capture your entire being and transform you into a different kind of man, more in tune with the forces of nature. He probably watched too many Westerns.

"Yeah. Don't sound so jealous. They're a lot of work."

"I'm not jealous."

"You are. Everyone is. And horses are cool, but a lot of work. And like I said, when you're done riding, then what?"

"So you came to the ocean."

"I was in 'Frisco, first. But then I met this guy who had a really cool business making drums. He wanted me to see his operation and stay for a while. But it's way back in the woods. After a while, it started feeling like I never left home — no one around, nothing to do but wait for skins to soak and dry. Cleaning them. Kinda gory."

"No girls at his place, I bet." Thomas laughed. He sounded like a braying donkey. A jackass. Luke didn't seem to notice. He stared straight ahead and he didn't smirk, from what Thomas could see out of the corner of his eye. Maybe his laughter only sounded ridiculous in his own ears.

"No people whatsoever. Just the guy and his drums. And a few families living about a half mile away. And they didn't party, sooo…"

"You're headed to Canada."

"Or Seattle."

"Or wherever the journey takes you," Thomas said.

"That's right."

They rode in silence for nearly a mile. Thomas's palms were damp on the steering wheel. He lifted his hands off briefly, then repositioned them. The road was like a long dark ribbon, unspooling behind them, tightening the distance to Pacifica in front of them. Only seven miles now. He needed to think fast, but he couldn't. How had he done it before? He couldn't remember a single conversation. Maybe the pleasure wiped out his memory of the preliminary dancing around.

"You're a very philosophical guy," Luke said. He pressed the button and popped open the glove box.

"There's nothing in there," Thomas said.

Luke rummaged through the maps and registration, pulling them onto the open door of the compartment. After a moment, he shoved them back in. "Didn't think so, just curious."

"Why do you think I'm philosophical?" Thomas said.

"The quiet type. Quiet and deep. Hiding things."

"I'm not hiding anything."

"You're very deep."

Thomas laughed, less donkey-like this time. "If you say so."

"The way I told you it was a journey and you tied that back around just now. Very deep. A thinker."

"Maybe."

"So what are you thinking about now?" Luke said.

"Nothing."

"Girls?"

"Not really."

"You mentioned them, so I assumed girls, or a particular girl, might be on your mind."

"No."

"Why did you bring it up? Specifically, as you say."

"Now who's being deep, tying the conversation back around?" Thomas turned slightly and saw Luke looking at him, a small smile moving slowly across his face, as if a movie was playing in slow motion.

"So why did you bring it up?" Luke said.

"No reason. Isn't that what everyone's thinking about when they go to a new place? Meeting new people, but most of them wanting to meet girls?"

"Not everyone."

Thomas eased off the accelerator.

"Are you dropping me off already?" Luke said.

"No. Maybe...are you hungry?"

"Sort of."

"We could stop for a burger."

"Cool. Your treat?"

"Sure."

"I don't want to take advantage. Since you're already giving me a lift."

"You're not." He felt Luke still turned in the seat, looking at him. He was pretty sure... He put on the turn signal and pulled off at the next exit. He drove slowly around the curve of the off-ramp. He wanted things solidified before they ate. Didn't want to keep taking soft, quiet steps around the topic.

"Imagine the odds of picking up someone you click with," Luke said.

Thomas smiled. "Yeah. It doesn't always happen that way."

"Mostly it *doesn't* happen."

"You like strawberry shakes?" Thomas said.

"As a matter of fact, I do."

"And after we eat, do you want to hang out for a while?"

"Whatever you want," Luke said. "I'm cool, *Paul*."

Was Luke happy with a ride and a burger? Or would he want

more? Or maybe, if this was the rare occurrence Luke halfway indicated it was, Luke just wanted him.

Ten

Mary was surprised by how easy it had been to hand a check to Thomas. He was innocent in a lot of ways. It never crossed his mind she was hiding something from him, although some of that was on her. She'd never hidden the truth from him, so he wouldn't expect her to start now.

She sat alone on the deck, her thoughts circling around each other like gulls flapping madly over a school of fish. This was her fifth cup of coffee and she still didn't know what she was going to do about the missing money.

Gordon had left the house early. He wanted to see whether he could walk all the way to the Monterey peninsula. He went alone, which was a relief. She wouldn't have been able to bear it if she'd seen him walking away, Caroline beside him, dancing and splashing through the waves. When Caroline stripped off her clothes to go swimming the night they'd taken acid together, Mary assumed the acid had stirred that impulse. She was wrong. Caroline loved swimming naked. More than that, she liked shocking people in any way she could. The day Thomas arrived home for the summer, Caroline had been walking around the deck without a shirt. Maybe seeing her had put Thomas off her friends from the start.

She stepped over sleeping bodies as she made her way from

the deck through the living room. She set her cup and saucer on the kitchen counter. Rinsing it now would wake them. She was a mother hen, watching over her brood, making sure they were fed and rested. To what end, she had no idea, but it felt good. She liked the routine and the simplicity, the familiarity of it. Taking care was what she'd done all of her life. Even before she was thirteen, she'd been molded into a caregiver by her stepmother's insistence that she look after her step brothers and sisters.

It was still foggy, and windier than she liked, but a walk would do her good. She could mull over what she should do about the missing cash. It wasn't that she needed the money, but she felt exposed, knowing someone had been in her room. Knowing she might not be safe, knowing one of her visitor's had a weak or nonexistent conscience. Had the thief closed her drapes? Had someone stood a few feet from her bed, digging through her purse while she slept?

She crept into her room, took off her jeans and put on a pair of Capri pants and a nylon jacket with a soft flannel lining.

On the beach, the sand was cold and soft. She walked quickly to the edge of the water, glanced at the ship, and turned in the opposite direction. She'd gone about a quarter of a mile before she realized it might seem she was chasing after Gordon. She did an abrupt about-face and walked as quickly as she could back toward the ship. She turned her attention toward the pier, trying not to think of the ship's silent, stony presence. How could she not be frightened of it after it took her mother's life? The image still lived in the back of her mind — her mother's arms bound to her sides by a tightly wrapped shawl. Although, it wasn't as if she would have survived without the shawl. The fact she didn't know how to swim had assured her death. The church considered it murder — taking your own life.

As she passed beneath the pier, she wanted to squeeze her eyes closed. Her ears too. But it was impossible to barricade her mind, to keep the voice and the thoughts of whatever was harbored inside the ship from weaving its way into her own thoughts, making itself a part of her. She walked faster, leaving the pier and the ship behind her. She veered closer to the water. Waves washed over her feet and ankles. There were only five or six people out walking, most of them so far ahead their forms were blurred by the fog, giving them the appearance of ghosts themselves. She smiled. Ghosts weren't simply imagined beings. But even people who believed the appearance of spirits from beyond the grave was nonsense had to recognize how the concept had worked its way into common language over the centuries.

One of the figures walking toward her was knee-deep in the water. When the waves went out, Mary saw that the gait and mannerisms belonged to Caroline. She wore a hooded sweatshirt and a gauzy skirt that sent goosebumps up Mary's legs, thinking of walking in the breezy morning air with fabric as insubstantial as tissue paper covering her legs. The hem of the skirt was sopping wet, and it hung unevenly below Caroline's knees. Her hair was tangled. As she drew closer, Mary saw that the cuffs of her sweatshirt were also wet and misshapen. Her entire appearance was of someone who'd slept on the beach in the clothes she was wearing now. And yet, she was beautiful. At twenty-six, every part of you looked good — any article of clothing from a thrift shop and any shapeless hairstyle was acceptable. If you could even call her long, uncombed hair a style.

It bothered her that she was mentally tearing apart Caroline's appearance, as if Caroline's clothing and hair were character flaws. Caroline was a good friend, the closest friend she had right now. What had Caroline done, really? She'd stretched out on the couch. Gordon was already sitting there. Of course her legs ended up lying across his. It didn't mean anything. It wasn't as if Gordon had made a pass at her. They were friends. All of them were friends — housemates. Jealousy was a petty, childish, unevolved emotion that would tear them apart. She would not allow it to eat away at her pleasure. She pulled her hand out of her pocket and waved at Caroline.

Caroline smiled and waved back. Everything was okay.

When they were a few feet away from each other, Caroline kicked at the water and sent a spray in Mary's direction. Mary giggled and leaped away from the waves.

"You're up early," Mary said.

"It's beautiful at this time of day."

"I agree. A lot of people don't appreciate that. Especially when it's foggy."

"The fog makes it mysterious."

"Haunting," Mary said.

"Very."

Mary turned and started walking back toward the ship with Caroline. "I think it's haunted."

"The ocean?"

"No, the ship."

"I can see that. Because it's so old."

So old? It wasn't much older than Mary. Did Caroline know that? Probably not. Caroline knew very little about her, not nearly as much as Mary knew about Caroline. And Mary had tried to blur the edges of her age when they shared stories of their past. Why draw attention to it? Gordon said age didn't matter. It was the life they experienced together that was important. "Not just that. Who knows what's buried inside of it."

Caroline shivered. "You're scaring me!"

They moved back so the waves lapped at their feet. Once your skin was numb, the water no longer felt cold.

"I'm a little upset about something," Mary said.

"Don't be upset. It's a groovy morning."

"You don't know what happened."

"What?" Caroline darted out at a wave and kicked the foamy edge. Pieces of foam clung to her skirt, gluing the fabric to her legs.

"Someone took money out of my purse."

"I'm sure it was for something important."

"But it's stealing."

"Maybe they bought beer for everyone. Or food."

"But they should have asked."

"You've bought a lot of food. They probably assumed…"

"It's stealing, taking it without asking."

"Stealing is an ugly word."

"I know. That's why I'm upset."

Caroline looped her arm around Mary's. "Please don't be."

"It makes me nervous. Wondering who's staying in the house. I don't really know them."

"It's just money."

"My money."

"Don't be like that." Caroline leaned her head on Mary's shoulder.

"Someone was in my room when I was sleeping. They closed the drapes."

Caroline lifted her head and let go of Mary's arm. She laughed. "You're upset about that?"

"It's unsettling."

"It's sweet."

Like Thomas. That's what Beth had said about Thomas. "I asked Thomas if he'd done it, and he said no."

"It's all good," Caroline said. "Someone was looking after you."

"I don't like people in my room when I'm sleeping. Looking at me when I'm not aware."

"You're a strange one, Mary King."

Mary hadn't realized Caroline knew, or remembered, her last name. It was comforting. It made her feel less alone, less uncertain about relative strangers living in her home. Because now she knew, they *were* strangers, and some of them might not be of the highest character. "It's perfectly normal to not want people prowling around your private space. Taking things. It *is* stealing."

Caroline danced out into the water and spun around. She flung her arms out to the sides and tipped her face up toward the sky. "I took it! Don't be upset. I thought you wouldn't care. I saw you sleeping like a sweet little baby. The sun was on your face and I closed the drapes."

That was a lie. The sun didn't come into her bedroom, the houses on the opposite side of the narrow street blocked it.

"Acid and mushrooms, psychedelic visions, aren't free. I thought you were part of it all and wanted to share."

"I do. I'm sharing a lot."

"Then it's cool about the money."

"You used it for drugs?"

"Don't make them sound eeee-vil." Caroline spun back in Mary's direction and bent forward slightly, walking backwards through the waves, exaggerating her expression so that her eyes seemed to bulge out of their sockets. "Druuuugs. It's cool, right?"

"Yes. I'm having a great time."

"Excellent." Caroline stood and turned so she was at Mary's side again.

"I wish you'd asked. Or told me."

"And I will. If it happens again I will do that."

"Thank you."

"I just assumed we were sharing." She leaned around so Mary

could see her face. She gave her a charming smile. "We share everything, yes?"

"I suppose."

They walked in silence for a few hundred yards. They passed a log, stripped clean by the ocean, all but one of its branches shaved off. It had been tossed and thrown for months, maybe years. It was possible the fallen tree had been rolling around in the ocean, traveling between continents for most of her lifetime. Who knew what current eventually brought them to shore, randomly selecting this stretch of this coastline. The single remaining branch had a sopping wet blue shirt caught at the end.

"I was sorry I didn't get to try the mushrooms," Mary said.

"Did you want to?"

"Yes."

"You should have mentioned it."

"I didn't know that was the plan."

Caroline laughed. "Nothing is planned. It just happened. Next time, for sure. There's still some left, okay?"

Mary nodded, unsure whether Caroline noticed.

Caroline chattered on about the differences between mushrooms and acid. Mary didn't care. She cared only about sharing the experience. Maybe the LSD had made her paranoid. She'd heard it could do that. Wasn't it a bit of paranoia she'd experienced when Caroline dove into the dark waves that night? And she'd heard the frantic, suspicious feelings created by LSD could linger. Your brain chemistry forever altered. Or was it the ghost? She turned away from the ship.

"What's wrong?" Caroline said.

"Nothing."

"You're sure?"

"I'm fine." Mary turned back and smiled.

They passed under the pier. A faded red child's tennis shoe was tangled in a mass of seaweed the size of a human body. The way it was coiled, it might have been wrapped around a body and no one would know.

Caroline gave her a hug and trotted across the sand to the deck stairs, Mary wandered back to the support posts holding the pier. The conversation, the entire encounter with Caroline, had left her deeply unhappy. If it were possible, she felt even more excluded than she had during the mushroom escapade. The lie about the sun on Mary's face flowed out of Caroline's mouth so easily, and there was a genuine quality about it — so detailed, so kind. Who lied about a kindness? There was something perverse in that. Was Caroline lying about the money, too? Protecting someone? But it made no sense to implicate yourself in an immoral act. A crime. Not a simple sharing of money, a deliberate misinterpretation of the idea of sharing. Of course they were all sharing. No one counted how many joints they rolled or who smoked each one and how many puffs they took. She was happy to share her house. The space was wasted on her. Gordon had purchased food several times. Caroline and Beth had gone to the store without Mary contributing any cash. Hadn't they? The first day? And maybe since then.

Society needed more sharing, less scorekeeping. But what did that mean — was everything shared? It couldn't possibly apply to lovers. Some of them did though. She wasn't naive. They shared sexual partners as easily as they shared joints. And that was fine, she supposed. Among kids. But she and Gordon were different. He was older than the others. And Mary was an adult woman. So was Caroline, but not in the same way. Caroline's experience of the world and the current state of her life was that of a teenager.

She picked up the lone shoe. She held it by her fingertips to keep the wet sand off her hands. She walked back to the enormous log and tugged the shirt away from the protruding branch. She carried both items back to the house and left them at the foot of the stairs. She didn't know why she did it…picking up lost clothing. It had become a compulsion over the years. Some things, she couldn't imagine how people managed to leave them behind. The shoe was a good example. Did they leave the beach barefoot, brush the sand off, and get into their cars without donning their shoes, not realizing until they'd driven ten or twenty miles that they'd left something behind? She wondered if any of them ever returned, hoping to find what they'd lost.

Eleven

The drive back from Pacifica was a steady hum of mindlessness. Nothing but the dark road in front of him, illuminated only by his headlights. The ocean beyond the cliff to his right was invisible, even under the brightly glowing moon. He felt it there, thrashing about, but with a steady rhythm. A controlled thrashing.

Luke hadn't asked for money. And he hadn't finished his strawberry milkshake. He'd handed over the half-full cup to Thomas. It sat beside him now, wedged against the back of the empty passenger seat with his jacket and his shoes. He was driving barefoot. It felt good, as if he and the car were one. Almost like riding a horse, he imagined — physical contact felt through your whole body. The milkshake had turned to thick, runny goop, but he continued to take sips from it every few miles. The intense sweetness added to his pleasure. It wasn't good for him and it almost turned his stomach, yet it tasted delicious.

When he reached Santa Cruz, he pulled off the highway and drove to a service station. He dumped the cup of pink liquid into a trashcan. While the attendant topped off the gas tank, Thomas put on his socks and shoes and bought a bag of potato chips. He needed to get the gummy coating of artificial strawberry off his tongue.

At home, the front of the house looked as impassive as ever, only the glossy cherry door distinguishing it from its neighbors. His mother's bedroom window was partially open. The drapes were open as well, the sheer curtain fluttering in the breeze that rushed up the narrow street as if it were late to dinner. He unlocked the door and went inside. The living room looked relatively tidy. On the back deck, several people were arranged in their usual circle. A thick cloud of smoke hovered over them. A candle sat in the center of their circle, casting a yellow glow onto a few of their faces. Mary's eyes were partially closed and she wore a dopey smile, as if she weren't all that intelligent. He turned away.

He went into the kitchen, poured a glass of water, and grabbed an oatmeal cookie off a plate sitting on the bar. As he started out of the room, he decided he was hungrier than that. He took two more cookies. When he reached his bedroom door, he set the water glass on the carpet to free his hand to open the door.

The room was dark. He picked up the water glass, stepped inside, and closed the door with his hip. He felt along the wall with his forearm until it bumped the light switch. He nudged it up. Paul was lying on the bed. His eyes were closed but he smiled knowingly, fully alert. He wore nothing but blue jeans that hugged his hips several inches below his navel. His hands were tucked behind his head, sparse golden brown hair exposed in his armpits. His feet were bare.

"What's this about?" Thomas said.

"Nothing." Paul's eyes remained closed.

"Please get off my bed."

"There aren't a lot of beds in this house. Why do you get to claim one of them on a permanent basis?"

Thomas set the water glass on the dresser. He stacked the cookies next to it, then picked up the glass and took a drink. He stared at Paul. Maybe the silence would force him to open his eyes instead of lying there like a smiling Buddha. He picked up a cookie and took a large bite. He chewed slowly.

"Are you going to explain?" Paul said.

"It's fairly obvious. This is my home."

"I thought it belonged to Mary."

"I'm her son."

"But you don't live here."

"I stay here in the summer."

"It gets old, sleeping on the floor."

"Then why don't you get a job and find a place to live?"

"I have a place to live. Like you, I'm enjoying the summer here. The beach is the place to be. I guess you know that."

Thomas finished the cookie and took another sip of water. He walked around the foot of the bed. He adjusted the spine on the shutters. He reached up for the hook on the top set, unlatched it, and swung the shutter open. Moonlight streamed into the room. A glossy reflection spilled across the water. The ocean was calm, hardly moving, gentle waves lapping at the beach. He wasn't sure how to get Paul off his bed and out of his room. He didn't want a scene.

"What are you looking at?" Paul said.

"The moon."

"Very seductive, isn't it."

"Why aren't you outside with the others?"

"I wanted to get some rest. On a real bed."

"There's a bed down the hall."

"Yours is nicer."

Thomas turned away from the window. "Well you've had your rest, now it's time to leave."

"Are you going to sleep?"

"Maybe."

"It's only nine-thirty."

"I'm tired."

"Where were you?" Paul sat up, pulled the pillows toward the center of the headboard, and leaned back.

"That's none of your business."

"Oooh. A mystery. A secret rendezvous."

"It was nothing like that."

"Then what? A party? A girl? A job interview? Slumming?"

"What does that mean — slumming?"

"Covers all the other possibilities. Which one?"

"None of those."

"So slumming."

"I said none of those. Please get off my bed. I'm really tired."

"Why so tired?"

"Talking to you is tiring."

"That's because you're trying too hard."

Thomas sat down in the armchair. Despite sitting in the car all day, sitting in the burger place for longer than it took to eat, and lying around in the crevice of an outcropping of rocks, a cave-like alcove on the beach near Pacifica, he was tired of standing. His instinct was to tell the guy he'd get Mary to throw him out. How foolish. Calling his mother for help. He grimaced.

"Are you feeling okay?"

"I'm fine."

Paul scooted toward the side of the bed nearest the window. He patted the mattress, thumping it hard as if he wanted to slap it into submission. "Come sit here."

"No."

"Why not?"

"I don't share my bed."

"With anyone?"

He hesitated. He had no idea what Paul thought after the other day. Thomas was pretty sure his body hadn't given any obvious signs of responding to Paul's touch, but he couldn't be sure. The guy seemed to have some second sight that allowed him to know things he shouldn't. Or maybe only a second sight into Thomas. If he kept insisting he shared his bed with no-one, Paul would assume that included females. He glanced at the door. Maybe his awkward behavior made him completely transparent. He felt trapped in the conversation, and in his room. He could go out again, but where would he go?

"It's okay," Paul said. "I like women *and* men. All human beings."

"Why are you telling me that? I don't want to know."

"I thought it would be useful information."

"It's not."

Paul rearranged the pillows and sat up straighter. "Can I have that cookie?"

"No. There are plenty downstairs. Help yourself to one of those."

"Then I have to leave this nice bed. Possession is nine tenths of the law."

"Not in this case."

"I told you what I like because I thought it would help you relax. And you should also know that I mind my own business. I'm not a kiss and tell kind of guy."

"So?"

"Your secret is safe with me."

"I don't have a secret. What do you know about me? Are you even twenty-one? You're a kid."

"Does that makes you feel better? Dismissing me, belittling me?"

"I'm not belittling you."

"I can feel that you want me."

"Well your feeling is incorrect."

"You don't know you want me, or you didn't. Until I touched you."

"I don't want to talk about this any more." Thomas stood up and went to the dresser. He finished the water. The result was he realized he had to piss, but he was not going to do that while this guy was sitting here acting as if he knew everything about Thomas's life.

Paul slid to the edge of the bed. He stood up. "I guess I called it wrong.

"I guess you did. Go ahead and take the cookie on your way out."

"You're not fooling me," Paul said.

"You called it wrong."

"I meant I called it wrong that you'd be interested tonight. Not about what you want underneath all that education and proper manners and looking out for mamma."

He wanted to smash his fist into Paul's nose, watch blood spurt all over the creamy bedspread. At the same time, urged by the blood pumping in his own veins, he wanted to push Paul onto his back and climb on top of him. When he spoke, his voice was hoarse — "Please leave."

Paul stepped around the bed. He cupped his hand around Thomas's shoulder. "Hey brother, it's not so bad. You're a good guy. I don't want to hurt you. It's okay to be who you are. You don't owe anyone an explanation." He glanced at the cookie, crossed the room, and opened the bedroom door.

A moment later he was gone.

Thomas collapsed on the bed. He jumped up and locked the door. He grabbed the last cookie and flopped on the bed again. It was July, but he was ready now to go back to school, where life was organized and predictable. He had classes and reading and programming assignments. He had research papers to occupy his mind. He had people telling him where to go and what to do. The freedom of summer was not what he wanted.

Twelve

The sun was going down. Mary sat on the deck drinking a glass of champagne. Remarkably, the house was nearly empty. Thomas was locked in his room sulking, which appeared to be his agenda for the summer. Beth, Caroline, and Paul were upstairs napping — all three of them in a single bed. She couldn't imagine the nap lasting long. She half listened for a thud on the floor to announce someone had rolled or been flung over the side of the bed. Gordon was in her room, also napping. After thirty-five minutes lying on her back beside him, stiff as a corpse with rigor mortis, fretting again about who really took the money out of her purse, analyzing Caroline's pronouncement of guilt, and trying to determine why she felt paralyzed to do anything about it, she'd gone into the kitchen and poured a glass of champagne.

The waves crashed like a thunderclap, but beyond the breakers the surface of the water was calm, dotted with pelicans and gulls. Most of the beach-goers had left for the day, but a few couples and families played in the surf, their figures turning to dark, indistinct forms in the setting sun.

She took a sip of champagne. At some point, she would have to figure out her life — what all of this meant, what her long-term relationship was with Gordon and Caroline and the others.

But for now, maybe until Thomas returned to school, she should simply enjoy herself. Of course this couldn't go on forever. Yet the long, sometimes pointless, but still fascinating pot-fueled conversations were more interesting than anything she'd experienced in her previous life. Getting stoned was fun. She liked not thinking about the future. She liked laughing at silliness, liked having her mind taken over by a single object, and she liked the peaceful feeling, free from craving and wanting something she couldn't define.

The door behind her slid open.

"Hi." Caroline's voice was rough and phlegmy with sleep. She flopped onto the chaise lounge beside the chair where Mary was seated. Mary took a sip of champagne and placed her glass on the small table between them. "How was your nap?"

"Ugh."

Mary smiled.

"I didn't really sleep. Just waking dreams, if you know what I mean."

"I do."

"It's quiet," Caroline said. "Except for the waves."

"And they have their own kind of quiet."

Caroline heaved herself out of the lounge chair. "Will you be here for a few minutes more?"

"Certainly." Mary picked up her glass. "At least until I finish this."

"I'll be right back." Caroline yanked open the door and went inside, leaving the door standing open.

A large white gull circled about fifteen feet beyond the deck railing. It settled in the sand. After a moment, it took off, circling closer to the railing. It landed on the railing with its back to Mary. She admired the black tail with its white spots. It made her think of the edges of a strip of movie film. The bird took a few steps to its left, then turned and studied her. She lifted her glass toward it. The bird cocked his head. She laughed and took a sip.

The bird lifted its wings, turned, spread them wide, and took off in a frantic flapping as Caroline stepped back out onto the deck. Gordon was with her. They pulled two chairs up to the tiny table.

"Would you like to take mushrooms with us?" Gordon said.

Caroline smiled and cocked her head, reminding Mary of the gull.

Gordon continued, "just the three of us. Caroline said you felt left out the other night."

"It wasn't really that…"

"We assumed you knew you were always welcome to trying anything. To join any conversation or walk or dance or swim," he said.

"You don't have to tell me that," Mary said. She wanted to add that it was her house. They were her guests. They shouldn't treat her like a special case. Didn't they see it was making her feel excluded even more?

"We wanted to make sure," Caroline said. "It seemed like your feelings were hurt."

"Don't make an issue out of it," Mary said. She drank the rest of the champagne in her glass and stood up.

"Do you want a refill? I'll get it." Gordon took the glass out of her hand, somewhat forcefully, she thought.

"Do you want a jacket, Mary?" Caroline smiled.

Mary felt as if she was Caroline's grandmother. "No thank you. I'm not cold."

"The sun's going down and it gets cold so fast. I'm getting one for me."

"I'm fine."

Both of them went into the house. Gordon returned first with the champagne and a glass of water. "I'll get two more glasses of water. Just a sec."

Caroline returned carrying several jackets and blankets. "We thought it would be more awesome on the beach. Like when you and I took acid."

What was all this *we* she kept referring to? Was Caroline aware how it sounded?

She's with Gordon. They're letting you down gently. But there is no such thing as a gentle let-down, is there? They betrayed you. They've taken over your house and she stole from you. She closed your drapes to unsettle you. And now, she's seducing Gordon.

Mary glanced at the ship. It was dark and solid, staring back at her with its cold presence. Whispering things she didn't want to hear. As if all the knowledge of the universe swam in the water-filled containers that kept it sunk into the sand, instead of floating as it was meant to. She took one of the jackets Caroline offered. It was pointless to keep refusing, trying to prove something to herself. If she insisted she wasn't cold, and later shivered, they would laugh at her for being stupidly proud.

Gordon returned with two more glasses of water. As she sipped the water, she couldn't think of anything but the fact that too much liquid would force her to return to the house to use the bathroom. She pushed the thought away. It was time to try something new and exciting. What was she doing thinking about urine and telling the lie that she wouldn't get cold? It was night and they'd be sitting on cold sand. "Thanks for the jacket," she said.

They walked down the stairs and started across the sand. When they reached the tide line, Caroline unfolded the largest blanket, flapped it in the air, and settled it over the sand. They sat down. Gordon handed around the delicate dried mushrooms. Mary didn't wait for the others. She put a few in her mouth, chewed twice, and swallowed.

It was difficult to see the others' faces despite the nearly full moon and the reflected glow off the water. The beach was covered in darkness and they'd turned off the outside lights that normally shone across the deck and spilled onto the beach. She wished Gordon was sitting closer. They were evenly spaced, points on a triangle without lines drawn to connect them. She felt nothing and didn't want to highlight her lack of experience by asking how long it would take, or what she would feel. She'd heard it was like LSD, but gentler. She hoped that meant the fearful thoughts she'd experienced when Caroline dove into the waves wouldn't torment her this time. Although now that she thought of it, those thoughts weren't stirred up by the drug, they were prompted by Caroline. What she'd done had been dangerous in several ways, and Mary had been right to feel afraid.

"It will work more gracefully if we talk, instead of just sitting here waiting," Caroline said. "Let's tell stories."

Mary considered whether she should tell the story of the ship. But was there a way to do that without mentioning her mother's suicide? She didn't want to talk about that when she was high. She might not remember later what she'd said. Things might come out that she wasn't ready to share with them. Caroline had seemed intrigued when Mary mentioned the ship was haunted. It wouldn't take much to get a conversation going about ghosts. That would be trippy, along with a brain trip. She giggled. Was it funny? Or was the drug beginning to transform her mind?

"I have a story," Caroline said.

"Tell us." Mary inched closer to Gordon but the blanket bunched under her and grabbed at the loose sand and she failed to close the gap between them. Despite the darkness, she could see Caroline shift her position, leaning toward Gordon. Without moving, Caroline seemed to be sitting much closer to him than she had been earlier, much closer than Mary was. Gordon was oblivious. She was starting to think that was his natural state — unaware of anything outside of his own head.

"It's not really a story. It's something Gordon might be able to help with."

Mary smiled. Her lips felt as if they were made of bread

dough, stretched too far so there was a spot at the center where they sagged. She pressed her lips together, trying to retain the smile at the same time. It was dark. They couldn't even see her smile. All she saw of Caroline's face was the occasional flash of her teeth and the gleam of her eyes.

"I took some cash out of Mary's purse," Caroline said.

Mary felt queasy. Was it the mushrooms or Caroline's continuation of the lie? Unless it wasn't a lie. Or the tone of her voice? Where was the giddy feeling that came with acid? She wanted it now. She wanted that feeling of adoring Caroline, the sense that their souls were melting together. The feeling that the world was a beautiful, friendly, loving place. Instead, she felt as if the world was decaying around her. There was a faint odor of fish coming from the water. She was suddenly aware of the thick, dead skin on the bottoms of her feet. Her scalp itched and she could feel moisture under her armpits. At the same time, the cold air was causing mucous to collect at the tip of her nose. She sniffed.

"Don't cry," Caroline said. "I don't want to make you more upset. But I thought he could explain things better than I was able to."

"What am I explaining?" Gordon said.

"I took some cash. I used it for the shrooms. And beer. But Mary feels violated. She even said it felt like stealing."

It didn't *feel* like stealing! It *was* stealing. Wasn't it? Now, she wasn't sure. If you were the only one who looked at something a certain way, did that change the meaning of it? Maybe, among housemates, there was no such thing as stealing. In a world where there was peace and everyone loved each other, maybe things should be different. It wasn't as if she'd earned the money herself. It came from Henry. But she deserved it. She'd managed his home and raised their sons. She'd been faithful to him. She'd loved him. That was worth something. It was worth a lot. You couldn't even put a dollar figure on it.

"Stealing is a harsh word," Gordon said.

Caroline's voice rose. "That's what *I* said!"

Mary closed her eyes. She wished they had a fire so she could see their faces even a little. Caroline sounded as if the fact that she and Gordon both had vague ideas about the definition of theft meant they were speaking the truth. As if Mary should believe Caroline's interpretation now that Gordon confirmed it. He was the expert, the voice of authority, and that settled the matter. "I feel betrayed," she said.

"Oh no." Caroline got up on her knees and crawled toward Mary. She wrapped her arms around Mary's shoulders and pressed her head against Mary's.

Mary hugged her back. She felt confused and very alone. Was it the mushrooms? She had no way of knowing. She only knew she wasn't enjoying this. She wanted them to tell her what to expect from the tiny petrified plants, and she did not want to debate the definition of stealing. The purse belonged to her. The money inside belonged to her, and Caroline should not have taken it. And if she hadn't, she should not take the blame for it to protect someone else.

Suddenly, Gordon's arms were also around her. Both of them were rubbing her back and arms. They assured her it was okay, assured her the money had been used for everyone's benefit. Caroline hadn't meant to betray her, hadn't meant to frighten her by coming into her room and leaving evidence she was there but never speaking about it until she was forced to. Now, Mary was certain the drug had taken affect. Maybe it made you stupid with confusion and syrupy emotion.

They sat in a huddle of arms and legs for quite some time. Eventually Mary's knees tightened. As if Gordon and Caroline sensed her discomfort, they moved away. Caroline curled up in a ball on her side. Gordon turned and stared out at the ocean. No one spoke. It was like that for an hour, maybe two, or more. At some point, Mary lay down on her side as well. When she woke, Caroline was gone. She sat up and moved close to Gordon. They sat with their arms around each other.

"I told Caroline to stay out of your room," he said.

"That's not what I…"

He squeezed her shoulders. "It's okay. I understand."

"I don't think you do."

"Is there more you want to say?"

She couldn't think. She couldn't find words to explain, wasn't even sure what she wanted to explain.

"She shouldn't be going through your things," he said.

"I don't like people watching me when I'm asleep. It bothers me to know someone was in my room and I wasn't aware."

"It makes you feel vulnerable."

She hadn't been able to admit it, but that was it, exactly. Still, she had a vague feeling he didn't truly understand. She pressed herself into him. He put his hand on her cheek and turned her face toward his. He touched his lips against hers and held them there for a moment. Slowly he began to kiss her more deeply. It was the most incredible sensation she'd ever experienced. Was this the mushrooms? Or him? Or something else?

Hours, or moments later, they were in her room. Gordon was asleep before Mary finished washing up. He was sprawled across the bed, his head turned to the left, breathing with soft, barely audible inhalations and exhalations. She sat on the side of the bed. Her body behaved as if she'd swallowed an entire pot of coffee. Every five minutes she had to use the bathroom. Her hands trembled slightly. She stood up and walked out to the kitchen. She drank a glass of water but the trembling wouldn't stop. Her hips felt as if they'd been injected with adrenaline. It might be good to go back to the beach, take a vigorous walk to burn some of the chemicals out of her bloodstream. She grabbed the discarded jacket off the couch and went outside. She hurried down the steps and ran across the sand toward the water. Her hair flowed behind her, legs pumping as if they belonged to a fifteen-year-old. She wanted to run right into the water, but stopped near the edge. She turned and walked toward the ship. When it was first towed into the bay, the ship had been magnificent, its lights shimmering on the water at night, full of life. Now, it was nothing more than a barge, stripped of its buildings and all its former glory.

When she was fifteen, she'd often walked out onto the ship at night. She'd spent a lot of time on the boat when she was fifteen.

During most days, she'd been there with Johnny, a boy she knew from school. He loved to fish. It was all he wanted to do — stand at the side of that boat with his line in the water. Mary had started talking to him one day. She wanted to know whether he got bored, staring at his thin, almost invisible line, hour after hour, hoping for a bite. She told him it would make her crazy to stand still like that. Johnny said there was nothing boring about it. At any moment the line could jerk and he'd have to use everything he had to reel in the fish. Mary pointed out that if it was a small fish, he wouldn't have to put out that much effort. He disagreed. You still needed your hands to coordinate, to maintain a solid stance, to think about what you're doing. She'd sat for a while and watched him. Looking at him was more interesting than staring at a nylon line that disappeared in a tiny ripple on the surface of the water.

He told her about the different kinds of fish he'd caught — mackerel, mostly. Some salmon. They talked about school and books. She brought a deck of cards so they could play, but he said he couldn't leave his pole unattended. When she stood next to him and stared into the swelling blue-gray water, he kissed her cheek. The next day, he kissed closer to her lips.

He told her about his three sisters and how he understood all about girls because of them. Mary doubted it was true. *All girls aren't the same,* she said. She told him how she'd climbed out her second story bedroom window when she was eleven, making her way among the tree branches, and down to the ground so she could go out to the boat even though her father had forbidden it. A lot of girls wouldn't do that.

"Did you get caught?" he said.

She realized telling him had been a mistake. She tried to think how she could adjust the story so she didn't have to explain about seeing her mother's body dragged out of the ocean.

He asked why she was crying.

She looked away. What did it matter? He was nice enough, she might as well tell him. "Some men were lifting a woman's body out of the water. It was my mother. So yes, when my father came, I was caught disobeying him, but he never said anything. Because of what happened."

After that, Johnny no longer talked about fishing, boring or not. He said he hadn't read any interesting books. He wanted to talk about her mother. Why did she do it? How did Mary feel? What did her face look like? Did Mary dream about it? How did it actually happen — did her lungs fill with water? Did she smash her head against the concrete? Was there any blood? Had a shark taken any bites out of her?

Mary stopped going out to the ship for a long time after that.

Now, she wanted to walk out there and scream out to whatever was down there. She wanted to demand that it stop tormenting her and tell her what she was supposed to do. About Gordon. About her friends stealing from her. About drugs. She liked getting high, but the point was to get *high*. She wanted to feel *good*, not like this. If whatever lived beneath the ship was able to form thoughts, why couldn't it say something useful, instead of stirring up more terror? She'd had enough of that already.

Thirteen

Thomas had surprised her. He made a large pot of stew with the tenderest beef she'd ever tasted, potatoes, young carrots, red wine to give it lots of body, and as an unusual touch, he'd added green beans — also young and incredibly tender. Stew was a perfect choice after two days of thick, heavy fog. He served it with bread and unsalted butter and they drank red wine. She skipped her usual champagne — the Cabernet was made for Thomas's stew. More surprising, he'd remained downstairs, talking with the others.

Several visitors she'd known only by sight had left. Perhaps that was why Thomas had emerged from his cave and become a social human being. There had been an awful lot of them. They'd made a constant mess of the living room, their used dishes and beer bottles like an infestation of ants that was slight on the back deck, growing thicker as it entered the living room and dining area, turning into a full blown swarm in the kitchen. She had to admit she was exhausted from all the washing up. Caroline helped often enough, but the majority of the work still fell to Mary. She shouldn't be so critical of Thomas, he simply wanted to look out for her but felt helpless to do so.

After lingering over a second helping of stew, Thomas washed the dishes while Mary and Gordon dried them. She wrapped tinfoil over the top of the large serving bowl that contained the last of the stew. She folded a sheet of plastic over the bread and placed the wine bottles and corks in the trash. Gordon carried it outside to the large can.

Thomas refilled the wine glasses and they went into the living room. Caroline stacked several records on the turntable and they spent the evening drinking wine and talking. No one suggested rolling a joint, and there were no mushrooms to be found.

Overnight, the fog rolled out to sea. At five-forty, the sun was already spreading pale yellow, like melted butter across the cliffs. Mary was sitting on the deck, wrapped in her thick terrycloth robe, drinking coffee. Thomas came out with a plate of leftover bread, the butter dish, and a small bowl of boysenberry jam.

His damp hair was neatly combed. He was dressed in blue jeans and a pressed cotton shirt, his feet were bare. Sometimes she was overcome by how handsome her sons were — all of them with thick, nearly black hair and those cornflower blue eyes. It surprised her that no college girls had driven down for the summer, chasing after Thomas. He'd shown no interest in Caroline or Beth, although she supposed that was his intense aversion to pot and their general approach to the world.

He sat beside her.

"That looks delicious. Thank you."

"You seemed hungry," he said.

"How can you tell I'm hungry from the back of my head?"

"I can tell a lot about you. I've known you all my life." He smiled.

"I've known you longer than your whole life."

"Touché." He sipped his coffee. "To that point, you were awfully quiet last night."

"Sometimes it's nice to sit back and listen to everyone else."

"I suppose. But you didn't look like you were always listening. You were somewhere else."

She was hesitant to tell him what she'd been thinking about, was unable to stop thinking about. Telling him something unpleasant would accomplish nothing good. On the other hand, telling him would help her growing feeling of isolation. It was upsetting that she could sleep in the arms of such a fascinating, mostly considerate man and still feel so alone.

"Are you upset about something?" Thomas cut a slice of bread. He smeared butter across the surface. He topped it with a layer of jam and handed it to her.

She took a bite. "This is so good. Thank you."

He prepared his own slice and ate half of it before he spoke again. "Something is bothering you."

"Gordon hurt my feelings. It's nothing, really. Those things happen in relationships. You'll understand when you find someone you're serious about."

He took a bite of bread and chewed quickly, gulping it down in his eagerness to talk. "I don't like hearing that. What did he do?"

"I said it happens. It's petty."

"What was it?"

"Remember, I asked you about closing my drapes?"

"What?"

"A few days ago. Last week…I don't remember when. I was taking a nap and someone came into my room and closed the drapes while I was asleep."

"Oh."

"Gordon made me feel foolish. He doesn't understand why I don't like knowing someone was in my room, watching me sleep. But I've never liked that. It makes me feel exposed."

"I can understand that."

"It's petty."

"You want someone you care about to understand your feelings. Even when they're petty."

"Aren't you wise for your age."

"I don't think it's wisdom. It's obvious."

"Anyway, I'll get over it."

"Why do you have to get over it? Maybe he needs to wake up."

"I knew I shouldn't have said anything. Don't judge him."

"Too late."

"Thomas, please."

The sliding door opened and Paul stepped onto the deck. "That looks good."

"It's for Mary," Thomas said.

Paul pulled a chair up to the tiny table, barely large enough for the plate of bread and the two cups and saucers of coffee.

"Help yourself," Mary said. "One slice is enough for me."

Paul grinned. He tucked his hair behind his ears. "Thanks." He carved off a perfect slice of bread. He pushed the butter aside and spread jam on the bread. He took a large bite.

Thomas sat back in his chair. He folded his arms across his chest. His expression was unreadable. She prided herself on knowing what was in her boys' heads by the shape of their lips, the position of their eyelids, even the diameter of their pupils. She knew some of those weren't truly visual cues, that their pupils were controlled by light not the thoughts passing behind them, but there was still something that enabled her to know. A sixth sense. Maternal knowledge that defied explanation. Still, at this moment, she didn't know. He seemed more bothered than was called for by an unwanted sharing of the bread. It was ironic that both of them had the same ongoing battle over the idea of sharing. Perhaps it was a family trait, this hoarding of things. Greed. But she'd never thought of herself, or Thomas, as greedy. It wasn't right that other people got to define what was personal and communal property. Her head ached from thinking about it.

"Groovy day," Paul said. "It feels like summer again."

"Coastal fog is normal in the summer," Thomas said.

"Normal but not what you want."

"You don't get to choose the weather," Thomas said.

"Not saying I do. I just prefer the sunshine. Mellow out."

"I don't need your suggestions regarding my mood," Thomas said.

Paul smiled and turned so he was facing the water.

Why had Thomas already abandoned his pleasant attitude of the evening before? It seemed as if he thought he'd done his duty by preparing a meal and putting on a polite demeanor for three or four hours. He was going to undermine the whole thing if he returned to being surly and generally unpleasant. If this was what she could expect, she preferred that he stay in his room. At least she'd be the only one to feel his hostility, the others forgot he existed.

"It is a spectacular day," she said.

Paul scratched his head wildly, leaving his hair disheveled. She had the distinct impression he'd done it to irritate Thomas. To have the last word, leaving Thomas without an opportunity to strike back.

She stood up. "Do you want some coffee, Paul? A warm-up, Thomas?"

Paul shook his head. "A coke, thanks."

She turned toward the door. Thomas pushed his chair several feet away from the table. "I'll get it." He took her cup and saucer and went inside.

"I'm sorry that Thomas is being rude. He's…I think he…"

"It's cool."

"It's not cool at all," she said. She shouldn't talk about Thomas behind his back, but he'd asked for it. Paul was a nice kid. Charming to everyone, love spilling out of every gesture. Kindness seemed to ooze out of his pores. She studied his golden brown arms and legs, more exposed than covered with swim trunks and a loose sleeveless shirt, similar to what basketball players wore.

Paul cut another slice of bread. He covered it with jam and ate it. managing to appear as if he was smiling while chewing. He swallowed. "He's used to having the house to himself. I understand."

Of course Paul understood. It was his nature. Thomas tapped on the door with the top of the coke bottle. Paul got up and opened it. Thomas handed the bottle to him and the coffee to Mary.

"I think I'll go for a swim," Thomas said.

"Good idea." Paul set his soda bottle on the deck.

"By myself," Thomas said.

Mary laughed.

"What's so funny?" Thomas began unbuttoning his shirt.

"Skinny dipping?" Paul said.

"No." Thomas removed his shirt. He unbuckled his belt and peeled his shorts away to reveal swim trunks. He glared at Mary. "Why are you giggling?"

"You sound like you're two years old — *by myself*," she mimicked his voice.

Thomas turned away. He folded his clothes and placed them on the back of the chair.

Paul stood up. "It's a big ocean. I'm going for a swim."

Thomas hurried down the steps and jogged across the sand. A moment later, all she could see was his dark hair and navy blue trunks, his body blending with the sand. The sky was clear and filled with yellow splashes from the quickly rising sun, but it was still cool.

Paul walked down the steps and started across the sand. He seemed in no hurry to catch up to Thomas who was ploughing into the waves as if he were escaping a pack of wild dogs. He dove under a breaker and emerged a few seconds later. He began swimming toward the horizon. Gradually he moved in an arc toward the ship. She wished he wouldn't.

Paul walked into the waves with long, graceful strides. She half expected him to walk on the surface of the water, like the golden, long-haired god he was. The exchange between the two of them made her feel as if they were performing for her. Acting out some kind of demonstration to win her approval. The impression made no sense, but she couldn't shake it.

They were still swimming when Gordon joined her on the deck. It was so solid in her mind, she described her senseless thought that Paul and Thomas were fighting for her approval. Gordon said it made perfect sense — Paul might be needy for a mother figure, Thomas felt his position as the baby of the family was threatened. He'd never been edged out by a younger sibling.

Against her better instinct, and because she'd craved a solitary, meaningful conversation with Gordon for so long, she spilled out all her irritation at Thomas. His prudishness, his rude behavior, the way he locked himself in his room like a personification of the SuperEgo. Gordon put his arm around her and listened without saying much, which made her feel content.

Fourteen

After swimming back and forth fifteen or twenty times from the ship to the point across from his mother's house, Thomas was exhausted. Paul was still bobbing in the shallow water, body surfing the waves onto the sand. If Thomas swam to shore, he'd be conceding that Paul had won the game, whatever game that was. But Paul had won every game, and Thomas was worn out. A single slice of bread was not enough to sustain him in a battle against waves and the current and his own unconditioned body. He drifted closer to the ship, treading water for a while. He could let the current carry him between the supports for the pier, get out of the water on the starboard side of the ship, but Paul would see him as he crossed back toward the Rio Del Mar section of the beach, and once again gain the upper hand, laughing as Thomas went out of his way to avoid him. He dove under a swell, swam for a few yards, and surfaced. He swam to shore with his head out of the water so he could time his passage through the breakers and identify the point where the ocean floor sloped up so he didn't stumble.

Paul didn't follow him across the beach after all.

He realized halfway up the stairs that he didn't have a towel. His clothes were neatly folded over the chair where he'd left them. Apparently his relationship with his mother had gone through a metamorphosis. Last summer, she would have taken his clothes inside and hung them in his closet. She also would have left a beach towel and a glass of water for him. She might even be waiting to inquire about his enjoyment of the ocean. He bent over and shook the water out of his hair. He straightened and studied the glass door, trying to think what to do. After all his complaining about the mess of her guests, he couldn't drip salt water and sand across her carpet and up the stairs.

He settled in the chaise lounge. The sun would dry him soon enough, although that wouldn't take care of the sand crusted to his feet. He closed his eyes and drifted into a half-sleep state.

A chair scraped across the wood.

"Are you asleep or sun bathing?" Gordon said.

Thomas kept his eyes closed. "Drying off. I forgot to bring a towel."

"I wanted to talk to you about something," Gordon said.

"Oh yeah? You didn't say two words when we went to the grocery store."

"Well now I have something to say."

Thomas waited. A gull shrieked overhead. A moment later, another echoed the cry. The sun was growing hotter, yet his chest was still damp. "So what's up?"

"You're a drag on Mary's happiness."

"Did she say that?"

"No. But it bothers her how you're isolating yourself, that you're trying to make us feel unwelcome."

"Well you are, in my book," Thomas said.

"At least you're honest."

"Always."

"It's not your house."

"It's more mine than yours. It'll never be yours, if that's what you're planning. To marry her and help yourself to her property."

"I understand your hostility."

Thomas wished he hadn't been so rash with his accusation. If Gordon went trotting back to Mary and told her what he'd said, she'd be extremely upset with him. And for good reason. It really was her business what she did with this guy. She might even ask Thomas to leave. Would she? Gordon was right about that — Thomas was in no man's land. He hadn't lived with his father since he was eighteen and he hadn't grown up in this house. Not that it would have given him any rights to it. But it truly was Mary's in every sense of the word. He should show more gratitude, and respect, but it was hard to respect this guy. Gordon was talking as if he viewed himself as some sort of pseudo father figure. What the hell was he up to? Maybe the idea that Gordon wanted to legally mooch off his mother wasn't that far off base. The thought might have come to him because it was the truth. A truth he'd felt on a mildly subconscious level for days. Still, he needed to proceed cautiously. It wouldn't do to alienate his mother. The way things were going, he was definitely the more likely candidate to end up dismissed from the commune. "I'm not a party person. I need quiet, and time alone. I apologize if that comes off as hostile."

"I think there's more to it than that."

"No, that's it."

"I think you feel threatened."

"Not at all."

"I think I'm threatening. My presence forced you to face Mary's sexuality and that makes you uncomfortable."

"I don't think about things like that."

"Exactly."

"What are you, an amateur shrink?"

"Mary is having a complete awakening to the possibilities of life."

Thomas sighed. How could he make the guy go away? Or at least shut up. He had no interest in talking about his feelings and definitely no desire to talk about his mother's sex life. What a pervert. A pervert trying to be daddy. It wasn't going to happen, but neither could he afford to piss him off.

"These are troubling times," Gordon said. "We need to live in harmony as much as possible. If we do that, perhaps we can alter the direction our political leaders seem to want to take the world."

"I doubt it."

"We have to try. The war…"

"Ignore the war, that's what I do."

"I will not ignore it, and I will not pretend it's not going to destroy a generation of men. My brother was killed over there."

Thomas had been telling the truth — he did ignore the war. He had one job. To study and earn his graduate degree.

Congress and the president could handle the war. They understood what was going on. "I'm very sorry to hear that. It must have been tough."

"Tough doesn't describe it at all. It ripped out my guts."

"No disrespect, but do you really think sitting around smoking pot and dropping acid and...whatever else it is you spend your time doing, that's going to create harmonic magic and end the war?"

"My brother was slaughtered. Have you ever lost someone close?"

"No. But I..."

"And for no reason? No reason at all? The US government murdered him in cold blood."

"That's..." Thomas stopped himself. No matter what he thought of Gordon and his drug-sniffing, freeloading behavior, he had no right to tell the man his views on the subject were extreme. Maybe it did feel like his brother had been murdered.

"There's not a lot I can do," Gordon said. "I can't bring him back, that's for sure. They're hell-bent on saving that little piece of the world for the fucking stars and stripes. I believe in the power of peace and human will, so that's what I'm doing. You can dismiss it and say it's airy-fairy pie-in-the-sky, but at this point in history, what else do we have? You can't stop the war machine with your bare hands, so why not try the power of average people coming together on the same wavelength? Maybe we can change the vibration of the planet."

More than anything Thomas had wanted to say all summer,

he wanted to tell Gordon to let him know how it all worked out. But he had to respect the sacrifice of the man's brother.

Gordon was breathing heavily. "Anyway, I wanted to talk about Mary. I got off track. I get riled up. I'm a passionate guy."

Thomas nodded.

"I don't like seeing my woman unhappy."

"Oh, please."

"It riles me up."

Thomas sat forward. He reached behind the chaise lounge and adjusted the angle of the back. When he was seated in an upright position, he turned to Gordon.

Gordon didn't blink. He wasn't smiling. Stubble covered his cheeks and jaw, a light, almost reddish brown. Partially hidden near his earlobes was a scattering of gray. Thomas wanted to laugh. He considered the words — *it riles me up*. Was it a threat? "Her happiness isn't in my hands."

"*Oh* contraire."

Thomas smirked at the butchered French. "What's that?"

"You influence her total happiness. You don't own all of it, but you play a part. All the people she loves play a small part. That's the way the human family is designed — interconnected."

"So what's your point?"

"Show some love, man. Join the party."

"I don't smoke pot."

"Why?"

"It kills your brain cells."

"Not true."

"Well it's my brain and I don't want it altered."

"It could use a little altering."

"That's my decision."

"Okay, so no party, but…"

The door slid open and Mary stepped onto the deck. She closed the screen. "Hi. Mind if I join the party?"

Gordon's face slid into a smile that had a touch of smugness. He probably thought the coincidental wording of her question proved he was right about everything.

"Did I interrupt something?" She sat sideways on the second chaise lounge next to Gordon. He looped his arm around her neck and pulled her toward him. She was wearing a two-piece bathing suit with a flimsy, transparent bluish thing over it. The effect was one of looking at her body under water. Her hair was piled in a messy heap on top of her head.

"No interruption, babe."

She smiled.

"We were talking about the war," Thomas said.

Gordon turned toward Mary. "I was having a little man-to-man chat with Thomas."

"About the war?" Her voice was light, slightly questioning. She sounded puzzled and a little nervous.

"It came up. But I was suggesting Thomas's isolationism was painful for you."

"Oh. It's not so…Well thank you." She kissed Gordon's cheek.

"I love you so much," Gordon said. "I want everyone to do all they can to make you happy."

She looked like she was going to cry. Thomas shifted his body so he was angled away from them. The other chaise lounge was too close. Gordon's knees bumped up against the edge of Thomas's chair. He could smell both of them. Their breathing was loud, shallow, synchronized.

"I love you." She kissed the edges of Gordon's lips. She put her hand on his thigh and stroked it gently.

Thomas stood up.

"Don't leave." Mary looked up at him. Thick liquid seeped over her lower lashes.

"I was just drying out from my swim," he said.

"Oh. How was it?"

"Great. But I'm dry now. I'll go grab a shower."

"You don't have to clean up on my account," she said.

"Just feels better to get the sand and salt off."

"It does." She smiled at Gordon.

Thomas grabbed his clothes. He picked up the plate with the heel of bread. He stacked the butter dish and jam on it and opened the screen door.

"Nice talk," Gordon said. "I think we know each other better now."

"Definitely." Thomas went inside and pulled the screen closed. It was possible he had it in him to commit murder. He'd never considered it before, but now he thought it would be easy. Much too easy.

Fifteen

Without Mary knowing how or when it happened, the house was overflowing with people once again. More people than ever. She thought she'd counted twenty when she made turkey sandwiches for lunch. Caroline and Beth helped with the sandwiches, chatting as they smeared mayonnaise on bread and folded thin slices of turkey in half, building them into large piles with pieces of tomato balanced precariously on top. It was so much fun hanging out with Caroline and Beth, she'd lost count of the number of sandwiches. Where had they all come from? Santa Cruz, probably. San Francisco. People were hitchhiking all over the place. She couldn't go to the grocery store without seeing six or seven people, thumbs extended, their belongings piled around their feet as if they'd just washed ashore.

For dinner, Gordon and Paul had walked up to Manuel's Mexican restaurant and carried back large pans of enchiladas and tacos, containers of beans and rice, and bags of tortilla chips accompanied by cups of homemade salsa. It was a feast that left everyone slightly tipsy from the beer they drank with it.

She'd been in a good mood for days now. Ever since she'd walked into the middle of Gordon's conversation with Thomas. Gordon absolutely loved her, far more than she'd realized. Every time she thought of it, she smiled. She wanted to spin across the floor, dance like a little girl. She was in love. Better than that, she was loved! Her paranoia was simply childish insecurity, stirred up by that malicious, insidious ghost sitting in the harbor, filling the bowels of the ship with her bitter, cautionary thoughts.

There was nothing in the world like being in love. The greatest high of all. Although that didn't mean she wasn't still eager to use other means to get high. She wanted to feel like this all the time, every moment of the day — soaring up in a clear sky, diving and laughing with the beautiful white gulls against the blue. Reaching up to heaven. This was how life was meant to be. And pot and LSD and mushrooms helped make it more spectacular, opening your mind to the possibilities. They washed away inhibitions so you could see, really *see*, the truth. People were terrified of revealing their vulnerabilities and fears. All of these exciting chemicals stripped away the walls erected by social convention. They allowed you to break free to be true and honest and unafraid. That was the only way for a true connection — for love and friendship to happen.

She was glad she'd told Gordon and Caroline how exposed she'd felt knowing someone entered her bedroom, glad for her fleeting moments of shame that had opened her up to her new friends, to new love. Exposing her self doubt allowed Gordon to see how he loved her and to find the courage to express it boldly. She was even glad that Caroline had taken the money. Or if it wasn't Caroline, glad the money was taken, glad that Caroline was free enough to take the rap. It meant nothing. Cash was simply scraps of paper that society put far too much value on.

Tonight they were all taking acid. They'd go out on the beach, build a bonfire, and trip out together, beyond the stars.

She flew around the kitchen, feeling she was high already, folding up paper plates and napkins, stuffing them into the trash, emptying the suds from the bottoms of beer bottles, and covering the leftover food. She filled several paper sacks with bags of potato chips and corn chips. She arranged ten six-packs of beer on the counter, ready to put into a cooler to take to the beach.

She went into her room and closed the door. What was the proper outfit for a psychedelic trip? There was no advance warning the other times, so she hadn't thought about clothing. She wanted to be warm and comfortable, but she wanted to look good for Gordon. She pulled off her shirt and flung open the closet door. She'd forgotten about her shopping plans. Next week she would definitely plan that shopping trip with Caroline. Refreshing her appearance would bring them even closer.

If she wore a blouse-y peasant top, it would cover her blue jeans, which were all wrong — not the low-slung hip-hugging style the girls were wearing. The trouble was, she didn't want to cover a seductive top with a thick sweatshirt. Maybe she'd just suffer the cold.

The bedroom door opened. "Hi." Caroline stepped into her room, leaving the door open. Mary turned so her back was to the door.

"Don't be shy around me," Caroline said.

"I'm not, it's the others."

Caroline laughed. "They can't see around corners. At least not yet, maybe in an hour, right?"

"Right." Mary turned partially. "I don't suppose you have a pair of jeans I could borrow?"

"I think my clothes would be too big for you."

Mary looked at Caroline. Her legs were slightly longer. Their hips looked about the same size. Caroline's waist was narrower, but Mary wanted jeans that didn't squeeze around her waist like something from the fifties. Did Caroline not want to share her clothes? That was a laugh. She moved hangers along the pole. The peasant blouse was the right choice. Maybe she'd be brave and wear it without a bra. Although, the fact she'd instinctively hidden herself when Caroline opened the door told her she'd have to dig deep to find the required confidence.

"Do you have any more blankets?" Caroline said.

"Look in the closet in Thomas's room."

Caroline rolled her eyes. "The door's locked."

"Just knock and ask him."

Caroline laughed. "If he opens it."

"Knock harder."

"Sure thing. I'll tell him…"

Mary slid more hangers along the pole. She had a beige peasant blouse with red embroidery and a yellow one decorated with green and orange and blue. The beige would be better, but it was more sheer than the yellow. Was she brave enough? Why did she care? Besides, it was dark. "Tell him what?"

"Never mind."

Mary stopped moving hangers. "Tell him what?"

Caroline blushed. "I could tell him his mother said to open up."

Mary's jaw tightened. She took the beige blouse off the hanger. "You could. Whatever works. Or people can sit on their sleeping bags."

"Sure. Okay. See you in a few." Caroline walked out and closed the door.

Mary got a pair of blue jeans out of the bottom dresser drawer. She took her clothes into the bathroom. She put on the jeans. She took off her bra, dropped it into the clothes hamper, and pulled the blouse over her head. She loosened the neckline so her shoulders were exposed. This also had the effect of making the blouse a little looser and only the outline of her breasts were visible. Once the acid took over, it wouldn't matter. And why did it matter now? Gordon loved her. He would be crazy about the blouse. She felt comfortable and free. She unfastened her ponytail and brushed her hair for several minutes until the bristles glided along the strands of hair like a fish through water. She added more color to her eyelids and touched up her eyeliner. She turned off the light and went out to the living room. Gordon was seated on the couch, waiting for her. Most of the others were outside on the deck. The sun was down, the sky inky blue, fading quickly to black.

"Nice," Gordon said.

Her cheeks and collarbone felt warm. She lifted her hair off her shoulders and gathered it in the back.

"Even nicer," he said. "Ready?"

"Was everyone waiting for me?"

"Nope. Caroline's getting blankets. Some of the girls ran to the store to get more Coke." He stood up and they joined the others outside. Caroline appeared at the door with an armload of blankets. She trotted down the stairs and headed toward the fire. Flames shot into the darkening sky, sparks snapped and fluttered in the still air.

Mary and Gordon sat on a beach towel placed sideways, close to the fire. She would have preferred a blanket but this was a night to let go of all her preferences and give herself over to whatever happened. Gordon put his arm around her. She turned her face toward his and he kissed her. He slipped his hand under the hem of her blouse and wrapped it around her breast. She sighed as her body melted like a stick of butter left in the sun. He massaged her breast until she felt she was going to weep. She moved her mouth away from his and sat up straighter.

"Where are you going?" he said.

"Just…well, there's plenty of time for that." So much for her vow of releasing herself to whatever came her way.

The others were taking up spots on the blankets and towels. Paul stood to Gordon's left, handing out scraps of paper dotted with acid. Mary took one and placed it on her tongue. Gordon did the same. He bit her ear. She squealed. He laughed and bit it again. He put his hand back under her blouse and felt around. She giggled. He pulled his hand out and spread his legs in a V. She moved around, nestling herself between his legs and leaning back against him. He ran his hands through her hair and moved it around so it hung over her left shoulder. He stroked it some more and she let her neck relax, allowing his chest to support the weight of her head.

The concrete ship was a dark presence directly in her line of sight. She wished she'd thought of that before they'd chosen a place to sit, but it was nice being close to the fire. With Gordon at her back and the flames leaping higher than their heads, she was perfectly warm. She closed her eyes. Bottles clinked and bags of chips rustled as others approached the area around the fire. She smiled. It was nice they were helping. She'd forgotten all about the things she'd left on the counter. The beverages would likely be consumed, but she doubted anyone would think about eating once the party got going — once their trip started. She giggled. Gordon put his hands on her ribs. His fingers were cold. She giggled again. He tickled her and she laughed harder.

After a while, she and Gordon stood up. Others were moving away from the fire as well. Some were dancing to tinny music coming out of Beth's radio. She wasn't tripping. She'd be able to watch over them, make sure nothing got too crazy. She'd smoked a joint and now she was nestled on her blanket, a dreamy expression on her face.

Caroline ran in a large circle around the group, kicking sand, singing *twinkle twinkle little star, how I wonder who you are.*

Gordon put his arms around Mary and they began dancing slowly, even though the *Cream* song called for something more energetic. Soon, Paul joined the dance, wrapping his arms around both of them. A few minutes, or hours, or seconds later, two more joined the swaying cluster of people. Caroline charged at them and pushed them down. They screamed with laughter. Mary lost track of Gordon as others piled onto the heap of fallen bodies. Then, she lost track of time, and everyone.

Now, she was lying on the oversized towel. Her eyes were closed. The towel was bunched up beneath her. She wrapped her arms around herself. Cold air brushed across her bare feet. She shivered. The fire had died back considerably. The far away cries of people splashing in the surf floated across the beach. Keeping her eyes closed, she reached out her arm and patted the area around her. No Gordon. She giggled. She reached behind her and felt another towel. She pulled it over her feet. Sleep felt so good. She wanted to drift forever, whorls of color spinning inside her head, entertaining her as if there were nothing else on earth that matched the fascination of color. She was content. At this moment, she was happy to be free of Gordon grabbing at her breasts, tickling her. She laughed. On the other hand, it would be nice to have his body keeping her warm.

Tears ran down her face, but she didn't feel particularly sad. She licked them. She wondered if the ship was watching her cry. Gloating. She'd wanted to tell Gordon about the ship, about the ghost. Caroline knew. They should all know. They were out in the water right now and the ship, the presence inside of it, walking on the deck, hovering above it, was watching them. Listening. What if someone drowned? She opened her eyes and sat up.

The intensity of the flames seared her eyes and they began to tear up again. She glanced to her side. They'd all gone into the water? They left her alone again? Making plans that she somehow missed, as if they had a secret code that passed among them. She heard someone moan, but couldn't tell if it came from the water or behind her. She twisted and a shiver of pain shot down her neck, stiff from the awkward angle of sleeping on the sand. There were several groans. She turned. Behind her, the prone form of one of her friends moved up and down. A woman sighed. There were two of them. She blinked to clear the moisture out of her eyes. They were naked. They were making love right in front of her. Maybe they hadn't noticed she was there. She felt her face flush. She turned back to the fire. The moaning grew loader. The woman giggled. Caroline? Mary crept closer to the fire. The woman laughed louder and the man began laughing with her. Mary turned and moved to the side, allowing the flames to cast their light over the couple.

Gordon and Caroline.

A wrenching, tearing sound rose up from Mary's bones. She lurched to her feet and started to run. Her foot twisted in the towel and she was thrown forward. Her mouth was filled with grains of sand that clung to her teeth like the mussels gripping the legs of the pier. It had the effect of releasing everything inside and she began crying so hard she thought she might vomit. She picked herself up and ran, stumbling on the loose sand, not sure where she was headed, her eyes vacant with tears.

She passed beneath the pier and ran closer to the hard-packed wet sand. Her eyes began to clear and she could see the edges of the foam sparkling in the moonlight. She felt as if her heart had been pressed between two boulders, squeezing her lungs into a tiny crevice, making it almost impossible to breathe. She slowed to a walk, moving quickly. She wanted the boat and Gordon and Caroline far behind her. How could they hurt her like this? Gordon loved her! Caroline was her friend, her best friend. Her blood sister! If she could hold Caroline's head under the water right now, and squeeze the life out of her, she would. She shivered at the thought. It was the second time in her life she honestly thought she might want to kill someone. From time to time, fantasies of ending Henry's life still passed through her thoughts. She never would, of course. But the thoughts were strong and solid, like true desires.

She wanted to walk forever. The stretch of sand came to an end at New Brighton Beach. Beyond, there was nothing but boulders between the base of the cliffs and the ocean. On warm, sunny days when the waves were gentle, she sometimes climbed on the rocks, but not very far. They were slippery.

The sky vibrated slightly and the waves sounded impossibly loud. Her lungs, her stomach, her heart — everything ached. Maybe, instead of walking for a mile or more down the beach, she should turn left and walk into the water, pushing forward until it covered over her, squeezing out her own life, not Caroline's. Just like her mother had done.

Good idea.

The whispering voice was strong and vicious.

It was *not* a good idea. Why should she give them the

satisfaction of knowing they'd hurt her? Of knowing she was so needy, so unlovable, her life was nothing without Gordon? Without her *friend* — Caroline? Besides, she was a good swimmer. She wasn't sure she could subdue her instinct enough to let the water suck her down to the floor of the ocean. She faced the water and stopped walking. It was so dark and beautiful and dangerous. She kept herself angled so she couldn't see the ship. She sat down. Wet sand soaked through her jeans. Her body shook, but not from the cold. She bent her knees and wrapped her arms around them. She pressed her face against the cool skin of her arms and let more tears fall out of her eyes, running across her wrists. They dripped onto the sand, salty tears and salty water. She licked her lips.

After a while, the tears stopped. She lifted her head and stared at the water. It really would be so pleasant to swim out as far as she could. The boulders inside of her chest would drag her down. She wouldn't be able to fight the weight of them. She would swim for a while, but then, her arms would grow weak and the ocean would take over.

She felt something beside her. She turned to the right. A large white gull stood looking at the water. The feathers were so bright, its body seemed to light the sand around it. The orange beak gleamed. It was only two or three feet away. She'd never seen one so close. She felt it contemplating the waves, trying to decide whether it would run forward and dig for sand crabs the next time a wave receded. Maybe it was just resting. Surely they slept at some point. It was late, past midnight, she thought. The gull must be tired. Life was tiring. Relentless. Confusing. But it must be simpler for the gull. Eat and fly, sleep and reproduce.

The gull turned its head and studied her.

She stared back, feeling his wild nature slip inside of her. "What should I do?" she said.

The gull opened its beak slightly. **Take what you want.**

Get rid of him, get rid of all of them.

Mary laughed. The thing haunting the ship wasn't enough torment? Now her mind was taken over by a seagull and something from beyond the grave. She was nothing but a hollow vessel for other creatures to occupy. Or maybe it was the acid talking. It lingered in your body for eight or ten hours. She was only a few hours into this. She had a long way to go, and now she was on her own. She couldn't even hear the others. Were they still swimming? Maybe they'd all been sucked under. She was too tired to check, or care.

They're using you.

"They're my friends." Her voice was a rough, weak whisper, as if she didn't believe her own words. What did it really mean to use another person? The very definition of friendship was give and take. Yes, she was sharing financially more than they were, but she had fun with them. They were taking years off her life. She felt she was living a life she'd missed with her too-early marriage. But what did that mean? Was she paying them to be her friends? Only if you looked at it with undiluted cynicism. She didn't want to be like that.

Get him back. The gull studied her, tilting its head to get a better look. **You have to fight for every scrap. Never stop fighting. Take what you need.**

She couldn't believe it was speaking to her. It must be the acid. Yet her head was clear, her thoughts seemed lucid. It wasn't that she heard a voice, but it was clearly the gull, describing the reality of his world. Humans were simply animals with better developed minds and language, it was entirely possible a gull could communicate his thoughts to a human being.

The gull edged closer. She should be afraid. It had a lethal beak and it might be hungry. Gulls regularly devoured dead flesh. What was to keep it from viewing her as an enormous feast? He would invite friends.

You need to stop taking that stuff. You're destroying your mind.

She turned toward the ship. A figure stood on the bow. Mary gripped her legs as tightly as she could. Her arms shook from the effort and her teeth began knocking against each other. She clenched her jaw to stop the chattering, but still her teeth rattled. The figure was white but shimmered like silver. It was shadowy, changing shape as it stood there, staring at Mary. It wasn't her mother, not the figure she'd witnessed in the past. It began to move toward her, seeming to fly, a terrible noise came out of it, lashing through Mary's body.

She screamed. She jumped to her feet. The gull rushed to the edge of the waves, spread its wings, and took off over the water. Mary turned away from the ship and began running. Her legs felt strong and the heavy pain inside her had dissolved. She felt as if she could take flight and join the gull, soaring over the ocean.

She ran for a long time. When she slowed and turned to look back, the figure was gone. The gull had landed a few feet behind where Mary stood. She walked close to the water and let the waves race toward her, soaking her feet and the edges of her jeans. She tightened the string in the neck of the peasant blouse until it covered her shoulders. She walked to the boulders, found a dry area, and settled down to let the acid wind its way out of her body. The gull chose a spot beside her. It remained to keep watch. Her mind was empty — sharp and waiting, like a bird's.

Sixteen

Thomas was woken by a crash a few minutes before sunrise. He jumped out of bed and ran down the hall. One of those idiots had fallen off the bed. It wasn't a surprise — four people had been sleeping in a single bed.

He went downstairs for a glass of water. He drank a full glass and filled it again to take back to his room. He walked along the edge of the living room. As he turned to go up the stairs, he glanced at his mother's bedroom door. It was open. He walked into the hallway and looked inside. The bed was made, not a wrinkle or crooked throw pillow, as always. He returned to the living room and looked out at the deck. It was empty. He stepped over bodies. They were sleeping wherever they'd fallen, one of them naked, flopped on her side like a washed up coil of seaweed. He placed his glass on the coffee table, and went outside.

He kicked at the rumpled blankets and towels on the sand around the dying embers of the fire. They'd left his mother's nice blankets scattered on the beach like trash. Beer bottles were coated with sand, sitting wherever they'd been dropped. He looked toward the water. Gordon sat studying the horizon as if his insipid brain didn't contain a single coherent thought. Thomas looked up and down the beach. For as far as he could see, it was deserted. The sun crested the cliffs and shone in his eyes. He put his hand across his forehead and looked out again. No sign of his mother. He started across the beach, his pajama bottoms dragging in the sand. He hoisted them up and walked faster. "Gordon!"

The man remained motionless. Thomas shouted — "Gordon!" He jogged to Gordon's side. "Hey! I'm calling you."

Gordon looked at him and said nothing.

"Where the hell is my mother?"

Gordon turned back toward the water. Thomas grabbed his shoulder. "Do you know where she is? She's not in the house."

"I haven't seen her."

"Then get off your ass and start looking for her!" He yanked Gordon's upper arm. "I'm calling the police."

Gordon pulled away. "Calm down. She probably went for a walk."

"When? I don't see her."

"It's not possible to see all the way to the end of several miles of beach."

"Which way did she go?"

"I don't know. We were blitzing by the fire, swimming, tripping…she just walked off."

"And you let her go? Stand up." He yanked Gordon's arm again.

Slowly, Gordon rose to his feet. His hair was damp and tangled, his beard more than a stubble, hairs lying flat on the skin, softer but more untamed. There was a stain on the right leg of his jeans and his t-shirt had a tear in the back. His feet were caked with wet sand. "I'm sure she's fine."

"Why would you be sure of that? She was high and she's been gone all night!"

"Not all night."

"Well when did you last see her?" He grabbed Gordon's shoulders and shook him, hard.

Gordon let Thomas have his way, not resisting the violent shaking, or cringing in expectation of a punch to the face.

"I didn't have a watch with me."

"This isn't a joke, you jackass."

"It's not my responsibility to look out for her. She's an adult."

"I thought you idiots looked out for each other when you're taking LSD."

"We do. But she wandered off."

Something in Gordon's voice didn't sound right. He wouldn't look directly in Thomas's eyes, but maybe he'd never been able to do that. Thomas couldn't recall. He squeezed Gordon's bicep, twisting slightly, hoping to cause pain. He began dragging Gordon toward the concrete ship.

"Wait. You go this way and I'll go in the other direction," Gordon said.

"I can't trust you to actually look for her," Thomas said.

"Of course you can. You don't know which way she went."

"Of course I don't know. I wasn't out here."

"Don't get hysterical," Gordon said.

"I'm not hysterical."

"You're freaked out."

"If anything happened to her, I'll kill you," Thomas said.

"Whoah. Settle down, man."

Thomas let go of Gordon's arm. "Get your ass in gear and if you find her, you come look for me immediately. Understood?"

"No problem."

Thomas regretted not changing into shorts or jeans, but it was too late now. He couldn't take the time to go back. He had to find her. People did crazy, stupid things when they took LSD — jumped out of windows thinking they could fly… she might be… he started running, holding onto the waist of his pajamas to keep them from sliding down. Damn these stoned, mooching losers.

He walked for over a mile before he saw her. She was seated on a boulder in front of the cliffs. He choked back a sob. He stopped for a moment and rolled up the ends of the pajama pants, something he should have done earlier. He took a deep breath and walked toward her.

She turned her head slowly. She looked so small. She wore a beige blouse that was completely inadequate for a night on the beach. The legs of her jeans were soaked. Her hair was hanging down the front of her body, covering her shoulders, as if she'd tried to use it to keep warm.

When he reached the rocks, he stopped. "What are you doing?"

"Watching the sunrise."

"You've been out here all night?"

She nodded. She looked calm, happy almost. But her eyes

were swollen. Her skin looked gray and her lips were blanched the color of white peaches.

"Are you okay?"

"I'm fine."

"I was worried about you."

"I'm sorry."

"Why were you out here alone all night?"

"I wasn't alone. The gull was here." She glanced to her right. "He's gone." She looked up at the sky, searching for something. She lifted her arm and waved.

"Come here," he said.

"There's no rush."

"You must be freezing. And hungry. Did you take LSD with them?"

She nodded. She stood up slowly and began making her way across the boulders. He climbed up on the pile of smaller rocks and held out his hand. When she was a few feet away, she took his hand. He steadied her arm as she climbed down. She brushed at her jeans.

"Are you cold?"

She shook her head. He put his arm around her anyway. They started walking. "What happened?"

"I had a beautiful and frightening trip. More beautiful than frightening. The gull gave me insight, told me about the world. He disagreed with what that horrible ghost was saying."

He shivered and let go of her shoulders. Did she realize she sounded mad? Psychedelic drugs sometimes did irrevocable damage to the brain. He wasn't sure whether to ask what she meant or ignore it, hoping it went away as the stuff cleared out of her system.

"He was so majestic. They all are," she said.

"Yes, they are."

"The males more so, but the females have their own quiet beauty, don't you think?"

"Yes."

"I've never seen one so close. It was only a foot or two away from me."

"They're not pets."

"I know that. But it was quite friendly. It came right up to me and stayed for a long time. All night."

"Why didn't you come inside?"

"I was enjoying myself."

"You could have drowned."

She laughed. "I don't think so." She glanced at him. "Why are you wearing pajamas?"

"I woke up to a house full of passed out people. Gordon was sitting on the beach and had no idea where you were."

"Oh. I guess not."

They walked in silence. "Why are you doing this?"

"Doing what?"

"Getting wasted. Letting these people take over our lives."

"*Our* lives?"

"Yes."

"You have a life somewhere else. I've been quite lonely, if you want to know."

"I do know. You told me." He moved closer and put his arm across her shoulders again. Her skin through her blouse was icy cold and slightly damp.

"You don't have to take care of me."

"You're not taking very good care of yourself. You could have died out here, done something crazy when you weren't in your right mind."

"We all die at some point."

"Is that what you want?"

"Not at all, but you can't control when it comes."

"Actually, you can. To some extent."

She said nothing. He remembered his instruction for Gordon to locate him immediately. He wasn't giving the same consideration. Although, he'd been accused of being hysterical, freaking out. Gordon wasn't worried, so what was the urgency? The guy really wasn't very bright.

She walked faster. "I know what I have to do."

He had no choice but to follow like a child reprimanded in the grocery store, contrite and obedient. He felt his life unraveling… no home, no mother, his father long-gone, if he was ever really there. He had no sense of how he fit into a society in which a female was paired off with every male. Desires that were abhorred by everyone he knew drove him to hitchhikers and bar hoppers like stray cats. A guy — a *friend* of his mother's — living in his house who acted as if he saw through him, trying to push him to do something that would destroy his life.

"If you don't like it, Thomas, you can leave."

But he couldn't. Not yet. There was nowhere to go until the fall quarter began. If he thought about it too much, he understood there was no place in the entire world for him, except maybe some back alley where he, too, would end up with a mind sodden with chemicals that felt good at first, then turned on him. "I'm worried about you. Is that so bad?"

"I'm worried about *you*," she said.

He looped his arm through hers, hoping to smooth things out, treat her like the peer she wanted to be. She was an amazing woman, and he understood her behavior more than she knew. He didn't like it, but he understood. He was afraid she was causing more pain for herself, afraid her life was stagnating and soon she would be too old to create a new kind of existence for herself. Forty-seven was already well into middle age. She might look thirty, but that wouldn't last much longer. "Why are you worried about me?"

"You're so full of hate. My friends are not bad people."

"But they don't do anything. They get high and sleep, they eat and have sex. They're parasites."

"It's summer. What's so bad about taking time off to have fun? Those things are what make life good — the best parts, actually."

"Those things are meant to complement your life, not be the center of your existence, the only thing you do. I don't care if it's summer or not. No one gets a three-month vacation once they're out of high school. Work is good. The body needs it. The mind needs it."

They were nearing the concrete ship. Mary pushed his arm away and turned up away from the water's edge.

"Are you tired?" he said.

"No."

"So what happened last night?"

"You know what happened."

"I don't know what happened to you. Why did you walk away from the group?"

"They went swimming."

"They swam naked, I presume? And wild as you are, you weren't up for it?"

"That wasn't it."

"Something happened."

"Acid takes you to strange places. I needed to be alone."

"It's dangerous any way you look at it, but wandering off by yourself is not good. If you go to *strange places*, there should be someone watching out for you."

"They were swimming."

She wasn't going to budge and he guessed why. They'd shoved her aside and she was too proud to admit it. She thought she had a houseful of friends, but they viewed her as an outsider, no matter how many hits of acid she swallowed or puffs of pot she inhaled. No matter how she changed her clothing style and hair to match theirs or how many meals she *shared* with them. She wasn't like them. They knew it, but she didn't seem to, and it made him ache for her. In some ways, the two of them were in very similar situations — isolated, trying to find a spot, always relegated to the fringe, unwelcome.

"Are you planning to do it again?" he said.

"Do what?"

"Take hard drugs like that."

"Acid isn't a hard drug. That means heroin. Dangerous things."

"Are you going to do it again?"

"Definitely. I'm going to ride this as far as it takes me. I'm going to fight for what's mine."

"You can't be twenty-five again. I know that sounds cold, but it's true."

"Age is irrelevant."

"Not always."

"There's Gordon." Her pace slowed ever so slightly. She didn't wave. After a few more steps, she stopped and turned back toward the water. She waded in and stood rock solid as the waves swirled around her ankles. "I do worry about you," she said. "A lot."

"You shouldn't."

"You're closed off. It seems like you're trying to pick fights. With Paul. With Gordon. Why do you care so much?"

"I told you. I don't want to see you get hurt."

"My mother's death hurt me. Your father hurt me."

"Okay, well you don't need any more."

"Stop turning it around to me. I'm talking about you. Why do you fight with them? Do you know Paul from school? Or somewhere else?"

"No. Why would you think that?"

"Because there's an intensity there. Like you have a history. You treat him as if you've known him for years. It reminds me of the connection you have with your brothers."

"That's ridiculous. Let's get going. I'm sure Gordon's concerned."

"We'll see him soon enough." She tossed her hair behind her shoulders and lifted her chin toward the waves. "The sun feels good."

He disagreed. It was rather cold. Wearing nothing but pajama pants, getting his feet and legs wet, the fabric soaked, had left him with a chill that penetrated his bones and made him think he wouldn't be warm again for quite some time.

He drove to the Santa Cruz Boardwalk and spent the day watching people wander from one amusement to another, eating candied apples, cotton candy, and salt water taffy — a festival of sweets. He bought a bag of the chewy stuff for himself to keep his mouth occupied while he let the shrieks and laughter close around his head. Along with the noise that submerged his thoughts, he liked the numbing effect of watching the parade of men, quite a few of them wearing nothing but swim trunks. For all his lecturing of his mother about the mind and the body needing work, he liked being idle, not thinking. It was possible he spent too much time thinking, planning, worrying, trying to find a way through all the clutter to his innermost thoughts.

Some men thumbed their noses at society. They abandoned

the desire for conventional careers with large, conservative corporations. They seemed content to live in low paying jobs, rent apartments or homes in questionable areas, enjoy a life in the shadows. They chose love and companionship over anything else society had to offer. He admired them. He envied them. But he wanted both. It wasn't right that he'd been born with a desire for men, an outright aversion to being touched by women, and was barred from having a normal life because of it. Meekly accepting the hand-to-mouth existence and rundown living space was grossly unfair. An outcast.

He unwrapped a piece of chocolate-flavored taffy and put it in his mouth. He chewed slowly as saliva exploded around the sugar, rushing to break down the candy into something his body could digest and rebel against. He swallowed. The moment one piece had been devoured, he wanted another. Was this what getting high was like, always wanting more? Good feelings fading too fast? The constant craving. Just like sex. He'd had a nerve-exploding experience with Luke, and already it felt as if it had never happened.

To have someone you were attracted to, someone who also had an attractive mind, share your bed every night, wake beside you every morning of your life, must be like heaven. It was a simple pleasure, and a need that pervaded every part of life. He wanted it for himself.

The world was cruel to the people who didn't fit in. He saw it in the river of bodies passing in front of his eyes. Most of them were in pairs or groups of three or four. Occasionally there was one alone — a boy who was extremely overweight, further ostracized by a face littered with blemishes. His expression was angry, straining to avoid tears at the same time. And a few minutes later, a girl with a large purple mark spread over her cheek and jaw. She was accompanied by two other girls, but the two had their heads close together, talked mostly to each other. She trailed behind, her expression a similar blend of grief and rage. He wondered if his face had that appearance.

Was that what Paul saw in him? Paul could see on Thomas's face that his body responded to Paul's touch. Paul saw the craving, the wanting, the loneliness crying out for affection that wasn't meted out like a mother supervising a child's consumption of candy. It wasn't a phony *connection* enabling Paul to sense Thomas's desire. It was revealed to the casual observer. His mother might see it as well. Even Gordon. The thought made him nauseated. The candy was cloying inside his mouth. He spit the piece he was chewing into the waxed paper wrapper and dropped it in the trashcan near the end of the bench where he was sitting. Did his brothers see it? Every single person he knew? He thought he presented an appearance of being in control, a man with a good education and a bright future. A quiet, reserved, dignified man. A man with a lot of potential. Instead, maybe they all knew there was something defective about him.

He stood up and dropped the remaining taffy into the trashcan.

Seventeen

Mary hated Caroline. All of her bad feelings spilled out onto Caroline, even though Gordon was equally, if not more, to blame. It sickened her to know she still wanted Gordon, but she shoved that feeling aside, shoving her self respect into a cabinet, just as she'd put her wedding gown and her children's baby clothes into a cedar-lined chest. Maybe in the same way, she'd take it out again at some point and be able to marvel at the different person she'd been at one time.

She was beginning to wonder if she didn't know what love was. She'd loved Henry, but then she hadn't, so was that not love after all? If you could stop loving, did that mean it was never love to begin with? She certainly knew she loved her sons, the kind of love that would be there as long as her heart was beating. They could ignore her, criticize her, even speak unkind words — which was rare — and still she loved them. If they committed crimes, her love wouldn't be diminished. So maybe that meant she had the same pure love for Gordon. It didn't matter what he'd done, she wanted him still. She wasn't sure if wanting was the same as loving.

The world was driven by animal desire. The gull had reminded her, urging her to take what belonged to her. Caroline might have the attractive power of recklessness. She might have the allure of young, undamaged flesh, but she did not have the steely resolve and the ability to hold on that Mary had exercised all her life. Caroline was not going to move into Mary's house, eat her food, steal her cash, use her stereo and TV and beautiful sheets and blankets, and then snatch Gordon away. She'd taken advantage of his disoriented state, and the male inclination to grab whatever opportunities presented themselves. He belonged to Mary. The moment she'd seen him walking toward her this morning, she'd known he was bitter with regret.

He was sleeping now. She hovered outside the bedroom door. The moment she heard a sound coming from the room, she'd slip inside. She was ready. She wore the yellow peasant blouse and a soft, flowing skirt she'd taken from Beth's things. Everything was meant to be shared — it was their core belief. Everything but Gordon.

Her head still felt a bit trippy, but it was a pleasant sensation. The wood and fabric of the living room furniture seemed alive, assuring her that she was well cared for. She was aware of her heart beating, of the air moving in and out of her lungs. Each time she blinked or swallowed, she felt the sensation like a small explosion through every pore.

The others were out on the beach. Five of them were tossing a red and yellow beachball, the rest were sunbathing. Maybe Gordon was inadvertently revealing that he was closer to her age than theirs, needing a serious nap in a real bed, not a bit of a snooze on a towel in the sand with the cacophony of people and birds filling his ears, disrupting his dreams. She stepped close to the door and pressed the side of her head against it. Silence. She tucked her hair behind her ear and pressed it hard against the wood again. She heard breathing, but it might be her own. He'd been asleep for over two hours. It was time to go inside and gently wake him. She smiled. She'd done the same when her boys were babies. But Gordon, like her eldest, took a long time to wake fully and could be grouchy when he wasn't ready. Still, if she took off her clothes…he couldn't be grouchy about that.

Her heart thudded in an irregular pattern, smashing itself against her ribs with a splattering sound like bare feet on wet sand. She wished it would quiet down. What if he was in trouble, acid eating at his brain so it no longer controlled his heartbeat? What if the silence said he was near death, and if she didn't open the door right now, it would be the end? She put her hand on the knob. She turned it slowly, her fingers firm, so it wouldn't slide out of her grip with a jarring clunk.

The door opened with a faint creak. He was lying on his stomach, his head turned toward the window. Only a sliver of his face was visible. She stepped inside and closed the door, gently turning the knob back until the latch clicked. The window was closed and the curtains hung motionless. Now she heard his breath, smooth and easy. The room smelled of dirty feet and oily hair — she tried to keep her breathing shallow, not gulping the smells. She desperately wanted to open the window, but there was no doubt the sound would jolt him awake. She walked to the chair in the corner and slipped off her espadrilles. She pulled the skirt down over her hips and lifted the blouse over her head. She stepped out of her underwear and shivered despite the warm, stuffy atmosphere. How did she know he still wanted her? Maybe he and Caroline were a thing now and he was simply using her bed, like he used everything. She looked down at her legs, rough with goose bumps, trembling uncontrollably.

No man would turn his back on a naked woman and Caroline wasn't here. She tiptoed to the door and locked it. She crossed back to the window. As if he was aware of her approach, he turned onto his back. He looked angelic. He hadn't meant to hurt her. She'd known from the first time Caroline tore off her shirt in front of all those guys that the girl wanted trouble. She needed everyone to look at her. She craved their attention, and the more shocked the attention was, the more she basked in it. Her mother a debutante — Caroline might loathe the trappings of it, she might have a different style, but the desired outcome was the same. She wanted everyone gazing at her, admiring her, applauding her every move. It was possible Caroline had slept with every guy in the house and Gordon was simply the last one on her list.

Mary walked to the side of the bed. She put her hand on Gordon's shoulder. He didn't move. She pulled the blankets back and sat on the edge of the bed. Slowly, she lifted her feet and slid her right foot under. Gordon groaned and flung out his arm. The back of his hand slapped her thigh, but his eyelids didn't quiver with recognition of her presence. She sat motionless for several minutes, one foot under the blankets. His breathing became steady again. She lifted the blankets higher and covered both her legs. For several more minutes she sat, waiting. She listened to his breath and her own. She lowered herself the rest of the way, turned on her side, and pulled the covers over her shoulder. She didn't want to fall asleep and risk him leaving the room. She propped herself up on her elbow and studied his face.

The doorbell rang. She cringed, but his lips remained slack. She hoped Thomas, or someone, would see who was at the door. After a few minutes of silence, she eased the breath out of her lungs.

When she woke, Gordon was looking at her with a solemn expression on his face. Her chest convulsed. Why couldn't he understand that she hated being observed while she slept? He must have forgotten. Or it was such a foreign idea to him, he didn't comprehend why it was disturbing.

He put his fingertip on her nose. "How are you?"

All the responses that came to mind were inadequate or set the wrong tone. She wanted him to speak first, wanted to know what he was thinking. She didn't want to be forced into blindly showing her feelings. Hadn't he done enough to bruise them? Was he really asking her to parade her humiliation in a stream of needy, pleading words?

The silence grew thicker between them.

He moved his hand to the side of her head. She closed her eyes. It was a matter of pride and getting the upper hand. She was not going to uncover her heart. It should be obvious. He owed her a tremendous apology. He owed her complete devotion.

"I'm sorry," he said.

It was the wrong thing to say. She did not want him apologizing after all. She was not going to be asked to forgive. She wouldn't offer it. Well then, what did she want? She wanted him to tell her how unsatisfying Caroline had been. That was it. She wanted him to dismiss the event as meaningless, to dismiss Caroline as unimportant.

"You know that, don't you?" he said.

She opened her eyes and glared at him. She couldn't tell if he recognized the anger and the demand in her face.

"Say something," he said.

"I have nothing to say."

"You always have something to say."

"No, I don't."

"I didn't mean to leave you," he said.

"What?"

"Last night. I don't know what happened, but I couldn't find you. And I'm sorry I wasn't there for you."

"Because you were too busy having sex with her!"

He leaned up on his arm. "Oh, Mary."

"Don't play dumb."

"What do you think you saw?" He put his hand on the back of her head. She pushed it away.

"Right in front of me. You were doing it with her right there in front of me. Laughing at me."

He smiled tenderly. "Mary. Come on. We were on acid. You must have hallucinated your fears and insecurities."

"You're lying."

"Whoah. That's heavy."

"You are."

He sat up. "I'm sorry you can't sort this out, but I'm not a liar. Did you have a bad trip?"

"Nothing was bad about it except you. And her."

"You sound so full of hatred."

"I'm angry." She turned her back to him. "I'm hurt," she whispered.

"Over nothing."

She closed her eyes. It seemed so real, but everything seemed real. Only a short time ago she felt the living room furniture was alive. She thought a gull had communicated its thoughts to her! "I suppose if I told you the ship is haunted, you'd think that was a hallucination also?"

"Is it haunted?"

"Yes."

"I can believe that."

She wasn't sure why she'd told him now, after keeping it to herself for so long. Yet, he believed her without any hesitation. Was he gaslighting her? It had been so clear, their bodies luminous in the firelight, the sounds of their pleasure, and then their laughter. Maybe he said he believed her about the ship to confuse her. If Caroline would disappear, if she would leave and never come back, things might be better. The sharp pressure of a headache ruptured at the base of her skull. "What do we have?"

"I don't understand your question."

"Between us, what is it?"

He put his arms around her and pulled her so she was lying across his upper body. "You and I have a spiritual union."

"I think so."

"I think I'd die if you believed I'd broken it," he said.

"Would you? Die?"

"In some ways, I faced death last night. My trip was not the best. It was so dark — starless, moonless — and I was so alone…"

"Alone?"

"Most of the night. After you left. I tried to find you, but it seemed as if the sky swallowed you. A huge, vicious seagull tried to attack me. When I went back to where I thought the fire was, everyone had disappeared. They took the fire with them."

She thought about how this sounded, and wondered if she sounded the same when she talked to Thomas. In your own mind, it was so lucid, so logical. But hearing another's experience described transformed it into senseless raving.

"I felt dead inside. My body was stiff, I couldn't move. For a while, I was lying on the sand and it seemed to be covering me. I was deep inside the earth with it pressing against my face and my bones. I couldn't breathe."

She slid away from him, turned onto her back, and laced her fingers together, resting her hands on her belly. "How are things?"

"What do you mean?"

"Who are we to each other?"

He rolled toward her and folded himself around her. He pressed his face into her neck, burrowing into her hair like an animal creeping into its nest. "We have an unbreakable connection."

She wondered why the hallucination had involved them laughing at her. It was a manifestation of her insecurity. She just needed to be sure Gordon belonged solely to her. No more mushrooms with Caroline, no more walks. No more private conversations and jokes and plans. Caroline would be on the sidelines.

"You and I are the leaders of this group," he said. "You and I are the parents of these children. They're all children looking for their place in the world."

Mary turned her back toward him again. She smiled. She hoped he was telling the truth, but wanting to believe him was good enough for now. She'd see how it played out. He was so deep and had ideas and thoughts that had never entered her mind before. She ached to know every part of him. He'd woken up places inside of her she hadn't known were there, peeled back doors over tiny crevices of sensation that made her feel as if she were living in another dimension. Every part of her body felt good when he touched her, every part of her mind was alive when he spoke. She wanted to drown in him.

After they made love and slept a while longer, Mary got up, took a quick bath, and dressed. Gordon showered while she went out to the living room. A guy she'd never seen before was sitting on the couch. Paul was lying on the floor at his feet. The stereo was playing Jimmy Hendrix.

"Hi. I don't think I've met you," Mary said.

Paul looked up at her. "This is Luke. He's a friend of Thomas."

She smiled. How wonderful that Thomas not only had a close friend, he was someone willing to make the trip to the coast to see him. Things were already turning around. "Good to meet you," she said.

"Hey," Luke said.

"Thomas isn't here," Paul said.

"Do you know where he went?" she said.

Paul shook his head. Luke shrugged.

"He'll be back soon, I'm sure. Do you want a beer or a coke, Luke?"

Luke stretched out his legs around Paul, shoving his feet under the coffee table. "No, I'm good. Thanks."

"Are you staying?"

"I might. This is a cool place. I had no idea."

"Thank you."

"Not just the house, the beach. Cool people."

"I think so."

She settled on the chair facing them, eager to know more about Thomas's friend. "Are you studying at Berkeley?"

He shook his head. He stood, crossed the room, and increased the volume on the stereo. It wasn't loud enough to preclude conversation, but it made talking more difficult. It was distracting. Did he like the song that was playing or was he trying to stop her from asking questions? She smiled. He smiled back. He looked friendly enough.

There was a thud of footsteps on the stairs. Caroline appeared in the opening of the living room. She wore a semi-transparent white dress that fell to the middle of her calves. There was nothing underneath it. Her hair shimmered and swayed with the dress as she crossed the room. She sat on the arm of the couch beside Paul. He put his hand on her lower leg. After a moment, he sat up and moved his hand up under her dress, resting it on her hip. As he massaged her hip, the movement of his hand made it look as if she had a growth on her leg — pulsing with excess blood.

Mary stood up. "Does anyone want something to drink?" She glanced toward the bedroom door. Gordon should have finished his shower. She smiled expectantly. Any minute the door would open and he'd enter the room, grabbing all the power with his charismatic voice and gestures, his eyes that insisted everyone keep theirs focused on him.

All three of them shook their heads. She wanted something. If nothing else, a moment of escape. "I'm going to open a bottle of champagne. Are you sure I can't bring you a glass?"

"Nope. I am in a perfect state of bliss," Caroline said. "I need nothing." She gave a very thin smile.

Mary was reminded of the Mona Lisa. She shivered, certain that Caroline noticed the involuntary convulsion.

"I guess I'll have some," Luke said.

She turned quickly and went into the kitchen. She tried to see them through the opening above the bar, but the angle wasn't quite right for her to watch their faces. She took a bottle of champagne out of the refrigerator. The last one. She opened it and poured two glasses. She took a quick sip from her glass. She felt cut off from everyone but Gordon, as if a machete had sliced through her life, severing every tender sinew that had connected them. If anything went wrong with Gordon…but it wouldn't. Things were perfect. Again. She took another sip of champagne and splashed a bit more into her glass. If he left, she'd become a captive in her own home.

She returned to the living room. Still no Gordon. Luke was now sitting on the floor beside Paul and Caroline leaned across Paul's lap, her head close to Luke. He was talking quietly. Caroline giggled. She tucked her hair behind her ear. It fell forward. Luke reached over and moved it behind her ear again. He said something Mary couldn't hear. She walked to the stereo and adjusted the volume down.

"Oh, man," Caroline said. "I love that song. Can you crank it?"

"It's hard to hear," Mary said.

"It's fine," Luke said. He smiled said something to Caroline.

Mary still couldn't hear. Something bristled inside of her. He was a stranger, visiting her home, waiting for her son. He should be friendlier. She walked to the couch and handed the glass to him. He took a sip and held it out for Caroline. She took a long, slow, slurping swallow. "Sooo good," she said.

Mary sat down and drank half the contents of her glass. She wasn't sure whether they were trying to make her feel she was intruding, if she actually was intruding, or if the LSD lingering in her nerves was stirring up paranoia. Where was Gordon?

The front door opened. It closed and the dead bolt turned. Keys clanked as they were tossed on the table. Thomas stepped into the living room. His gaze went immediately to the three on the floor in front of the couch. He shoved his hands in his pockets.

"Hi, *Thomas*." Luke handed the champagne to Caroline and stood up. "You said such great things about this place, I decided I had to see it for myself. How're things going?"

Thomas stared at Paul and Caroline who gazed back at him with equal intensity.

Luke nodded his head toward the others. "They said it's cool if I crash here for a while."

"Not a problem," Thomas said. He glanced at Mary and smiled, his lips stretched flat across his teeth as if he didn't want them exposed. His lips looked dry and slightly chapped.

She felt something…explosive? Anger? No, that didn't seem right. Was it a testosterone-fueled territorial conflict? Were they silently fighting over Caroline in her see-through dress? But Thomas had never acted interested in Caroline before, why now? The dress wasn't that impressive. It wasn't any more flamboyant than Caroline's bikinis, or her cutoffs without a shirt.

Mary sipped her champagne. It was almost gone. She felt confused and frightened.

Eighteen

His mother had asked him to run out and pick up a few bottles of champagne. He couldn't have been happier. Anything to get out of that house, that room brimming with the most confusing stew of desires he'd ever experienced. The rage between his mother and Caroline was palpable, ready to break into a bloody cat fight. What had happened during their acid trip? It appeared that it hadn't been the blissful journey Mary wanted him to think it was. Their snarling looks and bared teeth signaled an impending feline battle. Paul was a complicated morass all on his own, and Luke. Who the hell did that guy think he was, showing up uninvited?

He turned onto the entrance ramp to Highway One. He could have gone to a local store, but he needed to drive. Needed to think. Needed to escape from that house and that room. The music thumping as if it was chosen to suggest something was about to happen.

Luke knew his name. And now, Luke also knew who Paul was. Thomas was doubly exposed. How did he find out? He pulled left and passed a slow-moving truck. He stepped on the accelerator, pushing the car past sixty-five, then eased off. The goal was escape, not a race to Capitola and back that ended too quickly, hurling him back into that quagmire. He checked the side mirror, signaled, and moved back to the slow lane. The glove box. Luke had been rummaging in the glove box. He must have looked at the registration. Thomas King — Mary King's address. At least Luke had kept his mouth shut, so far. Hadn't done anything crazy to make them all wonder what the hell was going on. Although Thomas was certain Paul had a pretty good idea.

When he reached the 41st Avenue exit, he turned off. He drove to a tiny market that carried the champagne his mother liked. He pulled into the lot. He sat in the car for several minutes, his mind a wasteland of incoherent thoughts. It might be best to run, but then Luke would tell Mary everything. Part of him wanted to tell her about his life, the things he really wanted. That same part of him was sure she wouldn't love him any differently. But he needed to be absolutely certain, and he wasn't. It was equally possible she would turn her back on him, unable to make sense of something she probably knew nothing about. She had three other sons. What did she need him for?

Two scruffy looking kids, hard to tell whether they were male or female through the windshield of his car, sat near the entrance to the market. In front of them was a hat set out for collecting spare change. Why did the owner allow it? It turned away customers who didn't want to be faced with aggressive requests for money. The panhandlers pushed hard — *Just your spare change. You'll only go home and drop it in a jar and forget it. You won't even know it's gone and it'll mean everything to me*. Then, whether they were refused or rewarded — *Peace, man.*

He pulled his keys out of the ignition. He walked slowly

toward the entrance, hoping someone would emerge and capture the beggars' attention before he reached the sidewalk. He slowed his pace, glancing over his shoulder to see if any other cars had pulled into the lot after him.

As he drew closer, he saw that one of them looked familiar. A girl. It was one of the girls staying at the house. She'd been there from the start, that's why he recognized her despite the beaded band wrapped around her forehead as if she'd recently emerged from a teepee. She wore a suede vest over a white t-shirt and blue jeans that were torn and black around the cuffs where they'd dragged on the ground. Beth — he was pretty sure that was her name. It wasn't as if he needed to know, he hoped to avoid her glance and her recognition.

"Thomas!"

He tried to smile without looking too friendly. "Hi."

"I guess I can't ask you for spare change." She giggled.

"Why not?" What a stupid answer. Now he was obligated to give some. The last person he wanted to give money to was someone who was already siphoning money off his mother on a daily basis.

She lowered her voice as if she intended to whisper, but she was still audible to her friend and to anyone else who happened to step out through the automatic doors. "Because Caroline sent me here. I'm collecting money so we can put the cash back in Mary's purse."

"What?"

"Oh. Oops. Maybe you don't know."

He did know, but he needed time to digest it. His mind was still cluttered by the scene in the living room, trying to figure out what he was going to do when he returned. How he was going to be rid of Luke, not that he wanted to, not entirely. Besides, his track record for ridding the house of unwanted visitors was not good. "Yeah. I know. So Caroline took it?"

Beth shrugged. "She just said Mother Mary is super upset and feels betrayed and we need to win back her trust."

"Panhandlers are a blight."

She smiled. "It's not like people use their change. This keeps the river of life flowing."

"That's an interesting perspective."

She smiled.

"Hopefully the store will exchange this for bills when we're done. We can't give it all back to Mary in coins." She smiled.

Was she high? Why did she keep giving him that silly smile, like she needed to punctuate every sentence with it, showing her teeth that looked like products of very expensive orthodontia? "Well, then. Good luck to you." He stepped on the rubber mat and the door swung open. He walked into the store and let out a long breath. After he had four bottles of champagne in hand, he stood in line at the cash register. He wished he'd brought his checkbook. That would prevent him having unwanted change in his pocket. He was not going to contribute to more freeloading, not going to help subsidize a thief.

He paid with cash and pocketed the change. The clerk wrapped the bottles in narrow paper bags and nestled them into a larger bag. Thomas took it in his arms like a very heavy child, carrying it on his hip. The door swung open and he went out.

It wasn't only the intrusion of panhandlers he disliked. He was embarrassed for them. Beth was a good-looking girl. He didn't understand why she had to dress in a costume that made her look like she came out of the wild west. Didn't she feel ashamed, sitting on a filthy sidewalk, begging? It didn't seem like it. She seemed proud of what she was doing. She acted like it was owed to her. She was contributing nothing to the world, wasting her time and her potential.

She looked up at him. "I thought about it and I decided it makes just as much sense to ask you for your spare change as it does anyone else. Right?" She held out her hand.

"I wrote a check." The lie was out too quickly and he was sorry.

She narrowed her eyes. "You don't have anything? Not even a dime? A penny?"

He shoved his hand in his pocket, also too quickly. He pulled out two dimes, three pennies, and a wad of lint. Now he was ashamed for both of them. He felt he should tell her to forget the whole thing. The money taken from his mother wasn't about the cash itself, it was about how they were treating her. It was about honesty and ethics and obeying the God-damn law. He set the bag of champagne on the ground, plucked the lint away from the coins, and handed them to her.

She smiled. "Thank you. Every little bit helps."

"Caroline made you come out here?"

"She didn't make me."

"Do you know who took the money?"

"Not really."

"Yes, or no?"

"Caroline. She didn't think it was stealing."

"Of course not."

"Honest. Because we're all sharing. Mary borrowed my skirt."

He wasn't sure whether Beth was stupid or had created a fantasy world for herself. Drugs. It was easy to blame the drugs. He picked up the bag of champagne. "Good-bye."

"See you later, alligator!" She laughed.

As he turned, he heard the market door swing open. "Got any change?" Beth said. He hurried across the parking lot, put the bag in the trunk, and got into the car. He sat for several minutes. Now what? Back home to face thieves, a promiscuous mother, and his secret life. He started the car.

Despite Mary's best efforts at enforcing a single rule, the house once again smelled like pot when he closed the front door behind him. In the kitchen, he unwrapped the champagne bottles and opened the refrigerator. It was crowded with containers of leftover food and bottles of soda and beer. He moved the beer to one side, put the champagne in the back, and moved the beer so it surrounded the champagne, like a defending army. Maybe her champagne would last longer, enjoyed only by Mary, if more effort was required to access it.

Caroline and Luke were sitting on the couch. He darted out of the kitchen, hoping he could escape up the stairs without being seen. He had his left foot on the second step when Caroline's voice careened around the corner.

"Thooooomas! Come sit with us. Your friend has been waiting all day for you."

As he backed up until he had a view of where they were sitting, he realized he was stupidly hoping Luke would grow tired of his subtle intimidation game. A more frightening thought developed out of that — what if Luke thought there was blackmail potential here? A man with a well-off mother, a college kid dabbling in dangerous, deviant sex… He felt Luke studying him, waiting. A chill spread through his body. Even his eyeballs and tongue felt cold. He went into the living room. "I thought Luke was just here to enjoy the party. He and I don't really know each other that well, and…"

"Don't know each other well?" Luke said.

Thomas swallowed the excess saliva that released itself into his mouth. He sat in one of the armchairs. Just as he got comfortable, the last record in the stack came to an end. "Let me put on something else." He jumped up and turned his back toward them.

"Luke has had some very interesting experiences," Caroline said. "Traveling all over the country. Like I did."

"I'm sure you've had a lot to talk about." Thomas lifted off the three records and put them in their sleeves. He knelt to look at the selection. He chose two of his mother's albums by *The Supremes*. As soon as he slipped them over the spindle he realized these two would mock his selection. He lifted them off and returned them to their jackets. He settled on *Jefferson Airplane* and *The Grateful Dead*.

He sat down and Caroline and Luke chattered on about the beach, music, hitchhiking. Thomas remained silent. When those topics wound down, he looked at Luke. "You should go check out the beach, if you've never been down this way. The concrete ship is cool."

"Why don't you show him around," Caroline said. "Since he's your *good* friend. And he came all this way, just for *you*."

What had Luke said to her? It had been a mistake, leaving the house, not being here to try to get some sort of control over the situation. She spoke in such a dramatic tone, he wasn't sure if she was high or trying to irritate him, or if she actually knew the details of his relationship with Luke. But she was smiling. Would she accept that so willingly, turn it into a game, rather than being repulsed? Not wanting to spend time around either of them? He had no idea.

"Don't look so nervous," Caroline said. "You always look worried. Mellow out. Life is good. Why don't you come out with us tonight and get high?"

"Not my cup of tea," he said.

She laughed. "So hoity-toity! I feel like you're my father."

"Not everyone wants to bum around until they're middle aged."

"You should have fun before you're too old," she said. "Your mother figured that out. She's the party girl. And look how old she is. You don't want to wind up missing the best years of your life, do you? Go show the ship to Luke. Walk around in the sun. Have a beer, at least."

"I drink beer sometimes." He didn't know why he was so defensive. He didn't have to prove anything to her. What did he care about her opinion? She must know there was something between him and Luke, otherwise she wouldn't be saying such ridiculous things, taunting him. Trying to make him nervous.

"Go on Luke." She pushed him away from her.

Luke stood up. "It does look cool. I'm gonna check it out." He didn't even glance at Thomas. He seemed nervous. Maybe he was a stand-up guy after all.

"You can grab a beer. There's plenty," Thomas said.

"No. I'm good." Luke went outside, closed the door, and disappeared down the stairs to the beach.

"Why so worried, Tommy?"

"My name is Thomas."

"Why so worried?"

"I'm not worried at all."

"Liar."

"I'm concerned about all the people treating this place like a hostel. I'm concerned about people taking money out of my mother's purse, and panhandling."

Caroline arranged herself in a reclining position, her head on the armrest and her hair draped over the side. "She told you?"

"She didn't have to. I knew. And I saw Beth. You're a pimp."

"I'm nothing like a pimp." Her voice was lazy. "That has to do with prostitutes."

"You sent Beth out to solicit money for you."

"She wanted to help. Everyone's trying to help out around here."

"You're not doing a very good job."

"Is that right? What are you doing, exactly?"

"I live here."

"So do we. For now."

"I'm glad you put it that way," he said. "I don't appreciate having thieves in the house."

"I'm not a thief."

"Yes you are."

"I didn't even take it. So maybe there are thieves, if that's how you choose to view it, but it wasn't me."

"Then why did you say it was? Beth said…"

"I told Mary I did it. I didn't like her blaming attitude. She was acting so superior. Like she earned all this money herself."

"She did."

"How?"

"None of your business."

Caroline laughed. "I know how. On her back, if you get my meaning."

Thomas lunged across the room as if he'd been propelled by the increasing intensity of the drums winding themselves into a frenzy in the background of *Somebody to Love*. As soon as he reached the couch, he stopped. He couldn't assault a woman. "Take that back."

"Take it *back*? Are we in third grade?"

"Apologize."

"She didn't hear me."

"Apologize to me."

"What for?"

"What you said."

She stood up. "You are too boring, young man. You need to get high and get laid." She went to the screen door, flung it open, and walked onto the deck. She left the door open and went down to the beach.

The record ended and the stereo clicked as the arm lifted off. It dropped the next record onto the turntable and the needle lowered itself delicately into the first groove. He closed the door and went into the kitchen. He took an apple out of the fridge and filled a glass with water. Climbing the stairs felt like hiking the face of a cliff. When he reached the top he was out of breath and water had splashed all over his hand and wrist. He took a bite of the apple and opened the bedroom door. The shutters were closed, as he'd left them. He put the water glass on the dresser, sat in the armchair, and ate the apple. The bed was a mess but he'd been distracted that morning. Woken by the crash down the hall of someone falling from their bed. The morning, his search for his mother, seemed like it had happened a week ago. He leaned his head back and closed his eyes.

They weren't going to leave. And now Luke. It was too much work, trying to hide everything. Yet until these people showed up, until today, with Luke, he hadn't really felt like he was hiding. He was simply private, keeping things to himself. Now, everyone wanted to expose the darkest corners of his mind. Was that what they were all after, with their mind-expanding chemicals? *Feed your head?* No more secrets, no more pretending to be someone you were not. He could see the appeal in that. He imagined feeling light, and free, not thinking so much. What happened when you took those things? He imagined it was frightening, disorienting. But maybe not. Maybe the drug covered over that and you were simply excited with everything you saw and touched and tasted. Maybe it made life as wonderful as you'd always wanted it to be, but it had never been that way since you were a little kid. And even then, maybe not.

Nineteen

Mary's relationship with the sunken, crumbling concrete ship was complicated. She'd loved it as a child, hated it a year later when her mother's body was pulled up onto the deck, hated it more when people said terrible things about her mother. They called her a sinner. Killing yourself was classified as murder by the church, and therefore by God. At least that's what she'd been taught to believe. Now, she knew things weren't so clear-cut. She sometimes loved the ship with the childlike affection of something that was simply a permanent piece of her life.

The sky was growing light as she walked on the ship. Her mind was spacious and rested. She'd had a good night with her friends and an even better night feeling her skin against Gordon's, her feet touching his, her head tucked into the curve of his neck, his jaw pressing on her skull, her ears filled with his voice. It was brave of her, she thought, to come out here where she might be assaulted by a voice she didn't want to hear, the voice she hated. But she needed to get out of the house. Even though she was alone with Gordon in her room, there were too many people everywhere else. She felt their psyches pressing up against the closed door, trying to gain entrance — hearts beating, blood pumping, oxygen moving in and out of their lungs, minds whirring through strange dreams that played out, unseen, in the very air of the house.

She walked to the farthest point on the boat and looked out toward the horizon. All her life, living at one corner of this bay, and she'd never gone out on the water. An immobile ship was the only vessel she'd ever stepped on. Falling apart, just like her. The boat wasn't much older than she was, but it was aging faster, for now. She smiled. It made her feel less in the grip of its spirit, knowing it hadn't aged as gracefully as she had. It was entirely possible it would dissolve into the ocean before her life was over.

The sun was over the cliffs now, gently warming her back, even though the air was still chilly. It felt like Gordon's hands on her head, weaving his fingers through her hair. The night before, eating spaghetti and then smoking pot with the others, he hadn't left her side for a single moment. He held onto her hand until their body temperatures became the same, his fingers indistinguishable from hers. He sat close beside her on the beach, handed the joint only to her, put his arm around her shoulders after she passed it to the person seated to her right. He stroked her hair and made her feel like her presence was essential to his existence.

She breathed deeply, taking in the freshness of the water and the unblemished morning air. She should have brought a cup of coffee with her, but she'd wanted to walk without the baggage of a cup or a beach towel. Gulls circled, plunging into the water when they saw the glint of anchovy scales. A few pelicans bobbed on the swells, less anxious for food. Perhaps their bellies were already full and the gulls were eating leftovers. She turned and looked back toward the pier. A few fishermen leaned over the railing, their lines dribbling into the water. The hamburger stand wouldn't be open for a few hours, but once they started cooking burgers the fresh morning aroma would be consumed by beef fat.

A woman was walking down the center of the pier. Her body swayed dramatically, as she took long strides. Her hair flowed over her shoulders and her long sleeveless, yellow and brown dress dragged on the planks of the pier. As she moved closer, Mary saw it was Caroline. She had a fabric bag hugging one hip, the strap a bold, black stripe across her torso.

Mary turned away and walked toward the bow. She didn't want to talk to Caroline. She hoped Caroline was simply out for a walk, that she hadn't come looking for Mary and hadn't noticed her. There was nowhere to hide, as there had been when she was a child. The ship was stripped of its buildings — the dining room and dance hall. Mary crossed her arms and wrapped her hands around her upper arms, as if she could make herself smaller, less visible. A moment later, she released her grip on her arms. Although she wasn't keen on the interruption, there was no need to shrink away from a conversation with Caroline. Gordon had made it clear that Mary didn't need to fight for him. All she had to do was be herself. Love him and trust the things he'd said to her. Caroline was nobody.

There was no way to know, standing on solid concrete, when someone was approaching. Still, she wasn't going to turn. She would let things unfold as they wished.

"Hi, Mother Mary."

Mary turned slightly. Caroline smiled and held out her arms. "A hug? All is forgiven?"

"Why did you call me that?"

"It's who you are, isn't it? Watching over all of us? Gordon is our leader and you're his mate — the mother of all of us."

Mary felt a chill come from deep within the ship. It rose up from the icy water splashing into the broken hull, through the solid concrete, and grabbed her feet, filling her body with a burning cold. What had Gordon said to Caroline that caused her to adopt such a flowery, communalistic, fanciful view? "I'm not anyone's mother."

"Yes you are."

"You know what I meant."

Caroline smiled. "Don't hate me. I want to be your friend."

Despite her desire to feel strong without hugging herself, Mary found her arms crossing and her hands wrapping around her upper arms again as if they were moved by an outside force. "Why would I hate you?"

"Are you cold?"

Mary shook her head.

"What happened between Gordon and I…it was just a moment. I wasn't trying to take him away from you."

"What happened?"

"Making love…while you were right there."

"But it didn't…" She couldn't let Caroline know how stupid she was. How she swallowed every word out of Gordon's lips.

She couldn't believe how trusting she'd been, nodding as he assured her it was a hallucination. And now she was trapped. She couldn't go to him and accuse him of lying. Unless she planned to be done with him altogether. She closed her eyes. She needed to be strong inside. The gull, hallucination or not, told her to fight for what she wanted. And her body wanted Gordon, there was no escaping that. "It's not possible for you to take him away or give him back. He's not someone's physical property." Yet, it was entirely possible and she wished she hadn't said it. She was not going to spend every minute fighting for supremacy. She needed to simply rest in the confidence of Gordon's love without making an effort to bring Caroline down.

Caroline smiled and lowered her eyelids slightly, revealing smokey eye shadow. "If you say so. The important thing is that we're friends."

As the sun rose higher, the wind increased, sending a chilling breeze across the bow of the ship. Mary shivered and squeezed her arms more tightly.

Caroline stepped closer. She rubbed Mary's upper arm, her hand warm through the sleeve of Mary's jacket. "Oh, you're freezing. You poor thing."

"I'm not…"

"I have something for you." Caroline lifted the strap of her bag off her shoulder and over her head. She opened the bag and dug inside. She pulled her hand out, holding a wad of cash. "This isn't all of it, but we'll get the rest."

"What is this?"

Caroline pushed her hand closer. The bills fluttered across Mary's knuckles.

"Take it, please."

"I don't need any money from you."

"It's yours. So you won't feel betrayed. The money I took from your purse."

"It doesn't matter," Mary said.

"It does. It matters very much."

"Not really."

"It does to me."

"I don't want it. The point wasn't the money."

"You have to take it. We're very upset that you feel betrayed."

"I *don't* have to take it."

"Well I can't keep it. Use it for food. Or beer. It belongs to you, Mary. Just like the house belongs to you. And Thomas belongs to you, and hopefully, Gordon might someday belong to you."

She didn't like the things Caroline was saying. She felt foolish and old and crotchety. Caroline was making fun of her. She implied that giving money to Mary was arranged by Caroline and Gordon. Secrets whispered behind her back.

He doesn't love you.

She shivered violently at the words as they echoed inside her chest. In a single gesture, she was once again very unsure of her standing with Gordon. Taking the money would further undermine it. She took a few steps away from Caroline. The breeze grew stronger, whipping her hair across her face. She brushed it away and turned toward the water so the wind would blow it away from her face. From the corner of her eye, she saw Luke sauntering toward them, grinning as if he'd combed the beach looking for Mary and was thrilled to have found her.

Caroline moved closer. The bills brushed across the fine bones on the back of Mary's hand like the feathers of a bird trying to find a resting place.

"I need you to take this. We agreed we'd return it to you."

"Who is we?"

"It doesn't matter. Beth helped collect it."

"From where?"

Caroline waved the fist of bills over her head. "From people who wanted to give. It's yours."

Mary closed her eyes. She imagined Caroline relaxing her grip, bills flying up in the air. The gulls and pelicans would investigate, then turn up their beaks. The bills would drift away from the boat and land on the water. They'd remain on the surface for some time, and eventually become soaked through and settle onto the sandy bottom. If she grabbed Caroline's arm at the right spot, applied pressure to the underside of her wrist, that's exactly what would happen.

Taking the money would turn her into a woman whose feelings needed coddling. She wouldn't be an equal part of the group after all. And maybe she wasn't. She never had been. That's what Thomas kept trying to tell her, but it couldn't be true.

"What's up?" Luke said.

Mary opened her eyes.

"This money belongs to her," Caroline said. "Make her take it."

"Far out. I wish someone would shove extra cash in my face. If no one wants it…"

"Someone stole it from Mary. She's very upset about it, but now she's pretending she doesn't care."

"Why would she do that?" Luke said.

"Pride."

"I'm standing right here," Mary said. "Please don't talk about me as if I weren't."

Caroline shoved the money back in her bag. She looped the strap over her head and patted the bag against her hip. "Okay. Far out. You changed your mind."

Luke sauntered to the edge of the ship. "This thing is so cool," he said. "I can't believe they sank a huge ship on the edge of the beach. For kicks. Unreal. Take that, military-industrial complex." He laughed.

"It's haunted," Mary said.

"For real?" Luke said.

"Yes."

"How do you know?"

"How do you think I know?"

"You really think you saw a ghost?" Caroline's words came out in a puff of breath, as if her vocal chords had locked up and it was all she could manage.

"Yes. Several times."

"Was it scary?" Luke said.

"Once or twice, it was terrifying. Other times, not so much."

"I'd love to see a ghost," Caroline said.

"Not me." Luke put his arm around Caroline. "You..."

A huge wave hit the side of the ship and spray rained down on them.

"It knows you're talking about it!" Caroline pulled away from Luke. "Groovy!"

"It's just the ocean," Mary said. "High tide."

"I think it's the ghost. When can I see it?"

"It's not a sideshow," Mary said. "It appears when it wants something."

"Oooh. Now I'm kind of scared," Caroline said.

"You should be."

"No thanks," Luke said.

"I love scary things. When you're scared, you're alive. Life should be wild — swimming in the ocean at night. Diving off the ship. Crazy trips. Meeting new people every day."

"If you say so," Luke said.

"Scare me." Caroline turned toward him. "Do something that will make me so scared I'll scream my lungs out."

"You're nuts," Luke said.

"I want to live!" She yanked the fabric bag off her shoulder. She ran to the side, spun the strap like she was readying to throw a lasso, and hurled the purse into the water.

"Awww. Why'd you do that?" Luke ran to the side and looked down. "It's floating."

"Dive in and get it," Caroline said. "You can have the money."

Mary wished she could slip away from them. Caroline was scaring her. It felt as if Caroline wanted a certain response from them, but Mary had no idea what that was.

"Go get it!"

"I can't swim," Luke said.

"How can you not swim?"

"I grew up in the desert. I never laid eyes on the ocean until I was nineteen."

"You must have had a pool. A lake. A river." Caroline pushed her hair out of her eyes, peering at him as if he were a species she was unfamiliar with.

Luke shook his head. He hunched over and shoved his hands into his pockets. "If you want to feel so alive, why don't you dive in?"

"It's not my money."

"You're afraid. You like to say crazy shit, but I bet you never follow through."

She tossed her hair behind her shoulders, a futile effort as the wind blew it back across her face. It wrapped around her neck. She peeled it free. "I've done a lot. You have no idea."

"This is a ridiculous conversation," Mary said. "Should we go back and make coffee?"

"We need the money," Caroline said.

"Well I'm certainly not diving from here, so you'll have to get it yourself." Mary started walking toward the pier.

Caroline grabbed her wrist. "But Beth worked so hard to get it."

"What did she do? She didn't…?"

"She spent days in front of all kinds of stores, talking to people who would rather spit on her than give her a few nickels. All for you. Because she wanted you to feel loved."

"I don't feel badly because I'm missing a hundred dollars," Mary said. "I feel badly because someone came into my room when I was asleep. Someone went through my purse. I felt invaded."

"Well she put up with a lot to get that money. Has anyone ever spit on you?"

"Never."

"I've been spit on," Luke said.

"Literally?" Caroline blinked. She widened her eyes and stared at him. Then she blinked rapidly.

Luke was slim and dark-haired, very good looking, not someone you imagined attracting venomous reactions.

Her rapidly blinking eyes said she couldn't imagine a situation where such a thing might happen to him.

"People don't like drifters," he said.

Mary waited for him to add more. She didn't think being a drifter, hitchhiking or whatever he meant by that, was cause for spitting. It made her feel ill. "Why are we talking about this? Let's go back to the house."

Caroline moved closer to Luke. She put her arm around him and squeezed as if she were comforting a child. "I'm sorry you can't swim. And I'm sorry someone was so awful to you." She looked at Mary. "Thomas is a good swimmer. He can come get the money."

"No."

"Why not?"

"Let it go."

"But Beth…"

"You threw it over the side, you explain it to her. It's just money." Mary started walking again.

"Let's stay here," Caroline said. "It's groovy. It's getting windier. And the waves. Maybe the ghost will show herself… himself? To us. Which is it?"

"The ghost is a woman," Mary said. Why on earth had she mentioned it? She was only trying to impress them, to gain their affection, to feel as if they admired her or that she had something they didn't.

Caroline ran to the side. She flung up her arms and turned her face toward the sky. The wind whipped through her hair and thrashed her dress like an unfastened sail. The fabric gripped her body and wrapped itself around her legs. She leaned over the side as if she planned to dive after all. She wobbled slightly. Luke grabbed her and pulled her back from the edge. He took her wrists in his hand and lowered her arms. "Careful."

"Oooh! I like it when you grab my arms," Caroline said. "Tie me up. It's exciting to be a captive, don't you think?"

Mary walked away from them. The girl thrived on confusing everyone, on directing the spotlight to herself, on trying to manipulate all of them in some strange, unknown drama that played out inside her mind. Maybe she'd taken too many trips.

Maybe there was a limit to how much of that stuff your brain and body could handle. Maybe there were limits to life.

Luke kept Caroline in his arms, pulling her away from the side of the ship. "Crazy talk. You're a crazy girl."

"I am!" Caroline let out an ear-shattering scream. "Lock me up! Tie me to the boat so I don't do something crazy. That's what everyone wants to do! Tie me up. Put me in a straight jacket." She laughed hysterically.

Mary wanted to get off the ship, but she couldn't leave them out here. She wasn't sure Luke could control Caroline. It wasn't as if Mary would be much help, but she felt her presence might be steadying. She would have to talk to Gordon about how they could get Caroline out of the house. It seemed as if she was becoming dangerous. She wondered if Gordon would agree.

Twenty

Thomas had gone downstairs at three o'clock in the morning and filled a paper sack with a few bottles of soda and an opener, several apples, and a handful of cookies. He made two ham sandwiches and wrapped them in waxed paper. He stuffed a few napkins into the bag and took it up to his room. He closed the door and locked it. The house had remained quiet until about nine-thirty when he heard Caroline on the back deck, shouting about the concrete ship and straightjackets. He laughed softly. How appropriate. Maybe that's what he should do — call a mental hospital and have all of them packed up and taken away. He wished he could.

After that, there were sounds of people waking up — water rushing through pipes, the rumble of voices, thumps and thuds as they went up and down the stairs. The sounds were punctuated by a few minor crashes when someone flung open the sliding door with too much force and it wobbled inside its metal frame. He showered and dressed and opened the shutters. He sat in the armchair and ate an apple and read *James Bond*.

Surprisingly, no one knocked on his door. He thought for sure Luke would come looking for him. But it seemed that Luke had integrated himself into the group. He'd smoked grass the night before and lounged on the couch listening to music. He ran around on the beach and walked out on the ship to look at the water. He might have originally pursued Thomas to the coast to continue where they'd left off, or to extort money, but his agenda had changed. Unless it hadn't. Maybe his agenda was the same as the others' and Thomas was insurance, allowing him to stay in the house unchallenged. Luke could be confident he was welcome as long as he kept the secret.

Thomas grabbed one of the cookies and ate it in two bites.

It was a long day. He finished one *James Bond* and started on *The Valley of the Dolls*, which seemed appropriate. He looked over his class schedule for the coming Fall quarter. He wrote a letter to his advisor and letters to each of his brothers. Finally, it was dark. He realized he hadn't stashed enough food. The sandwiches and cookies were gone. All that remained was a half-eaten apple, its flesh turned brown. He ate it anyway. He was still hungry.

It was getting dark and they were probably heading out to smoke dope. It would be a long time before it was safe to go downstairs. He was disgusted with himself — locking his door against them, sneaking around while they slept. Would it be so terrible to go out there right now and try some pot? But he couldn't trust himself. He didn't really know what effect the stuff had, and he'd been drunk enough times to know you often did things that surprised and scared yourself. You occasionally did things you couldn't remember.

He stood up and stretched. He got down on the floor and did fifty push-ups. He needed to burn off some adrenaline and would have liked to do jumping jacks, but he was stuck with soundless exercise. He turned onto his back and did a hundred sit-ups.

When he woke, the house was silent. He was lying on his back on the floor near the foot of the bed. He went into the bathroom, splashed cold water on his face, and used the toilet. He looked in the mirror. His beard had sprouted like spring bulbs abruptly poking their stalks through hard, dead earth. He rubbed his hand across the lower half of his face. He brushed his teeth and went back into the bedroom. He was a caged tiger, muscles burning with the need for work. He opened the shutters and looked out. The deck lights were off, and the beach looked deserted. If he went downstairs, he could leave by the front door without being seen. He'd walk down the street, around the row of houses to the beach, and go for a swim.

When he slipped into the entryway, he heard the TV murmuring. He opened the door quietly, stepped out, and closed it with equal care. He'd removed the house key from the ring. He tucked the key into the pocket of his swim trunks. With a rolled up towel shoved under his arm, he walked as quickly as his bare feet would allow, down the sloping sidewalk to the small sign announcing Rio Del Mar beach.

He jogged across the sand and placed his towel by one of the posts supporting the pier. After jogging to the wet sand, he burst into a full sprint and plowed into the water. He pushed forward, ignoring the cold tearing at his skin. A wave broke in front of him and he dove under it. God it felt good. His muscles were filled with blood and oxygen, no longer quivering. The water rose and fell around him. He swam past the breakers and turned on his back. Stars covered the sky. To his left, the ship was a silent, hulking presence. He turned over and swam away from it to ensure he wasn't tugged too close, grabbed by the current, and shoved up against the rough side.

Again, he rolled onto his back and let the water support him. It no longer felt cold, his skin partially numb, adapting to the temperature. He shouldn't just float here, his body needed to work. But it seemed as if a cry for movement wasn't what had plagued him after all. It was the need to escape the claustrophobic smells and sounds of that house. As he yielded his arms and legs to the water, he thought about yielding everything, allowing his mother to do whatever she pleased. That's how it was anyway, he needed to stop resisting her. It was him against ten, or twenty others, however many there were on any given day. He had no chance of winning.

With a greater supply of food, he could realistically remain in his room every day. He could reverse his schedule. Sleep during the day and come out here at night. It would make for a pleasant summer vacation — nothing but reading books and swimming in the ocean.

The trouble was, the situation was making him recognize that he was in as much of a limbo state as the hippies and dopers and panhandlers. At some point, he needed to figure out how he was going to live his life with a satisfying career in computer engineering and also find physical and emotional satisfaction. A complete life. With all the political upheaval, drug experimentation, women breaking away from previous constraints, why couldn't it be that way for him? Why couldn't the world see that sometimes, more often than most of them realized, men loved other men, and women loved each other? It shouldn't be so difficult.

It's not.

He jerked up and began treading water. Had he spoken his thoughts out loud? Did someone hear and respond? "Hello?"

The water echoed as it splashed against the ship. The current had pulled him closer to its side, as if the ship itself were drawing him near. He swam with his head out of the water, taking long, smooth strokes, kicking hard to get away from it. He treaded water again and looked up, trying to determine if someone was up there. Had he spoken out loud? He turned and looked in the direction of the horizon, even though there was nothing to see but complete darkness. The stars, glittered like the cold, hard tips of spears, waiting to pierce his skin.

Where had that voice come from? He faced the boat and tried to shout, but his voice trembled and lacked force. "Anyone up there?"

It was impossible to see. The concrete side, washed and stripped by salt and water, was an enormous wall beside him, but up above, the ship was shrouded in darkness. He swam parallel to the shore for several minutes, increasing the distance between him and the ship. He looked up at his mother's house. Except for the bedside lamp in his room, the house was completely dark.

He turned. Someone was moving about on the ship — a woman draped in long, golden, flowing fabric. Was it Caroline? It wouldn't surprise him if she was out here in the dark, running around looking for thrills, looped out of her mind.

"Who's up there?" His voice echoed back at him. She didn't stop moving, drifting up and down the ship. He couldn't make out a face, only her long, silvery hair and that glowing fabric covering the rest of her.

There was no way to get up onto the boat from the water. If she wasn't going to answer, he should let it go. He dove under the water, trying to wipe the words and the image of the woman from his mind. Maybe he was hallucinating. He was exhausted and gripped by panic over what Luke or Paul, or both them, might do to the shape of his life. He was afraid of his very self. He swam under water until the pressure in his lungs screamed for release. He surfaced and looked up at the ship. Nothing. He began swimming to shore.

I'm watching you. I know your secret.

He began to cry softly, which made it difficult to swim. Was he going to drown out here, tormented by someone who wanted to play with his fear, and ultimately expose him? It sounded like a woman, but how did he know? In some ways, the voice sounded like his own, echoing his own thoughts. It could be anyone. Not his mother though. Oh God, not his mother. Tears streamed across his face. He could hardly see. He dove under the water again and shoved himself through the waves, letting the salt water cleanse his face, pushing himself away from the ship. He surfaced and continued toward shore. His breath came in erratic bursts, forcing him to gulp in too much air, drawing cold salty water into his mouth along with oxygen. By the time he reached a spot where he could stand, water had leaked into his lungs and he ached from trying to cough it out. The hacking, gagging sounds filled his head and drowned out the rush of the waves.

When he finally straightened, he saw Paul standing on the shore. Moonlight fell across Paul's face and shoulders. He was smoking a joint and smiling. He blew out a cloud of smoke. "Hi, Thomas."

Thomas grimaced and flopped onto the sand, still coughing. He was freezing cold and for a moment, couldn't remember whether he'd brought a towel. Yes. By the pier. He looked over but couldn't see it.

"Is this what you need?" Paul held up a crumpled towel.

"I have one. It's..." He pushed himself to his feet. "It's somewhere..."

"This is it." Paul moved closer. "I kept it warm, I hope."

Thomas grabbed it. He didn't like seeing Paul but was grateful because the towel was warmer than if it had been sitting on the sand the entire time.

"Rough swim?" Paul said.

"I swallowed water."

"I noticed."

Thomas scrubbed his hair with the towel, then slid it across his chest and his shoulders. He coughed, but with less violence.

"It's not safe to swim at night," Paul said.

"It certainly is."

"So proper. You sound like Mary."

He wrapped the towel around his shoulders. He wished he'd thought to bring one to tie around his waist, but he hadn't expected to emerge from the water choking and terrified. "It's not any less safe to swim at night than in daylight."

"No one knows you're out there."

Someone had certainly known he was there. The person speaking to him from the ship, or maybe swimming nearby, now that he thought of it. Could someone swimming speak so clearly, with such strength in her voice?

"You look worried. Scared, actually. If something happened, how would you get help?"

"You apparently knew I was there."

"I just came out for a toke, and you rose out of the waves like Poseidon."

Thomas laughed.

"Do you want a hit?"

"No."

"It'll ease the fear."

"I'm not scared."

"Your voice says otherwise."

Thomas gripped the towel harder, trying to pull it more tightly around him. He shivered.

"Do you want another towel?"

"I'm going inside, as soon as I stop dripping."

"I didn't see you leave the house."

"I went out the front door."

Paul smiled and nodded. He sucked in smoke from the skinny cigarette pinched between his thumb and index finger.

"I wasn't sneaking out, if that's what you think."

Paul nodded again, holding his breath. A moment later, he released a thin stream of smoke. "It will give you a whole new perspective on the world if you would just try it."

"How many times do I have to tell you I'm not interested."

"Yet you're still standing here."

Thomas started walking. Paul remained where he was. Thomas passed him, turning his head so he didn't inhale the cocoon of smoke.

"Come on. I can see you're miserable." Paul grabbed his arm. "It's not going to destroy your college education to try it one time. At least explain to me why you're so opposed. In fact, explain to me why alcohol is okay and this isn't. I really, honestly want to know. Because I don't get it."

Thomas stopped. He was no longer cold, warming uncomfortably under Paul's scrutiny. "I guess I don't really know. I do know it's illegal, and…"

"So was alcohol at one time."

"But I didn't drink it then, I wasn't even alive."

"I bet your mother did."

"She was a child."

"Her parents."

"I have no idea. It's irrelevant. I also don't like smoke in general. I don't like the smell of pot and I don't like the dopey way people behave when they use it."

"You're so stubborn. You're fighting us — everyone knows you don't want us here. You're fighting something that might connect you with other human beings. You're fighting who you are. It's almost as if you're fighting life, that you want to be dead."

"I am not suicidal. I resent you suggesting that I am."

"I didn't mean you're going to kill yourself, just that you wish you were dead. Two different things. And you might as well be. Why don't you join us tonight? We don't judge."

"Why would I feel judged?"

"Oh come on, Thomas. I know what's going on with you. I know who Luke is."

"What did he say?"

"I told you from the start that you and I had a connection. I know what you want."

"Why don't you speak plainly and tell me what you're getting at," Thomas said.

"Because you're so ashamed. I don't want to embarrass you."

"I'm not."

"I know you're gay. I know you want me, and you're completely taken with Luke. And there's nothing wrong with that."

"I didn't say there was."

"But you *feel* there is. You've taken the world's view of your desire and made it your own. There's a battle inside and you aren't going to win. You need to change how you think."

Thomas felt a sob rise up in his chest. How could this kid — *a kid!* — see through him like this? How did he know so much? He felt naked, as if he were standing in the middle of a stadium, a spotlight directed at his unclothed body, every imperfection exposed. He worked so hard to present a cool, polished image. How did this punk *know*? What inadvertent signal had he sent out? "What did Luke say to you?"

"He didn't say anything. He didn't have to. I already understood. When he knocked on the door and said he was a friend of yours, I knew. Of course, you also advertised it when you acted so messed up the minute you saw him."

Thomas felt something swimming in his stomach, rising up his esophagus, pushing at the back of this throat. He swallowed and tasted bile mixed with seawater. "I just can't."

"You're wrong." Paul held out the joint. "It won't hurt you. I promise."

"Why would I trust you?"

"Why not? I think I might be the first person in your entire life who really knows you."

The bile was gone and he felt like crying. He was not going to turn into a blubbering infant in front of this guy. He needed to escape. And yet, the marijuana smelled sweet and alluring. He was tired. So tired of being careful. So tired of thinking, choices twisting inside his head until he felt the blood vessels might knot themselves together and refuse to continue delivering oxygen to his body.

"Come out and smoke a joint with us. Get to know us. We aren't monsters."

"You smoke with my *mother*. Don't you see how…"

"Your mother is not who you think she is."

He didn't know what that meant and had no interest in finding out. He started walking. He heard something beyond the crash of the waves. He turned, but kept walking. There was a faint, high-pitched tone, a woman's voice whistling a melody. Or humming. Singing? He stopped and looked at the ship.

"What's up?" Paul said.

"Do you hear that?"

"Hear what?"

"That whistling. Or singing?"

Paul shook his head.

"Can you see anyone up there, on the ship?"

Paul shook his head and took a puff on his cigarette. "And you're worried about this stuff damaging your brain?" He laughed. "Maybe you drank too much ocean water."

"I heard someone. Out there."

"What do you mean?"

"A woman was talking. Like she was right next to me. And I saw…"

After a few moments, Paul said, "Saw what?"

"Nothing."

"So you've been dabbling in the mushrooms instead of weed?"

"No."

"It sounds like you have. A woman swimming with you, watching you?"

"I swallowed a lot of water. I imagined it, I guess."

"You don't sound very sure."

Thomas studied Paul's smile. It had remained unchanged the entire time they were talking. Why did Paul immediately assume he was having a hallucination? Was it possible someone had slipped something into a soda, or the coffee? It was odd that he'd fallen asleep doing sit-ups. And seeing that woman on the ship, the voice. Of course. Why hadn't he thought of it before? He couldn't trust these people at all. They were all crazy. High most of the time. Did they even come down from the previous high before they started taking more stuff? "Well. Nice talking to you."

"Are we at a cocktail party?" Paul laughed.

"No. I just need to get going."

"Where do you need to be at three-thirty in the morning?"

"Sleeping." Thomas laughed. He walked quickly toward the pathway that merged with the sidewalk leading up Beach Drive. He forced himself to ignore the urgent need to turn and see whether Paul was watching him, to see whether he still had that smile on his face.

Twenty-one

Manuel's Mexican Restaurant had opened on the fringe of the entrance to Seacliff Beach two years earlier. On summer evenings, it was almost impossible to get a table before eight o'clock, but on a Wednesday at lunchtime, it was relatively quiet. Mary ordered a glass of white wine and Thomas ordered a Corona. She sipped her wine, pleased to be sitting alone with her son.

Thomas dipped a chip in the bloody red salsa. "It feels good to get out of the house." As he bit the chip, salsa dribbled on his chin. He wiped it off with his index finger and licked the tip.

"Why is that?" she said.

"You know why." He ate another chip. "Help me eat these."

"I don't want to fill up before I get my meal."

He pushed the basket to the side, then took another chip and gobbled it without salsa.

"I hope you won't spoil our lunch by complaining about everything," she said.

"I won't. And I hope you won't spend it telling me I'm unfriendly."

"It's your loss."

A waiter approached carrying two large plates. He set a taco with rice and refried beans in front of Mary and chile rellenos and an enchilada with rice and beans, in front of Thomas. "Another glass of wine? Or a beer?" he said

"Not yet. Thank you," Mary said.

Thomas cut a piece of enchilada and held it on the end of his fork. Steam rose off the tortilla.

She wished she'd ordered an enchilada to go along with her taco. It looked delicious. She ate a forkful of rice. "I want you to be happy, and I wonder whether you'd be happier if you went back to school."

"No one's around."

"No one at all?"

He shook his head.

"None of your friends stayed for the summer?"

"No one I can crash with."

"I see."

"Are you kicking me out?"

She shook her head. She picked up her glass and took a sip of wine. It was the opposite of what he thought. She wanted him to join the others. She wanted him to accept Gordon as a legitimate part of her life. A man who might become her husband at some point. She wanted him to stop spending all his time alone like some kind of hermit. But if he was unhappy, he should return to Berkeley.

She couldn't start harping, especially when he'd so nicely asked her not to. If she didn't want to hear his complaints, it wasn't right to force him to listen to hers. Sometimes it was easy to forget he was an adult. You were so used to telling your children what to do, correcting their behavior, molding them into creatures fit for society, it was hard to flip the switch and stop providing guidance. Now it was considered nagging.

"Then what?" he said.

"Nothing, let's enjoy our meal."

"Kind of difficult now." He took a long swallow of beer. He set the bottle on the table and looked around for the waiter.

Mary took a bite of her taco. It calmed her, tasting the moist chicken and the comfort of a light corn tortilla wrapper, with plenty of lettuce to give it a satisfying crunch. She was barely finished chewing when she took a second bite. She swallowed and sipped her wine. "Do you miss the routine of school?"

"It's nice to get a break." He paused to ask the waiter for another beer. "I'll be glad when I'm finished, I think. I like being there, but I'm anxious to get out into the world."

"Do you think you'll stay in California?" Her voice shook. She didn't want it to, and she'd thought she had it under control. She wouldn't be one of those weepy women who didn't want their children to spread their wings. It would be nice to have all her sons nearby, but it wasn't realistic. They needed to live their own lives, wherever their jobs or their families took them.

He shrugged. "Tell me more about that ghost you mentioned."

"What made you think of that?"

"I was talking to Paul…"

"Oh, that's nice."

He grimaced.

Why did he have to make that face? All she'd said was it

pleased her to know he was being sociable. She sipped her wine. The ghost was a safe topic. As long as Thomas didn't go off on a tangent about hallucinogenic drugs. "I've seen it a number of times over the years. Sometimes, it takes the form of my mother. It feels like her. But other times, I'm not sure. I don't know what it is."

"How do you know it's a ghost and not your own thoughts troubling you?"

"I've seen it."

He nodded.

"Did you see something?"

He shook his head.

"Speak to me. Don't just bob your head this way and that. I know it feels uncomfortable, but I'm the last person who will think you've lost your mind."

"I saw what looked like a woman. And I heard someone speaking. And singing, or humming."

"What did she say?"

He picked up his beer and drank some. He seemed to be looking over her head, barely listening to her, avoiding her gaze.

"What did she say?"

"I don't remember word for word," he said.

"Yes you do."

"How do you know?"

"It's not something you forget."

"I'd rather not say. Alright? Besides, I wanted to know what's led you to believe there's something real, that you even believe such a thing is possible."

"When you hear it and feel it. When you see it, you know."

"I suppose. It couldn't be drugs?"

"I saw it before I knew what drugs were." She didn't understand why he brought up the subject but now seemed to be trying to discredit her. She supposed most people were afraid to admit they believed something that might make others laugh at them. Especially someone studying technology, working toward becoming an engineer. He looked upset, almost near tears. She recognized the look from so long ago, a little boy crying because…why? She could no longer remember when or why he'd last cried.

"Maybe you were sleepwalking, when you thought you saw it as a child. Or so overwhelmed by the loss of your mother. And now the drugs…"

"Explain it away all you want." She took a large bite of her taco.

"I'm just not sure."

"You brought it up. Where were you?"

"Swimming."

"Near the ship, I assume?"

"Yes. I had another thought." He turned away, staring at the bar as if he expected to see someone he knew. He turned back and began cutting his enchilada into bite-sized pieces. "I wonder if your friends put LSD in some of the beverages."

She wanted to smack him. She'd thought they would have a nice lunch. When he asked about the ghost, her heart felt like it was melting — thinking they might have something interesting to talk about, thinking he wasn't dismissing her experience as imagination or delusion. This was far worse. He hadn't even given her friends a chance. He'd looked down on them the minute he walked in the door that first time.

All these years she'd tried to think of her boys as mostly hers. Henry had rarely been around when they were growing up, and when he was, he buried himself in the newspaper. When he left her, the boys gathered around like she was their queen, and their life mission was to protect her at all costs. It seemed as though she'd fooled herself into thinking they were more like her, that they had more of her blood in them, and had adopted most of her habits and views of the world. Not Henry's. These past few weeks, Thomas was proving he was not who she'd thought. He was cold and critical and aloof. He was downright rude. This was her house! He didn't pay for a thing — not his education, his housing at school, even his car. He should respect the people she chose as her friends.

She took a sip of wine and glanced at his face. He knew she was upset, yet he refused to apologize. Maybe she'd been all wrong about Caroline. The poison that had seeped into her home was coming from her own son. Not Caroline, a woman who had started out as a very good friend. There was no way to blame Thomas for Caroline and Gordon having sex right in front of her, trying to hurt her, for Gordon's lies, but maybe Thomas had influenced it. Not that he'd suggested anything to Gordon, or planted cruel thoughts in Caroline's mind, but his general bad vibes. All of human life was connected — by blood, by energy, by love. Thomas and his hateful attitude had infected Caroline, driven her to try to hurt Mary. Why hadn't she seen that before? Caroline had wanted to be her blood sister! She wasn't after Gordon at all! Caroline and Gordon were simply good friends — bound like all of them by their nights on the beach, their expanding consciousness. Once Thomas arrived, everything turned sour and nasty. He hurt them all with his ugly expressions. He was greedy and territorial, causing them to think of things like stealing. Those kinds of behavior came from people who refused to evolve.

The rage and hatred surrounded the table, contaminating the food, and her wine. She pushed her plate away.

"Aren't you going to finish?"

"I'm not hungry."

"Don't get upset. It's only a suggestion, but I think it's something we should consider."

"*We*?"

He looked at her as if he couldn't grasp her meaning. He probably couldn't. He assumed a biological connection trumped a spiritual one. It was the reverse. Who was this person sitting across from her? Maybe he was a complete replication of Henry. Or a stranger unrelated to either of them.

"The fact that you think you've seen things out there, that you think you have memories of it from your childhood — all of that's fed by hallucinogenic drugs," he said.

"You have no idea what you're talking about."

"I don't know a lot about drugs, sure, but I know that LSD and things like that alter your brain chemistry. I'm concerned."

She wanted to point to his promise not to complain, but what was the point? It was his nature. And what he'd done now was far beyond complaining. Instead of being rid of Caroline, she should ask him to leave. But he'd ignored her mild suggestion earlier, and she didn't have the courage to demand it. No matter how he behaved, she couldn't stop loving him. It was just that right now, she was pretty sure she hated him. The thought made her cringe.

"Are you feeling okay?" he said.

"Not really."

He pushed back his chair. "What's wrong?"

"I need some time to think. Some time alone."

He laughed. "I know what you mean."

She glared at him. She took a sip of water, knowing it was also potentially infected with his malicious thoughts. "Why were you swimming in the middle of the night?"

"I couldn't sleep."

"And you were high?"

"I didn't think so, but out there in the water…it was something I can't describe. Quite terrifying. I hate admitting that, it makes me feel weak, but it was."

"You do know that acid doesn't just sneak up for a short little thrill and then evaporate. A trip lasts for hours."

"Other things happened."

"Such as?"

"I fell asleep doing sit-ups."

She felt her mouth open. She snapped it shut. He was an idiot. She closed her eyes for a moment. She opened them and studied his angry, confused face. His blue eyes darkened to navy in the dim light, or by something coming from inside of him. "I do think it might be good for you to go back to Berkeley."

"School doesn't start for weeks."

"I realize that."

"So you *are* throwing me out?"

"I don't think you fit in."

"I'm planning to stay in my room, leave all of you alone to your parties."

"What about Luke?" she said.

"What about him?"

"He came here to see you. As far as I can tell, you haven't given him the time of day."

"That's my business." He stood up. "If you don't feel well, I'll get the check."

She nodded.

"Just so you know, I'm not leaving," he said.

"It's my house."

"I know that, but I wouldn't be doing my duty as your son if I left you alone there. I'll stay out of your way, I won't complain any more, but I'm not leaving you by yourself."

"I don't need your protection."

"Too bad."

The waiter handed the check to Thomas. He glanced at it and placed some cash in the waiter's hand. "I don't need change." He walked around to Mary's chair and held the back.

"Please move," she said.

"I was going to help you up."

"Not necessary."

He backed away. She stood up, took her purse from under the table, and walked to the door. She wanted to cry, and she still wanted to smack him. But more than that, she was curious to know what the ghost wanted with him.

The bedroom door opened and Gordon stepped inside. He closed it softly. "What did you want to talk about?"

"It's nothing." Before lunch she asked if they could talk later, but now everything had changed. She couldn't tell him the negative vibe was coming from her own son. That there'd been some subtle shift and perhaps Caroline's seeming madness wasn't that at all.

He kicked off his shoes and climbed onto the bed. He pulled the pillows out from under the bedspread and stuffed two behind his back. He arranged the other two beside him. "Tell me what's going on with you."

"Really, it's nothing."

"It was important to you earlier, how can it be nothing?"

She got onto the bed and scooted close to his side. She laid her head on his chest. He stroked her hair and traced his finger over her lips.

"Talk to me," he said.

"I was worried about Caroline. She seems…off center."

"She can be."

"How long have you known her?"

She felt his body move as he shrugged. "What difference does that make?"

"I don't know if she's always been a little...out of control, or it's something new. Did you just meet her this summer?"

"Last winter. We crashed at the same place in San Francisco for a few weeks."

"And you've been hanging out together ever since?"

"Is this jealousy talking?"

"Not at all." She was angry, maybe jealous, that he'd suggested it. Why was *she* always painted as the one with a problem? Caroline accused her of being selfish, while ignoring her own theft. Gordon blamed her for feeling jealous, never considering that he was too easy-going, so easy-going he acted as if they weren't even a couple. It didn't occur to him that *he* should change, only that she was flawed. Thomas thought she was foolish and silly and needy and so many other things she couldn't name them all. He was so busy pointing out what was wrong with her, he gave no thought to the modifications that would improve his own behavior.

"What are you worried about?" Gordon said.

"She said some scary things. I was watching the sunrise on the ship and she came out there. We started talking. Then Luke showed up."

"What happened?"

"She was shouting."

"Why does that worry you?" He nudged her onto her back and bent over her. "You sound like a mama bird, worrying about her chicks."

"That's what she called me."

"What?"

"Mother Mary."

He kissed her nose.

"I don't like it."

"Lighten up." He straddled her and bent down. He started kissing her.

She closed her eyes and let his weight and need take over her body. But despite his hands and tongue, her mind remained separate. She'd spoken too quickly. She should have waited to see how he responded to the Mother Mary comment. She couldn't shake the feeling that he'd suggested it to Caroline. Which meant they were still having private conversations. Worse, so private she wasn't aware they were happening. Before, at least she'd seen them whispering in plain view.

The bed creaked as he changed position, lying on top of her, every part of his body pressing on hers. He kissed her neck. He began unbuttoning her blouse, pushing each tiny button back through the slot that had secured it, his fingers so gentle it seemed as if he treasured the delicate nature of the buttons.

In the living room, someone put the *Stones* on the turntable and increased the volume. The music surrounded her, filling the house with a heartbeat. As the drums and winding chords swelled, they carried her thoughts to another place. She was tired of thinking about Caroline. And Thomas. Maybe both of them were poisoning the atmosphere.

It was equally possible the ghost was having its influence. Caroline loved the ship, and they'd been standing right there, talking about the spirit. It was surely listening, and immediately after that, Caroline flung the money into the water and began screaming about her desire for bondage. Even that night on the beach, around the fire, the thing inhabiting the ship had been there, watching them in the darkness, weaving malicious thoughts into their minds. It was far more insidious than LSD or psychedelic mushrooms.

Twenty-two

Thomas deeply regretted his promise to live out the rest of the summer in his bedroom. After six days without human contact he wondered if his vocal chords were still capable of producing sound. There were moments when he had to look in the mirror or touch his body because he wondered if he'd ceased to exist. Had his mother given him a single thought? Did the others think about him locked inside? Did they laugh? Did they listen at the door to see whether there were sounds of life?

His dreams were strange, not that all dreams didn't have a strangeness to them. Now, they were more vivid. Sometimes the colors were neon, making his eyes ache. Other times, scenes played out in gray tones and the people who appeared were impossible to recognize. The subject matter was incoherent, yet the meaning perfectly clear — endless swimming as his arms grew limp and useless and his lungs filled with seawater, orgies with people he didn't know, wandering endlessly on the concrete ship looking for ghosts, for his mother, his father, his next class at UC Berkeley. He was more tired when he woke than when he slid beneath the sheet. His room was too stuffy to allow using a blanket, and the lack of a covering with substantial weight on his body made his sleep restless.

At night, once he saw the deck light go out, he eased himself quietly out the front door and went for a long swim, keeping far away from the boat. He hadn't heard any voices, singing or speaking, and hadn't seen even the suggestion of a ghost. Each night that passed without incident, he was more convinced his terror had been drug-induced. He just wasn't sure how they got the stuff into one of his beverages. As far as he could remember, he always opened his own beer and soda bottles. The meal he'd eaten with them had been too many hours prior to the experience. Unless they baked it into the cookies he'd been gobbling up. Filtered it through the mayonnaise he put on his sandwich, or injected it into each slice of ham.

These thoughts made him feel his rational mind was slipping away. Although he suspected them of messing with him, he didn't think they were smart enough and probably not calculating enough to do such things. But it tormented him. How had a psychedelic substance found its way into his body?

Or was this a psychotic breakdown? Disassociating from his true self had damaged his mind. Paul was right. He might as well be dead. If he couldn't live a life with the companionship he longed for, why go on living?

Being alone in this room was better than what he would face if he tried to express his desires — a solitary life in a far less pleasing environment. No ocean outside his window. Instead, he'd look out on grungy buildings blotting out his view of the sky, apartments filled with bums and drug addicts, elderly people abandoned by their families and barely subsisting. Delinquent children with criminal parents.

The bedroom smelled of soiled sheets and ham and coffee. He cleared out the dirty dishes every night, but still it had a sad, dying odor. It was seeping out from his pores. He'd started showering twice a day, made sure he shaved regularly even though it was tedious and there was no purpose to it. He combed his hair and brushed his teeth. Still the room smelled. The stench of fear and death. How on earth had he ended up in this situation? He'd been a straight-A student in high school. In college, he made the Dean's list every quarter. He was excelling in graduate school. This couldn't be the sum of his life.

He wrote a letter to his father. The next day he tore it up.

Tonight, maybe he should swim toward the horizon, telling himself that turning back was forbidden. His body would give out and he'd slip beneath the waves. But he didn't want to die. It wasn't fair that all of his mother's *friends* got to live out their carefree lives. They worried about nothing! They were satisfied without careers, without any certainty in their relationships. They laughed all the time. They were fascinated by endless conversations that danced in the air around the glow of fire or candlelight, given more power by the crash of waves.

He ate two oatmeal cookies. He tore open a bag of corn chips and tossed a handful into his mouth, washing them down with beer that wasn't as cold as he would have liked. He folded over the top of the corn chip bag and stood up. He stripped off his shirt and pants and went into the bathroom. He took his swim trunks off the shower rail. They were still damp. He fought with the wet fabric as it grabbed at his skin, resisting his effort to tug them into place. He pulled down the beach towel that was hanging over the shower door. He sniffed it. Although it was dry, it smelled damp and not quite clean.

It was only one-thirty in the morning. He could hear music and the sound of voices downstairs. He smelled pizza, but he couldn't stay in this room a moment longer. He was going for a swim. Not toward the horizon, just the usual. He couldn't form the desire fully in his mind, didn't want to acknowledge it was there, but he knew that deep inside, he hoped to run into Paul. Or Luke. Anyone, really.

Despite his unacknowledged desire, he crept down the stairs. He opened the front door with the same stealth as always. He walked to the beach, left his towel beneath the pier, and walked into the surf. He stood for several minutes while his body temperature adjusted to the cold water. The waves swirled around his knees, tugging him forward. Against his better judgment, he glanced toward the ship. The only sign of life was a single white gull, staring back at him as if it wanted to know what Thomas was looking for. Thomas studied the bird. Life must be so easy. No thinking mind, as far as anyone knew. Just pure existence — the hunt for food and the pleasure of flight.

If he did swim out toward the horizon, not turning back, he would drown. He could be reborn as a wild bird, if you believed in that sort of thing, which he did not. He turned away and plowed farther into the water. A wave swelled in front of him. He lifted his arms out to the sides to stabilize himself, then pushed his feet off the bottom, rising with the swell and feeling it pass by him before it curved into an arc and crashed onto the shore. When the next wave rose in front of him, he dove beneath it.

The shock of being fully submerged in icy water stopped his circling thoughts. He surfaced and swam out fifteen or twenty yards. He glanced to his right. No matter how he tried to keep away from it, the ship loomed beside him, so much more intimidating than when it was viewed from the beach. It seemed to be moving toward him. He curved to the left, putting distance between himself and the immovable mass of concrete. He stopped and looked up. The bird was gone. There was no ghostly figure moving about. Further proof someone had managed to drug him. He swam parallel to the shore for about a quarter of a mile. When he was pleasantly tired, he turned and swam back, stopping well before he was in the vicinity of the ship. He bobbed in the swells for a while, and then swam to the beach.

It was brutally cold walking back to the pier for his towel, but better than swimming too close to the ship where he might have another unwelcome experience. It was funny how his logical mind was certain he'd been drugged, while his primitive brain did everything it could to avoid the chance of another fright from a ghost. He laughed and jogged to the pier.

Luke and Paul stood near his towel. "You're alive," Luke said.

Thomas laughed. He reached for his towel. Luke put his foot on it. "You are seriously screwed up, man."

"I know," Thomas said. He was stunned by his honest reaction. A hard swim in cold water seemed to have stripped his brain of the ability to filter itself.

Luke moved his foot. He picked up the towel, shook off the sand, and handed it to Thomas.

"Thanks." He began drying himself, conscious of their eyes on him, studying the movement of his muscles beneath his skin. He felt slightly aroused by their interest, a sensation that was immediately replaced by panic. He glanced toward the house.

"Everyone's watching TV," Luke said.

Paul pulled a joint out of his pocket. He had a lighter in his left hand. He put the joint in his mouth, snapped the lighter, and touched the thin tip of twisted paper to the flame. It caught and settled into an ashen glow. Paul inhaled, held the smoke inside, and slowly released it. He handed the joint to Luke, who did the same. Luke held it out to Thomas. He shook his head.

The two of them turned and began walking down the beach. After a few minutes, they were barely visible. Thomas felt like crying. He ran the towel over his body again and sat down in the sand. He was cold and miserable, but he wasn't going back to his room. He wasn't moving until he came to some sort of decision about his life. He couldn't be locked in that room again, but neither could he be who they wanted him to be. He wasn't like them.

You are.

He shivered.

You are. You are. You are.

He began crying softly. If he had a knife, he'd carve off his ears, dig his brain out of his skull. He pushed his hands against the sides of his head until it ached. He pressed harder, as if he were trying to crush it. What was he so afraid of? No. That wasn't right. He had a legitimate reason to be afraid. It was easy for Luke and Paul to do as they pleased without fear of being shunned. They were bums. They'd enjoy their parties now, and by the time they were thirty, their lives would be over. They'd be sleeping on the street, begging, possibly dying from living in filthy conditions. Their beautiful young bodies would deteriorate early and their lives would end. But at least they would enjoy the next few years. Was it better to have four or five happy years and endless misery after, or to scatter your misery over your entire lifetime?

He felt a hand on his shoulder. He yanked his hands away from his face and wrenched himself around to see who had snuck up on him.

No one was there. He cried out. He tried to stand up but it seemed as if his muscles had turned to pudding and his bones had lost their rigidity. He managed to push himself forward onto his knees. He scrambled around so he was facing the pathway that ran along the beach. The legs of the pier stood like a gathering of very stiff people, looking at him but not seeing him, their faces vacant. He squinted. One of them must be the person who had touched him. He crawled forward, leaning to one side, hoping the altered perspective would reveal which one was a human being, rather than a pillar of solid wood. There was no one.

"Who's there?" His voice echoed, pathetic and terrified. He glanced down the beach, worried that Paul and Luke heard him crying like a scared little girl. They were laughing at him. He couldn't see them, but that didn't mean they couldn't see him. Even if they couldn't make out his form, they surely heard him whimpering. He sat back on his heels. He shoved his hands into the sand, and this time, his legs cooperated. He stood and wrapped the towel around his waist. "I know you're there." His voice was stronger. Standing upright helped. "Stop messing with my head. It's not funny and I'm not impressed at what a coward you are."

He heard nothing but the crash of waves. He turned and looked toward the water. The stern of the boat was visible beyond the last legs of the pier, staring back at him through the pillars. It was entirely possible the ship was swarming with ghosts. All those people who had danced in the ballroom. People who had eaten meals and enjoyed games, talking and laughing. Most of them were probably dead now, but their voices and all their craving and wanting and needing lingered inside the concrete shell.

After a few minutes, he moved closer to one of the legs sunk in dry sand at the left side of the pier. The post itself was dry and clean, unlike those past the water line that were deformed by the enormous clusters of mussels clinging to them. He sat down, leaning his back against the pillar. He sat with his legs bent slightly to the side so he'd be ready to jump if someone touched him again. His eyes ached from scanning the water, the beach on both sides, straining to see in the darkness. He wasn't sure what he was waiting for, aside from some magical blast of otherworldly revelation to tell him in which direction his life should go. All he knew was he couldn't return to that room. At least out here, there was plenty of space to breathe, and he could drink in the smell of water and sand and cold air. He was no longer drowning in the odor of his own hungry flesh.

"Hello, Thomas."

He turned to see his mother walking toward him. She wore an ankle-length cream-colored dress that flowed around her body like liquid. It had long loose sleeves, and a scooped neckline revealing the tops of her breasts. Her hair was down, draped over her shoulders, blowing gently as she moved. Her feet were bare. She held a glass of champagne in her left hand, which startled him because all his life she'd held her glass in her right hand.

Was it her? Or an apparition? There was something not quite right about her appearance but he couldn't say what it was. His hands shook. "Hi." His voice was too loud, barking like a seal along the columns of the pier, out to the water that sloshed against the boat, echoing back to him.

"May I sit here?"

He nodded.

She handed the glass to him. It was cold. The champagne undulated. It was real enough. She settled herself beside him and he handed the glass back to her. She took a sip and smiled at him. He felt as if he were a child again. This was the mother who read stories to him and sat beside him while he did homework. The mother who made sandwiches and roast chicken and stuffed sole and kept the house clean. Not the mother who raged and drank a little more than she should because her husband tossed her aside like a discarded burger wrapper. The husband who humiliated her in front of the people she'd known all her life, dragging along a younger, superficially more beautiful woman and insisting with the sheer force of his will and position in society that this woman be accepted as a suitable replacement for the mother of his children. As if Mary had never existed. But she had four sons proving her existence.

"How are you doing?" she said.

He shrugged. The feeling he was eight years old wouldn't leave him. It wasn't uncomfortable though. He liked it. Life was simple then. He wasn't consumed by questions that couldn't be answered. He was focused on what he liked to do, not on exploring his inscrutable mind.

"I've missed you."

He was glad she didn't say *we've* missed you. He wondered if it was deliberate — her careful choice of pronoun.

"I don't think you've having a very good summer vacation," she said.

"I've had better."

She smiled and took a sip of champagne. He was glad she did, because his senses were starting to dissolve again, making him wonder whether this was his mother or some expression of her existing only in his mind. He wanted to touch her dress to be sure, but that seemed childish.

"Why have you been hiding in your room?"

"I don't know."

"Life is short and senseless and confusing."

"I know."

"You don't know how short it is. How quickly it can come to an end," she said.

"I guess not."

"You should join the party before it's over."

"I can't."

"Drugs will help you find out new things about yourself. About the world."

"They can also help you lose yourself forever. You must know that."

"It's better than never finding yourself."

A wave smacked the sand. He jerked his head toward the water, his whole body convulsing in response to the sound. It seemed as if the ocean wanted to get his attention.

Listen to me.

He turned back, half expecting her to have disappeared. "I feel like I'm dreaming," he said.

She smiled.

"Did you put LSD in my food?"

"Don't entertain such ugly thoughts."

"You did?"

She sipped her champagne. The level of the liquid seemed to be the same as when she'd first sat beside him. "There *is* a ghost, you know. More than one, I think."

"In your mind." He sounded like a petulant child. He'd

studied history and grammar and math, biology and chemistry and literature. He had a bachelor of science degree in software engineering and he'd gained admission to a graduate program. Yet it seemed as if outside of the intellectual pieces of his brain, he hadn't evolved beyond the age of eight. He was playing hide and seek with himself.

"Why won't you tell me what's wrong?" she said.

"There's nothing wrong."

"You aren't happy. And it's not about drugs or strangers living in our home. It's not about my unconventional relationship with Gordon. There's something you're not saying."

He squeezed his eyes closed. How could she possibly know that? She was guessing. And she was trying to divert his attention from her bad behavior.

A moment later he opened his eyes. She was gone.

He jumped to his feet. It was a dream. It was all a stupid dream, telling him nothing. Something was swallowing his mind. They all claimed clarity through pot. And LSD. Yet if she'd already slipped it to him, or they had, there was no resulting insight. They lied.

He saw Paul and Luke walking toward him. Their shoulders touched, the backs of their hands brushed against each other. They appeared to have finished the joint. They came closer, not looking at him. He opened his mouth to speak, but no sound emerged. As they passed by, it seemed as if they didn't see him.

The woman hadn't been a ghost. He was the ghost. Perhaps he'd swum out too far and drowned after all.

Twenty-three

After they spent the day swimming and lounging around the beach, it was decided they would go out for hamburgers and milkshakes. Mary swallowed her worries and urged Gordon to go without her. "I need some time alone. I'll do a bit of picking up," she said.

He kissed the top of her head. She felt herself soften in the presence of his height, his lithe build, his taut muscles. She wanted to collapse into him, but this was important — being alone in her house. Alone, except for her son the troll sequestered in his bedroom as if it were a cave carved in the side of a mountain.

"It's sweet of you to do that," Gordon said. "I'll bring you a burger."

"No. I'm going to make something light. I can't eat all of this beef and pizza and whatnot. It's making me tired."

He pulled a shirt over his head and shoved his feet into leather sandals. He walked to the window and pulled the chord to close the drapes.

"Will you leave them open?"

He shrugged and pulled the chord again. The drapes, still moving from the momentum of being closed, swung in the opposite direction, taking a moment to settle.

He would be with Caroline, but there were seven others, the group having contracted again. She was confident there would be no time for secret conversations or subtle touches beneath the table. And if there were, it could happen just as easily if she were sitting beside him. She took a deep breath, stood on her toes, and kissed him.

When they were gone, she went into the kitchen. She wondered whether Thomas had noticed them leaving. It was unlikely he heard much from that side of the house, but she really had no idea what he did and didn't hear up there, if he listened at all, if he slept most of the time.

She took a swordfish filet out of the refrigerator. She sliced it into two pieces, a larger one for Thomas. She sprinkled the fish with oil, herbs, and salt and pepper. She put the pan under the broiler and made a salad of cooked broccoli, small white beans, green onion, and tomatoes diced into pieces the size of a fingernail.

When the fish was nearly done, she got the portable record player from the hall closet and an LP of Vivaldi's *Four Seasons* from the stereo cabinet. She carried them upstairs and set them outside of Thomas's door. She put her ear to the door and listened. She heard nothing. She went downstairs and got a bottle of white wine, the corkscrew, and two glasses. She set them beside the record player outside his door. She put the dinner onto plates, tucked the utensils and two napkins into her pockets, and climbed the stairs with deliberate slowness. She tapped on the door with her knee.

He opened it immediately. "What's this?"

"Dinner."

"I can see that."

"I'd like to have dinner with you." She pointed her foot toward the things on the floor. "I brought music and wine. Will you get them?"

He stepped to the side and she entered the room. She put the plates on the dresser. Although the shutters were open and the window cracked, the room smelled stale. Now it would smell like fish. He probably wouldn't appreciate that, but he needed to eat something healthy. Not the leftovers and sandwich fixings and cookies she'd seen disappearing from the kitchen.

He opened the wine and filled the glasses while she plugged in the record player. She flashed the album cover at him. "Rock and roll is great. I do love it. I don't think it's saying too much to tell you it's changed my view of life, but classical is what feeds the soul when the world seems dark. Rock and roll can surely take you on dark trips, but classical stays with you into the grave."

He shivered visibly. "How would you know? You're not dead."

Turning away from him, she put the record on the turntable. She spoke softly. "Is this how it's going to be?"

"Sorry. No."

She turned on the power, lifted the arm, and settled the needle onto the record where Vivaldi's composition moved to *Summer*. It moved into place and the graceful strains of the opening filled the room.

Thomas sat on the window seat and she sat in the armchair.

They toasted each other with a simple *Cheers*. It was best, under the circumstances.

He took a bite of swordfish. "This is delicious."

She smiled.

They ate in silence for several minutes.

Mary took a sip of wine. She put her glass on the dresser. "You can't live like this. You have to tell me what's wrong. And I don't think it's just the drugs. Or my friends."

"How do you know that?"

"Because I feel something. There's a tension that's eating you alive."

He speared a piece of broccoli and put it in his mouth. She watched him chew. He took far longer than was required. Finally, he swallowed. "I feel trapped, maybe that's what you sense."

"Then why don't you leave? You stay here like you're waiting for something."

"I have nowhere else to go."

She nodded. She picked up her fork and continued eating. She loved the feel of fresh, wholesome food filling her stomach. She loved fish. She thought she could eat it every day and not miss beef or chicken for the rest of her life.

He broke off another piece of swordfish. "This is really good."

"So you said."

"They're just so aggressive." He put the swordfish in his mouth, chewed, and swallowed. "I thought we were all supposed to just *be*. I feel like I'm required to smoke pot. If I don't, I'm shunned. Drop acid or I'm not cool. I keep having the same argument over and over. Why is it so hard to understand that I prefer to face life with a clear head?"

"And how is that working out for you? Facing life with a clear head?"

"So far so good."

"Is it?"

He shoved several pieces of swordfish into his mouth.

"Slow down and savor it."

"I am."

"I hear you leaving the house at night," she said. "You don't think that's a little strange, that you're so afraid of people you have to sneak out when everyone's sleeping?"

"I'm not afraid. I just don't want a joint shoved in my face every time I walk into the room. I want to go for a swim with a clear mind."

"No one's shoving a joint in your face."

"That's where you're wrong. You haven't seen them. And I think you want me to validate your choices by joining in."

"That's not true." She picked up her fork, but didn't eat. "It worries me that you swim at night. It's dangerous."

"I don't see why." He sipped his wine. "I'm a good swimmer."

"There are sharks."

"They come in the daytime too."

"If something happened, you'd be all alone."

"Having a crowd of doped of people on the beach while I swim is not going to save me from a shark attack just because the sun's out. Besides, no one can save you from a shark attack."

She put a broccoli floweret in her mouth and chewed slowly. When it was gone, she put down her fork and took a sip of wine. He wasn't going to change, but she wasn't sure if he was being stupid, or there was something seriously wrong with him. He'd said he was watching out for her, but that didn't explain everything. If he wanted to watch out for her, shouldn't he show his face once in a while? She refilled her glass. She stood up and walked to the window seat. She poured wine into his glass and returned to her chair. "There are other dangers besides sharks."

"I don't want to talk about that again," he said.

"If she has something to say to you, she's not going to give up."

He nodded. "Good to know."

"I guess neither one of us is going to change our opinion."

"I guess not. But I'm glad you're not upset with me about what I said. I know you wouldn't do anything so sneaky. I'm sorry for suggesting it."

"What?"

"The other night. I'm sorry I said that."

"What other night?" The music grew more intense, swelling around them. She thought she should turn it down, but she didn't want to stop the flow of whatever he was trying to say.

"When we were sitting under the pier," he said.

"I wasn't."

"You remember…you were wearing that white dress."

She swallowed the last of her wine. He would laugh at her, or get angry, but it didn't matter. "You saw the ghost."

He didn't laugh. He drank his wine and turned his attention to breaking apart the last of the swordfish. He stabbed at a few scattered white beans, securing one to each tine of the fork. He put them in his mouth and stabbed more, turning the consumption of her salad into something that reminded her of a dart game. When his plate was cleared of beans and his wine glass empty, he looked up at her. "I'm sorry I said it."

"Said what?"

"I'm sorry I asked whether you'd slipped LSD into my food. I thought you might have done it so I'd have my own hallucinations. So I'd believe your haunted stories about the ship."

Tears rushed into her eyes. She swallowed, but it didn't help her breathing. She swallowed again, harder. "Is that what you think?"

"I don't know what I think. I just wanted to tell you I'm sorry for thinking that about you. I know it happens — people putting LSD in Kool-Aid. I couldn't understand what I heard when I was swimming, what I thought I saw. I don't believe in ghosts. They're superstitions that developed before education was available to common people. I'm not implying you're uneducated, but that's when those beliefs were prevalent — when all the knowledge was in the power of the ruling class, and…"

"Stop." She stood up and took his plate away. She stacked hers on top, with the half-eaten piece of fish and the last of her broccoli salad. It had been such a promising dinner. She finished her wine and took his empty glass. She set the dishes on the dresser. She lifted the needle off the record. She went to the door and opened it. "You can bring the dishes down later."

"Wait."

She shook her head. "I don't know what's happening to you. Maybe you have too *much* education. Maybe she's twisted your thoughts." She closed the door.

Immediately after everyone returned from their burgers, most of them had piled back into two cars and headed to The Boardwalk. Riding a roller coaster while stoned was a mind-blowing trip, according to Caroline. All but Luke had wanted to try it. He'd gone for a walk on the beach. Mary sat on the deck, sipping champagne, waiting for him to return. She couldn't let go, couldn't stop thinking about Thomas. Luke must know something.

A crowd of gulls stood on the shore, making quiet noises as the night settled around them. They looked out to sea, but she wondered whether anything in the water was visible in the darkness, even to them. Maybe they were just resting. The waves crashed hard. Whitecaps shimmered farther out. The ship sat there as silent and empty as always. She glanced at it. Would her mother appear tonight? Was that who Thomas had seen, mistaking her for Mary?

He'd seemed so certain. She hadn't gone to the beach…unless she'd had a minor blackout. In her experience, it was always clear the spirit wasn't flesh and blood.

Each of her sons was unique, of course. They'd all presented different challenges when she was raising them. But Thomas, who was so easy as a baby, such a happy little boy, a good student all through school, was turning out to be the most difficult as he crossed the bridge into the adult world. As a child, he'd wanted to spend time with her more than the others had, yet at the same time, he'd been more independent at a younger age than the others. From the day he turned sixteen, he'd gradually erected a wall, telling her less and less about his life. Their conversations grew more superficial. She hadn't noticed it right away, but the past year, when she considered the changes in him, she saw it had started back then. At first she attributed it to his father's despicable behavior at such an impressionable point in Thomas's life. The others were grown by the time Henry paraded his tawdry affair in front of them. But now, she thought it was more than that.

She picked up her glass and held it close to her lips, enjoying the sharp tap of the bubbles that continued their tiny explosions. She took a sip and let it fizz across her tongue and around the insides of her cheeks. Sometimes she felt like a child, the way she enjoyed the carbonation in champagne. It never ceased to give her an extra burst of pleasure along with the taste and the soothing effect of the alcohol.

Luke emerged from the darkness. She hadn't seen him approach and suddenly he was a few yards away from her deck stairs. His brown t-shirt and dark shorts had partially hidden him, but perhaps her thoughts of Thomas, and the brooding presence of the ship had consumed her attention more than she'd realized. She was fixated on it, if she was honest. Staring at it and hoping whatever haunted it would find rest and leave her alone, and in the same heartbeat, longing for another glimpse of her mother, the sound of her voice. She refilled her glass and waited for Luke to climb the stairs.

He stopped on the last step. "I didn't see you."

"Have a seat."

"Uhm. Okay. You sound like I'm in detention."

"No. That's not it. We haven't talked much. Why not?"

"Can I get a beer?"

"Sure."

He went into the house. He took longer than she would have thought necessary to grab a bottle of beer out of the refrigerator and pop off the cap. Maybe he used the restroom. It was easily five minutes before he returned to the deck. She hoped he wasn't afraid of her. She hadn't meant to sound like she was ordering him to sit beside her.

He flopped on the chaise lounge several feet away from where she was seated at one of the small, round tables.

"What's up?" The beer bottle clicked against his teeth.

The sound was so loud and solid, she shivered, thinking it must have hurt, but he said nothing.

"I thought a chat would be nice. Where do you and Thomas know each other from? I didn't catch that."

"Just met on the road, like lots of people."

"That doesn't sound like Thomas."

"Maybe you don't know him as well as you think you do."

What did that mean? Probably nothing. What mother knew her adult son in the same way his friends did? There were huge pieces of his life that were complete mysteries to her. If she was pressed, she wouldn't be able to name half the courses he'd taken, and she knew nothing about computers, although everyone said they were poised to take over the world. They'd be running everything in twenty years — cleaning your house and doing your grocery shopping. She looked forward to a robot cleaning her house, but she enjoyed going to the market and picking out her own produce. She couldn't imagine a machine doing that effectively. How would it know what she wanted? What shade of yellow the bananas should be or how firm she liked her peaches?

"No offense," he said.

"None taken."

"I mean, we just started talking and even though he's in school and I'm not, we hit it off."

"Started talking where?" she said.

"Why does it matter?"

"I'm just making conversation, trying to get to know you."

"Where we first spoke to each other has nothing to do with getting to know *me*."

"Fair point. Why don't you tell me about yourself?"

"Like what?"

"Whatever you think is important. Why you're not in school. You could start there."

The beer bottle clinked against his teeth again. She couldn't figure out if he was doing it on purpose or his hand was shaking.

"I like to travel. Hitchhike."

"Is that where you met him? You said on the road…"

"I thought you wanted to hear about me? Is this just snooping into Thomas's life? Making sure your baby boy isn't up to no good?" His laugh turned to a giggle.

"Of course not," she said. He'd managed to avoid the question, and if she asked again, it would prove the lie of what she'd just said. "I'm sorry. It just seems like you're avoiding telling me, and that makes me think there's something you don't want me to know. That you're keeping a secret for him."

"If he has secrets, you should be asking him, not me."

"I'm not asking you to betray him," she said. "You're twisting what I say."

"I don't think I am. You seem very curious."

She took several sips of champagne, hoping he'd continue on another track, feeling outwitted and ashamed that she was prying into her son's life. But what was the problem with telling her where they'd met? It was a simple question, a common question. Luke showed up at the house and announced himself as a friend. The natural question was how do you know each other? She should ask Thomas, but he'd probably react the same way — accusing her of poking into his life where she didn't belong. It was a simple, polite question! Having the answer withheld turned it into something dark. "Go on," she said.

"I've been to thirteen states in the past four months. Mostly the southwest. I was in west Texas for a while, but those tarantulas chased me out. I didn't want to wake up with one of those beasts staring me in the face. Or worse."

She shivered. "I feel the same way."

"I try not to stay in one place for more than a few days. A rolling stone, right?"

"What do you do for money?"

"People are generous. Except crazy girls who throw cash into the ocean."

"That was disturbing," she said.

"Sure was. Did anyone try to swim out and get it?"

"Not that I know of."

"She's a trip," Luke said. "Asking for trouble, is what my mother would have said."

"Is that right?"

"Yup. Sure thing. She's asking for it."

"That sounds like you're wishing her harm."

"She's *asking.*"

"I don't want any problems," Mary said.

"If there are problems, they'll come from her, not me. I just go with the flow. I let others take the lead. If that chick wants to do something crazy, I'm happy to help."

"Don't take advantage of her. She's fragile." Mary hadn't known until this minute it was the truth. Caroline was like one of the glass animals she kept on the windowsills to catch the light. One of the clear ones, with legs so thin you thought they might snap at the touch of your fingertip. There was something brittle about Caroline's smile, about her eagerness to strip off her clothes in any situation, about her passionate approach to everyone, even relative strangers.

"She's a big girl. It's 1967. Women are all independent now, not my responsibility."

"I don't like what you're saying. It sounds like you're making a threat of some kind." The champagne tasted metallic in her throat. She put down her glass.

"You're imagining it. You feel threatened, you imagine threats."

"That's not true," she said.

"I think it is."

"Well I disagree."

"She wants to challenge death. She told me."

"Why would she say that?"

"She told me stuff. She's kinda screwed up."

"That's why you should be gentle. And kind."

"But she wants things. Too many things. She wants to have sex with every man on the planet. She wants someone to control her. She told me herself she knows she's out of control. When she was a kid, she had a nanny who tied her to the chair, tied her to the bed. Because she was out of control. Throwing things, tantrums, running away."

"That's terrible."

"She liked it. She liked having someone take charge because she knew she couldn't control herself. It's still that way. Crazy." He laughed.

"It's not funny," she said.

"But crazy, all the same."

She felt a headache stabbing at the inside of her forehead, sharp pain in the hollow below her left ear. Luke was scaring her. He made her afraid for Caroline and afraid of what he was thinking. She didn't know him at all. She had to find out where Thomas had met him.

Twenty-four

The dishes were still stacked on the dresser where Mary had left them. He'd taken the wine and his glass to the window seat and finished the entire bottle. He was left woozy and annoyed with himself. There was no chance of a post-midnight swim when he was buzzed. They insisted swimming at night was dangerous. It was not, but too much alcohol sliding through his bloodstream changed the picture.

Knuckles rapped on the door. He jumped up. She wasn't angry after all. It had seemed plausible that she might slip him some LSD, hoping to lure him into her new world, but when he'd seen her eyes develop that blank stare, the pained twist of her lips, he'd realized what a terrible thing he'd accused her of. Now he could apologize with more sincerity, make sure she understood that sitting alone in his room caused his thoughts to turn in on themselves and he wasn't thinking straight, looking for anything to explain away a mystifying and frightening experience. There had to be an explanation that didn't involve the supernatural, and LSD was the likely candidate. Unless pot also caused hallucinations? Maybe all the lingering smoke had affected him.

He crossed the room and opened the door.

Luke grinned. "I came up for a visit."

"Oh." Thomas gripped the door, holding it in place.

"Well?"

"I guess."

"Aren't you the welcoming host," Luke said.

Thomas stepped back. Luke walked into the room, pushed the door closed, and went to the window seat. He leaned close to the panes and looked out. "Hard to see much in the dark, but it appears you have an excellent view." He turned and looked around the room. "Nice pad."

"Thanks."

"Your mom takes good care of you." Luke settled onto the window seat, leaned back, and stretched out his legs. He crossed his ankles. He wore shorts and a dark t-shirt with the silkscreened image of someone Thomas didn't recognize. "Have a seat." He gestured toward the armchair.

Thomas sat down, hating himself for following orders. The hours he'd spent with Luke were some of the best in his recent experience, but he'd never imagined they'd see each other again. He hadn't *wanted* to see the guy again. Except…he had wanted it. Living a divided life was tiring, never really knowing what you were after — wanting two opposing things in the same moment.

"What are you thinking about?" Luke said.

Thomas shrugged. "What do you want?"

"I want to know why you're ignoring me."

"It's complicated." Thomas leaned his head back and closed his eyes. He thought the lights flickered. He opened his eyes, looking directly into the glare of the bulb in the bedside lamp, visible beneath the shade from his slumped position. He sat up straighter. The bed looked rumpled even though he thought he'd pulled the spread securely when he made it.

"Why is it complicated?"

"Come on," Thomas said. "You know why. I live here with my mother. There are all these people."

"The people don't matter. You're only worried about her."

"Well does your mother know all about your personal life? Does anyone?"

"Yes. My parents know. And I accepted the consequences. Like a man. My father spit in my face. But at least he knows who I am."

"So that's why you're a drifter?"

"I travel."

"You don't have a job. You mooch off people you meet. You can't live the rest of your life that way."

"I aim to try."

"It's not right," Thomas said.

"Being called a pervert because I'm attracted to men isn't right either."

Thomas glanced at the wine bottle, wishing he hadn't been so quick to finish it. He could go downstairs and get another, or offer his guest a beer, but that would risk someone finding out Luke was in his room.

"Thirsty?" Luke said.

Thomas shrugged.

"I could have ratted you out. Your mother is quite curious

about how we met."

Swordfish and broccoli clamored in his stomach, pushing their way back up his esophagus. He burped and tasted vomit. Luke looked friendly enough, smiling with what seemed to be affection. But why had he said that? His tone sounded threatening. Thomas wanted everything to go back to the way it had been last summer. A quiet, uneventful vacation at home. Sex confined to his fantasies, not two guys circling around him like a pack of dogs. One afternoon, and now, what was it going to cost him? He leaned his elbows on his knees and put his head in his hands. It felt heavy, like a block of concrete sinking quickly to the bottom of the ocean.

Luke got off the window seat and sprawled on the bed. "Come here."

Without looking up, Thomas shook his head.

"Look at me."

"I need to think."

"You know you want to. Everyone in this house is migrating from bed to bed. No one will know, and even it they did, they won't care."

"Not everyone."

"Oh, your mother? Maybe not, but her guy is. He's gotten it on with every woman here."

Thomas bolted up. "He has not."

Luke smiled. "You're a little naive, you know that?"

He did know that. And he couldn't believe Gordon would betray his mother like that. At the same time, it wasn't surprising.

"This house is like *Peyton Place*. All kinds of shenanigans under the covers. And you're so worried you're the only one who wants to sleep with a person deemed inappropriate." He laughed.

"You didn't tell her, did you?"

Luke smiled.

"Please tell me you didn't. It's not your information to pass on."

"I didn't know it was top secret."

"Yes you did."

"She was very, very curious. Couldn't stop asking about it. She really wasn't interested in any other topic of conversation."

Thomas stood up. He started toward the bathroom, certain he was going to be sick.

"You okay?"

"Not really." He walked to the bathroom and leaned against the doorframe. For some reason, he felt ashamed at the thought of vomiting with Luke lying ten feet away, listening.

Luke sat up and moved to the edge of the bed. "Let's go smoke a joint. That'll relax you and we can see what happens."

"I'm not feeling well."

"It takes away nausea."

"Does it?"

"Sure. Everyone knows that."

It sounded appealing. He hated throwing up, it was disgusting, and painful.

Luke got up again and went to the window. He opened it and looked down. "Everyone's back. They're already lighting up. I see your mom taking a toke right now."

Thomas closed his eyes and bent over slightly. Maybe he should go. If Luke sat around getting high with his mother, there was no way of stopping her from digging for an answer to her question. It sounded like Luke had already hinted at their relationship. Why was she curious? Why had she even been talking to Luke?

Was Thomas going to have to sit out there every night, join every meal, babysit them when they dropped acid or ate mushrooms, to ensure his mother didn't find out? Maybe it was time to tell her. Even if she flipped out entirely, he didn't think she'd cut off his tuition. That was paid by his father anyway, and it wasn't as if his parents had any kind of relationship where they discussed their plans. He was pretty sure they hadn't spoken in nearly two years.

He tried to imagine how she would respond. He imagined her feeling validated that she'd been right to suggest he was keeping something from her. He didn't think she could be that upset at his failure to align with society's norms. Look at her choice for romance. Still…

Luke walked around the bed. He came up close to Thomas. "What do you say?"

"I don't do drugs."

"Aww, man. Come on." He waved his arm toward the dresser. "You drank a whole bottle of wine."

He was tired of fighting. It was possible he would enjoy it. Possible his mind would slow down and take a rest. And it was the only way to keep an eye and an ear on his curious mother.

"Okay."

They went downstairs. When Luke opened the sliding door, everyone turned to look, as if Thomas were being announced upon entering a great ballroom.

No one commented on his presence, for which he was grateful. He sat beside Luke. He crossed his legs and inched himself back from the circle to be sure his knee didn't brush against Luke's. Beth was seated on the other side of him. He was grateful for that as well. She was quiet and kind. Mary looked at him and turned away. He hoped she was glad to see him, that his willingness to finally join the others dissolved some of her anger. Or hurt. She was probably more hurt than angry.

The joint made its way around the circle. Luke took a hit and handed it to Thomas. Instead of being concerned about damaging his brain, all he could think of was inhaling smoke and the likelihood he would cough uncontrollably, prove himself a first-timer, as they all knew, and be the recipient of their silent, or not so silent, ridicule. He took a small puff, hoping to forestall coughing. The smoke burned inside of him, ripping at his throat.

"That's not enough," Luke said.

He couldn't respond without exhaling prematurely, losing control of his lungs. He put the cigarette to his lips and sucked gently, hoping it satisfied them. All of their eyes were watching to see what he would do. He felt like a child, inexperienced and naive. Wasn't that what Luke accused him of? Naiveté. It was humiliating. He released the smoke in a single huff and coughed.

He handed the joint to Beth. He felt nothing.

After the joint had circled another time, it had shrunk to a tiny stub. Paul rolled a new one and lit it.

After a second hit, Thomas still felt nothing. What was the big deal? His throat burned and his bones hurt from sitting on the deck. He was cold and he couldn't move without the risk of touching Luke. Not only did he want to avoid an accidental touch that his mother took notice of, he didn't want desire for Luke to spread through his body faster than the smoke seemed to be doing. He never should have come out here. They were staring at him, watching him, laughing at him. Wondering how he'd respond.

The joint made its route two more times. Now he felt slightly...relaxed. Less concerned. Let them stare. Let them silently mock him. What did it matter? They were all strangers. They weren't *his* friends. He could care less what any of them thought. Mary might be angry or upset or hurt, but he was her son — she couldn't hate him. She might say things that made him feel terrible, but she would never change her basic opinion of him. Mothers loved their children no matter how stupidly they behaved. No matter what course their lives took. Didn't they? Wasn't it instinct, or something? A biological imperative.

He looked out toward the water. The waves were soothing, coming to shore like caresses rather than crashing and rolling like stampeding horses. He couldn't see them, but felt their rhythm through his entire body, rolling through his chest, washing the interior walls of his heart, stripping it as clean as the sand. The night seemed to creep closer, growing darker, as if stars were blinking out. He knew it was fog moving in, but it still felt like each star had a switch and they were snapped off one by one. A few glittered over the concrete ship, but did nothing to illuminate it. Could his mother be telling the truth about a ghost? She wasn't prone to lying, it was the drugs that made him disbelieve her. Maybe it was a delusion that comforted her over the tragic loss of her mother at such a young age.

His experiences of someone speaking, singing, knowing his thoughts, the apparition he thought he'd seen, had the substance of a dream. But as he listened to the water, and looked at the faces surrounding him, they too appeared dream-like. Faces of strangers. How did he know they were strangers? Every human being on the planet had the same eyes. There was minimal variation in shape and position, noses and mouths in the same arrangement. How was it that such infinitesimal variations in features presented such wildly different appearances? He'd never mistake Mary for one of the other women. Luke and Paul were unique and distinctive in every way. He closed his eyes for a moment. The thoughts were puzzling, but he felt no compulsion to find the answers to his questions. Simply watching them drift by, turning in different directions, weaving their own course, was satisfying.

He stood up.

"Where are you going?" Luke wrapped his hand around Thomas's ankle.

Thomas stepped back, forcing Luke to move his hand. He

wasn't so high he'd allow a man to touch him with such affection in front of others. Still, he definitely was high. And now, he saw the appeal of this kind of thing. It was more enjoyable than alcohol in several ways. He was curious to see what his mind would feel like when it was over. "Going for a walk."

Luke stood. "I'll come too."

Thomas wanted to say no. He glanced at Mary. She was watching him. There was a polite smile on her face. She didn't understand what was happening, she was just pleased that he was here with the people she called friends. That he was no longer judging them. Or so she thought. He smiled.

Her smile broadened.

If he walked away, Luke would follow. If he told Luke he wanted to be alone, there was no way to predict how Luke would respond. Luke might refrain from provoking him, now that he was high. It was equally possible he'd create an embarrassing scene. It was hard to imagine shame in his current state of calm, but it would still be there, trying to penetrate the cloud that surrounded him.

Paul stood up. "A walk sounds good."

There was no escaping them. It might all be good. He didn't have to talk to them.

He walked down the steps. Luke followed, then Paul. Thomas crossed the sand, feeling the shadow of their presence behind him like a string of ducks. He laughed. They ran to catch up.

"Finally having a good time?" Paul said.

He didn't answer. If they were as blissful as he was, why the caustic question? He walked to the edge of the water, then turned and headed toward the pier. It stood dark and silent above him. He moved quickly, taking long, sure strides.

"What's the rush?" Paul said.

"He's trying to leave us behind," Luke said.

Again, Thomas didn't respond. There was a great deal of power in remaining silent. Why was he realizing that for the first time? They could attribute motives, and critique his behavior all they wanted. It didn't make it true. Defending himself turned every conversation into an argument. Other people debating his thoughts as if they could see inside his skull! He laughed and began running.

"Cool!" Luke darted ahead of him and turned, jogging backwards.

Paul caught up and stayed close by Thomas's side. Thomas slowed to a walk. Thankfully, no one spoke, leaving him alone inside his fuzzy head. When they reached the rocks at the end of New Brighton Beach, they turned and started back.

"We should go for a swim," Luke said.

"No towel. No swim trunks," Thomas said. His voice was rough, after not speaking for so much time. He cleared his throat.

"No need," Luke said. He stopped and peeled off his shorts and shirt.

Thomas kept walking.

"Come on." Paul stripped off his shirt and jeans.

Thomas began running. From far away, he heard them laughing, but their laughter sounded more disappointed than condemning. He ran until he was about forty feet from the pier. He looked out at the ship. A woman appeared, standing on the bow. He shivered. He turned and looked for the others. They were in the water, impossible to see from this far away.

Stop lying. Stop suffering.

He closed his eyes and pressed his hands over his ears. Why was the woman shouting at him? He glanced back down the beach again, knowing he still wouldn't see them.

A blast of cold rushed through him. He shivered violently, afraid he would fall down, his limbs and body completely out of control.

The woman on the ship moved toward the pier. Her hair was long and whitish gold, flowing behind her like ribbons. Her dress, if you could call it that, and not a shroud, was white. As she moved closer, seeming to fly, yet not, her face became more visible. It was white and gave the effect of being transparent, although there was nothing he could make out beneath the skin, if that's what it was. Instead of eyes, the face had gaping sockets that consumed the entire space where there should have been cheekbones. The mouth was a dark gash, no teeth, no lips to speak of.

He shook harder and fell to his knees, knowing he should run. It was coming for him. He groaned in anticipation of unimaginable pain, or a horrible death. Or no death at all, a lifetime of terror where he wished for death.

You're killing yourself. No one else. You.

The thing vanished. He was lying on his side, covered with

sand, crying like a newborn. He tried to lift his head to see if the others had witnessed his collapse. He couldn't see them. The beach was empty of life. There were no birds, and the sound of the waves was muffled. He couldn't see a single light from the houses or hear a human voice. He lay there crying softly for a long time.

Twenty-five

Despite the relaxing effects of the pot and Gordon's leisurely, gentle, and soul-shattering love making, Mary had hardly slept. She'd woken at three, so alert her eyes wouldn't close. She'd turned on her side and focused on the shadowy folds of the drapes, hoping her lids would grow tired and close on their own, but it hadn't happened. She changed her position seven or eight times. Finally she sat up. For several minutes, she rubbed Gordon's upper back, half hoping the pressure of her fingers would wake him and they could make love again. But he slept without moving, his breath barely audible. She ran her fingers through his hair. She slithered down again and pressed her body against his.

At five, she'd gotten up, put on a long, loose dress, braided her hair, and gone out to the kitchen. The coffee pot was loud, but nothing penetrated the unconscious condition of her friends. It was the deep sleep of the young — untroubled, exhausted from complete absorption of all their senses and muscles — like puppies.

She poured two cups of coffee and carried them upstairs. Tiptoeing up the stairs at five-thirty in the morning wasn't really necessary, she had hours before the others woke, but still she moved quietly. She was pleased that Thomas had joined the group last night, but she needed to talk to him before the others woke up. Luke was giving her an uncomfortable vibe.

He opened the door after a single, quiet tap. Perhaps he didn't sleep the untroubled, contented sleep of his peers. She'd been right to come up here. Maybe he felt the vibe from Luke as well.

He took the coffee cup from her hand.

"Do you want to go for a walk after coffee?" she said.

"Sure." He glanced at the shutters. He took a few quick sips of coffee and put the cup on the nightstand. "Let me get dressed."

She sat on the window seat. When he came out of the bathroom, her cup was empty. His cup, forgotten it seemed, remained on the dresser.

Outside, the sky was clear, pale gray as the edges of the sun bled across it. The tide was low, the waves quiet as a lake. A huge flock of gulls stood in their usual morning formation, gazing at the water. A few pelicans joined them, enormous beside the others and awkward with a seeming excess of joints.

When she and Thomas reached the footpath, she turned and started toward the pier.

"Let's go this way," he said.

"I thought we'd walk on the boat."

"I'd rather not."

"It's beautiful out there right now. The sea is so gentle."

"Let's walk on the beach." He turned away from her, headed toward the steps, as if he was going to walk where he chose, no matter which direction she wanted to go.

She hurried after him. "Let's walk on the ship."

"I thought you didn't care for it much?"

"I hate it and love it. On a beautiful morning, when I feel restless, I love it."

"I don't."

"What's the matter?"

He stopped and faced her. His eyes were bloodshot. His nose was glossy and slightly red at the tip. His face looked pale beneath the dark hairs covering his cheeks and jaw. "You were right. I think it's haunted. I guess…"

She bit the inside of her lip, trying to stop herself from smiling. "What happened?"

"It's too hard to talk about right now. Maybe later. I didn't sleep."

She nodded. She stepped to the side and looped her arm around his. "Let's walk, then."

They went to the water's edge. Mary gathered her dress in her hand, pulling it up toward her knees. She waded into the surf, soothed by the cold, slowly gliding water. "If you don't want to talk about what happened on the ship, then tell me what you thought of your first high."

"Isn't that a weird thing to discuss with your mother? It was weird enough sitting across from you."

She laughed. "I don't think I'm a typical mother."

"I guess not."

They walked for a while.

"It was fine," he said.

"Fine? That's all you can say?"

"I see the appeal."

"Will you do it again?"

"I'm not sure. I wonder how much the things I saw and heard were influenced by pot."

"It doesn't cause hallucinations." She walked deeper into the water. It didn't really matter if her dress got splashed. "Did she frighten you?"

"I said I don't want to talk about it."

"Why?"

"Because I don't. I need to think."

"Can't you think and talk?"

"No." He walked into the water, soaking the hems of his jeans.

Mary hurried to catch up. "If you don't want to talk about that, how about Luke?"

"What about him?"

"He seems nice."

"What does that mean? Do you know people who aren't nice?" he said.

"As a matter of fact, I do. Where did you meet him?"

"Why does it matter?"

"That's a strange answer to an innocent question."

"I don't really remember."

He was lying. He must know she recognized that fact. Of course you remembered where you met people. It wasn't as if he'd lived twenty or thirty years as an adult, visited hundreds of cities, been involved in multiple organizations and held various jobs where he'd met thousands of people. He either met Luke at school or somewhere around Berkeley. Or in Santa Cruz. Those were the choices. "That's odd."

"Not really."

"I remember where I meet everyone."

"Well good for you. I hardly know the guy and I can't recall. It might have been a party or…"

"He said he doesn't live in Berkeley." Tension radiated off him. She was pushing too hard, but she couldn't stop. She wasn't going to be dismissed as a nosey mother, made to feel as if she was imagining things.

"My whole life isn't in Berkeley."

"I thought it was."

"Why are you nagging me?"

She kicked at the waves playfully, splashing his legs. Her kick was harder than expected and she managed to soak the front of his jeans.

"Stop it."

"Stop splashing you or stop asking about your life? We've hardly talked all summer, and when we do, it's an argument. It wasn't like this before. I don't understand what's going on with you, and your behavior has become more troubling since Luke arrived. I just wondered how you know him and why he's here." She put her hand on his arm.

He shook off her hand. "Why are any of these freeloaders here?"

"So he's a drifter? Like my friends?"

"He's not my friend. And they are not your friends. As long as you feed them and provide cash for drugs and a warm place to sleep, they'll stay. Cut that off and see how friendly they are."

"Why do you have such a sour view of human nature?"

He walked faster. She hurried to catch up, slogging through the water. Her dress was soaked up to her hips. The wet fabric slowed her movement, hugging the water as if it wanted to sink into the waves, taking her with it. She gathered the skirt more tightly and wrung it out. Water poured down her legs, but it didn't make the fabric any lighter. She kept it bunched in her hand and ran awkwardly until she reached his side. "Thomas. I'm sorry. I'm just trying to talk to you. I'm interested in your life. I care about what's going on inside your head. You might be an adult, but you're still my child."

He stopped and folded his arms. "I'm not a child. And you can't pretend you're twenty-five around all of them and expect to act like my mother at the same time. Even if you weren't acting like an idiot, I'm an adult and I don't need to explain my life to you."

She backed up. Her left heel landed hard on a broken clamshell. She winced and moved to the side. "I didn't think I was asking you to explain your life. I asked where you met your friend. I thought it was a simple enough question, but your reaction makes me even more concerned that something is going on that's upsetting you."

"You're imagining things. You imagine a lot of things. Your whole life is a fantasy."

Tears pushed at the backs of her eyes. This wasn't what she'd expected. It started out so nicely, such a beautiful morning. It still was. The sun was up over the cliff now, warming her face. Hopefully it would dry her dress.

She wasn't sure if she should be afraid for him. Maybe he was right. She'd invited strangers to live in her house. All she knew about them was what they chose to tell her, and that could be a complete fabrication. In fact, all she knew about Thomas's life was what he wanted to reveal, and he'd chosen to lie. There was no possible way he could fail to remember where he'd met Luke, and the more he argued that point, the less she believed him. There had to be a way to break the stalemate. Maybe the old adage about catching flies with honey. She was putting him on the defensive. Silence was best.

She took his arm. "Let's just walk and enjoy the sunrise."

"Sunrise is over."

Apparently he wanted to make an argument out of everything. She was curious about his reaction to the pot, curious to hear about his encounter with the ghost. It seemed that none of her curiosity would be satisfied. "Do you want to keep walking?"

"If you stop haranguing me."

"I can do that."

She felt the ship behind them, watching, listening as it waited for one of them to speak again. It was always listening. That's how it got under your skin. It heard the things you said on the beach, even if they were whispered. She was fairly certain it even heard the things that passed through your mind.

She hoped she wasn't losing her son. Her other boys had moved so far away and she knew she clung to Thomas more than she should. He was her baby. His childhood was the last time she remembered being foolishly happy. When he was small, she'd been too busy with all her kids to notice what was happening to her marriage. Once Thomas became semi-independent, she felt that she'd woken out of a dream and noticed something had changed between her and Henry. He proceeded to shatter her life, expecting her to smile and be gracious as he moved out of the house and began living his very public love affair. Thomas was her rock. She had to figure out how to mend things between them. The problem was, Thomas didn't seem to want them mended. "What would you like to talk about?" she said.

"To be honest, I'd rather not talk at all. There's too much talking."

"How can you say that? Spending every day and eating all your meals alone in your room?"

"I like quiet."

"There's a limit to how much solitude people can bear."

"Who says? Maybe there should be a limit to talking."

"I see your point," she said.

They'd gone for nearly a mile, possibly more. She felt more alone than if she'd been walking by herself. She felt the weight of his brooding silence, his hostility. It made her heart ache and made her tired all over again, after the long night of turning around in her bed until she was wrapped in sheets like a mummy. Not necessarily sleepy, just very, very tired. It was possible the party was coming to an end. Her friends were not worth losing her son. And everything wrong between her and Thomas could be traced back to her friends. "I wonder if I should ask everyone but Gordon to leave," she said. "Even Luke."

"Do whatever you want."

"I thought you wanted them to leave?"

"It's your house."

"I'm very frustrated with you, Thomas. There's nothing I can say that you don't argue with. Nothing I can say to make you happy."

"You can't make another person happy. You shouldn't try. If you're just throwing them out to appease me, you don't understand anything."

"What don't I understand?"

"I don't want to talk about it."

For the second time in just a few weeks, maybe the third, she wanted to slap his face. How could he act like a man one moment and a child the next? She stopped. "I guess we should turn back."

They reversed their direction. She thought she might cry. "Don't be angry with me," she said softly. "Whatever I did. Everything I did, I suppose. I'm trying."

"You can't fix it. Just leave me alone and let me handle my own life."

"Okay."

When they got close to the house, they cut across the beach at an angle, as if they'd silently agreed they didn't want to waste any steps in their eagerness to get home and be rid of each other.

After Thomas trudged up the deck stairs and went inside, she walked quickly to the pier. The hem of her dress dragged across the dry sand, turning into a crusty cardboard-like garment around her lower legs. She walked quickly to the end of the pier and sat on a bench facing the ship. It felt as if the world had frozen around her. Water lapped at the legs of the pier and the sides of the boat.

When the sea was quiet and the sky blue, the gulls drifting lazily overhead, the idea of something living inside the ship, something dead but not, was impossible to believe. It was confusing the way Thomas mentioned encountering a supernatural creature, then immediately discounted it as a drug-induced hallucination, as if he didn't know his own mind. Thomas didn't realize that not knowing one's mind was caused by the ghost. He was afraid to admit to his fear. Now that she thought about it, she believed he was afraid of Luke. And possibly, that was the antagonism she'd also sensed between Thomas and Paul. Everything he did was wrapped in fear. He was young and strong and well-educated. Smart. What did he have to be afraid of?

A couple passed by her, headed toward the ship. What would they do if she rushed over to them and warned them to watch out for a malevolent ghost? They'd think she was crazy. Anyone would.

The woman had short, curly hair. She wore a bikini held

together with strings. Her skin was pale, even against the white bathing suit. The man had equally curly hair and wore blue jeans cut off at the knees.

Mary was overcome with a desire to be that woman. Neither of them were thinking of ghosts. The woman wasn't worrying about adult children or trying to protect her guy from a predator. Why did they get that kind of life and she'd been denied happiness when she was young? She'd felt she was happy for a short time with all her children and a charming, successful husband. But looking back, the whole thing was a lie. It was so unfair. Half her life had been wasted. All of her youth. Why did some couples get to have happy lives that continued while their children grew up, lives that became even more satisfying when they returned to the state of two?

She turned, removing them from her range of vision.

She stood up and hurried off the pier. The stiff fabric beat against her legs and sand clung to her skin. She walked across the beach and up the stairs to her deck. Two stubs from smoked joints sat in plain sight, unnoticed in the darkness. She picked them up and dropped them into one of the empty beer bottles. She grabbed up the other five bottles and hugged them to her chest. The vapor trapped inside touched her face with a fog of stale beer. She averted her head as she opened the door, balancing the bottles, and stepped into the house. The sleeping bags contained the mounds of dreaming bodies. From a few, long clumps of hair were exposed, spread across the carpet. If she squinted, it looked like the floor was dotted with furry rodents.

She stepped around them, went into the kitchen, and opened the door under the sink. She pulled out the trash and dropped the bottles in, not caring that they rattled and crashed against each other. She glanced back at the living room. No one moved in response to the noise. She washed her hands.

Weariness dragged at her limbs and her eyelids. Her head felt so heavy she didn't think she could keep it in place. She went down the hall and opened her bedroom door. Caroline sat naked on top of Gordon's prone body. She was touching his face. She didn't turn at the sound of the door and Gordon didn't appear to notice Mary's presence.

Mary stepped back out and closed the door. She bent over, trying to breathe. Strangely, there were no tears and she had no desire to cry. Instead, rage pumped through her blood vessels. She opened the door again. As she started to speak, the scene registered a fraction of a second later than it should have. The room was empty. The drapes were pulled to the sides, the window was partially open, and the curtains floated on the breeze. Her hand fell away from the doorknob. She went to the bathroom. It too was empty. The lights were off and there was moisture on the shower curtain. She returned to the bedroom and sat on the bed.

Had the drugs made a permanent change in her brain and she was now hallucinating without their help? She'd heard of such things. Was it a vision of the future? Or a vision of something that had already happened? Was it a scene projected by the ghost, intent on twisting her heart until the pain was unbearable?

She got up, closed the door and locked it. She took off her dress and crawled naked under the blankets on the side Gordon used. He and Caroline might be out somewhere together but she was too tired to hunt for them. She hadn't noticed any empty sleeping bags, but she hadn't checked each one.

She closed her eyes. She might be able to sleep all day. Maybe she should. Maybe a dream would advise her what to do. She'd never felt so alone in all her life, not even after Henry walked out the front door for the last time. At least then, she'd had the company and outraged comfort of her sons.

Twenty-six

It was dark when Thomas woke. He'd slept all day. His sleep had been dreamless — something to be grateful for among the multitude of things disturbing him. The moment he'd mentioned his experience with the ghost, he'd regretted it. Of course it was induced by marijuana. It didn't matter if those stupid people insisted the drug didn't cause hallucinations. They were all in one enormous collective hallucination, what did they know about reality?

His mother had seemed so excited that he was admitting to the possibility of a haunted ship. She wanted to drag him down with her. She wanted him to accept the infestation of useless people, she wanted him to accept her embarrassing attraction and blind devotion to Gordon, and she wanted him to bare his soul to her as if he were a child. He didn't need her any more. He would figure things out himself, without her input. His sex life was none of her business! What had ever made him think he needed to explain himself to her?

He got out of bed and went into the bathroom. He turned on the cold water, stripped, and climbed into the shower. The water lashed at his skin like a whip with icy metal tips. It felt good, reassuring to know he was alive and sober. Never again. He soaped himself, rinsed, and got out. He dried himself and opened the bathroom door.

Luke was sprawled across the bed. “Hi, handsome.”

Thomas stepped back into the bathroom and grabbed a towel. He wrapped it around his waist. “Get out of my room. How did you even get in? The door’s locked.”

“Not any more.”

“How…”

“A lock on a bedroom door? A child can get past that. It’s a deterrent only.”

“Please leave.”

“I don’t think so.”

Thomas walked to the door and opened it. “Out.”

Luke laughed. “Make me. Tie me up and carry me out.” He laughed harder, opening his mouth wide, revealing a discolored tongue.

“I want you to leave. Please respect me enough to do what I ask.”

“Why? Shut the door.”

Thomas clutched the doorknob. If he closed the door, Luke won. If he kept it open, anyone might come up the stairs and see them. He closed it. “What do you want?”

“I think you and Mama Bear have even more money than I realized.”

“Don’t say that.”

“Mama Bear? Or money?” He giggled. “You are too funny. You’re making this too easy.”

Thomas shivered. He tried to keep his arms pressed against his sides so Luke didn't notice the tremor. He was genuinely scared, more than he had been when that ghoulish face on the boat had been turned in his direction, the figure rushing toward him like it wanted to devour him.

"It's so obvious you're terrified of anyone finding out what you are."

"Don't talk like that."

"About what you are? As if you're an alien being? But you are. Unless you become a nameless faceless vagrant in a huge city, you'll never find a place where you can be what you are."

"I…"

Luke sat up. He pushed the pillows against the headboard. "Come sit here. Take off the towel first."

Thomas pulled the towel tighter and readjusted the half knot he'd made along the top edge.

"Shy. I know." Luke crossed his arms. "Anyways…you're as scared as a cornered bunny rabbit. So I imagine you can provide me more cash than I dreamed of."

"Why would I give you a dime?" Thomas knew, in a distant corner of his mind, he absolutely knew why, but some other part of him insisted this couldn't be happening. Luke liked him. They were the same. Sure Luke was less concerned about being found out, but he still wanted to keep his private life to himself, didn't he? Didn't everyone?

"You're just stupid, Paul…Tommy. Whatever you want to call yourself. You think you're superior with your exclusive college and your fancy degrees and your beachfront house and your upper class mother and your sense of ownership. But you're not smart at all. You're stupid, picking up a random guy and doing things that could get you locked up in every state in this country."

"I thought you…"

"You thought I liked you? That we might have a relationship? If you thought that, why did you leave me without a ride and without any cash? You thought you could buy me with a hamburger?"

Stupidly, Thomas's mind argued back that Luke also had a milkshake and fries. And now what? One way or another, he'd be forced to tell his mother, either by asking for cash or allowing Luke to betray him. Not five minutes earlier he'd felt so solid in his right to a personal life that was separate from hers.

"I think five hundred will do."

"Five hundred dollars?"

Luke nodded. "For now."

"I need to get dressed," Thomas said.

"Realized you're not in a strong position? Standing naked? Soon to be exposed to the world?"

"You wouldn't do that," Thomas said. He leaned against the dresser. He coughed and tried to take a deep breath, but couldn't seem to find the strength to pull more than a few ounces of oxygen into his lungs. He coughed again.

"Calm down."

"I'm calm."

"You're headed toward a panic attack."

"I have nothing to panic about."

"I think you do. A prestigious graduate program? A protective mother? I assume a prominent father somewhere or other. With a reputation to maintain."

Thomas moved to the chair and sat down. He put his head in his hands and leaned forward. He had no idea where he would get five hundred dollars without asking one of his parents. There had to be a way to get this guy to stop.

"Lots of guys are owning who they are these days, fighting to be recognized as part of society. I guess you're not one of them," Luke said. "It's kind of sad."

If only he were dressed, he could think more clearly. There must be a way to delay this, to buy some time. "I certainly don't have five hundred dollars sitting around my room."

"A down payment is fine."

"A down payment?"

"Whatever you have in your wallet will keep me quiet for the next…oh, let's say twelve hours."

Thomas glanced at the clock. It was ridiculous to care about when the twelve hours would be over, he wasn't doing this. But it seemed a so-called deposit was the only way to get some time to think about how he would get Luke out of the house and out of his life. He stood up.

"Attaboy."

Thomas slowly pulled open the top drawer of the dresser. He took out his wallet and opened it.

"Seventy-four dollars. I already looked. A lot of cash for a young guy like you, on summer vacation, no real expenses, and no job." Luke chuckled.

Thomas pulled out the cash and folded the stack of bills in half. He put his wallet on the dresser.

"I'd put that away if I were you," Luke said. "You never know when someone might come into your room, looking for something useful."

"What would they steal? You're taking all the cash."

"Driver's license. Fake ID, my friend."

Thomas turned around. "Here." He held the bills a few inches from his body.

"Bring it here."

"You're leaving, so come get it and then you can continue on out the door." Thomas shivered.

"Getting cold? You might as well bring it here, I'm going to outlast you. In everything."

Thomas shivered more violently. The double meaning made him more determined to remain where he was.

"I have all night," Luke said.

Thomas wanted to get dressed. He wanted Luke out of his room, although first he wanted to wipe the knowing, seductive smirk off Luke's face. He wanted to figure out what he was going to do to fix this, but none of that could happen unless he yielded and carried the cash to the bed. He took a step to his left.

"Come on. That's right."

He took a few steps closer, hating himself. He stopped.

"I didn't mean to frighten you, little rabbit. Bring me the money, buy your freedom for twelve hours."

Thomas tossed the bills toward Luke. Predictably, a few fluttered onto the bedspread, and some got no forward movement at all and dropped to the floor around Thomas's feet.

Luke laughed. "You just made more work for yourself."

Thomas felt like crying, but waiting to pick up the bills just prolonged the agony. Luke would wind up making him do something even more degrading. He knelt and gathered the bills into a messy stack. He started to get up.

"Stay like that. On your knees. It's how you feel, isn't it?"

"I don't feel like anything."

"But you are. A beggar. Bring them here, on your knees."

Thomas stood up. "This is bullshit." He shoved the bills at Luke.

"Careful brave boy, I have powerful information. Never forget that. Never." Luke smiled.

Thomas walked around the bed and stood by the door. "Now you need to leave."

"But we haven't arranged when we'll meet up so you can give me the rest of the bread." He folded his arms across his chest. He lifted his chin slightly and shook his head, shifting his hair off the sides of his face.

"I won't be able to get you that much money in twelve hours."

"That's a problem."

"You have to be realistic."

"Mary has plenty of cash." Luke closed his eyes. "Oh. I see. You don't want her to know you prefer boys but you can't get that much cash without her asking what it's for." He threw his head back, crashing it against the headboard with a loud thunk. He laughed as if he felt nothing from the blow to the back of his head. After a few minutes, his laughter dissolved. "I suppose I could give you more than twelve hours. Or, we could make a trade."

Thomas grabbed the doorframe. His nails scraped the plaster. A shiver ran along his arm and drilled itself behind his ear. He clutched the edge of the towel with his other hand.

"I'll stay in here with you. We can cuddle and keep each other warm. That's worth a lot to me. It's worth five hundred. Or I should say four-hundred-and…" He looked at the ceiling. "… Twenty-six bucks." His tone became serious. "Someone to hold me and love me. That's worth quite a lot." His eyes were no longer mocking. Instead, they were glazed with sadness.

"No. That won't work," Thomas said.

Luke glanced toward the window, although there was nothing to be seen from his position on the bed. He wriggled slightly, shoving himself into a half-reclining position. "It's a good deal. And no one will know what we're doing in here. It's the best deal you're going to get."

"I can't. I don't know why you refuse to understand my situation."

"I understand your situation perfectly." Luke's words were sharp. "You're a spoiled rich kid and you're scared of losing the position you were born into. You'd rather live alone and lie to every single person you know. Your secret is more important to you than anything. But what I've found is that secrets are a profitable business. I just never expected to uncover so many in one house. I stumbled upon the pot of gold at the end of the rainbow." He laughed.

"If you care for me at all, you won't do this."

"What on earth gave you the idea that I care for you?"

"When I picked you up, when we…"

Luke smiled. "Oh. I'm sorry. Yes, I do care for the way you make me feel. But I'm not concerned about your secret. Or how it's messing with your head. I have bigger problems. I have the problem of feeding myself, a problem you've never encountered. I have the problem of finding a safe place to sleep every night, a problem you can't even comprehend."

"What other secrets?"

"What?"

"What other secrets have you uncovered?"

Luke smiled. "If I told you, they wouldn't be secrets."

"Other people are paying you money? How many people are you extorting five hundred dollars from?"

Luke smiled.

"Most of them don't even have any money." Even with nothing but the towel covering his body, he was uncomfortably warm. The back of his neck and his armpits were thick with sweat. He felt a smear of it developing on his forehead. A bead of water broke away and ran down the the bridge of his nose.

"Should I open the window?" Luke said.

Thomas shook his head.

"You're thinking your mother has secrets. And I'm collecting even more than you realize."

"No, I wasn't thinking that."

"You are. You realized she's the only other person with money. Or so they say."

"What does that mean?"

"You'd be surprised the money that's available when someone doesn't want to be found out."

"Who?"

Luke laughed. "For someone who wants to keep his privacy, you aren't very considerate of others'."

"I just…"

"I know. I know. Things are not what you thought they were. You thought your mother's drug use and her too-young boyfriend were the worst things. But maybe they're not. Maybe those are only the tip of the iceberg."

"You're making this up," Thomas said.

"Am I?"

"You want me to…"

Luke stared at him, smiling. He tilted his head to the side. "I want you to do what?"

"Nothing."

Luke shrugged.

Thomas glanced toward the bathroom. "I need to get dressed."

Luke waved his arm. "Nothing's stopping you."

"Are you blackmailing my mother?"

Luke giggled. He pulled his knees up and hugged his shins. "I can't tell you that." He picked up the bills and stroked them along his cheek. "Mmmm. Secrets."

"You're lying."

"Do I get to sleep here tonight?"

"No."

"Come on. We had a great time together. I know you want me to."

"Wrong. I don't want you."

"Okay, your worried brain doesn't, that's true. But the rest of you is dying to have me stay."

"I don't like you."

"Aww. Now you hurt my feelings."

"How do I know you won't take my money, or get whatever else you want, and still tell everyone about me?"

"Trust."

"That's a laugh," Thomas said.

"It's all you have. I can tell you a secret."

"What would that accomplish?"

Luke shrugged. "So you know I'm serious."

"Oh."

"It's about Caroline."

"You're blackmailing her, too?"

"Such a nasty word."

"Well are you?"

"She's very forthcoming. She has a secret, even though she loves to tell people her life story."

That wasn't surprising. As far as Thomas could see, Caroline never wanted to stop talking.

"She's gonna be a mama."

"She's pregnant?"

Luke nodded. "Yup."

"And why is that a secret? It's not like these people care about their reputations."

"She doesn't want to be a mama. Gordon's the papa. And she's not a fan. Not what she pictured at all. The guy is like forty years old. She tells everyone she's twenty-something, but she's only nineteen. She has lots of partying still to do. A baby launches her straight to middle age. Destroys her body. She's trying to figure out how to undo that problem."

"She paid you not to tell anyone, and now you betrayed her?"

"Only because it's you. Because you'll do whatever I tell you to do."

"I won't."

"I think you will," Luke said.

Thomas let go of the doorframe. He swayed slightly. He needed to sit down but there was nowhere to go. He took a few steps back and looked in the mirror. His hair was drying. He clutched the towel and strode across the bedroom. He yanked open the second dresser drawer, pulled out a pair of jeans and a t-shirt and shoved the drawer closed with his foot. It stuck, one side protruding. He returned to the bathroom and closed the door. Maybe it wouldn't be so bad to tell his mother everything. She'd keep his secret, and Luke didn't know anyone else that mattered. He was doing this because he sensed Thomas's fear of

Mary, not anyone else. Luke wasn't going to find an administrator at UC Berkeley or get in touch with his father. It was all fear and threats. He would tell Mary and she'd share whatever secret she was harboring and they'd be free of this guy together. They'd send the whole bunch of them back where they came from. Including Gordon.

Twenty-seven

Mary was obsessed with finding out where Thomas had met Luke. Their total loss of memory on the matter was not believable. It made sense if you forgot a person entirely, if you ran into them years later and couldn't recall where you'd known each other, only that the face was familiar. She couldn't come up with any explanation for why they were so determined to hide the truth from her. Was it possible Thomas was involved in something criminal? Luke had been so cold in his insistence that Caroline was *asking for trouble*. Everything he said had a hard edge. The steely look in his eyes made her think he'd had a rough life. That was how her mother described people she thought were not on the up and up — *he's had a rough life*. It covered a lot of sins and disasters — *rough life*.

Was Thomas in some kind of gang? Were they collecting protection money? She didn't know a lot about criminal activity and that was the only thing that came to mind. Bank robbers, maybe? Curiosity was keeping her from sleeping, and even a hit of weed or an extra glass of champagne failed to ease her mind. Thoughts raced but they went nowhere. She'd tried talking to Gordon about it, but he didn't understand why it bothered her so deeply. He informed her she was being silly and nosey and wasting her energy on something unimportant.

She didn't like him saying things like that. She wasn't silly. She was a concerned mother whose instincts were screaming that something wasn't right. Thomas was strong and fit from a lifetime surfing and swimming in the ocean. How could he be afraid of the boy? And Luke was definitely a boy.

Anger twisted her stomach like the taffy machine at The Boardwalk, pulling and stretching her intestines into a different consistency. Gordon should respect her. He should consider her thoughts important and worth discussion. Sometimes it seemed as if he didn't even hear what she was saying, he already had an answer ready. And his answers were like gusts of wind, scattering her concerns out of his path. She'd waited too long to have a serious conversation with him. She was trying too hard to be like the others, to avoid coming across as someone old and needy and demanding of commitment. The worst sin was to tie a man down. But the fun had gone out of their way of life. You couldn't drift forever. You couldn't just let things be, sometimes decisions had to be made. Sometimes action was required.

When they were in bed, she was transported to paradise. He made her body feel like the most desirable thing he'd ever touched. His hands on her skin made her tremble until her nerves rose to a feverish plane, releasing cries of pleasure that made her blush when she remembered them later. The things he said when he was touching her made her feel beautiful and timeless. She was treasured and safe in his arms. All her thoughts and concerns melted away. Then, while he slept, they crept back in and gnawed at the inside of her skull.

She turned onto her side and pressed her face against his spine. She took a deep breath. The scent of him filled her sinuses. She relaxed into him. She worried too much. This was supposed to be fun. Hadn't she invited these people into her home, opened her arms to whatever experiences came her way because she felt she'd missed out on a significant part of life? She'd been too young to enjoy the nightlife on the boat when it came into the harbor, when the excitement of the twenties still pervaded the world. She'd come of age when the entire state, the country, was in a state of depression. Then she'd raised children with a bloody, horrific war as a backdrop. Just when the world started to enjoy itself again, her husband decided to leave. Finally, it was her time, and now, worry was destroying her pleasure. She was on the cusp of middle age. Some would say she was well into middle age, but she didn't feel that way. She felt as excited and full of life as she had when she was twenty. She'd given everything to her children and her home and her former husband. She deserved this before it was too late.

Still, she didn't simply want a companion at her parties. She needed someone who loved her and would stay with her for the rest of her life. Maybe she wanted too much. Now that she knew such things were possible, she didn't want to live without the feelings Gordon aroused. This was what love felt like. She loved him with her entire being, and she was sure he loved her. So why couldn't he act like they were bound together for eternity — lovers like Cleopatra and Mark Antony? If she meant as much to Gordon as he did to her, shouldn't he drink in her words as eagerly as she swallowed his, revel in her soul, not just her body? That's what love meant. Making love was the culmination of those other things.

A sigh escaped from his lungs as she pressed closer. She wrapped her arm around his waist, holding onto him as if he were a life raft and the waves were threatening to suck her beneath the surface. She kissed the center of his spine. "I love you so much," she whispered.

He was silent. Of course he was asleep, she couldn't expect him to answer, but a part of her hoped their connection was so deep he would speak from inside his dreams. She ran her hands over his chest, stroking him. She wanted his desire for her to wake him, proving that even in an unconscious state he needed her.

After a while, her shoulder began to ache, her neck was stiff from lying in the same position for so long with her face pressed hard against the bones and muscles of his back. She rolled in the other direction and pulled her legs up close to her belly. It didn't mean anything — that he hadn't woken spontaneously. He was tired. She stretched out and pulled the covers up to her earlobe. She rehearsed their love making from the night before, touch by touch until, finally, she drifted to sleep.

When she woke, the drapes glowed with morning light. Gordon was in the same position he'd been earlier. Now, she was annoyed. He slept like a bear in hibernation. He had no concern for her anxious thoughts and he belittled them as if she were a child in whom he had only minimal interest...childish thoughts to dismiss with a condescending attitude.

She rolled toward him and nudged him slightly. He turned onto his back and twisted his neck so he was facing her. "Good morning, gorgeous."

She kissed him, afraid that anything she said would start the day on a sour note.

"Sleep good?" he said. He slid his arm under her shoulders and pulled her closer. "I'm going to eat you up." He nuzzled his face in her neck.

Against her will, her body stiffened.

"Are you okay? Bad dream?"

"No."

"You seem tense. Worrying again?"

She willed herself to relax. At least he was in tune with her thoughts, although he made it sound as if worrying was a personality defect. Worry was a gift of animal instinct. When there was a threat, the mind looked for escape alternatives. That's all she was doing. But what made her think there was a threat? Was that what she read between Luke and Thomas? Was the boy threatening him? But why?

"What's on your mind, pretty lady?"

Her stomach twisted in yet another direction. Why did she have to dissect each of his words as if it was layered with a hidden message? But she couldn't help it. *Lady* implied someone older. Not a carefree girl running on the beach, a wild woman making love in front of a fire. An explorer of the universe expanding her mind to investigate undiscovered corners of the human psyche.

He tickled her.

She giggled. "Don't."

"She speaks!" He rolled on top of her.

It was too much. She didn't want to whine and complain, to push him away. He retreated when she talked too much. This way, he would be thinking only of her and how much she meant to him. She yielded to his mouth and the pressure of his body.

After they made love, they slept again. This time when she woke, the room had grown stuffy and stale. She sat up.

Gordon moved and rested his head on her legs. "What should we do today?"

"I think we need food. But maybe you and I could go out for breakfast…or lunch. And then we can go to the market." When he didn't immediately answer, she said, "Just the two of us."

"Many hands make light work."

She wanted to laugh. Too bad that wasn't the prevailing view when it was time to cook or wash dishes. She hated the resentful feelings that seemed to spill out of every crevice in her heart. She didn't want to feel these things, yet, they wouldn't stop flooding through her. "Wouldn't it be nice to spend time alone?"

He put his mouth on her breast and sucked it for several minutes. Her mind began to break apart, as if a fizzy tablet had been dropped into the center of her brain, popping and dissolving, warm, melting pleasure running through her nerves. She forgot what she wanted to say.

After a few moments he pulled away. "We're alone now. We've

been alone all night."

She wanted his mouth back on her breast, wanted him on top of her, inside of her, becoming part of her, but a wanting craving soul screamed back that she needed more than that. "I meant time for talking."

"Why do we need to talk alone?"

"There are so many things I don't know about you. So many things you don't know about me."

He laughed softly. "I know everything I need to about you." He pulled her toward him, running his finger down her spine.

"That's kind of insulting," she said.

He put his hand on her neck and pressed her head against his chest. "You're amazing. I feel like our souls are merged. Why would it be insulting that I know every part of you? It makes me excited that you know every part of me."

She tried to pull away but his grip was too tight. Her voice against his chest was meek. "You know my body. I know yours…" As she spoke, a loose hair from his chest worked its way into her mouth. She tried to spit it out, but it gripped her tongue. It was coarse and persistent. She worried it would find its way down her throat if she tried to say more. She tongued it toward the back of her lips where it felt like something living. She tried again to spit it out, but it slid between two of her teeth. "You don't know my mind, everything about my life."

"How can you say that?"

He gripped her neck with warm, strong fingers, whispering into her hair as if he wanted to implant his words directly into her brain. Just like the ghost, the chill of another's words seeping into your mind, taking it over so you couldn't distinguish your own thoughts. She shivered.

"What's wrong?" he said.

"You're hurting me."

He eased the pressure of his fingers, but kept her forehead and the tip of her nose pressed against him. The hair continued to slide around inside her mouth. She coughed.

"Every night we expand our consciousness. We're all one. Everyone in this house, and those who have passed through, are a single mind. We know each other better than people with whom we've spent half our lives. We're connected on a higher level. The force of our collective consciousness is bringing the energy of love into the world. It's spreading every day. The peace that flows out of us will flow across the planet, dissolving conflicts, ending the war. All wars. We can't get trapped by the trivial details of a family tree or a diary of activities. Don't you see that? The things you're saying make me feel you haven't truly been there with us."

"Please let go of my neck. I'm uncomfortable."

He took his hand away and she rolled onto her back. She stuck her thumb and forefinger into her mouth and removed the hair. Being rid of it made her feel less frantic. It was exhausting trying to explain herself to him. Was he deliberately not understanding? Or were they from entirely different generations after all? She hadn't thought the age difference was too great, but perhaps they hadn't had any similar events in their lives to form a connection beyond sex. The thought made her want to cry. She loved him. She couldn't live without the shattering sensations he drew out of her body, as if he were a magician, making things appear out of nothing. But in reality, magicians tricked the eye. There really wasn't any magic at all.

He stroked her hair. "What are you trying to say?"

She turned so her back was toward him. Tears seeped out of her eyes. She was old. Too old for all of them. They didn't know her at all, and more than anything, maybe even more than soul shattering sex, she needed someone to know her mind and her heart. Of course, she wasn't sure, right now, that *she* knew her heart. How could she expect Gordon to know it? The one thing she did know was that she loved her children with every cell of her body, and she was desperately worried about her youngest son. He might be a man, but he was still her baby. He was still the person who grew from a tiny seed inside of her, forming lungs and a heart of his own, a brain and limbs and a personality. He was still the baby she'd held and cared for, the boy she'd taught to speak and navigate the world. And something was terribly wrong. "I'm worried about Thomas." It was not at all what she'd wanted to say. Did this mean she'd given up on Gordon? That she'd chosen motherhood over her own happiness? Or maybe, she now knew with certainty that Gordon would never provide the love she craved.

"Why?"

"He shuts himself up in his room. He won't talk to anyone, he judges everyone. He seems upset and angry. It's almost as if he's…scared."

Gordon laughed. "You are a worrier. He got high with us. It just took him a while to overcome his conservative upbringing." He tickled her waist.

She squirmed away. "Don't. I'm trying to talk to you."

"Okay, Mother Mary."

"Why does everyone call me that? Who came up with that?"

"It's just a game. Don't be so serious. You can't be worrying over your son. He's an adult. Set him free."

She bit down gently on her tongue. She wouldn't say anything more. He could never understand. She released her grip on her tongue. "Where do you think we're going, you and I?"

"On a magical trip."

"I'm serious." She closed her eyes, waiting, although she couldn't say what she hoped to hear from him.

"Why do we have to be going somewhere?"

"Are we a couple?"

"Stop trying to put everything into a box."

She turned toward him. "Stop telling me that everything I think is somehow wrong. I'm just trying to understand what kind of relationship we have. Are you only with me? Or are you flirting with the others? Sleeping with them?"

"Look." He sat up. "I've never pretended to be someone I'm not. I've been completely up front with you."

"I don't know who you are."

"Yes you do."

He was wrong. She knew nothing about him except that he'd

been a schoolteacher and dropped out of that life to wander around and get high. That was it. And maybe that wasn't even true. "Are you sleeping with Caroline? Did you?"

He took her in his arms, cradling her against him, pulling her up so she was half lying across his upper body. "Mary. Stop it. You're looking at the world all wrong. Love is so much bigger than any one person. We're all one. We're all lovers, or meant to be. If war is to end, if death can have any meaning…" he gasped for air.

She turned her head to look at him. His face was slick with tears. Mucous bubbled at the entrance to his nostrils. She moved away and took his face in her hands. "What's wrong?"

He continued to suck in deep gulps of air as if he was afraid of running out. "Nothing. I'm okay. We're all *oh-kay*. The only thing that matters is love. Let me love you." He lifted her gently to the side and pressed himself against her. He lowered his head and sucked on her breast, his nasal passages suddenly clear.

She closed her eyes and let herself disappear.

Twenty-eight

She and Gordon didn't go out for lunch after all. When Mary came out of the shower, Gordon had disappeared. *Gone for a walk* someone said, someone she didn't recall seeing before.

Hours passed. Caroline had disappeared as well. *Needed time to think*, Luke said. *I'm not sure where she went.*

A bunch of them were watching TV. Such a shame on a balmy day, the water sparkling like an ocean of sapphires.

Toward the middle of the afternoon, Mary went to the market by herself. When she returned with thirteen sacks of groceries, the house was quiet. She put the bags on the kitchen counter stepped into the living room. It was deserted. Lumps of sleeping bags and scattered clothing covered the carpet and every piece of furniture. A sweatshirt was draped over the TV. She yanked it off and dropped it on the floor. She returned to the kitchen and put the food away. She was not going to cook dinner. She was not even suggesting food when the time came for people to be hungry. They were rarely hungry on a normal schedule anyway.

After the paper sacks were folded and tucked in the cabinet beneath the sink, she grabbed her purse and went out. She walked up the hill, following the road that led out of Seacliff Beach State Park. She turned right and walked a half block to Manuel's. She asked for the table in the corner near the window.

While she watched the people walking by, she ate a chicken taco and drank a glass of beer. When her food was gone, she ordered another beer and sipped it as slowly as possible. Hippies and teeny boppers drifted in front of her eyes, laughing and talking, heading to, and away from, the beach.

When she returned home it was close to dusk. Caroline was in the kitchen. She stood in front of the refrigerator, holding the door open, staring inside as if she expected dinner to leap out at her fully formed. "I'm hungry."

"Help yourself." Mary turned to leave.

"What should we fix for dinner?"

Mary shrugged. "I'm not hungry."

"But everyone else is."

Mary smiled. She held up her purse. "I need to put this away."

"And then you'll help me figure out something to eat?"

"You handle it. I can't even think about food." She patted her belly and walked out of the room.

In her bedroom, she shoved her purse in the closet as far back as it would go. She piled shoes in front of it and closed the door. The bed was in the same rumpled condition they'd left it in hours ago. Had it only been that morning? Of course, it was nearly noon when they'd gotten up, so morning wasn't accurate. She really should wash the sheets, but it was too late now. Once they managed to figure out something to eat, everyone would be heading to the beach. She tossed the pillows on the floor and yanked the sheet up to the top of the mattress. She smoothed it and tucked it in. She did the same with the blanket, pulled up the spread, adjusted it to hang evenly, and tucked the pillows beneath the top fold. She opened the drapes that had remained closed all day and cracked the window to allow fresh air inside, even though the evening was growing damp with low, thick fog. It wouldn't hurt for twenty minutes or so. The room would be pleasantly cool later.

Someone had decided it was a good night for dropping acid. Because the fog was the kind that prevented you from seeing more than thirty or forty feet in front of you, it would enhance the trip, although possibly not in a good way. She supposed they were right to call her Mother Mary — she fretted over their well-being. Fortunately, she'd managed to avoid cooking for them, so that was a partial victory. It saddened her that she now thought of their relationships as a battle between victors and vanquished.

Gordon had reappeared as if he'd emerged out of the fog like a prophet from another realm. He sat on a chaise lounge, smoking a joint. No one else was out on the deck. They were clustered in the kitchen, eating ham sandwiches that Caroline and Paul were slapping together as fast as they were devoured. A girl with short, curly hair stood by the refrigerator handing out bottles of beer. She wore a bikini top and an ankle-length, batik skirt. Her feet were bare and so filthy Mary shuddered to think of her walking across the living room carpet. Once they were gone, she would need to hire a firm to scrub the carpets. She hoped they wouldn't need replacing. More and more, she found herself thinking about what she would do when they left. She didn't know when that might happen, or why they would leave without her initiating it, but the thoughts passed through her mind with the rhythm of a train clacking past, each car slightly different, but in the end, the same.

She hurried past the kitchen bar, tossing a half-smile in their direction. She went outside and closed the glass door. She put her hand on Gordon's head and buried her fingers in his hair. It was damp with fog, maybe. Unless he'd gone for a swim.

He tilted his head back. "Hi." He held up the joint.

"No thanks."

She untangled her fingers from his hair and walked around to sit beside him. He moved his legs to make room for her on the lower half of the chaise lounge. She waited for him to speak. She wouldn't ask where he'd been all day. It was too degrading, after his lecture that morning.

"How was your day?" he said.

"Pleasant."

He laughed. "Pleasant?"

"Yes. Pleasant. I picked up groceries and…"

"Don't lay a guilt trip on me."

"Pardon?"

"I can't be the only one to go shopping with you."

"Of course not. I didn't…"

"Why else was it pleasant?" he said.

"I had a delicious Mexican lunch."

He took a hit on the joint and held it out to her. "Are you sure you don't want some?"

"Not if I'm taking acid."

He took another hit.

"Are you okay?" she said.

"Blissed out. Ready for our trip."

"Cool." The word sounded false. She wondered if he heard the same wrong note, if he thought she was pretending to be someone she wasn't. Her voice echoed strangely, as if the fog were a soft curtain around them. Fog settled onto her face and the backs of her hands. She was warm enough in jeans and a white sweatshirt. Her feet were bare. The fog wasn't particularly chilling, just insistent, trying to cover her hair with a dusting of moisture and make its way beneath her clothes.

After a while, the door slid open and Caroline and Luke stepped onto the deck. A moment later, Paul joined them. Just as Mary was about to point out she didn't want pot smoke or fog in the living room, a few others came out and closed the door.

They drifted down to the sand. Mary glanced up at Thomas's window. The shutters were partially opened. Was he watching? Longing to join them, or hating them?

Paul was handing out slips of paper with drops of acid. She took one and swallowed it quickly. She was ready to climb into the stars, leaving her tedious thoughts and concerns scattered across the earth. Thomas was a big boy. He could take care of himself. If he wanted to sulk in his room, worried about some kid he had issues with, that was his business.

They settled in a circle on blankets and towels that someone had put out earlier. There was no fire this time, which was just as well. It wasn't legal, and if Thomas was inclined to do something dramatic to break up the party, she didn't need a fine for having a fire on the beach on top of everything else.

Soon, her mind was flying. She was laughing at nothing. She got up and climbed onto Gordon's lap, straddling his hips. She kissed him and he kissed her back, long and deep, pulling her so close she felt he wouldn't be able to breathe without her. She moved off his legs and settled beside him, letting the idle chatter and silliness drift past her with the same delicate grace as the fog. Trying this on a foggy night was a good idea. It was mysterious and fun and the possibilities were tantalizing. She dug her feet into the sand and leaned against Gordon.

Someone started singing a folk song. A few of them — the girl with curly hair and Paul and someone she didn't know — stood and began swaying, half dancing to the tune. Caroline stood up. She untied her halter top from behind her neck. It fell forward, covering her hips like a small apron. She untied the back, removing it completely. She shimmied out of her jeans. She reached behind her neck and pulled her hair up in a fan over her head, letting it cascade around her shoulders and arms as she spun. She took small steps to keep her balance, flinging out her arms. "Let's go for a swim! Who's up for it?" She spun several more times.

A few people laughed. Beth undid her bathing suit top and took it off.

Caroline lunged away from the circle of people. "I'm going to swim all the way out and around the ship!"

Luke moved close to her side. "Careful, Mama. I don't think that's a good idea."

Caroline tipped her head back, gazing into the fog. "I'm not the mama! She is." She laughed and danced around the outside of the circle until she was behind Mary. She rested her hands on Mary's head. "The one who feeds us, except when she's angry. The one who knows the secrets of the beach. The one who speaks to the haunted ship."

She bent lower and pressed her face into Mary's hair.

"You will be soon," Luke said. "Be careful."

Caroline turned and ran toward the house. She hopped up the steps to the deck and lifted up a thick rope coiled beneath the bench. She held it up. "We'll tie ourselves together so no one can drift away or get caught by the waves. Or a shark." She laughed.

Mary didn't like Caroline laughing at her in front of everyone, making her seem ridiculous for believing in ghosts. What was going on? Was Caroline pregnant? She looked up at Gordon.

"Let's go!" Caroline shouted.

Beth was naked now. Paul stripped off his clothes. A few others were lying on the sand, curled on their sides like cats. The girl with wavy hair stood apart from the circle, humming to herself, dancing in slow circles, going somewhere different, away from the rest of them.

"I don't think you should," Luke said.

Caroline worked her face into a dramatic pout. "It'll be righteous. Don't spoil my fun."

"I'm gonna tie you up with that rope." Luke began tugging at the rope. "You say all this shit and you never follow through."

"A tug of war!" Caroline laughed.

"You said someone needs to get control of you."

"I haven't lost control, silly." She giggled. "I'm trying to get this party going."

Gordon stood up and went to Caroline. He put his arm around her. "It's a not a good idea."

She wrenched herself away from him. "Leave me alone, old man! I don't belong to you." Luke continued twisting the rope. He pried at her fingers, trying to loosen her grip.

Gordon put his arm around Caroline again. She dropped the rope, pushed away from him, and ran toward the water.

Tears formed behind Mary's eyes — a great ocean, as if her bones and muscles and organs were dissolving into salty water, rushing through her body. She couldn't stand up, her body was liquid. She would splash onto the sand and be absorbed into nothing. She started to cry. She slapped her hands over her face, trying to prevent her insides from spilling out. She wiped her face and lowered her hands, forming fists and digging them into her thighs. What was going *on*? "Is she pregnant?" No one seemed to hear. No one even looked at her. Maybe she hadn't spoken out loud. "Is she?"

Gordon followed Caroline. She was no longer visible through the thick fog. All that remained was her trilling, shrieking voice as the cold water hit her skin.

Luke grabbed the rope and ran after her. His shape became dim and fuzzy. He disappeared into the whiteness.

"Gordon!" Mary tried pushing herself into a standing position.

Gordon continued walking slowly toward the water, also becoming indistinct in the fog.

"Gordon! Come back. I need to talk to you."

"Not now."

"Yes! Now!"

He kept walking.

She ran after him and grabbed his arm. He continued moving forward as she stumbled to keep up. "Why won't you talk to me?"

"It's not a good time. Caroline's headed for trouble."

"She's already in trouble. Is she pregnant? You *did* sleep with her?" She was sobbing. She wanted to hit him, but he kept moving away from her.

"Don't be so clingy, Mary. I need to make sure she's safe."

"You need to talk to me!"

He shook his head and started jogging toward the water. She hung back. She didn't want to get wet. It wasn't a good idea to go into the water with all this fog, with their senses distorted. The movement of the fog gave the impression the ship was coming toward them — a ship of ghosts emerging from the ether, headed to pick up more passengers.

Gordon waded in, not seeming to notice the water soaking his jeans.

Caroline and Luke were tussling near one of the legs to the pier. The tide was low, and they'd gone out to where the pier legs were covered with great bulges of mussels. Luke hung onto

Caroline's arm as she thrashed and twisted.

"Stop," Gordon splashed through the knee-deep water. Luke turned and in a single, well-coordinated move, raised his arm, formed a fist, and punched Gordon's jaw. There was a loud crack. Gordon sat down hard into the shallow water.

She knew she should go to him, but the water was so cold — shards of ice on her toes. She couldn't move. The ocean was turning into a sheet of ice, longing to wrap its arms around all of them, pulling them close to the side of the concrete ship, plunging them beneath the surface, holding them down, pressing the air out of their lungs until they turned into limp, rubbery, drifting strands of kelp, lifeless eyes gazing out at the airless space around them. She looked out at the ship. She'd never swum around it, although her sons had. The idea terrified her. Some kids swam into the cracked area at the center, diving into the cavities exposed when the hull split, staying in the enclosed spaces until their lungs were ready to burst. Her chest ached thinking about it. She was having trouble breathing. She backed away from the water. Gordon remained seated, watching Caroline and Luke. Gentle waves washed around his upper arms and chest.

Luke pulled Caroline closer to the leg of the pier. He pushed her up against it. Her skin glowed whiter than the fog, her hair clung to her collarbone and breasts like dark strands of seaweed. She laughed. Luke wrapped the rope around the pillar and then around her waist. She laughed louder, on the edge of hysteria. "Yes! Tie me up so I don't swim out to the end of the world. Tie me *up*! Take control of me, Luke. I love you Luke." She whipped her head toward Gordon. "Not you! Get away from me."

Luke walked around the leg of the pier, wrapping the rope across her shoulders, around her rib cage, then angling it lower so that it crossed her legs in several places. Each time he moved behind the post, he disappeared as the pillar obscured his slim body.

From where she stood, all Mary could see was the shadow of the pier legs, Caroline's white skin criss-crossed with thick, wet rope, her hair plastered over part of her face. Gordon sat in the water, entranced by their performance. Why wasn't he stopping Luke from tying her up?

It seemed as if an outside force were directing the three of them. They'd stopped moving now, waiting for something to happen. Caroline did nothing to resist the restraints.

They're crazy. They're all crazy. This isn't a psychedelic trip.

Mary closed her eyes. She was so tired. A thin stream of laughter at the absurdity of everything she'd witnessed wound through the back of her throat. She wanted to lie down in the sand and sleep for a long time. But the sand was damp and cold. She shivered and opened her eyes.

They've swallowed your soul. There's nothing left.

Barely visible in the thick fog, a figure in a cape, a hood covering its head, stood at the side of the boat. It looked out toward the sea. Mary felt the chilling fingers of her mother stroking her heart, pleading with her to walk into the water.

Come with me. Please. Please come with me.

Mary's heart vibrated against her rib cage. The cold was so deep she was certain she'd never be warm again.

The figure on the ship moved toward the bow, becoming more indistinct as she was enveloped by fog. After a few moments, she reappeared at the edge of the waves. The hem of her cape was frayed and soaked with water. A briny smell came from her. Mussels and sea anemones clung to the heavy fabric. She turned toward Mary. There was no face, only a dark, gaping hole with long silvery hair floating out from the sides of the hood.

Please come. You know you want to. No one here wants you, but I do.

A sob shoved its way out of Mary's chest. She turned and ran across the beach. She glanced back over her shoulder. The woman remained at the edge of the surf, water rising up around her as the tide came in, faster than the force of the moon dictated, rising as if it would flood the entire beach in moments. She ran faster, slipping on the soft dry sand. She looked up. Thomas stood near the window. Was he looking at her? Or the ghost? Simply watching the partiers?

When she reached the others, she slowed, breathing rapidly. It could hardly be called a party. They were lying on the blankets, staring at the inner cavities of their own minds. No one was speaking. If it weren't for the rise and fall of their shoulders, the occasional blinking of their eyes, she'd think they were all dead. Maybe they were.

It was later. Mary wasn't sure how long she'd been standing on the deck. Her neck was stiff from tipping her head back, straining to see the sky through the fog, watching the stars attempt to force their way through the white blanket. The stars weren't visible, but she sensed their effort, felt them exerting every molecule of strength to make themselves known. They moaned softly, pushing against the fog but finding it as impenetrable as a concrete wall. It didn't stop them from trying and she felt they were bleeding now, their edges torn from smashing themselves into something solid, drops of blood falling on her eyes, her cheeks, her lips.

As she lowered her head, she saw the fog had lifted a few feet off the ground. The group on the sand hadn't moved. Beth stood in the center of the circle of reclining bodies, her skin like cream, her hair like silk. She looked out over the water as if she were searching for someone. She began walking. She stepped outside of the circle of sleeping, dreaming, tripping friends. She made her way across the sand with careful steps. Her body was flawless, her hips a perfect curve. A young woman's body was a work of art, a fresh beauty that most girls weren't even aware of. They moved through the world with unselfconscious grace, unaware of what they had, and how quickly it would be lost. No matter how well-preserved Mary's body was, fitting nicely into a bikini, or lying on her side in a comfortable bed, draped with expensive sheets and soft blankets, she would never look like that again. The signs of decay were evident — cells dying every day, their replacements slightly less supple, the slow wearing down of muscles and the microscopic disintegration of bones, the introduction each day of a strand of hair that lacked the resilience of the one it replaced, the silkiness turning to something dry and withered. Even with imperfections, a younger woman's body was sublime. Mary's body was not unlike an overcooked piece of meat.

Beth reached the edge of the water. The fog was receding as if it flowed out to sea to make way for her. It still covered the ship and drifted along the pier, but Gordon, Caroline, and Luke were now visible. Gordon was no longer seated in the waves like a defeated dog, but he still gazed at the leg of the pier where Caroline's body clung to the wood like a starfish gripping its host, waiting for the tide to return and provide it with nourishment.

The specter had evolved into something shapeless. It hovered over the stern of the boat — a dark, opaque cloud.

Gordon took a few steps back. Beth reached his side. She put her hand on his shoulder and he turned. She wrapped her arms around his neck and pulled his face down toward hers. He placed his hands on her hips, tenderly drawing them close to his. They began to kiss. The fog rolled slowly away from the shore, melting out of the sky, revealing the stars, sparkling like a million eyes gazing down at them. The air grew soft and warm. The waves swelled and broke with a whisper, even as the tide rose like something living, breathing, stroking the sides of the ship as it took more of it below the surface.

Mary's heart cracked with the same abrupt splintering that had split the hull of the ship so many years ago. Gordon had never loved her. She'd never been loved at all. Her mother didn't love her enough to remain in the world, her father had loved his new wife more than his daughter. Henry tossed her on the curb like a worn out pair of shoes. Gordon loved only himself and his own desires and his own thoughts. She closed her eyes. Tears spilled from behind her lids, streaming down her face.

"Well. That's over."

Her eyes flashed open. Luke stood beside her. She'd only closed her eyes for a moment, not even that. How had he crossed the beach and walked up the steps without her seeing, or feeling his presence?

"You're pathetic," he said.

"Where's Caroline?"

"Do you care?" His smile was a sneer, his lips dark, as if he'd eaten a half-melted chocolate bar. "I don't think you do."

She strained to see Caroline through the remaining fog and the dark shape of the ghost descending over the end of the ship, shrouding the pier. She'd been there a moment ago. "Is she pregnant?"

"So she says."

"She's not?"

"Do you care? It has nothing to do with you." The unchanging shape of his mouth was wearing on her, his words disconnected from the expression on his face.

"You need to untie her. This has gone on long enough."

"I agree."

She wasn't sure whether he was referring to Caroline's body lashed to the pier, or the party, or something else. "When the tide comes in, she'll…"

He put his hand on her arm and pulled her toward him. She slid her hand beneath his, trying to pry him loose.

"What's wrong? You can't face the truth?" he said.

"What truth?"

"You want her to die."

"That's a horrible thing to say. Don't talk to me like that."

He let go of her and stepped backwards until he was at the top of the steps. "Good-bye, Mother Mary." He laughed. "A mother who wants to devour her children."

"I don't."

"You won't let them live."

"My children, my natural children, not this hippie fantasy family, are just fine. They have admirable lives."

"Is that right?" He smiled. "So, Caroline…live or die? Say the word."

She had no idea what he was talking about. Nothing really, he just wanted to frighten her. He was enjoying it. He and Caroline were out of their minds. All of them were. They lived in a make-believe world where they would magically be taken care of, where everyone loved everyone else, where there were no rules and no obligations. She didn't want anyone to die, she just wanted them to grow up. To leave her alone.

"Okay," Luke said.

"Okay, what?"

"It's probably time for me to hit the road."

"I think so…yes. Go untie that silly girl before the tide comes in, and then you should go." She turned and went into the house.

She closed the door and walked slowly through the living room.

In the kitchen, she put the kettle on the stove. She took out a teabag. Every movement felt like something full of weight and importance, slowed and colored by the acid. It was important she drink some tea. She didn't know why, but it was important. Tomorrow, she'd tell them the party was over.

Twenty-nine

When she woke, the bedroom was dark. It couldn't possibly be nighttime still, she felt she'd slept for eight or nine hours, even an entire day. She'd had a dream that went on forever. Her boys were small and they'd gone out to the beach to play. A thick fog descended and she couldn't find them. She heard them calling, but no matter which way she turned, the voices shifted to a new place. She ran back and forth on the beach, down to the water, splashing in the waves, beneath the pier, searching behind the legs where they might be hiding. She couldn't catch even a glimpse, yet they continued to call out to her, their voices frail and trembling.

She turned over and put out her hand, patting the bed to locate Gordon's body. The sheets were cold.

Beth and Gordon. Caroline with Gordon's child. Caroline tied to the pier.

She bolted up. Her head felt light, near to fainting. She bent forward. After a moment, she raised her head slowly and reached toward the nightstand. Her fingertips found the lamp. She dragged them up the base until she touched the switch and turned it on. Her cup of tea sat on the other side of the lamp. It was full. She dipped her finger in the liquid. It was icy cold. She shivered and slid her legs out of bed.

The jeans and sweatshirt she'd worn to the beach were on the floor. She dressed quickly and pulled her hair away from her face, wrapping it with a ribbon she pulled out of the nightstand drawer. She walked to the door and opened it. The house was dark. The murmur of people talking came from somewhere, but she couldn't identify the location. The kitchen, maybe. She made her way into the living room. Hazy moonlight came through the sliding glass door, illuminating most of the sleeping bags filled with slumbering bodies. No one was talking.

She went into the kitchen. It was empty. The clock pointed to three. She guessed it was close to midnight when she'd fallen asleep. Was it really only three? She squinted, as if she'd misread the size of the hands and it was actually twelve-fifteen, but of course, if that were the case, it would be daylight. She was annoyed with her stupidity. It had only been six or seven hours since she'd taken acid. In all likelihood she was still tripping, even though she felt she wasn't.

The murmuring continued. It sounded like someone repeating the word *please*. And another, whose words couldn't be deciphered. She went to the foot of the stairs. She climbed slowly, feeling as if the sound of the voices was coming out through the walls on either side of the staircase, falling down from the ceiling like dust shaken loose by a broom. When she reached the top, she turned to the right, ignoring Thomas's closed door. The whispering couldn't be coming from his room, he allowed no one inside. She quietly opened the door to the second bedroom. A couple was in the bed but they weren't speaking, arms and legs wrapped around each other so it was difficult to tell which limbs belonged to which person. She didn't have to see their faces. She knew who they were. She closed the door.

The whispering continued. Was it in her head, or was someone awake? The words were articulated but she couldn't make sense of them, other than *please*. There was something she needed to know, something she was supposed to hear, but she couldn't. It was the acid. She crept back down the stairs and stood at the entrance to the living room, feeling the gentle rise and fall of sleeping bodies. She stepped up to the bag nearest to the hallway. Could it be someone talking in his sleep? No, it sounded like a conversation. She looked out at the deck. It was deserted.

She went outside and walked slowly down the steps onto the sand. There was an anxious hammering inside her stomach. She'd told Luke to untie Caroline. Had he done it? He must have. She was certain he'd wanted to frighten her, certain that Caroline was one of the huddled forms burrowed into the warm flannel of a sleeping bag.

There were a few towels scattered around, pinned to the sand by beer bottles. She walked around them. Had she dreamt the conversation with Luke, or hallucinated that as well? It was so tiring, trying to determine what was real and what was conjured up by her own mind, injected by the ghost, or manufactured out of chemicals twisting her mind into new shapes.

The water lapped softly on the sand and echoed with a hollow sound in the skeletal tunnel formed by the aging wood of the pier. It was still partially foggy, but not as dense as it had been earlier. Through the darkness and the wisps of vapor she saw something that didn't belong. The shimmering white of Caroline's wet skin. It couldn't be. It wasn't real. She'd told Luke to untie her. She'd *told* him! She moved closer to the water. It touched her toes, tickling like icy fingers running across her skin. The cold made her feet curve involuntarily. She took a few steps back and squinted at the object tied to the leg of the pier, trying to understand what she was seeing.

Once again, she stepped into the shallow water. A wave crested and crashed at her feet, soaking her legs past her knees. She jogged backwards, too late, but a natural response.

She heard laughter. They were laughing at her. She whirled around and lost her balance. No one was there. The ghost? She turned back. The laughter continued. It forced her to turn again, it sounded so close, so real, yet there was still nothing but an empty beach behind her.

She walked into the water. Caroline's weight was supported by the rope. It cut up under her breasts, her shoulders collapsed forward and her arms moving gently, her hands trailing in the water as it ebbed and flowed. Her head was bent forward and her face wasn't visible, draped with wet hair.

Mary started to cry. She'd told Luke! No, this wasn't real. It was in her mind. The laughter had stopped. Now the only sound was the lapping water and the pigeons warbling and cooing in the rafters of the pier, their sounds echoing as pleasantly as the water. A pigeon left its perch and rushed at Caroline, landing on her shoulder. Another flew at Mary's face, flapping its wings with such force that a few strands of hair pulled loose from the ribbon and fluttered across her face. She turned and started to run. A wave surged forward and rolled against her hip, pushing her down. There was no time to put out her hands to break her fall and the water flowed over her. She coughed, swallowing salt water and sand, crying out, which sucked more water into her throat. She felt the tight, inescapable pinch of it seeping into her lungs. She coughed violently and pushed herself up. Her vision was blurred by the cold and the water. She fought past the next wave and looked at the leg of the pier.

Nothing but water and dark wood was visible. She must have hallucinated Caroline's body. Of course she had. Even sitting in the water was a hallucination. She was still in her bed, no longer searching for her sons, the dream landscape shifting nonsensically. What was she thinking? Walking in the waves when she was tripped out of her mind. Seeing bleeding stars and hearing laughter from people who weren't there, imagining birds flying at her face and tangling her hair, whispers coming from the walls. She laughed. She turned and struggled out of the water. She didn't look back at the pier.

She returned to the house and entered the living room. The whispering had stopped. There was no point in wandering around the house trying to find its source now. It wasn't real. She laughed. Of course it wasn't — she was tripping on acid. Why did she keep forgetting that? She wasn't going to let a few chemicals turn her thoughts inside out. Her mind was stronger than that. The best thing to do was to get into bed and sleep until morning. Then, without hesitation or discussion, she'd tell them to leave. She might still be tripping, but she could clearly see that Gordon didn't love her and none of these people could be called friends.

Thirty

Thomas had stood at the window all evening, watching them go crazy on the beach. There was a lot he couldn't see because of the thick fog — a few of them had walked away, headed toward the water. He heard shouting and laughter. He saw them dancing around in a circle, if it could be called dancing. They jumped and thrashed their arms around, jerked their heads back and forth. The movements weren't bona fide dances like the mashed potato or the swim — even those had some form and grace. This was like people in an asylum, driven by voices inside their heads, unable to control their bodies because their brains had come loose from their moorings.

It made him sick to think what his mother was doing, obscured by fog.

Finally, he moved away from the window. He picked up his beer and took several long swallows. It looked like he wasn't going to be granted a midnight swim tonight, not unless he wanted to walk through that crowd, drawn into senseless conversations with his mother's friends. Would she ever see that she'd purchased their attention and affection? Even with that, they treated her badly.

He sat on the bed and closed his eyes. When the beer bottle was empty, he set it on the nightstand. It was another sign of his weakness and his fear-driven life that he was allowing their antics to prevent him from swimming. What was wrong with him? The ocean belonged to no one. Surely he could find a way to skirt the cluster of naked people to enjoy a quiet, energizing swim. He stood up. There was one more beer on the dresser. Another beer, or a swim? The beer was likely too warm to be satisfying. He went into the bathroom and changed into his swim trunks.

A moment later, he returned to the window. Mary was stumbling across the beach. She stopped a few yards from the group that had collapsed from their dancing. They were lying on towels and seemed to be staring up into the sky, sightless except for what flitted across their own nervous systems. He waited for a few more minutes, watching her watch them. Finally she walked past them and disappeared from sight. He opened the window wider and listened to the waves smack the sand with a violence that made him shudder. He expected it, he felt the swell building, yet still he startled when each one hit the shore.

He grabbed a towel and opened the door. Paul stood in the hallway, positioned as if he'd been about to knock on the door. "Can I come in?"

"Are you high?" Thomas said.

"Why does that matter?"

"Because it does. All of you act as if nothing matters, and you're wrong. Things matter. How you treat people matters, taking advantage of a woman with a good heart matters. Picking up after yourself matters. It all matters!"

"Shh. Shh." Paul put his hand on Thomas's shoulder. "It's

okay. Yes, I took acid, but I'm lucid."

"In your opinion," Thomas said.

"Plcasc?"

"Why?"

"There's a bad vibe in the house. I don't like it — Luke."

Thomas opened the door and Paul stepped into the room. They walked to the window seat and settled at opposite ends.

"So what's to talk about?" Thomas said.

"Someone needs to ask him to leave."

"Good luck with that."

"Shh. Shh. Keep your voice down. Can't your…can't Mary ask him? Caroline is losing it, he pushed her too far. He's dangerous."

"He threatened me," Thomas said. "I gave him money."

Paul shook his head, as if he knew. It didn't have to explained how easy it was to threaten someone like Thomas.

"He said people are paying him to keep their secrets."

"No one but you," Paul said.

"How do you know?"

"You're the only one hoarding secrets. A secret. You want to hit me, you want to strangle Gordon, you want to…"

"I don't."

"It's all over your face."

"That's not true."

"Maybe no one else sees it, but I do. I've been where you are."

"How could you have been where I am?"

"I had a scholarship. To an Ivy League school. But I knew."

"Knew what?"

Paul ran his hand over the cushion of the window seat, moving invisible bits of lint and crumbs to the edge where he brushed them off with a flick of his fingers. "I knew I could form a shell and live inside of that, shriveling into nothing, until all that was left was the shell. Or I could have a real self."

"So you just go around telling everyone you like guys?"

"I don't advertise it, but I don't pretend I'm something else. What's the point? For money? For prestige? What does that get you when you're dead? Life is so big, the world is vast and I don't want to just exist like an object with no soul. I want to be who I am. I want to be real."

Thomas leaned against the window. The waves crashed with the same hard, thunderous sound they'd made earlier, but they no longer jolted him into an involuntary shudder. "I want other things."

"Yes, but do you want to be alone, to live as if you, the person inside doesn't exist? Live a life where not one single person on the planet ever knows you? I'm the first person who sees who you are. Doesn't that make you feel…I don't know…free? Like someone recognizes you?"

Without realizing what was happening, with the same involuntary reaction he'd had to the pounding waves, Thomas felt his head move, nodding in agreement. He wanted to punch the guy and he was afraid of him, but he did feel…different. Something solid that had formed itself around him, constraining his movements and keeping him from breathing, dissolved when

Paul was in the room.

"Your mother isn't who you think she is."

"You keep saying that."

"She's not going to punish you. Or exile you."

Thomas laughed. "Exile me?"

"Isn't that what you're afraid of? The one person who might actually welcome you?"

Thomas stood up. He went to the dresser and picked up the beer bottle. He didn't want it, but he had to do something. He couldn't sit there with this kid — a kid! — staring right through him, telling him things that most forty-year-olds didn't know. "From what I've heard, once they know you're gay, parents have a tendency to act like you were never born."

"It's a first step. No matter what you're afraid is going to happen, it's gotta be better than hiding your whole life."

The words floated in the air behind him. He didn't want to turn and let Paul see that his eyes were filling with tears. He felt like a little kid, a girl. Why was he crying?

He moved toward the window, keeping his back to Paul. He looked out. Nothing was visible but the foam on the waves. He felt Paul's hand on his shoulder.

"You don't seem high," Thomas said.

"Acid doesn't make you high. It opens your mind."

Paul's arms moved around him, circling his waist. Paul rested his chin on Thomas's shoulder.

There were some things that felt better than an admirable career and community respect. His mother would probably understand more than anyone — she'd lost her place in the community, and survived. She'd made a few mistakes, disastrous mistakes, but she wasn't locked in her room.

He and Paul stood there for a long time. Thomas wished it could always be like this.

Thirty-one

Light pressed against the drapes, giving them a soft glow. Mary sat up and switched off the bedside lamp. Although she'd determined not to let the whispering frighten her, she'd left the lamp on when she returned to bed, anxious that someone — something — might enter her room, unhindered by the lock. The house was silent and it all seemed to be a dream. She'd woken and turned on the lamp, fallen back to sleep and dreamt she'd followed the sounds of people whispering, seen Caroline's corpse tied to the pier. She laughed at her foolishness.

She was naked and her clothes were on the floor. Her head was clear. It was eight-twenty. She took a quick shower and put on jeans and a loose top. She opened the drapes and picked up her dirty clothes. A pair of Gordon's jeans was tossed on the chair in the corner. She folded them and gathered his toothbrush and razor from the bathroom. She carried his things into the living room and placed them on the coffee table. She went into the kitchen.

Luke leaned against the counter, drinking a beer.

"I thought you were leaving?" she said.

"In the middle of the night? That's harsh."

"How's Caroline?"

"She isn't with us any more." He placed the half empty bottle on the counter and shoved his hands in his pockets. "As soon as I see Thomas, I'll split."

Mary shivered. His words tried to imply Caroline was dead. "Where did she go?"

"Are you naive or being willfully stupid?"

"What do you mean?"

"As you hoped, Caroline drowned." He smiled.

Mary opened her mouth. He was trying to scare her. She clamped her teeth together. She'd wanted coffee, but she couldn't stay in the room with him. "There's nothing you need to say to Thomas. I want you to leave."

"You don't believe me." He laughed.

"Of course not."

"You wanted her to die because she took your man, and made a baby with him."

Mary folded her arms across her ribs. "You're not going to scare me. If you have a message for Thomas, tell me what it is and I'll pass it on."

"I don't have a message. He owes me something. And I have no desire to scare you. I'm just telling the truth. But I guess the truth can be scary. Deadly, even."

"I told you to untie her, so I know you're just trying to upset me."

"I did untie her. When the tide went out this morning, she went with it, for now. We can't have pigs sniffing around, can we?"

"I told you to untie her last night!"

He smiled. "I don't do everything you say, Mary. You're not my mother. Of course, I didn't do everything she told me to do either." He laughed softly, pleased with himself.

Mary hurried out of the kitchen. She scrambled across the living room, slid the door open, and stepped onto the deck. She ran down the stairs and across the sand. The rope was still wrapped around the leg of the pier where Caroline had been tied. Surely Caroline hadn't…of course not. Luke was laughing at her. He was standing in her kitchen, drinking her beer, and laughing at her gullibility. She went back inside the house. She ran up the stairs and flung open the door to the back bedroom. Gordon was lying on top of Beth. The room smelled of sex and sweat with an undercurrent of pot. "Gordon."

"Hmmm?" He buried his face in Beth's hair.

"Where's Caroline?"

"Not sure."

"Sit up, look at me."

Beth giggled softly and wrapped her lower leg around his thigh.

"Both of you. Sit up and look at me right now."

"It's cool, Mary." Beth laughed so gently it sounded like nothing more than her breath. "There's enough of Gordon to go around, plenty for all of us."

"I'm not talking about that. Where is Caroline? Did someone untie her?"

Gordon's voice was hard and dismissive. "I said I'm not sure. Why can't you let things be."

It wasn't really a question. She started to cry. She hadn't wanted Caroline to drown. Was she really dead? Had someone taken her body? No, the whole thing was a disturbing hallucination. It seemed so real. "I'm scared that something happened. Did you talk to Luke?"

Gordon's head moved slightly, hardly bothering to acknowledge her question or her fear, or her presence at all. She swallowed, feeling as if her throat were filled with sand. She walked slowly to the side of the bed. She pushed Gordon, trying to shove him onto his side. He stayed rooted to Beth.

"Tell me what happened," she said.

"We're kind of busy here. I don't know everything that happens."

She smacked his shoulder blade.

"Ouch."

The skin bloomed red where she'd hit him. "I need you to get dressed."

He rolled off Beth and looked at her. "You're losing it."

"Now!" She backed away until she was standing in the doorway.

The room seemed to shrink, becoming a haze of images, people dancing, kissing, walking on the beach. Her brain felt like it was detaching from the inside of her skull. She thought she might be sick. She put her hand over her mouth and closed her eyes, willing her brain to return to its normal state. It was too awful. Were all of them murderers? Including her? It hadn't been enough — to think she could simply demand they stop their game and walk away without making sure Caroline was safe. She never should have left. She should have seen what was coming. From the moment she met him, she'd sensed something wasn't right with Luke. Hadn't she? Or had she tried too hard to make him think she was cool? Tears filled her eyes. She opened them and spoke with a half sob. "Get out of here. Take the others, too. You can start with Luke. He's in the kitchen."

Gordon slid out of bed. He walked toward her, she turned her head so she didn't have to see his erection. He reached out and put his arms around her. She pushed him away. "Now. Or I'm calling the police."

"And what would you say to the police?" Gordon said.

"Oh, Mary. That's so sad," Beth said.

"It's okay," Gordon said. "Everything's cool. She belongs to a different generation. Her time has passed and she can't hack this scene. It's cool, we should go."

Beth climbed out of bed. "Okay."

Mary stepped into the hallway. She glanced at Thomas's door. She'd talk to him later, after they left. She needed to do this by herself.

She returned to the kitchen. Luke was gone. His empty beer bottle was on the counter. She picked it up and threw it into the trashcan, disappointed that the glass didn't shatter. She made a pot of coffee, filled a cup, and took it outside. She crossed the beach and walked along the pier toward the boat. She stepped onto the ship and took a sip of coffee. She looked out at the blurred horizon, glad that she couldn't see what was happening inside her home.

When the coffee cup was empty, she returned to the house. Gordon had been surprisingly effective at waking everyone and getting them to roll up sleeping bags and stuff clothing into backpacks. The living room was stripped clean. Gordon, Beth, and Paul stood in the entryway, filling the space with the smell of unwashed hair. She gave Paul a warm hug, clinging to him for several seconds before he went outside. Beth put her hand on Mary's shoulder. Mary pulled away. "I'm sorry you're angry with us," Beth said. "I think…"

"I don't want to hear it," Mary said. She put one hand on each of their shoulders and pushed them until they were forced to step onto the front stoop.

Gordon slid his arms into the straps of his backpack. It seemed to say something, that he was more concerned about getting his pack settled than holding onto her or speaking to her. When the pack was in place, he put his arms around her and pulled her close.

She stood unmoving in the circle of his arms. "Is she dead?" her voice was weak, muffled by his jacket. She wondered if he'd heard. When he didn't respond, she moved slightly. "Is she? Dead?"

"You know the answer."

"I really don't. I don't know what's a hallucination, what's a dream, what's a lie."

"She wanted thrills. Nothing was enough for her. She got the greatest thrill there is in this world. She looked like she was at peace."

Mary turned her head to the side. No wonder her neck was so stiff — she was constantly turning her face away from what was happening. She pulled away from him. She walked into the living room. She stood looking at the back deck and the ocean beyond.

She heard the front door close.

Luke was right. In her heart, she'd wanted it. For the rest of her life, she'd know she was responsible for a woman's death. She'd done nothing to stop it.

Luke had been more than right about several things. She was both naive and stupid. How had she ever believed any of them were friends? It was impossible to live as if she were twenty-three, trusting that she might find a man to love at this point in life. It was too late for her. And now, it was for the best. What man could love a woman who harbored murder in her heart?

Thirty-two

Thomas put a bottle of champagne in an ice bucket. He carried the silver bucket and two glasses out to the back deck. He returned to the kitchen and filled a bowl with pretzel sticks. He took it outside and put it on the table beside his mother. The sun floated above Pleasure Point. It was a dark orange color, rippled at the edges so it appeared to pulse like a beating heart.

He turned away from the sun. "I need to talk to you."

"I'm pleased to hear that."

He opened the champagne and filled the glasses. He handed one to Mary. He lifted his glass and tapped the edge of hers. "To the truth."

"I don't need a lecture," she said.

"I wasn't talking about you."

She took a sip of champagne. "This is delicious. It's the perfect temperature."

"There's no good way to tell you this, so I'm just going to lay it all out there."

She nodded.

He took a long sip of champagne and set his glass on the table. "I'm not like other men."

"Well certainly not like some of the men who've been living here." She smiled and raised her glass toward him. The descending sun sparkled in the liquid, turning it gold.

"Don't say anything. Or I won't be able to do this."

"Certainly."

"I don't know if you're aware, but some men…some people… prefer mates of their own sex."

"I wasn't born in the nineteenth century, Thomas." She sipped her champagne. "Oh. I…"

"Yes."

"How do you know?"

"I just know."

"Are you sure? Is this a new thing? Because everyone is experimenting?"

"I've known since I was a child."

She turned toward him. Her face was split by a shadow from the angle of the roofline. Her eyes were impossible to read. "And you never said anything?"

"It's not a usual topic of conversation."

"I guess not."

After a few minutes, she said, "Do your brothers know?"

He shrugged. It wouldn't surprise him if they'd guessed, or at least wondered, but it had never been mentioned. He didn't want to think about that right now. "It's very difficult. Very…I feel very alone." His voice was a whisper, sliding past his vocal chords without grabbing hold.

"What's that?"

He coughed and picked up his glass. He took a small sip of champagne. It gripped his throat and he coughed harder. "It's lonely. I can't tell anyone. You can't tell anyone. It could affect my employment chances, maybe my status at Berkeley…so many things."

"Yes, I suppose so."

"Some men, men who are caught in the wrong bars, are arrested. I've known guys who were fired. Beat up. One guy's in a wheelchair now."

"Oh, Thomas. I don't want any of that to happen." Her voice sounded near to crying.

"I'm careful. Most of the time."

"Luke?"

He nodded.

She put her hand on his leg. "I'm glad he's gone."

Her fingers were cool and firm. It felt as if she would never let go of him. It was insulting, that he'd allowed Luke to make him believe she'd be ashamed of him, that she'd shove him out of her life. "Paul and I told him he needed to leave."

"I wondered why he disappeared so fast. It seemed we were in the middle of a discussion, and suddenly, he was gone." She sipped her champagne "He said you owed him something."

Thomas put down his glass. "He wanted me to pay him to keep my secret."

"Oh, no." She squeezed his leg. "You didn't give him money, did you? Please tell me you didn't. Please tell me you didn't think I could ever stop loving you."

"Just a little — fifty bucks or so."

She blinked. Tears sparkled on her bottom eyelashes. She

turned her head.

He closed his eyes. When he and Paul had left his room and descended the stairs that morning, the morning after Caroline drowned, the morning they all moved out, the house had been silent. The quiet was punctured by the hiss of a metal cap coming off a bottle. They'd walked into the kitchen together.

Luke leered at them. He stuck out his tongue and wiggled it, lunging toward Thomas. Beer splashed on Thomas's foot and Luke laughed. Thomas grabbed his arm.

"Oooh!" Luke giggled. "The deviant is strong. A strong, tough man."

Thomas twisted Luke's arm. "If I'm one, so are you."

Luke laughed, half shrieking. "I'm not one of you." He nodded his head toward Paul, then Thomas.

"But we…"

"You are unbelievably dumb. You and your Mommy." Luke laughed hysterically. "I become what I need to be. I do what needs to be done. But I'm not a fairy, that's for sure." He laughed louder. "You should see your face! Poor Tommy. You thought I loved you. You thought I was into you. You thought I…"

Thomas let go of Luke's arm. He would shove his entire arm down Luke's throat if that's what was needed to stop the flow of abuse, burning his ears, turning his skin hot as the ugly words poured out of the laughing mocking lips. He punched Luke's face. Cartilage cracked and his hand slipped away from Luke's mouth, wet and foamy with beer. Blood poured out of Luke's nose, drenching Thomas's hand and wrist.

"Shit, man! You busted my nose. You're gonna pay for that." Luke stumbled back. His hip slammed against the counter.

Paul grabbed Luke's arms and pinned them against the counter. Luke twisted, laughing with a shrill edge to his voice that sounded like he was crying. Thomas punched Luke's jaw. Not hard, pulling back as Luke winced in anticipation. It wasn't as satisfying as the first punch, but he wasn't going to beat the guy up when he was defenseless. Thomas lowered his arm. "You need to leave."

"That's cool. But you owe me."

"I don't. I'm not giving you any more."

"You'll regret that."

Thomas shrugged. He went into the living room and picked up Luke's backpack. Despite the noise they'd made, the sounds emerging from the sleeping bags were of blissful, dreamless sleep. He returned to the kitchen. Paul dragged Luke into the entryway and Thomas followed. Thomas opened the door and Paul shoved a still giggling Luke onto the front step.

Thomas tossed the backpack onto the sidewalk. "I'll call the police if you come anywhere near this house."

"Big talk," Luke said.

"It's not big talk."

"They're more likely to arrest *you*, if they find out what I know. Faggot."

"Try me," Thomas said.

The words had echoed strangely in the deserted street, as if they'd come from someone else.

Now, he felt Mary looking at him. He opened his eyes. Hers were still wet.

"Such terrible things I allowed to happen in my home," she said.

"Paul thought Luke brought bad vibes," Thomas said, feeling his face flush. "He knew Luke was dangerous."

"More than we even felt," Mary said. "Leaving Caroline to drown." She started to cry. "I wonder if they'll find her body. I should have called the police, but without her body, and all of them gone. I…I don't know what to do. Part of me doesn't want to believe it, I still want to think it was just a dark, hideous acid trip. She can't be dead."

"But Gordon saw her."

"I know. And I'm responsible. I'm a murderer. And now, I'm covering it up."

"You're not responsible."

"I wanted her gone."

"Then we're both responsible," he said. "I wanted all of them gone."

"I mean I thought that I could kill her, I was so…"

"But what happened isn't your fault. She asked him to do it. And he went along."

"I should report it. I know I should."

"What can you report? Unless you hear of her body being discovered. Maybe sharks got her."

"Would they eat something already…already…dead?"

He shrugged. "I don't know."

"If I don't tell someone, that makes me a murderer."

"Stop saying that."

"I wished her dead, and now she is."

"It's not your fault."

"I did nothing. I didn't call the police."

"You still can, but what would you say..." He extended his arm, sweeping it out to include the house and the ship and the entire beach in his gesture. "...about all the things that happened here?" He knew she wouldn't. She'd never do anything that might drag him into an unstoppable chain of events. He refilled their glasses and they sipped their champagne without talking while the sun settled on top of the cliffs and then disappeared, leaving a splash of orange and pink across the sky.

"So, Paul, too?" she said.

"Yes."

"I felt something between you."

He shivered.

She put down her glass. "Why did you tell me about your... inclination? Why now?"

He looked out at the concrete ship. The darkening sky and the frothy still white clouds, the shimmering ocean, were too beautiful. This was how he was born, who he was at the very center of his being. It felt good to know that she knew him, not some fabrication of himself. "Paul helped. And the ghost..." He laughed nervously.

A smile tugged at the edges of her lips.

"It's no good burying your own soul," he said. "I wanted you to know who I am. It's hard, hiding it from every single person I meet, every member of my family, my friends. The whole world. I wanted someone on this planet to know who I really am."

"I'm honored you chose me."

He felt calmer than he had in a long time. Maybe ever. The house had been returned to its tranquil state and Mary had shed the things that threatened to transform her into someone unrecognizable. He had no idea what had happened that night. The events she'd related to him were flimsy — a few details stitched together, leaving gaping holes at the center, but he wasn't sure he wanted to know any more. He wanted to enjoy the rest of the summer and finish his degree and figure out how he was going to live his life. This was an admirable first step.

As if some outside force had proposed a toast that both of them heard inside their own minds, they simultaneously lifted their glasses to each other and took a sip of champagne.

1970

From the moment James Carmichael walked up to Mary on her neighbor's back deck, handed her a glass of champagne, and said — *You look like a lady who drinks champagne* — she'd marveled at the sudden change in the course of her life.

At the age of forty-seven, she'd spent the summer trying to live as if she were twenty-five. Now, at the age of fifty, when most would view a woman's life as a slow dissolving into the invisibility of old age, a man had fallen in love with her. *She'd* fallen in love with him. This time, it was real. Maybe it was her age, or the suddenness of it, but now she knew she'd never been in love before. This was nothing like Henry, made her marriage to Henry seem like a transaction for child-rearing and financial support. And Gordon wasn't love at all — he'd become a joke in her memories, a clichéd footnote in her life. He was the symbol of an extended hallucination.

James was a best friend and a lover and a housemate all wrapped up in one, quite a good-looking package. He was slim, his hair the color of pewter. His eyes were hazel with distinct flecks of green. His voice was so warm and smooth and familiar she felt she'd been hearing it all her life.

They cooked together, experimenting with dishes from Italy and Germany and India. They walked on the beach and took leisurely swims in the ocean, shivering inside a shared towel when they were finished. He loved classical music and rock 'n roll in the same doses she preferred. They'd danced in small clubs and shared meals in beachside restaurants.

Only one thing scarred her happiness, only one thing stood in the way of marveling over the half carat diamond he'd put on her left finger yesterday.

Now, she stood near the farthest accessible point on the ship. It seemed the only appropriate place to tell him the rest of her secrets. One secret, really. She'd sent him a note asking him to meet her here this morning. Strangely, or not, it was the anniversary of Caroline's death.

She needed James to know she was a murderess. Not with her hands, but surely with her heart. She was as guilty as the others for turning her back, even more guilty for wishing a woman dead. For never making any effort to report Caroline's death or locate her parents. For three years, she'd opened her eyes each morning, turned on her side and wondered who she really was. Every so often, she hoped they'd all conspired to make her believe Caroline was dead, but the moment the dreamy stuff cleared, she knew it was wishful thinking.

Her thinking was indeed wishful. Several times over the years, Caroline's spirit had appeared on the ship, proving Caroline was dead. The spirit's shrill voice told Mary she was a killer, reminded Mary that Gordon had never cared about her, that no one wanted her. From time to time, Caroline's ghost followed Mary along the beach, filling her walks with torment, destroying her pleasure in the rolling, crashing surf, spoiling the peaceful presence of the gulls and pelicans, the harbor seals and sea otters and dolphins. Sometimes, Mary found herself running back to her house, tripping up the stairs, and locking herself inside. She closed the blinds and stayed for days without seeing a soul.

Caroline's ghost hadn't materialized since James came into her life, but he needed to know before Caroline made her next appearance. He had to know what he was in for — sharing a bed with a killer, exposing his life to the women haunting the broken concrete ship.

She felt James standing behind her. He put his hand on her shoulder, but she didn't turn.

He moved closer and slid his hand down her arm, slipping it around her waist. "What do you need to tell me?" His voice trembled with a touch of fear. He let go of her waist and put his hands on her shoulders, turning her to face him.

She stepped away. "No. Stand beside me. I can't look at you while I tell you this."

She told him first of her mother's ghost, waiting to sense a tightening in his body that said he didn't believe her, that she was mad, she'd damaged her mind with drugs. Instead, she felt his breath remain steady on her cheek and his arm tighten, pulling her into him. Then, she poured out the story of 1967 as fast as she could form the words, her voice growing thin as she forgot to breathe in her rush to rid herself of it, to get to the end and find out whether she was going to be left alone again, never loved after all.

"I could have done something! I should have reported it, but I kept putting it off. I couldn't think what I'd say about all of them, about tripping on acid. I had no idea where they'd gone, no information about any of them."

"There was no body to report," James said.

"That. And when Thomas told me about his life, and I saw the fear in his eyes, I couldn't risk them finding out. If the police ever did locate Luke, or Gordon, or Paul…they would expose him. It was dangerous for men like Thomas. It still is."

"It's understandable," he said. "And without her body…"

She let him put his hands on her shoulders again and turn her until they were facing one another.

"It wasn't you," he said. "You're not guilty of anything except misplaced trust, thinking the best of people."

"I wanted her to die."

"Wanting and doing aren't the same. Not at all."

"It must be the same…her spirit won't leave me alone."

He put his arms around her and pulled her close. He rested his chin on top of her head. "You're with me, now. Maybe she'll go away. But if she doesn't, I'll be right here, holding your hand."

She leaned into him. The breeze washed around them and the waves crashed against the ship with a roar that was somehow comforting.

After nearly forty years, her mother's ghost lingered in the recesses of the concrete ship. She was certain Caroline's ghost would be similarly persistent, caught forever in the cavities below.

Mary would never be free of the haunting presence. But she was loved, and that made it bearable.

About The Author

Cathryn Grant is the author of Suburban Noir novels, ghost stories, and short fiction. Her writing has been described as "making the mundane menacing".

Cathryn's fiction has appeared in *Alfred Hitchcock* and *Ellery Queen Mystery Magazines*, *The Shroud Quarterly Journal*, and *The Best of Every Day Fiction*. Her short story "I Was Young Once" received an honorable mention in the 2007 *Zoetrope All-story* Short Fiction contest.

When she's not writing, Cathryn reads fiction, eavesdrops, and plays very high handicap golf. She lives on the Central California coast with her husband and two cats. Visit her website at SuburbanNoir.com or email her at Cathryn@SuburbanNoir.com

Haunting the Beach - Book Three

It's 1930 and the concrete ship is towed to its final resting place at Seacliff Beach. The town of Aptos is buzzing with anticipation for the grand opening of the restaurant and dance hall built inside the ship.

Everyone has a dream for the promise of a night on the ship. Mary fights to convince her parents the "adults only" rule is unfair. Her mother, Lorene King, anticipates a final chance to rekindle her marriage and her husband's colleague, Jacob Archer, knows it's the perfect setting to win the woman he adores.

The concrete ship, glowing with lights and filled with music has a dark side — It's prohibition and bootleggers know they can pick up their illegal deliveries when the parties are over and the lights go out. Greed and violence threaten to shatter the dreams of Lorene and those she loves. As the tragic events of Mary's childhood unfold before her uncomprehending eyes, she has a terrifying encounter with the ghost that dwells within the S.S. Palo Alto.

In the end, ninety-two-year-old Mary finally confronts the ghost that's haunted her since the ship first appeared in her life.

Coming in May 2016.

CPSIA information can be obtained
at www.ICGtesting.com
Printed in the USA
FSOW02n0447060416
18886FS

9 781943 142200